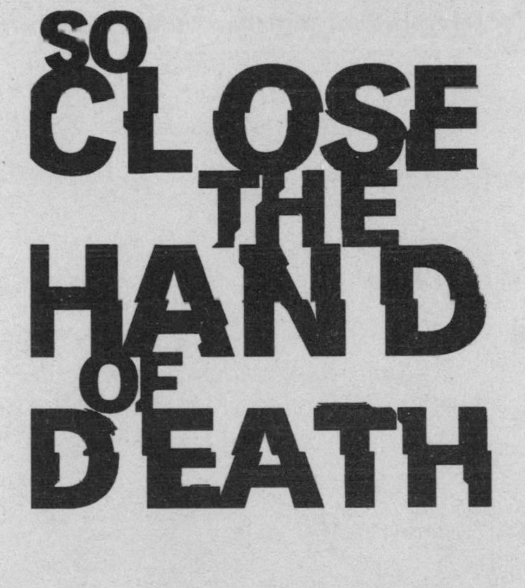

J.T. ELLISON

Recycling programs for this product may not exist in your area.

ISBN-13: 978-0-7783-2943-5

SO CLOSE THE HAND OF DEATH

For questions and comments about the quality of this book please contact us at Customer_eCare@Harlequin.ca.

www.MIRABooks.com

Printed in U.S.A.

Praise for the novels of J.T. Ellison

"Mystery fiction has a new name to watch."
—John Connolly

"*The Cold Room* combines
The Silence of the Lambs with *The Wire*."
—*January Magazine*

"Outstanding...potent characterization and clever plotting, and Ellison systematically cranks up the intensity all the way to the riveting ending."
—*Publishers Weekly* on *The Immortals*
[starred review]

"Flawlessly plotted, with well-defined characters and conflict...quite simply a gem."
—*RT Book Reviews* [Top Pick] on *The Cold Room*

"A tight and powerful story.
Judas Kiss moves at a rapid-fire rate...
rushing like adrenaline through the bloodstream."
—*The Strand Magazine*

"Carefully orchestrated plot twists and engrossing characters... Flawed yet identifiable characters and genuinely terrifying villains populate this impressive and arresting thriller."
—*Publishers Weekly* on *Judas Kiss* [starred review]

"A twisty, creepy and wonderful book... Ellison is relentless and grabs the reader from the first page and refuses to let go until the soul-tearing climax."
—*Crimespree* on *14*

"A terrific lead character, terrific suspense, terrific twists...a completely convincing debut."
—Lee Child on *All the Pretty Girls*

"*All the Pretty Girls* is a spellbinding suspense novel and Tennessee has a new dark poet.
A turbocharged thrill ride of a debut."
—Julia Spencer-Fleming

Also by J.T. Ellison

THE IMMORTALS
THE COLD ROOM
JUDAS KISS
14
ALL THE PRETTY GIRLS

Look for J.T. Ellison's next novel

WHERE ALL THE DEAD LIE

available September 2011

For David Achord, who gave me the tools.

And for my Randy.

By three methods may we learn wisdom:
first, by reflection, which is noblest;
second, by imitation, which is easiest;
and third, by experience, which is the most bitter.

—Confucius

Imitation is suicide.

—Ralph Waldo Emerson

November 5

One

Boston, Massachusetts
8:12 p.m.
To: troy14@ncr.tr.com
From: bostonboy@ncr.bb.com
Subject: Boston

Dear Troy,
All is well.
BB

Quiet, except for the pounding of his heart.

She was home now, the week of late nights at the office finally over. He'd been starting to wonder if she'd ever make it back and was amused at the relief he felt when he saw her trundling down the street, her heavy wool coat dragging her steps. He had been more concerned than he expected, considering the stakes. This was just a game for him, after all. A lovely game.

She'd walked right past the truck without giving him a second glance. A few feet more and she was at her building. The wrought-iron kissing gate was broken, listing slightly, ajar. She pushed it open with her left hand and plodded up the steps. He watched with his head bent, eyes slid to the side as she unlocked the door and slipped inside. She never turned her head, never thought for a moment that she wasn't safe. Her millionth mistake this week.

He'd give it just one more minute, let her get upstairs. He busied himself with the package, the hard, plastic electronic-signature tablet, the straps on the box, all the while counting.

One Mississippi. Two Mississippi.

Once he hit sixty, he followed her path to the door. He pushed his finger into the white button, heard the shrill bell ringing. A woman's voice, tinny and thin, said, "Yes?"

"Delivery for June Earhart."

She buzzed him in without saying anything else. The door unlocked with a snap and he pulled it wide, allowing enough room for the handcart to fit in, adjusting his cap lower on his head. He didn't want his face to be seen. There were cameras in the foyer, he knew from earlier reconnaissance.

He thought about his target. He loved the way June looked. Brown hair, brown eyes, five foot six, somewhat lumpy, but that was just because she enjoyed her food and didn't exercise. Not lazy, never lazy. Just… padded.

He'd watched her take lunch all this week: Monday was McDonald's, Tuesday Subway, Wednesday a couple of iced crullers and a sugary juice smoothie from Dunkin' Donuts. Thursday she'd stayed in, but this afternoon she'd gone for a grinder, thick with salami and ham and cheese, with a side of potato chips. He wondered if she would smell like onions or if she'd been considerate enough to chew some gum, or suck on a Tic-Tac. He'd wager the latter; June was a self-conscious woman.

Granted, she'd walked from her office to each of these places, but she'd passed the pita joint and the all-natural juice-and-salad bar on the way. She chose the fattening food, and he knew it was because she was afraid to be alone but needed a defense mechanism to justify her single status to herself. He knew she sat in her dingy apartment, night after night, reading fitness and yoga magazines, dreaming about what it would be like to have a hard, lithe body, knowing that if she did, if she put in the effort, then she would be irresistible. And irresistible meant the paralegal from the office next door would notice her.

But she was afraid, and so dreamed only, her traitorous actions affording her a little more time. He knew she planned to join a gym at the beginning of the new year—it had been scribbled in purple ink on a list of possible New Year's resolutions discarded in her kitchen trashcan. He bet she made that resolution every year. June was the type of woman who made New Year's resolutions in November and never, ever saw them through. A woman who dreamed. A woman who would buzz a total stranger into her building because she never expected to be a victim.

His kind of woman.

The handcart made the trip awkward, bumping, bumping, bumping along the risers as he climbed. It would have helped if June hadn't ordered wine—he could have carried a normal box up the stairs. But this fit the image he had of a delivery man. Safe and unassuming, too busy with his work to be a threat.

He was at the door of June's second-story walk-up

now. He straightened his cap, arranged the handcart in front of him, the heavy wooden box tied tightly to the metal. He felt in his pocket—yes, everything was there. He arranged his features into something close to a smile and knocked.

June opened the door, still a little out of breath from her climb up the stairs. She'd taken off the heavy coat but her scarf was still wound around her neck in a breathtaking knot. Face-to-face with her, he didn't realize that he'd frozen until she said, "Kind of late for a delivery, isn't it?"

Moving his lips even wider over his teeth, he said, "Yes, ma'am. Apologies, ma'am. Got behind today."

"I never thought the damn stuff would get here. Put it over there," June said, pointing to an uncluttered alcove just before the kitchen. The same alcove he'd been in last night, watching June watch television. She'd never known he was there, and he'd slipped out after she fell asleep.

He wrestled the handcart into the foyer and made for the alcove, reached into his pocket and depressed the call button on his disposable phone. June's phone began to ring. He saw a brief flicker of debate in her eyes, then she shrugged and let the door close behind him as she started toward the living room to attend to the call. The moment her back was turned, he attacked. He whipped her scarf up into her mouth so she couldn't scream, then picked her up and moved toward the bedroom. Might as well be comfortable about it.

She was struggling, so he clouted her over the ear, just enough to daze her. That did the trick. June's eyes got woozy and the panic in them dulled. He stripped her down and tossed her on the bed, but took care in removing his own clothing piece by piece, folding the brown pants with the seams in, the shirt with sleeves together, then in half. He'd need to reclothe the driver, he didn't want anything getting on the uniform. June was groggy but cognizant, and when he rolled on the condom and took her, she tried to scream and get away. But he was much bigger, much stronger, and she had no chance. All her wriggling made it go quicker than he'd prefer, but at the end, he wrapped the trailing ends of the scarf around her throat and pulled them tight…and felt another kind of release flow through his veins.

When her eyes bugged out he pulled the scarf tighter still, watching critically as her skin turned a mottled red, and the whites of her eyes began to fill with blood. After three long, excruciating, joyful minutes, she went completely limp beneath him.

He cleaned up quickly, the truck was sure to be noticed soon. When everything was in place, he unwound the scarf from her neck and tied it in a jaunty bow. He kissed June on the forehead, briefly felt sorry that she'd never make it to the gym, dressed carefully then left the apartment, locking the push button lock behind him. He was surprised at how quietly the door closed, a silent witness to the death of its owner and the stranger going gently into that good night.

The night air was brisk. Snow was coming. He turned up his collar and pushed the handcart in front of him to the delivery truck. He'd been lucky: the original driver was his size, and his uniform fit perfectly. He clambered into the truck, drove around the corner to a quiet, deserted cul-de-sac. He stripped, replaced the brown uniform with his own street clothes, struggled a bit getting the dead limbs of the driver back into the arm and leg holes, but finally had things in their proper places. He patted the empty-eyed driver on the head. Collateral damage, but necessary.

He looked out the window on either side. The street was empty, the lights off in the two houses that flanked him. He was confident he hadn't been seen. He slid out the side of the truck and started to whistle, a tune he'd long forgotten. *Strangers in the night...exchanging glances...*

One down. Many, many more to go.

New York, New York
10:12 p.m.

To: troy14@ncr.tr.com
From: 44cal@ncr.ss.com
Subject: New York

Dear Troy,
Hey man. I'm on schedule.
44

The bag was rustling, damn it. He knew keeping the gun in the bag wasn't a good idea. Every step he took, all he could hear was the *crackle, crackle, crackle* against his leg. How was he supposed to sneak up on anyone like this? And he couldn't take the gun out and carry it properly—this was New York, after all. A cop on every corner, a chicken in every pot. Tourists every few steps, wide-eyed and camera happy.

The directions had been explicit, though. The paper bag was required.

The dog made me do it. The dog, the dog, the dog.

There. He was back in character.

A light snow began to fall. He knew it was dusting his body, his head, but he couldn't feel it, he'd pulled a black watch cap over his bald scalp. He got too cold otherwise. He crossed Houston and jogged into Washington Square Park, skipping around a puddle. *Crackle, crackle, crackle.* Maybe if he put his hand in his pocket he could shush the noise, but no, he'd look furtive and strange walking with his hand deep in his cargo pants. He remembered the instructions. *Don't draw attention to yourself. Walk tall, shoulders back, meet the eyes of those you pass. No one remembers the ones who look at you. They only remember the ones who look away.*

The dog made me do it.

He spied his quarry. Two men leaning close in to one another, one blond, one dark, oblivious on the green park bench. He felt his heart soar. Everything was going according to plan. Unbeknownst to their wives, who thought their respective spouses were at the gym—or a card game, or a movie, a late dinner, a meeting run long, terrible traffic—the men came to this bench every night. They sat and talked and dreamed together. Sometimes, if they were feeling terribly risky, a finger would softly stroke a palm, or a bit of pressure would be felt against a thigh. And on the glorious nights—the ones they both looked forward to the most—after a decent interval of time, they'd slink, one after the other, to a small, dingy apartment they borrowed for their occasional physical assignations, make hurried love, then disappear back to their lives. No one could know. No one did know.

Except one. And now two.

The dog made me do it.

He walked right up to them, the fornicators. The wretched, abnormal bastards. He stopped three feet away, reached in his pocket and pulled out an American Spirit. He lit it, took a long, hard drag and blew a plume of smoke out of his nose. He knew he looked like a dragon, did it again for his own amusement.

They hadn't looked up. They were completely wrapped up in their conversation. He felt a moment of disgust—men weren't supposed to feel like that about one another, it wasn't right—but their distraction was good. He was just another guy on the street, taking a smoke break. He finished the cigarette, savoring the deep, husky burn in his lungs, then tossed the butt away into the bushes.

He glanced over his shoulder. Washington Square was strangely deserted. It must be the cold, or providence. The angel sitting on his shoulder squeaked. He ignored him, like he'd been ignoring him for the past six weeks. He was bored, and ready. Ready to have some fun.

The men leaned closer together.

He sniffed once, like he was deciding what to do, then whipped the gun out of his pants pocket. The suppressor coughed and blood burst from the wounds. Two shots, each to the head. They never knew what hit them. He crumpled the letter and tossed it at them, then fled. The sinners slumped together, gray sweats and red brains commingling on the hard cold bench, little spatters of blood dropping into the dusting of snow beneath them. He heard the drip as he left.

The dog made me do it.

He was a block away when his angel told him he wasn't crackling anymore. Son of a bitch. He searched his pockets and found nothing but the gun, his cigarettes and the lighter. The bag had come out with the gun and dropped to the ground, he'd been too caught up in the furious noises the angel was making to notice. Shit. He wasn't supposed to leave anything behind except the note. Shit, shit.

He snapped right out of character, panic invading his bloodstream.

The angel talked to him. *Breathe. That's good, man. Breathe. Keep walking. It's just a brown paper bag, not like anyone can identify where it came from.* He made a mental note to throw the receipt for the package of lunch bags away as soon as he got home, just in case. He didn't want to leave anything behind that might implicate him. Orders were orders, after all.

The angel was on a roll now. *Fucking dog. Who blames a dog? Some crazy ass motherfucker, that's who. Dog made me do it, my ass.*

He wasn't a very good angel.

Behind him, sirens started. He felt the panic start in the pit of his stomach, gone watery at the noise. He needed to go. He needed to run. He started to break away, but the angel yelled in his ear.

Walk, homey. Walk away.

He stopped, and took a deep breath. Remembered the look of surprise on their faces. Turned to look at a bar window as the flashing lights cruised past, feigning interest. Just another guy on his way home, thinking about stopping in for one more drink. Smiled into his beard.

All in all, it had been a good night.

San Francisco, California
11:00 p.m.

To: troy14@ncr.tr.com
From: crypto@ncr.zk.com

Subject: San Francisco

Dear Troy,
It's going well. Will be in touch if anything goes wrong.
ZK

His palms were sweating.

He fought the urge to vomit, swallowed hard against the rising gorge. The gloves felt tight, itchy, claustrophobic. Defying orders, he whisked them off. Cool air made his damp skin prickle. There. Better. He tucked the gloves into the back pocket of his black jeans. His grip on the gun became surer, stronger. The metal was slick, hot in his hand. He'd imagined this moment for years. Now he had a chance, a real chance, to fulfill his fantasies and make some money at the same time. Save himself from the day-to-day grind he was living. The hateful job that laid him off. The hateful house the bank was taking. The hateful car he could barely make payments on. He was homeless, broke and hungry to try his hand at murder. The money would be a nice bonus. This opportunity had come at the perfect time.

Twenty yards away, two figures writhed in the front seat of a Toyota Tercel. A whisper of music emanated from the darkened vehicle. The windows were steamed, he couldn't see any details. But he knew it was a couple. Teenagers, out for a late-night grope. Their names didn't matter to him. Their lives didn't matter. They were just props. An illusion.

He inched closer, careful not to shift the gravel. This road was neglected, full of ruts and dust. The close smell of stagnant lake water wasn't a deterrent. The old road was commonly known as a lover's lane, the perfect place to go for privacy. Only the moon lit his path.

Ten yards now, and the nausea was back with a vengeance. He paused and breathed deeply through his mouth, willing his heart to slow, felt the adrenaline pulsing through his body like the stinging venom of a million tiny fire ants.

It was here. The moment he'd been dreaming of for years. Finally!

He talked himself back. *Remember what you're doing here. Remember what's at stake. Think of what can be.*

That was better. The nerves were gone, he was caught up in the moment.

It was time.

He took the last few steps electrified with excitement. He pulled the Maglite from his jacket pocket, hefted it into place. He could hear moaning now, see the thin flesh of the girl as she rose and plunged onto her lover's body. Over and over and over. He felt a tingle in his balls, like he felt when he was watching a porno. Recognized his nervous excitement for what it really was—arousal. Realized he liked that feeling a lot.

Using the blunt end of the Maglite, he tapped on the driver's-side window.

A small shriek; he'd surprised them. Good. He placed the silver shield up against the window. Watched the boy's eyes go white. A quick fumbling—they probably had some alcohol or drugs within easy reach—then the electronic window whirred down. Music spilled into the air. He recognized the tune, some old-school lovin' jam. The boy's spooked face filled the window frame. The girl retreated to the passenger seat, surreptitiously plucking at her skirt.

The boy cleared his throat. His lips were red and raw in the harsh beam of light.

"What is it, Officer? What's the problem?"

"No problem," he said, and squeezed the trigger. He caught the boy right under the left eye. *Perfect!* He hesitated for a moment, staring at the neat hole, astonished by the amount of blood that sprayed across the seat. The gun was so much louder than he expected—on the range, with ear defenders blocking the noise, it wasn't ever this intense, his ears were ringing but he could make out another sound, someone screaming. The girl.

He was jolted back to the moment. She was fumbling with the door latch, damn, she'd gotten the door open. He moved around the front of the car swiftly. Reached her as she started to run. She was crying in panicked little grunts. When she looked over her shoulder and saw him advancing, she started running backward and fell hard on her bottom. Scrabbling crablike, her feet catching in the dry twigs and gravel, she tried to scoot away. He took the shot.

The bullet entered her chest with a *whump* and she fell back, arms and legs tangled up, eyes staring heavenward. It was a clean shot to the heart. It only took a minute for her to die. Her breathing labored for a moment, hitching as her body realized that it had ceased to be alive. He ignored her kittenish whimpers and stared at the blood. Fascinating: the viscosity, the color. He reached out and touched the growing pool; his hand came away shimmering with red.

He realized he had the most intense erection. For the briefest of moments, he imagined touching himself, the candy-red wrapping around the hardened flesh, and that was enough to drive him right over the edge.

Sated, trying to catch his breath, he stowed the gun inside his jacket and brought out the camera. He took fifteen shots, from various angles and distances, then returned to the boy and did the same. He glanced at his watch. Just past midnight. Time to go.

He loped off into the woods, along the well-trodden path that led to the lake, pleased with the night's adventure, already thinking ahead to the next step. His nerves were gone now. He got to use the knife next.

Nashville, Tennessee
Midnight

Taylor Jackson started awake, heart hammering in her throat. She rarely slept soundly, but she must have been deeply under; she felt like she was swimming through the murky gray matter of her brain, trying to get the synapses to fire and open her eyes. Something had wakened her, something loud and close.

She reached her hand under the pillow, felt the cold steel of her Glock. Trying not to rustle the sheets, she drew the weapon to her chest, got a good grip on it, then bolted upright from the bed, gun sighted on the blank darkness of her room.

She heard the noise again and felt a chill move down her spine. An owl.

Shuddering, she lay back down and secreted the gun in its resting spot. She crossed her hands on her chest and willed her heart rate back to normal. The ceiling seemed closer than usual, moon spikes traversed the luminous paint.

Just this afternoon, her friend—if you could call Ariadne that—told Taylor the owl was her totem, her spirit guide. The owl would bring signs to her world. Not that

Taylor really believed any of that mumbo jumbo; the Pagan priestess was full of warnings and prevarications. But hearing the owl hoot once more—that made three distinct hoots—she felt the dread begin to build.

If she *were* to listen to Ariadne, she had to call this a sign.

She didn't need an owl to tell her things were about to go south. It had only been forty-eight hours since she'd been forced to shoot and kill a teenage boy. Time was not healing her wounds. If anything, she was worse now than the day of the shooting.

She rolled over, trying to force the boy's face from her mind. "Think about something else," Ariadne had told her. "It will get better."

That was a lie, though. It wasn't getting better. As a matter of fact, things were devolving rather quickly. She knew what was about to happen. She could feel it in her bones. She didn't need hooting owls or witches to tell her trouble was coming; her own gut instinct was on fire.

Her greatest enemy was finally making his move.

She stared at the ceiling. The Pretender, that psychopathic son of a bitch, had kidnapped Pete Fitzgerald, her dear friend Fitz, her sergeant and father figure. He'd held him and tortured him, but allowed him to live. A testament to the power the Pretender had, he held life and death in the palm of his hand. She understood the point loud and clear—he could take her. Anytime, anywhere.

He left behind a present for Taylor, a mockery of her abilities, and a warning, in an old Airstream trailer in the mountains of North Carolina. There was a note attached to Fitz's detached eyeball, written in Hebrew.

Ayin tahat ayin. The translation quite literal: an eye for an eye.

Fitz may be breathing, but he'd been disfigured for life. She had no idea what other damage had been inflicted, could only imagine the worst.

But she'd know soon enough. She was heading to Nags Head, North Carolina, in a few hours to bring him home.

She rolled over, the sheets tangling in her legs. She kicked at the whisper-soft fabric, let them settle around her like an obedient cloud.

The darkness filled her again, her mind still working in overdrive. The feeling that everything was falling apart, that she'd lost her edge, crept back in. The past two days had been among the worst in her life. Two days of recalling every moment in her head, the gun kicking in her palm, the sting in her wrist as she fired again, and again, the ringing in her ears deafening, the look of pure shock, and hatred, in the boy's eyes. For the thousandth time she wondered, *Could I have done differently?* Of course not, he'd drawn down on her. *Suicide by cop,* they called the phenomenon. The disturbed suspect trying to get the officer to end it for him because he didn't have the courage to end it himself.

Her mind shifted back to Fitz, to the pain he must be in, to visions of what it must have been like having his eye taken out. She prayed he'd been unconscious. She felt the gorge rise in her throat. Just speaking to him had dragged her out of her funk, momentarily. When he'd called, to tell her he was alive and okay, he hadn't gone into the details of his ordeal. But he had given her a message from the Pretender, oblique and taunting. Two words, full of meaning.

"He said to tell you, 'Let's play.'"

She rolled back the other way, punched the pillow to get the goose down plumped up, then smashed her head into the softness. It wasn't just the shooting and Fitz's pain that had her disturbed.

Let's play.

The Pretender hadn't been terribly subtle. There had been phone calls to the house. The bullet and note left in her mailbox while she was out of the country, chasing yet another madman—always another madman out there, waiting to be found… The all-pervasive feeling that she was being watched. The lengthy silence from Fitz, his reappearance, was the real message. *See what power I have, Taylor? I can touch those closest to you, anytime I want.*

The Pretender wouldn't be satisfied with hurting her friends. Not anymore.

Let's play.

She wished Baldwin were home. His enforced return to Quantico meant he'd been away for the past two days. She didn't realize just how much she needed him, had come to depend on his logic, and comfort, until he was gone. She'd been faced with one of her biggest challenges, had made it through just fine, but she longed to have him near. A small flash of happiness came over her. She'd see him tomorrow, if his disciplinary hearing didn't keep him longer. If tomorrow ever came.

The clock read 12:17 a.m. now.

With a deep sigh, she got out of the bed. She pulled on a pair of black yoga pants, slid the Glock .40 into the waistband at the back. It was heavy, and dragged on the elastic, so she tightened the strings. There, that was better.

Her beloved pool table was just the length of a hallway away. Once in the bonus room, she turned on a banker's lamp, the green cap casting an unearthly glow across the shadows. She flipped on the television. It was tuned to Fox News, and one of her favorite shows was on. *Red Eye* never ceased to amuse her; she especially liked the Halftime Report with Andy Levy. If she couldn't cry tonight, maybe she could laugh.

She pulled the cover off the table and took her time chalking her stick, listening to the television with one ear. She racked, broke, pocketed the balls in turn, then did it again.

The owl affected her more than anything she'd experienced before. Maybe she'd finally bought into the witch's insight. Ariadne had told Taylor she had no choice in the shooting, that she'd saved lives, that it was the right thing to do. She'd told Taylor Fitz would live, but be hurt. That Taylor and Baldwin were inextricably linked, and she could, and should, depend on him. Ariadne had insinuated herself into Taylor's life, acting as a surrogate in Baldwin's absence. So Taylor hadn't been totally alone with her worries. Which was good, because she couldn't shake the feeling that everything was collapsing around her. The Pretender was coming for her, and this time, he wouldn't be satisfied with passing her in the night.

She didn't know why he'd chosen this particular moment to act, to reach out. Why he'd chosen her in the first place, truth be told. He was a threat to her very existence, *that* she did know. Alarms and guns and protection aside, he wanted her for something.

Let's play.

She broke again, the balls scattering in her vehemence, the cue ball sloppily careening off the table onto the floor with a thud. She bent to retrieve it, set it gently back onto the green felt.

Am I ready for him?

First things first.

She was going to North Carolina to collect Fitz.

November 6

Two

The Outer Banks, North Carolina

The Gulfstream's flight attendant, if asked, would have been circumspect and silent, as befitted her job. She worked for the deputy director of the Federal Bureau of Investigations, and discretion was her middle name. Which meant she saw a great deal that mere mortals weren't privy to. She saw her boss talking with other discreet and powerful men. She saw people transported who might otherwise come under scrutiny if they traveled by normal routes. She saw new widows and the now childless. She saw much, yet never spoke about it.

But the gray-eyed woman sitting midcabin in the expansive leather chair, a crystal-cut glass of Voss water untouched at her elbow, was a bit of a surprise. The flight attendant, whose name was Cici, had initially been charmed by the pleasant smile, mesmerized by the mismatched eyes, the right slightly darker than the left, like it hadn't made up its mind to embrace gray just yet. She'd loved the smoky, Southern drawl that emanated from the woman's mouth when she said good morning, the blond hair tied back from her face in a perfectly messy bun. Cici fingered her own limp locks and wished, for the millionth time, for some fullness, some body, so she could wind her hair up and leave it alone for the day.

She had been envious of the woman's height, about six feet tall without heels, and her whole look: a flattering black cashmere turtleneck, black leather jacket, low-slung jeans and black Frye motorcycle boots. She'd seen the holster and badge attached to the waistband of the jeans and felt a mild shock of surprise: this woman didn't look like a cop. But she was a cop—Cici knew from the manifest. A Homicide lieutenant from Nashville, Tennessee.

The lieutenant sat in the wide leather chair with an uncommon stillness—no fidgeting, no crossing and recrossing of legs, no drumming of fingers. Her hands were folded loosely in her lap, her head turned away slightly so she could stare out the window. This lack of motion left Cici feeling uneasy, and she tiptoed around the cabin so as not to disturb.

Cici also knew the woman was closely attached to one of Cici's favorite men in the whole wide world: Dr. John Baldwin. Baldwin was her boss's darling, and she understood why. His handsomeness aside—*oh, those green eyes are to die for!*—Baldwin was insightful, and caring. He was the glue that held her boss together, the son he'd never had. She knew that because Garrett Woods had told her so, once, when he'd been drinking something stronger than Voss water.

Baldwin had led men and women into battle, fighting the forces of evil that came across their desks, pushing back the tides of blood that swept out before their opponents' wickedness. He was polite, so much so that she sometimes wondered if it was an act. Who could be like that all the time? So contained. So like his woman. She'd often wondered just what made Dr. John Baldwin tick. Cici was no profiler, but she'd studied psychology in school. His calm facade was a veneer, she was sure of it. He had demons, coiled and writhing in his gut. Guilt, and shame, and hate. Everyone did, right? Right?

She felt that same sort of fight going on behind the lieutenant's gray eyes. Guilt, and shame, and hate. And if Cici wasn't mistaken—*remember, she was no expert and would be the first to tell you that*—if Cici wasn't mistaken, there was something else lurking in those loch-gray depths.

Fear.

Taylor felt the landing gear unfold and lock into place. The tarmac appeared beneath her, gray and chilly. The jet landed softly, came to a halt within minutes. Baldwin had arranged for his boss's plane to collect her in Nashville and fly her to North Carolina. She had to admit, flying in the Gulfstream was a habit she could get used to.

The attendant opened the galley door, bid her farewell. Taylor wasn't sad the flight was over; the woman was as twitchy as a deer in an open meadow, pale and staring from under nearly lashless lids.

She stepped down the stairs onto the tarmac, surprised to see little flakes of snow drifting swiftly from the slate sky. She could already feel it accumulating on her hair, so she shook it out and wound it back up into a ponytail.

Baldwin was waiting for her. His deep green eyes lit up when he saw her step down the stairs. He hadn't shaved since he left her Monday morning, and he looked like he belonged on a billboard, a perfectly groomed-to-be-scruffy model. She felt that strange pull of desire deep in her gut, and the uncontrollable joy at being near him again made a huge smile break out on her face. He smiled in return, grabbed her by the waist and kissed her deeply. When they broke for air they both spoke at the same time.

"Was your flight okay?"

"Is Fitz here?"

They laughed, and Taylor said, "You first."

"He's not here. The North Carolina State Bureau of Investigations agents have him. They're still doing a debrief, and he's scheduled for surgery this afternoon. He's going to be flown to Duke. There's a specialist who's been retained to help."

"We have specialists in Nashville. Why can't we bring him home?"

"Because the North Carolina SBI want to keep him in their jurisdiction for the time being. They have three district offices involved. This is a big case for them, a score. They want hands on him at all times. You know how it is. Besides, this guy at Duke is one of the best. They're going to clean up the eye socket, put in an orbital spacer so the ocular muscles won't collapse. Then they'll transfer him to Vanderbilt for the duration of his recovery. I've seen Fitz, but just briefly. I know he'll be thrilled to see you though."

See me. That spike drove right through her. "His poor eye. Is he in much pain?"

"He was stable enough to be checked out of the emergency room and taken to the police station for questioning, so I'm sure they've given him everything he needs. He's a tough old bird, too. He's going to be just fine.

They said the damage was fixable, and he'll be able to have a prosthetic in about a month."

"I want to talk to him. See if he'd rather go back to Nashville. They can't treat him like a suspect. It should be his choice."

They started walking toward the terminal. The private airstrip in Duck was tiny, accommodating only the smallest of jets and single-engine planes.

"Any other news?" Taylor asked.

"Yes, actually. The harbormaster discovered Fitz's boat. It's been docked at the marina here for a week or so. He went to collect the rent and knew immediately something was wrong, pulled out and called the cops. There's a lot of blood. The Nags Head Police found Susie's body stuffed in the head. Multiple stab wounds."

Taylor felt a wave of nausea pass through her. Susie McDonald was the best thing that had happened to Fitz in a long time. Taylor had liked her, Fitz had loved her. Her loss would be enormous.

"Poor Susie. Does Fitz know?"

"Just that she's dead, not the details. He was there when Susie died, though, so he probably has some ideas. He's in remarkably good shape, considering what he's been through. Losing an eye isn't life-threatening. Painful as hell, but he's going to be just fine. I'm sure he'll tell you all about it."

"Does the marina have cameras? Did they see anyone leaving the boat?"

"They do have cameras, but nothing has been found yet. We're early days, remember. I just got down here myself."

Taylor watched the snow fall in graceful dances. It was gathering quickly. The forecast was for at least three inches, quite a lot this early in the season for this neck of the woods.

"The Pretender isn't stupid, Baldwin. He's trying to draw me out. Hurting Fitz is a guarantee. He knows I'm coming for him, and if I don't, he'll come for me."

"Taylor."

"Seriously. No more foreplay. I want to see the bastard bleed."

He sighed deeply. "Which is why you've got a security detail on you 24/7 as soon as I send you home. I refuse to let him get his hands on you."

"I know. You've said that before. I don't need a detail."

He stopped short of the terminal door and pulled her around to face him.

"You listen to me. I am not kidding. This is building to a head. I know you can feel that, too. We have to be alert."

"I'm alert. I'm alert. Stop fretting." She patted her waist, the Glock nestled in its holster on her hip, then reached into the front pocket of her jeans and brought out a single .40-caliber Winchester jacketed hollow point.

"See? I'm even carrying the bullet the bastard sent me. I'm saving this one for him."

Baldwin's mouth twitched, she could tell he was fighting a smile.

"What's on it?" he asked finally.

She flipped the bullet into his hand. She'd used a marker to draw a lopsided *hamsa,* the hand of Fatima, on the casing. The eye felt like a talisman of sorts to her. It was juvenile, she knew that, but the action had given her great satisfaction.

"I have every intention of letting the Pretender know exactly how I feel about his eye-for-an-eye mentality."

Baldwin shook his head and sighed.

She pulled on his arm. "Come on. Let's go. What's happened since your hearing? Have you heard anything?"

He hesitated for the briefest of moments, then said, "Yes. But not now. We'll talk about it when we're alone."

Something was wrong. He was hedging. She could feel him pulling away slightly as they walked. The hearing at Quantico had been disciplinary—a case from Baldwin's past—she knew that, but he hadn't gone into detail. She was wrapped up enough in her own pain that she hadn't pushed. Maybe that had been a mistake.

Biting her lip, she followed him through the tiny terminal building, through the glass double doors and into the parking lot. The State Bureau of Investigations had sent a car for them. She could see it idling, black and square, so conspicuously federal, the foggy condensed air shuttling out of the tailpipes. The driver wore shades despite the lack of sun. It was oppressively warm in the backseat. Baldwin asked the agent to turn the heat down. He acquiesced, then pulled out onto the main road slowly. It wasn't icy yet, that would come later, but the snow was making everything slick.

The landscape was exotic and familiar at the same time. Taylor hadn't been to the Outer Banks since she was a girl, and never during the cold months. Snow drifted down onto the sand: a mismatched postcard. *Come celebrate winter at the beach.* It conjured images of roaring bonfires, happy dogs running up and down the lengths of sand, people in warm woolen sweaters braving the icy shores. Of the North, not the South.

She was surprised to find it so appealing. She was a Nashvillian born and bred, which meant she both hated snow and revered it with the wonder of a child. Aside from the huge Christmas storm they had last year, snow was more of an anomaly in Nashville. Ice, sleet, yes, but these fluffy, prancing flakes were utterly foreign, and completely charming.

She didn't know if she'd want it around all the time, to be sure. But this, the snow falling on the fine sand in silent whispers, felt right. Like forgiveness.

Baldwin took her hand and squeezed as if he knew her thoughts. He always seemed to be able to see right past her skin, past the bone, directly into her being. Granted, he was a psychiatrist, but this was more than having a clinical understanding. He *felt* the pain she was experiencing. He knew that every time she used her gun, another little bit of her soul stripped away into nothingness. She could only hope that if he continued to love her, maybe, just maybe, Baldwin could stop her humanity from slipping away.

"Have you been sleeping?" he asked.

She smiled. "The pool table's been getting a workout, but I slept some last night."

"You know I could give you something for that. Or Sam could."

"Sam's busy," she said, looking away. "She has a lot on her mind. She wasn't planning on getting pregnant again so soon. It's a strain on both her and Simon."

"Are you two fighting again?"

"No. She's… I just don't want to drug myself to sleep."

Because if I'm out, and he comes for me, I'll be completely defenseless.

Things between her and Sam Loughley had been

tense lately, but Taylor didn't want to share that with Baldwin. No sense in getting him more upset than he already was. It wasn't fun to be in a spat with your best friend, especially one you had to work with almost daily because she was the chief medical examiner. She'd known Sam since kindergarten, and they'd fought many times over the years. They always made up; it would happen again.

The trouble had started when James "Memphis" Highsmythe, late of New Scotland Yard and the FBI's new liaison back to his own group, had made a play for her. Taylor had foolishly flirted back, and Sam had called her on it. The situation was Taylor's fault, she knew that. But the whole thing wearied her. She assiduously avoided thinking of Memphis if at all possible, confident that the little crush he had on her would go away if the feelings weren't reciprocated. Hashing things out with Sam just meant she'd been thinking about Memphis, and the kiss they'd shared, and she just didn't have the desire to go there. Not now. Not with everything feeling so damn precarious.

He took her hand.

"Okay, okay. How'd the session go with Dr. Willig?"

"Victoria? Fine."

He sensed the lie, but didn't say anything. After the shooting, all the deaths, all those blameless lives ended, Taylor's commander, Joan Huston, had insisted she get checked out before she returned to active duty. More than the cursory checkup required by the department after a shooting. And that meant time with Willig, Metro's department psychologist. Taylor had spent a grand total of ten minutes with the shrink. She wasn't in the mood to hash through the details out loud.

She looked at the ocean, the roiling waves crashing on the sand, and identified a bit too much.

Recognizing that Taylor was through talking, Baldwin sank back into the deep leather seats and retreated into his own world to check his BlackBerry. She was relieved the interrogation was over. She was still learning how to share with him. She'd been alone long enough to learn true emotional self-reliance, and the fact that she had a soul mate beyond her childhood friends could be disconcerting. She still found herself holding back, not saying everything she felt. Dr. Willig would tell her that wasn't healthy, but she'd get there. She was going to marry Baldwin, and soon, which meant allowing those last few barriers to be battered. Thankfully, he was a patient man, and knew her well enough to back off when he felt her closing down.

They were quiet for a mile or two, until the car turned into a shell-covered driveway, the entrance to the Nags Head Police Station. The building was as informal as the rest of Nags Head—weathered gray shingles, white trim, a second story as a defense against the inevitable hurricane season flooding. The car came to a halt. Their driver got out and lit a cigarette before silently disappearing around the corner of the building.

A slim man came out the main doors, waving in welcome. He had brown hair and matching eyes, was dressed for the weather in chinos and a battered tan wool sweater.

They exited the vehicle and took the short sidewalk to him. The man smiled up at Taylor in appreciation.

"Good grief, you touch the sky, don't you?" he said.

She heard Baldwin stifle a laugh. If she had ten cents for every time someone commented on her height…

"I try not to fly too close to the sun. Nice to meet you," she replied.

They shook hands. "Steve Nadis, I'm the chief here in Nags Head. How ya doing?"

"Lieutenant Taylor Jackson, Metro Nashville Homicide. I'm good. And you?"

"Fine, fine. Got a whole host of strange cops and a few Feds roaming the place, but we're all good. Come on in, I just made some coffee. Colder than a witch's teat in a brass bra out here. Snow. This early, too. Strange weather for us. Dr. Baldwin, good to see you again."

"You, too, Chief."

They followed him inside the station, which held all the classic cop shop paraphernalia. Taylor felt immediately at home. There was something about being with cops—she never quite trusted people who weren't in law enforcement. Though she'd come across her fair share of jerks behind the blue wall, for the most part, she only felt like herself around people who had been there, who could relate to her permanent mind-set. It was what made her relationship with Baldwin work so well.

They passed a wooden counter and the office assistant working behind glass, then went through a rabbit warren of hallways until they reached the door that was informally marked "Chief" with a brown-and-white placard.

The comforting scent of roasted coffee beans drifted down the hallway.

Nadis gestured to two chairs facing his desk. "How do you take it, Lieutenant? I know Dr. B here likes his black."

"Light, please. Lots of cream and sugar." Taylor wasn't a huge fan of coffee, it had a tendency to tear up her insides if she wasn't careful, but she didn't want to be rude. She *was* chilled, something warm would help.

Nadis disappeared, whistling, and Taylor smiled at Baldwin. The Nags Head chief was a bit like a cheerful firefly. Fitting for a beach cop. Taylor had noticed there was a certain mentality in some of the more unique law enforcement regions. It took a special personality to live at the beach full-time, and a specific kind of person to govern those free spirits. Her own chief would be an absolute disaster in a laid-back town.

Nadis returned with the two coffees, handed them out, then sat at his desk facing them. The liveliness had disappeared from his face.

"We don't get a lot of murders out here. I have four good people in my CID, but I knew the SBI was already involved, so we gave them a shout. I hope you don't mind."

"Of course not," Taylor said. "I would have done the same thing if I was in your position. Tell me, do you, they, have any leads?"

"I'm afraid not. Like I told the doc here, there's a bunch of evidence that's been collected, and the state boys are running the show now. Your friend's been through a lot. Good fellow. I can see he's been a fine cop."

"He still is. I doubt this will derail Fitz at all." Her tone was sharper than she intended, and she felt bad when Nadis declined his head in apology.

"Of course he still is. I didn't mean that. Sorry."

She shrugged it away. There were more important things to deal with. "How did he come to be here, in Nags Head?"

"We found him yesterday morning, early, wandering

on the side of the road in his skivvies. Face was cut up. He couldn't tell us how he'd gotten there."

Baldwin interjected, "We assume they dropped him after they killed Susie. When the harbormaster found the boat, she'd been dead at least forty-eight hours, maybe more."

Jesus.

Nadis rocked back in his chair. "A couple of agents from the west branch of the SBI found his eye earlier in the week, in that trailer near Asheville. It's not a quick drive, over seven hours. His captor, or captors, would have had plenty of time to get him here. He was probably drugged."

"Or he's been here in Nags Head the whole time, on the boat. They found his eye four days ago. I wonder if the suspect just delivered the eye to Asheville to throw us off the trail," Taylor said.

Nadis looked at her with new appreciation. "Now that you mention it, that does make more sense. Sergeant Fitzgerald was pretty nonsensical when we found him. We took him to the hospital, got him cleaned up. He couldn't tell us much about what had happened, just his name and his badge number. He was in shock, of course. But we'd seen the alerts, called up to the FBI. Dr. Baldwin got on a plane down here, the SBI coots showed up first thing this morning, and Bob's your uncle. That's all we got right now."

"Why didn't y'all keep him in the hospital?"

"I figured you'd ask—our hospital is kind of small, and there was a food poisoning outbreak last night. They needed the bed, he was stable, so we brought him here."

Taylor didn't realize she was tapping her fingers on the side of her cup until Baldwin set his coffee down on the chief's desk. "I know Lieutenant Jackson would like to see her sergeant. Can we make that happen?"

"I think that's a good idea." Nadis glanced at his watch. "Those SBI folks have been going at him for a couple of hours now. He's probably ready for a break. But, Lieutenant, I need to warn you. He's seen a lot the past few days, been through a lot. You may want to—"

"Chief, no offense, but Fitz is like a father to me. I won't push him. But I would like to see him. If you wouldn't mind?"

"Okay." Nadis stood and gestured for them to follow him. The hallway seemed to go on forever, and led to a steel door. Nadis knocked twice as a warning, then inputted his code into a numbered lock, explaining as he did. "This is a secure area, we usually use it to let some of the local yahoos sleep off their buzz. We don't have a jail, per se, here in the building, just holding cells, so this works for our needs. The corrections facility is a mile down the road."

The door clicked open, and he led them through. A woman stood on the other side, staring into a window with her arms crossed on her chest. She was about five foot four, trim and athletic, with bushy brown hair tied back from her face. Her black suit was well made, and Taylor could see the bulge of a shoulder holster under her left arm.

She turned and saw the entourage, stepped away and introduced herself.

"You must be the sergeant's lieutenant. I'm Renee Sansom, SBI. Hey, Dr. Baldwin. My boys are in with your guy right now. You want to see him?"

Taylor shook Sansom's hand. "Yes, I would."

"He's been through a lot," the woman said simply,

then knocked on the window. Taylor knew it was a one-way mirror, acrylic, unbreakable, but for some reason avoided looking into the room. It seemed impolite to stare at him when he couldn't see her. And with so many warnings on Fitz's condition, she was starting to worry about him even more.

The door opened and two men stepped out, blue suited, wearing red-and-white striped ties. Two of a kind. They nodded professionally and the second one held the door open for her.

Taylor took a deep breath and entered.

Fitz had shrunk since she'd seen him last. He'd lost weight, his shoulders were hunched together. He seemed to be folded in on himself, protecting the kernel of pain that was driving him. Taylor knew he must be exhausted, and that hurt her as much as his obvious grief.

He turned as she entered. The left side of his face was covered with a large white pressure bandage, the skin of his cheek tinged with the yellow of Betadine, the iodine base discoloring the flesh around the dressing. But his remaining eye, round and dark blue, lit up when he saw her.

"Good to see you, little girl," he said gruffly, and she heard the tears in his voice.

And then she had her arms around him, holding on for dear life.

Three

Nashville, Tennessee

Colleen Keck typed in the blog title, her fingers moving quickly.

No Clues in the Hunt for a Missing Nashville Teen

She looked it over for errors, saw none. Good. Catchy. She took a sip of her Diet Coke, then started the entry, her fingers flying over the keys.

Nashville is still reeling from the horrific Halloween massacre last week, when eight teenagers were viciously murdered in Green Hills on Halloween afternoon. As the burials begin, more frightening news is leaking out: a seventeen-year-old varsity athlete from Montgomery Bell Academy has gone missing. Peter Schechter, a junior defensive end for the MBA football team and the lacrosse team co-captain, did not make it to a morning practice the day after Halloween and has not been heard from since.

His vehicle, a silver 2006 BMW 5 series, was found Saturday morning in the parking lot of the McDonald's in West End. His parents, Winifred and Peter Schechter, Sr., report that their son was responsible, hardworking and very settled in his routine. "It is completely out of character for Pete not to check in. He's religious about it. We're very close," said a tearful Mrs. Schechter.

Schechter's friends confirm that they were downtown, on Lower Broad, attending an eighteen-and-over Halloween night party at the bar Subversion, though no one remembers driving him back to his car. "We just assumed he'd left with someone," said Brad Sandford, a friend and fellow ballplayer. "We went home without him."

The police do not believe that Schechter left of his own volition, though they will not release details. He is not answering his cell phone, and no texts have been sent from his number. A source close to the investigation who has asked not to be identified confirms the police suspect foul play. An AMBER Alert is in effect, and a search is being organized. If you know anything about the whereabouts of Peter Schechter, please call 866-555-2010. All tips can be left anonymously.

Humbly submitted,
Felon E

Colleen read through her piece one more time, corrected a comma splice, and published the story. It automatically fed into her Twitter feed; she watched TweetDeck as the message went viral through the community, her hundreds of thousands of followers dutifully spreading the word that a new blog post had been published. She cracked her knuckles and allowed herself a small smile.

Felon E was her baby, her creation, her universe. While the world of true-crime bloggers grew exponentially, with new entrants on the scene almost daily, she was still number one, the top of the heap. Her blog echoed throughout the online world because of her accuracy, her tact and her compassion.

She utilized all the social networks to get the word out, and her fans did the rest. She'd come a long way from the crime beat at *The Tennessean,* though no one online had any idea who she was. Anonymity allowed her to utilize sources from multiple jurisdictions without complaint. The law enforcement folks she worked with knew they could trust her, that she'd never, ever reveal her sources. Her silence was golden.

She was admired by law enforcement, too. Many departments utilized her blog and announcements to get background out about hopeless or urgent cases, especially AMBER Alerts and Silver Alerts, work she was happy to do gratis.

To stay on top of the breaking crime news, she'd carefully cultivated contacts throughout the country, but her bread and butter came from friends in the 911 call centers. Major metropolitan areas, local county networks—she'd made deals with hundreds of folks. Those connections allowed her a jump on the competition. She had video and audio feeds live, an online police scanner running at all times, the Emergency Radio app on her iPhone, and an open policy from her contacts. They knew what calls were worth passing along to her. She accepted tips from the general public, too, but always,

always confirmed with two sources before she ran her stories.

After a high-profile bank robber had written in to the blog and asked to surrender, the media had been keeping a close eye on Felon E. There had been requests from every major news outlet for her to appear on their shows to talk about how she could keep on top of the country's crime, but she refused all interviews. She wasn't in this for her own glory. She was in it because she wanted to help.

At least that was what she told herself, over and over again.

The blog was raking in the dough. The advertising she sold on the site, and so judiciously monitored, paid more than enough to keep her afloat, enough that she could afford to send her five-year-old son, Flynn, to the pricey Montessori school down the street. It was a luxury she never thought she'd be able to find the money for, and while the bills got paid, there wasn't too much left for lavish possessions. No matter. Working at home meant no extraneous business expenses: fancy suits and gas and lunches out. No husband—and no desire to date—meant no need for overpriced cosmetics, and she didn't have to fuss with her hair; the expensive highlights she used to maintain like clockwork every six weeks had grown out, and that money went to pay her grocery bill. It all balanced in the end.

She toggled her mouse and tried not to look at the picture wedged at the back of her desk. It was no use. Shifty as a sneak thief, her eyes slid over the faded photograph in its dented silver frame. A dark-haired man holding a small blue bundle, smiling broadly with paternal pride. He'd been gone a week later, leaving her to manage a newborn and a funeral. She swallowed hard and let her eyes drift away before she could make real contact, before the memories of him overwhelmed her.

Angels and death, missing fathers and harried mothers. The past clashing with the reality of her present.

She'd explained to Flynn time and again that his daddy was with the angels. It just doesn't register when they're so young. You can't miss what you don't know, and Flynn had never met the smiling young man who'd fathered him. All Flynn really cared about was Colleen paying him attention when he wanted it, and being left alone for "me" time when he desired. His newly independent streak worried her, hurt her fragile feelings when he pushed her away from the door to his room and said, "I need some time for me, Mommy."

And pizza. He was passionate about pizza. Just like his father.

Flynn's daddy was an on-the-rise young cop who'd been mowed down in the line of duty. One minute here, the next gone. They said it was instantaneous. That he died bravely. That he never knew what hit him. She'd been at enough crime scenes to know they were lying—gunshots didn't kill you instantly, you lingered for several minutes while your organs got the message that they were no longer needed and shut down, one by one—but she'd nodded like she understood and hadn't asked anything more.

She'd held her silence all this time, though his killer hadn't been caught.

When Tommy died, Colleen was working at the paper, pulling down just about enough to cover the mortgage and little else. Though the foundation his coworkers had set up was flush, that money was earmarked for Flynn's college fund. The day-to-day expenses of a single-parent family were astronomical, and she quickly realized that even with the hefty insurance settlement, her job at the paper wasn't going to cut it.

She'd always been a crime buff, that was probably why she married Tommy in the first place. A cop whore, he'd called her, joking and laughing at her over dinner, his dark eyes dancing while he filled her in on his shift. After he died, some of the other brothers in blue had sat in his rightful spot across from her at the rickety kitchen table, relaying stories and keeping her spirits up while she draped a blanket across her body and nursed Flynn.

When her grief allowed her rational mind to surface, she knew she needed to find something more to raise her small family. She was a writer, after all, so she thought about writing a book. It would be fast, easy money; she could break into the market with a flashy true-crime story. Then one of her heroes, Dominick Dunne, died, and the extensive coverage of his career brought another thought to the fore. The idea of a crime blog started to germinate. She liked it. Quick and dirty. Instantaneous feedback, a running record. Like Dunne, she could be a voice for the victims, but she'd be behind the scenes, an angel of sorts. She preferred that no one knew who she was. She didn't like to sign her real name to her work; she never aspired to fame, or attention. It was better this way. Safer.

Colleen started populating Felon E with stories, announced it was under way on a few true-crime message boards, and it took off like a shot. She was still surprised at how well it was doing; within a year of the launch, she was able to quit her job and dedicate herself to running the blog full-time. She'd underestimated the fervor civilians had toward the intimate, gory details of the crimes they were surrounded by. She had a fascination, but she was a cop's wife, and a former crime reporter. She'd been caught up in the scene. Her readers were regular folks off the street, but bloodthirsty for all that.

She'd attracted a few nuts and the like over the years, but Tommy had taught her well. She could shoot the guns in the safe with the ease of many hours of practice, had the house wired to an elaborate alarm system. She knew self-defense techniques. She was smart and savvy and capable of disguising her whereabouts with the computer. She'd been a computer science major at MTSU before switching to journalism her junior year. That gave her two important legs up, an edge over other crime bloggers—the ability to code her site with lovely little traps for those trying to sneak in the back door, and the skill to do all her own web work, ensuring that precious anonymity.

So much for memory lane. She really should move that picture of Tommy—every time she looked at it, the whole scenario flooded into her brain. She really should. But she wouldn't.

Colleen stood and stretched, then slipped into the kitchen, past the cabinet that needed some work—it was practically hanging off its hinges—to the refrigerator with its broken ice machine. She cracked the lid on her fourth Diet Coke of the morning and started thinking of the angle for the next installment of the story. Teenage boys from upscale Nashville neighborhoods didn't go missing every day. But if she was going to make this story sing, she needed a scoop, something major. Something official.

Settling back at her desk, she set the soda down and opened her internet browser. She tried to post five original stories a day, with attendant follow-ups as they happened, so combing the net and working her sources took the vast majority of her time. The minute one good story was in the can, she was off to the next.

Where was Peter Schechter?

Her message icon was flashing, so she toured through her new email first. She received tons of tips from true-crime buffs across the country, so many that she could barely handle them all. To help her sort through the mass quickly, she'd coded some of her best sources in the major metropolitans so they would stand out. There were three messages blinking red and marked urgent, one each from San Francisco, Boston and New York.

She popped up San Francisco first; it had come in the earliest. All thoughts of a local boy going missing disappeared when she read the message. Her heart began to beat a bit harder. She read it through twice, then closed it and sat back in her chair. Could it be? And was she the only one who had this?

She tried not to get too excited. A diversion was in order; she opened the message from New York.

A buzz began in her ears, the rush of adrenaline sparking through her system, bringing every nerve ending alive. She opened the message from Boston and nearly passed out.

If this was for real, this was huge. This was so huge.

She flew into activity, responding to her three contacts, asking the most relevant questions she could think of. Then she went to her bookshelf, her reference material, her background. Nestled on the left-hand side of the third shelf was a book she'd opened so many times that the edges were frayed and the binding broken. *The Encyclopedia of Serial Killers.*

She stroked the cover reverentially, then flipped it open. The book was organized alphabetically by proper name, not the nicknames given to the men and women whose crimes were housed in these hallowed pages.

She had to take this in steps. She debated for a moment, then decided. San Francisco first. She turned to a dog-eared page at the very end, to one of the few killers who *was* categorized by a nom de plume, one of the all-time majors. The man who remained anonymous after all these years. The man who hadn't been caught.

She started with the Zodiac.

Four

The Outer Banks, North Carolina

Taylor was only allowed to spend twenty minutes catching up with Fitz before Renee Sansom knocked on the door and told them it was time to transport him to Duke for his afternoon surgery.

Taylor had tried asking questions, but Fitz was surprisingly evasive about the crimes he'd endured. He kept repeating the same lines: "I was drugged, I think." "I really don't remember anything." "All I know is what I told you." "He said to tell you 'Let's play.'" "He said you'd know what that meant."

She'd expected him to be forthcoming with her, but after ten minutes of trying and failing to get him to open up, hearing him reiterate his apparent memory loss, she stopped. She hoped he wasn't suffering from full-on PTSD, that he was just overwhelmed by the situation, that he remembered more than he was saying, or would remember when the shock wore off. But that was probably wishful thinking, considering what he'd been through.

She switched tactics. She asked if he wanted to go

back to Nashville for the surgery and was surprised to hear he'd rather stick to the plan they had for him, go to Duke and get the surgery there. She wondered if he wanted to stay close to Susie, lying in the morgue.

Pushing the worry and concern from her voice, she filled him in on what had been happening in Nashville. How much his fellow detectives Lincoln Ross and Marcus Wade were looking forward to getting him back to work, about the new member of the Homicide team, Renn McKenzie, and their latest boss, Commander Joan Huston. Fitz seemed to appreciate the distraction. He held her hand tightly through the time they spent together, and Taylor could feel the frisson of fear that coursed through his body on a regular loop. He was scared, and that freaked her out.

The Duke Medical Center Life Flight helicopter landed in the small parking lot in front of the police station. Fitz was loaded in, walking slowly, head down. Taylor and Baldwin waved wildly until the sophisticated chopper was out of sight. Taylor hated like hell not going with him, but promised to be by his side tonight, after he was out of surgery. She and Baldwin would take the Gulfstream up, and as soon as Fitz was cleared, they'd take him home.

The snow was whipping harder now, the storm in full gear. They trooped back inside the station, shivering. The door closed against the blustery day, they made their way to the conference room Nadis had evacuated for their purposes.

Sansom eyed Taylor and said, "Okay. It's time for your debrief. I need to know everything you have about this creep. Your boy there didn't want to talk to me, but I assume he told you quite a bit. Let's have it."

Taylor shook her head. "Fitz didn't tell me anything, actually. He says he was drugged, that he doesn't remember anything, and I believe him. Like you said, he's been through a lot. I'm not inclined to push him too hard. If he starts to remember, or seems more open to discussion, I'll be there to hear the story. In the meantime, I can give you enough background to get you started."

Sansom looked at her for a moment. "Our initial blood work doesn't indicate drugs in his system."

Taylor stared her down. "You know a complete toxicology will take weeks."

"Perhaps. Perhaps your sergeant is trying to hide something."

That got under Taylor's skin. "You can't possibly think he had something to do with this. He lost his eye, for Christ's sake. What do you think, he murdered his girlfriend, scooped his eye out with a spoon and drove it on up to Asheville?" She was breathing heavily, fists clenched, and barely felt Baldwin's hand on her arm. Restraint. But come on. Accusing Fitz of any involvement in Susie's murder was ridiculous.

Sansom continued to bait her. "I don't know, Lieutenant. It's awfully convenient. He wouldn't be the first to have a relationship go south and blame it on the local bogeyman."

"That's bullshit, and you know it."

Sansom had the audacity to smile.

"Taylor," Baldwin said, the note of warning clear, "let's just cover what we know so far, and take it from there."

"Fine," Taylor replied, biting off the comment she really wanted to make. She tried to see the case from an outsider's perspective. While she and Baldwin knew, in their bones, that this was the work of the Pretender, people who hadn't been privy to the earlier cases might be led astray by the crime scene. Any good investigator would look at all the possibilities. That was all Sansom was doing.

Taylor kept telling herself that, felt her blood pressure drop a notch.

Baldwin held Taylor's chair for her, and the three of them sat at a long table that Taylor suspected doubled as a lunch spot for Nadis's team. Spots of dried mustard coated the wooden edge of the table in front of her seat. She scooched down a hair so she wouldn't accidentally lean into it.

Sansom's two agents joined them, were introduced as Wally Yeager and Eliot Polakis. They each had a clean yellow pad in front of them, ready for notes.

"Baldwin, why don't you begin?" Taylor said. She wasn't quite ready to reengage.

"All right. I've been profiling the Pretender for a year now, and the profile is still in progress. It keeps changing. He's a chameleon. He adapts, copies, mimics, then disappears. Despite your thoughts about Sergeant Fitzgerald, I'm fully convinced this is the Pretender's work. Killing Susie McDonald, stabbing her and leaving her on the boat, taking Fitz, then removing his eye and letting him go, are only his second original series of crimes we're aware of, which obviously changes things yet again. There are a few items I can tell you up front—I don't think he's had a formal education, but he's above average in intelligence. He was raised in multiple homes, was probably a foster child."

"A foster child," Sansom said. "Hmm."

"He's also transient, just sets up base wherever he is, which makes him harder to track. He's in his early thirties, lacks confidence in himself, takes jobs as necessary to pay for his basic needs. He's computer savvy, knows his way around the message boards. He believes he's a scholar, a student of serial murder. He'll have books with him, anything and everything to do with serial killers. He considers himself as much of an expert as I am. And he has a fascination with blood that would have started at an early age. I wouldn't be surprised to find out that he killed very young, a sibling, perhaps. He's good with his hands, affable, charming, sexual. He can go unnoticed, or he can draw attention, whatever suits his purpose."

He leaned into Sansom, making sure she was paying attention. "Don't ever let your guard down if you do happen upon him. I'm dead serious here. He has no feelings, can't be reasoned with. He'll kill you without hesitating and never give it a second thought. If he's cornered, he'll do whatever it takes to get away. We're going to have a hard time bringing him in alive. He has nothing to lose. He isn't a glory seeker, trying to see himself in the news. He's a pure sociopath who enjoys killing by any available method."

Sansom didn't flinch at that, and Taylor thought she should. Of course, Taylor had seen him in person, or thought she had, back in Nashville last year, in a bar called Control, at what was supposed to be her bachelorette party. She'd felt the evil emanating from his skin like sweat on a hot summer day, visible and malodorous.

"Okay then. Where do we start?" Sansom asked.

Baldwin sat back in his chair and crossed his legs. "With the note you found in the trailer in Asheville. It's handwritten. I have one of the world's preeminent experts on sociopathic graphology ready to study that note. With any luck, she'll be able to tell us something about him that we don't already know."

Sansom turned to Taylor. "That's a start for you, then. I still have a kidnapping and murder on my books to clear. So let's get down to it. I'll show you mine if you show me yours. What else do you know about the Pretender? How are we going to catch him? Lieutenant, I'd like to hear from you. What do you think his next move is?"

"His next move?" Taylor laughed lightly. "Me. I'm his next move."

Five

Taylor had a flash drive with a PowerPoint presentation on it, one that had originally been given to her team when they were dealing with the Snow White Killer's apprentice brutalizing Nashville. The Snow White had killed ten Nashville girls in the 1980s, then sent a letter to the police telling them his reign of terror was finished. He was true to his word for over twenty years. But then, the previous Christmas, the long-dormant killer resurfaced. Out of the blue four girls were viciously murdered in the Snow White style. Taylor's team suspected a copycat, and they'd been partially correct. That was the first time the Pretender had come across their radar screens. But he'd existed long before he touched Taylor's world.

She popped the flash drive into Sansom's laptop computer; Yeager and Polakis got behind to watch.

Taylor narrated, trying to ignore the chill creeping up her spine. The last time she'd heard this information, FBI special agent and profiler Charlotte Douglas had been speaking. Charlotte had used the information as a weapon to make Taylor look bad. Her actions had backfired.

Taylor didn't think she'd ever forget arriving at that crime scene, the shock of seeing Charlotte's fire-red hair commingled with her life's blood, the setting sun echoing the bloody sheets.

Taylor forwarded the slides, covering the original killings of the Pretender, sharing the details as they knew them. By the time he'd hit Nashville, he had eighteen confirmed kills under his belt already. He'd committed another four under the tutelage of the Snow White Killer, then he'd gone off the rails. He killed three more girls before he was shot and ran. Adding Charlotte to the mix took his total up to twenty-six homicides.

Taylor heard an echo from the past, Charlotte's voice ringing through her head in triumph. *These four murders in Nashville have been directly connected to the other eighteen. You don't just have a copycat on your hands, you have an obscenely prolific serial killer with victims in five states. The CODIS results are definitive. His pattern is undeniable. It is quite likely that he will move on to another state, kill more young women, if you don't stop him here in Nashville.*

Despite her proselytizing, Charlotte Douglas had been right on the money. They hadn't stopped him. And now look where they were.

Taylor played with the remote in her hand. "As you can see, Susie McDonald makes twenty-seven confirmed kills. If the evidence matches the forensics we already have, of course."

"I thought you were certain this was tied to the Pretender. You have an eyewitness, after all, even if he says he can't remember anything," Sansom said.

Taylor ignored that last comment. "You know as well as I do that we have nothing yet to definitively prove it was the Pretender. We need the DNA results, the forensics, to confirm it for sure."

Sansom opened a folder, laid out an Identi-Kit sketch. "I was under the impression that you'd seen him before. We have this picture we're working from, and your sergeant thinks it was the same man."

Taylor glanced at the picture, at the electronic depiction of the man he'd seen. Remembered giving the description. *Cruel eyes. Square jaw. Dark blond with a military buzz cut*. Generic.

"Fitz told me he *thought* it could be the same man but he never got a solid look at his face. Yes, he gave a description, from a moment's glance at over four hundred yards through binoculars, of someone who *might* have been the same man we saw in Nashville, but we have no real proof he's the Pretender. We need to tie the crimes together with actual evidence, and with DNA, and the only way we're going to do that is by capturing him."

"Okay. I see your point. Tell me more about his earlier kills. I want all the gory little details."

Taylor clicked to the next slide. "In Los Angeles, he copied the Santa Ana Killer from the mid-fifties, the one who dismembered the bodies of the women he killed and left them in the desert. In Denver, it was the LoDo, the Lower Denver Killer, who preyed on prostitutes. He strangled them and left them posed on street corners. In Minneapolis, Minnesota, he copied the Classifieds Killer of the 1970s. Do you remember him? Old guy, placed ads in the *Star Tribune* for temporary secretarial work. They'd answer the ads and he'd gut them."

Sansom's eyes shone. "Yes, I'm aware of that case."

"Good. In New York, he became the Prospect Lake

Killer, strangling his victims and dumping their bodies into Prospect Lake Park on Long Island."

Taylor set the remote down on the table.

"Here's the thing. Nashville changed everything. He broke the pattern. The Snow White was the only killer he emulated who was still out there. All of the other original killers had been caught and jailed. Two had been put to death. While he was with the Snow White, he started to improvise."

"Why?"

Baldwin joined the conversation. "An excellent question. We don't have a good answer for that. The relationship between the two men began as some sort of… apprenticeship. The Pretender was studying under the Snow White just like a painter or sculptor would study under the tutelage of a master. Snow White had a very specific script he wanted followed, and his apprentice disagreed. He felt he was powerful enough to strike out on his own. And that's where we lost him."

Sansom was finally looking impressed. She stared at the computer screen for a long minute, then said, "So why has he changed his pattern?"

Taylor and Baldwin exchanged a glance.

"That's what we want to know," Baldwin said. "He's self-actualizing, testing to find his preferred method of killing. His MO is blatant though—he likes to imitate. He's been successful pretending to be other killers for years. He's a method actor, getting into the role by imitating the originals. He'll go back to that—I'm sure of it. But there's another component that's come into play, interrupted his plans. His attraction to Lieutenant Jackson. I believe that, ultimately, he's trying to impress her."

"Lucky you," Sansom said.

"You have no idea," Taylor replied.

"Has he threatened you directly?"

"Several times. It's been more cat and mouse in the past. He wants kudos for his work. He's reached out to me before. But this time, it got personal."

Baldwin tapped a pencil on the sketch. "I believe he's feeling rejected by the lieutenant. She hasn't been willing to play his game. That's upset him, and he's taking it out on those closest to her."

"Hmm," Sansom said. "How do you sleep at night?"

Taylor shrugged. "I don't. Not much, at least."

They were all quiet for a moment. Sansom seemed energized by the briefing, excited. She dismissed her two agents with a curt nod, waited for them to close the door, then smiled at Taylor and Baldwin.

"It sounds like a good time to get our hands on him. And why do you think he let Sergeant Fitzgerald live? And where do you think he'll go next?"

"A warning," Taylor said. "Fitz is just a pawn to him, a tool to get my attention. Where he's heading next is anyone's guess. No predictable pattern, remember?"

"Looks like the warning worked," Sansom said. "You're here."

Taylor simply nodded. Silence filled the room. Sansom watched her for a few moments, then scooted her chair closer.

"I want in on this. I want to help you track him down. Let me tell you what we have, and we can go from there."

"I seriously doubt he's still in North Carolina," Baldwin said. His BlackBerry beeped; he looked at the screen. Taylor felt his posture change, saw his spine straighten just a fraction. What was that all about?

Sansom seemed to sense the shift in Baldwin, too.

She leaned forward, eyes gleaming, tapping her forefinger on the file for emphasis. "Listen to me, Dr. Baldwin. We are going to act like he is still in North Carolina, at least for the time being. I've had crime scene techs sweep every square inch of the boat and the Airstream trailer. You want forensics? I've got them in spades. And I'll trade them for a chance to be in on this."

Baldwin broke his eyes away from his BlackBerry, cleared his throat. Taylor heard the tension in his voice.

"Agent Sansom, this isn't a game. You don't get to make the rules. You don't trade the information, you give it to me, willingly, then you step aside and let my team handle this. If you do this, and we catch him, you'll receive the credit you and your team are due. Rest assured, we want everyone to win here. For the moment, though, I'm afraid you're going to have to excuse the lieutenant and me. We have another meeting we need to get to."

Sansom openly bristled. "There's nothing more important than this right now. I can hold you both as material witnesses if I want. But I don't think that's necessary. I just want to help. You need me on this. I've already gotten clearance from my superiors to join your task force."

Taylor watched Baldwin's eyes cool, the green becoming a stormy sea. Normally the offer of help from an obviously capable agent would feel like a good idea, but Sansom rubbed her the wrong way. And Baldwin didn't trust Sansom either, that was clear. No, they'd be better off without her.

"We haven't set up a task force, and I can't say that we will. So no, Agent Sansom, I don't need you. I already have a team in place, all the positions are filled."

Sansom and Baldwin stared at each other for a brief moment, playing some sort of silent game of chicken. Baldwin's phone began to ring. He ignored it, eyes locked on the SBI agent. Taylor expected him to answer it, but he let it go, on and on, until it stopped with a beep she knew meant the call had gone to voice mail. The second it stopped ringing, it began again.

Sansom smiled, and Taylor sensed something was terribly, terribly wrong. She glanced sideways at Baldwin, saw his right hand was on his gun. She hadn't even noticed his arm moving. She went on alert. Sansom shifted, and Taylor coughed, using the noise as an opportunity to unsnap her holster strap. Despite her efforts, the click echoed in the room.

Sansom moved with a swiftness Taylor couldn't believe. She shoved the table toward them, catching Taylor hard in the gut, then bolted for the door. Baldwin was up and out of his chair in an instant. Taylor was a couple of seconds behind, her wind just starting to come back, her weapon drawn. But Sansom had the advantage, the element of surprise. She was out the door and sprinting away, her heels slapping the linoleum as she ran down the hall. Taylor and Baldwin exploded out of the room after her.

"Where's her team?" Taylor shouted.

"I don't know. Keep an eye out."

"What the *hell* is going on?"

Sansom darted out the heavy steel door. Taylor could see it had been propped open so the lock would be disengaged. A gunshot rang out, followed by a scream, and more shots, close together. They barreled into the hallway in time to see Captain Nadis slump over onto the floor. A bullet had caught him high in the chest, the blood pooled under him in a dark puddle.

"Stay with him," Baldwin shouted. Taylor knelt beside him, searched frantically for a pulse, found none. He was past her help.

Baldwin had taken up a defensive position at the entrance to the reception area. Wiping Nadis's blood on her jeans, Taylor lined up opposite him. She risked a quick look out, saw nothing but the stocking foot of the receptionist. She was down, on the floor, one leg sticking out from under her desk.

"It's clear," she said, low. He nodded, then eased around the corner. An engine gunned, tires spitting up seashell gravel in an effort to gain purchase. They rushed to the deck just in time to see a black sedan fishtail out onto the main road.

It was pointless to shoot at a fleeing car, dangerous, even, but they both started firing, bullets winging through the thin, chilly air. A few metallic thunks resonated back to them, but the car never stopped, it disappeared with a squeal of tires around the corner.

"We have to go after them," Taylor yelled. Baldwin lowered his weapon and grabbed her hand, holding her back.

"What are you doing? Let's go!"

"Taylor, it's okay," Baldwin said quietly. "They won't get far."

The distinctive *whump, whump, whump* of a heavy helicopter sounded in the distance.

"Is that Fitz's chopper?"

"No, it's one of ours."

The snow was tumbling down fast, littering flakes on Baldwin's dark hair that melted quickly. He turned to her, his eyes hard and cold.

"The message I got while we were talking to Sansom was from Garrett. Three people were found dead about twenty minutes ago, their bodies dumped on the beach just south of here. A woman, and two men. An SBI agent is on scene and says they're theirs."

"I don't understand."

Baldwin gestured over his shoulder. "The people in there, the ones we've been talking to all morning? They're plants. The real Renee Sansom, Wally Yaeger and Eliot Polakis are dead."

Six

Nashville, Tennessee

Colleen Keck was deep into her background on the Zodiac when her computer started going wild. She looked up, saw the words *Nags Head*. North Carolina? She flipped her online scanner over to the appropriate channel. Her mind was instantly processing this information as if it were linked to the earlier messages she'd received—what serial killer had struck in North Carolina? Was this part of the pattern from the murders last night? Was she simply reaching? She was a crime blogger after all, prone to seeing killers in every corner of her world. An overreactor, Tommy would say.

She was instantly grateful for the new protocols in many police departments that had allowed their personnel to shift away from 10 codes and into plain speak; while she was familiar with a wide array of codes from the major metropolitan areas, the smaller jurisdictions didn't follow the same patterns. Plain speak allowed everyone to understand. The scanner crackled.

"Officers down, officers down. We need backup, my location."

What the hell was his location? she wondered, writing the words down in her personal journalism shorthand. The disembodied voice went on, describing the scene.

"Update, there are seven officers involved in two separate shootings. We have a total of seven down. We need extra personnel, my location. Send out a BOLO on a black Lincoln Town Car, North Carolina plate, state owned, numbers to come. Suspects are armed and dangerous, repeat, armed and dangerous. Last seen heading west on Highway 64. Put roadblocks in place all the way out to 95. Switch to channel eighteen, code three, code three. Switching channels now." The scanner went dead. They'd switched to a private channel to avoid people like her. It wouldn't have mattered if the voice had continued, she wasn't hearing anything but the roaring in her own ears.

Oh, my God.

Colleen's breath came short, and she gagged a little, unable to resist a brief glimpse into her own hell after hearing the words *officers down*. Seven cops hurt in the line of duty. Seven families torn apart. *Seven.*

The memories assailed her anew, and she barely made it to the bathroom in time. She vomited in the sink, tears mingling with sudden beads of sweat that popped up on her forehead.

Oh, Tommy. Why did you have to leave me? Why did you have to be so freaking brave?

After a few minutes, her cries died down, and she gathered herself. She rinsed her mouth out with cool water, splashed some on her face, which managed to smear her already desiccated day-old mascara even further. She swiped furiously at the dark smears with a bit of toilet paper. Weakness was not allowed. Weakness was her enemy, the taloned beast that lived in her chest and couldn't wait to sharpen its fangs on her heart. She'd considered succumbing many times, but Flynn—her darling, sweet boy, the spitting image of Tommy—Flynn kept her strong. Strong enough to fight back the beast and its basilisk stare into her soul.

Empty. She was terribly empty. The less she had to give, the less she could get hurt.

The phone rang.

She had a moment's irrational fear—it was a call from the police, something's happened to Flynn—but she pushed the thought away firmly. This time of day, it was some sort of telemarketer. She allowed the answering machine to pick up, heard the long beeps of a facsimile machine.

Sniffing hard, Colleen went to the refrigerator. She poured a little orange juice in a glass, then opened the cabinet above the stove, the one locked against her child's roving hands. The small vial of Ativan was nestled in between some old painkillers and a never-used package of birth control pills, standing ready for when she and Tommy were able to resume post-baby connubial relations. Choking back another sob, she extracted the benzodiazepines, shot two into her mouth before she could change her mind, and swallowed. Thus indulged, she brushed her hair back from her face and tried to focus.

Something major had happened in North Carolina. Combined with the reports coming in from California, Massachusetts and New York, she felt it her duty to explore the cases further. They were connected, she was sure of that. Something told her that they hadn't seen the end, either.

Seven

The Outer Banks, North Carolina

Taylor felt the cold seeping into her stomach. No wonder Fitz had been so reluctant to talk to her. He must have sensed something wasn't right about Sansom and her goons.

Oh, God. Was Fitz safe? Surely this was an anomaly, not some sort of reengagement. Would the Pretender let Fitz go only to take him back into his custody? She took a deep breath. No. The helicopter that took him away bore the Duke Medical Center insignia. There was no way.

She was through taking chances.

"We have to get that helicopter diverted to Nashville, just to be safe."

Baldwin looked at her for a long moment. "I agree."

He made a call. Taylor could hear the voice of Charlaine Shultz, one of Baldwin's lead profilers, on the other end. She promised to take care of it immediately, and Baldwin put the phone into his pocket.

They could hear sirens wailing now, and the SBI

chopper soared past overhead in a swirl of dusty snow. The cavalry had arrived.

Baldwin touched her arm. "Come on, let's do a sweep. This place is going to be crawling in a few minutes and we'll need to give a SITREP."

As always, Baldwin was thinking ahead. Taylor wasn't in any mood to stop, hand over their knowledge to another officer, calmly give a situation report. No, she wanted to go after that damn car. But she joined him back in the police station. The scene inside was worse than Taylor remembered. Nadis and his receptionist were sprawled in their own blood, and they found another Nags Head officer and their SBI driver garroted in a closed-off room. Taylor barely recognized the silent smoker who'd picked them up from the airport. The scent of death was close in her nose.

Standing over the bodies, looking at the thin necklace of bruised and bloodied flesh on the officers' throats, Taylor felt ice sweep through her veins. The sight thrust her back in time, to more deaths on her hands. Garroting was the signature of another killer, one long since dead. She swallowed hard.

"Fake Polakis and Yeager were taking down the others while Fake Sansom talked to us," Taylor said.

"Looks that way. See, there are drag marks," Baldwin said, pointing to a series of black scuffs on the white linoleum that led to the small break room where the bodies of the men had been stashed.

"They must have taken them down one by one, then lugged them in here, out of the way. How did they pull this off?"

"I don't know. They were excellent though. If I hadn't been warned, we might still be in there. Or in there." He pointed toward the break room.

Taylor heard the sound of a car, the wheels crunching on the gravel. Their alone time had run out. She had that queer feeling in the pit of her stomach, the aftermath of adrenaline, when her senses were oversharp and she felt like she might throw up. A few deep breaths quelled her nausea, and the rage started to bleed in.

"I assume they were meant to take me?"

Baldwin shook his head. "I don't think so. They could have easily shot all of us and grabbed you at any time. I think fake Sansom was supposed to get on the team, go with us, and report back everything we knew. Drive us, like cattle, to a predetermined place and time so they'd have the upper hand."

"We gave her a lot of information."

"Nothing they didn't already have. Charlotte's PowerPoint wasn't anything new."

"The Pretender arranged for all of this. He has help."

"Yes." Baldwin was gritting his teeth, the muscles in his jaw jumping. "Yes, he has help. More than we could have anticipated."

Taylor breathed in deeply and regretted it. She slumped against the wall.

"So he arranged for Fitz to be dropped in Nags Head, where he could control the scene. Left the boat where it could be easily found, everything. He set us all up."

"Yes."

"He has to have people on the inside, don't you think?"

"Yes."

"And he knew I'd come rushing here, playing right into his hands."

Baldwin turned to her, lips set in a thin line. "Yes."

"A little less affirmation from you would be helpful, you know."

He snorted through his nose at that, and shot her a crooked smile. "Then stop being so right all the time."

The levity helped, and she felt herself settle. She'd spent years in training for these types of situations, and despite the personal nature of the crimes, the fact that the dance was directed at her, she felt certain they would win. It was what they did. Good triumphed over evil, even if it sometimes got trampled along the way.

She could hear shouting from the front of the station. They shared a glance. No sense taking chances. Baldwin drew his weapon; she followed suit.

"Be ready," he whispered.

They flattened themselves against the wall.

A moment later, the shouts came closer. A strong, deep voice slightly dampened by a Southern accent called to them.

"Dr. Baldwin? Lieutenant Jackson? I'm SBI supervisory agent Roddie Hall. I know you might be a bit spooked right now. Garrett Woods told me to tell you he's got a bottle of White Label in his bottom left drawer. I'm gonna toss my badge in there for you to look at, okay?"

Taylor felt Baldwin relax fractionally.

"Go ahead," he said.

The credentials landed with a thud close to Taylor's right foot. Baldwin nodded to her. She reached down and grabbed the leather case, then handed it to him. Baldwin glanced at it and signaled the go ahead. They both stepped around the edge of the door, Taylor low, Baldwin high, weapons trained on the man standing in the middle of the reception area with his hands up. It was clear that his shoulder holster was empty.

"Your boss is a little peeved with me," Hall said. "I don't think he's gonna be sharing that liquor with me any time soon."

"I can only imagine," Baldwin replied.

"Mind if I put my hands down now?"

"Go ahead. Slowly."

Hall looked relieved, dropped his hands to his side. He was a big man, prematurely gray, inhabiting a rumpled brown suit that was a size too large for him. There were red blotches on his white shirt. After a quick glance at Taylor's hands, he wisely didn't try to shake.

Temporarily appeased, Taylor and Baldwin holstered their weapons.

"What happened?" Baldwin asked. "How did they get the drop on your agents?"

"We don't know just yet. All three of them were shot twice to the back of the head. Executed. Thrown in a shallow grave on the beach. A guy walking his dog found them. The dog went nuts and started digging. You folks okay?"

"We're fine, but we have four officers down here. Three Nags Head and one of yours."

Hall shut his eyes for a brief moment as if in pain. Taylor readily understood the feeling. It felt like the whole world had gone to war, that every corner of her life was under attack.

But the Pretender had miscalculated one thing. By killing seven law enforcement officers, he'd just brought the entire nation's might down upon him. It wouldn't just be Taylor and Baldwin looking for him; every single agency in the country would push him to the top of their lists. He had assured that the chase was on.

Taylor's attention drifted. What the hell did the fool want? This was so much trouble to go to in order to have a showdown with her. Was he just egging them on for fun? She was so tired. She wished she could sit down, lay her head on her arms and puzzle it through. She pushed her weariness away and tuned back in.

"Agent Hall, what else do you know?" she asked.

Hall ran his hands across his forehead. "Not enough, obviously. Facts, then. Your sergeant, Pete Fitzgerald, was found yesterday morning wandering the road here. From what I've been told, he'd been missing for over a week. Our Western Branch agents were the ones who found his eye, they sent out an alert to all of us. We were looking everywhere in the state for him. Coming up dry, too, until he showed up. He spent a good part of the day and night in the hospital under lock and key, then the local authorities transported him here. We agreed it would be easier that way."

"Easier for you to treat him like a suspect, you mean," Taylor said.

That pushed Hall over the edge. His voice rose. "Easier to keep an eye on him and to keep him safe. Yes, we needed to question him. You'd do exactly the same if this happened on your turf. The BOLO's the only reason the local cops didn't slap him in cuffs on the spot—it had him listed as a kidnapping victim. Man covered in blood, missing an eye, talking about his dead girlfriend? They didn't know what they were dealing with."

"Easy, you two. No one's to blame for this," Baldwin interjected. He raised an eyebrow, silently admonishing her, then turned back to Hall. "Please, continue."

Hall sighed heavily and ran his hands over his sparse hair. "There's not much more to tell. We sent our team to meet with him first thing this morning. They must have been ambushed on the way. I just don't know how this could happen. This whole case has been on close hold since they found the boat. What time did you meet the suspects, Dr. Baldwin? Were they already here?"

"Yes. It was early, 7:00 a.m. or so. They were here before me, had already been introduced around. The people who would have seen their credentials are dead, so we can't ask whether they were federal-issue or copies. Hell, they might have bluffed their way in, they really did look the part. I didn't ask to see their creds. I wish to God I had. Sansom gave me her card, though."

He pulled it from his wallet. Hall looked it over, then motioned for an evidence tech.

"That's the real Renee's card, all right. Might get some prints off it if we're lucky."

Baldwin handed the card to his tech by the edges, watched Hall issue instructions, the tech scurry away. Hall turned back to them.

"They were well-ensconced by the time you got here?"

Baldwin nodded. "Yes. They must have been lying in wait for your agents, knowing they were coming to take Fitz into protective custody. Who arranged for him to be flown to Duke, by the way?"

"That was me. He was obviously a mess, and I know the doctor at Duke, we did our undergrad together. He's done some really groundbreaking work on optics. I figured it was the best place for him."

Taylor softened at that. "I appreciate that. We've had

the flight diverted to Nashville. I hope you understand. You're welcome to come talk to Fitz there."

"Yeah, I get it. Can't say I really blame you, we really screwed the pooch. I can't imagine how this happened."

Taylor crossed her arms on her chest. "You need to be looking closely at your staff. Someone leaked sensitive information out of the SBI. I hate to tell you this, but you've got a traitor."

Eight

Taylor and Baldwin went over the details with SSA Hall for another forty minutes, but nothing else shook loose.

Taylor had to admit, Hall was a good cop. He ticked off his checklist just like she would, methodical and thorough, not rushing, moving ahead to another point only once every available detail had been squeezed out of the moment. They'd all been bamboozled by the imposters, and no one wanted to make any more mistakes. She respected that, and tried to keep her impatience to a minimum. She was worried about Fitz, just wanted to get back on her own turf. Someplace she knew she could defend herself properly.

All those agents. She didn't envy Hall the job of informing the families, something that couldn't happen until they had all the details of the crime scene down pat.

She had a crazy thought, one that tore through her mind like a storm. *Could Sansom's imposter be the Pretender? Could it have been a woman all along?*

That would be almost too far-fetched. They had DNA from several of the crime scenes, but that was easily planted. She thought about how the woman leaned in to hear the details, her eyes shining at the descriptions of the kills.

No, that didn't feel right. It was possible, but so unlikely that Taylor forced it from her head. This maniac was a man who used women, then disposed of them like dirty Kleenex, tossed to the floor without a second thought.

When the SBI lead was finished with them and started working the scene, she called in to her boss, Commander Joan Huston, and filled her in on the situation. Talking to Huston helped settle Taylor's mind—her boss was as pragmatic as she was capable. Huston assured Taylor that Fitz had arrived and was scheduled for surgery with Vanderbilt's ophthalmologic team later in the day. Lincoln Ross was with him.

Taylor finally felt as if she could breathe again. Fitz was safe.

Now she could focus on the problem at hand.

The Nags Head Police Station resembled a kicked-over anthill. Crime scene techs swarmed the scene. The bodies had yet to be moved, there was too much evidence to collect first. Despite the chill, a lone lazy fly bumbled through the hallway, drunk on blood. She swatted at it and missed, cursing as it darted into a heating vent. It would be back, and it would bring friends. She hoped they could get out of here quickly.

She and Baldwin were taken to separate rooms to do an Identi-Kit on the three suspects. She missed the days of actual artists working on sketches; while the Identi-Kits were quick and convenient, they lacked a certain level of perfection, a way of layering in the slight details that a human could seize upon with a flick of a pencil. While the officer plugged her description of the suspects' features into the program, Taylor had a bizarre sense of déjà vu, of sitting with another artist, in another police station, giving a detailed description of the man she thought might be the Pretender.

This case. This goddamn case, with its maybes and theoreticals. She had to stop him. Nothing else existed for her now.

When they were finished with the artists, Hall debriefed them again, in the same room where they'd spent the morning talking to a killer.

"So I just got a call. A body was found out on Highway 64, out by Plymouth. Fits the description of the goon who impersonated Wally Polakis."

"How was he killed?" Taylor asked.

"Shot in the head, tossed out of the car. He was found sprawled on the side of the road, you know how bodies do when they're shoved out of moving cars."

"So the car will have blood in it."

"If we find it. There's so many back roads in this area, bridges and trails—they could dump the car, catch another ride and it will take us a week to find it."

"But they're turning on each other. That's good. Maybe they'll eliminate themselves and do us all a favor," Baldwin said.

Taylor gave him an unpleasant smile. "One can only hope. But it was probably prearranged. Too many cooks spoil the broth, especially when you're taking orders from a killer who likes to be top dog."

Hall rubbed his hands over his head wearily. "Girl, you're starting to scare me. Are y'all ready to go over it all again?"

Baldwin went first, describing what had been discussed and the shift in personality when the fake Sansom started to show her hand.

"They were good. Very good. All three of them must have had experience in law enforcement at some point," Baldwin finished.

"Lieutenant Jackson, break it down for me. What was your impression of the imposters?" Hall asked.

She'd had all morning to think about that. "They were completely above board. She made me uncomfortable, but only because she was implying Fitz was responsible for Susie's death. That got my back up, and I missed everything else." The apology was implicit, and Hall declined his head slightly, accepting.

Taylor toyed with her ponytail while she did one more mental run-through. "In hindsight, I can say she seemed a little too eager. Too excited by things she shouldn't have been. Her body language was all wrong. She leaned in when she should have pulled back. Licked her lips when she should have flinched."

A fine shiver ran through her body. "I've been up against this monster before. He scares the hell out of me. She wasn't fazed in the least by the presentation. That should have been enough to warn us right there. I should have noticed something was wrong. My sergeant was trying to tell me something, but I wasn't listening hard enough."

"I think it's safe to say they pulled a fast one on everyone, Lieutenant. Don't beat yourself up over it." He was trying to be kind, but Taylor didn't have time for it.

"I hate to point this out, Agent Hall, but if I had paid more attention, four people might not be dead. We need to go. Sitting around talking about him isn't going to fix things. We need to get back to Nashville. That's where the Pretender will head next, I'm sure of it."

"Why? Why are you so sure?"

She avoided looking at Baldwin, despite feeling her voice thicken. "Because everything I hold dear is in this room or in that city. I have to go home. Now."

Hall sat back in his chair and gave her a long look. He glanced at Baldwin, who merely nodded his head in agreement.

"Okay, then. Be prepared to come back at any time, but you can get out of here for now. Thanks for your help." He stood and shook their hands, lingering for a moment over Taylor's, all irritation gone. "I have to go let four agents' families know they're never going to see them again. You be safe, ya hear?"

Taylor and Baldwin climbed into the backseat of a Nags Head patrol car. The officer was young, and openly stared at them through red-rimmed eyes. Taylor shook her head slightly to discourage any questions. She wasn't ready to have a casual conversation about the morning's events, especially with someone who knew the victims. Seven dead, eight including Susie, nine if you counted one of the imposters. The North Carolina soil was running red with the blood of innocents, and each murder weighed on her mind. This shouldn't be happening. She should have been paying attention, should have felt that things were wrong. She had been so wrapped up in her own grief over shooting the teenager that she'd missed all of the warning signs. The Pretender knew her better than she knew herself, apparently.

The officer pulled out of the drive and headed back toward the airstrip. Baldwin worked his phone all the way there, allowing her a few moments with her dark thoughts.

Within fifteen minutes, she and Baldwin were safely

ensconced back on the Gulfstream, under the watchful gaze of Cici the flight attendant, and the pilot was getting clearance to take off. Baldwin waved Cici away, then leaned over to Taylor.

"Pietra just sent me a text. You're not going to believe this. All of the forensics were compromised," he said.

"What do you mean?"

"I mean someone managed to cross-contaminate everything the SBI agents collected from the boat and the trailer. A second blood source was introduced, mixed with bleach. Even if they isolate the DNA strings, it would never hold up in court."

Pietra Dunmore was Baldwin's forensics expert, back in Quantico. She was legendary in the forensics community, brilliant, capable and exceptionally loyal to Baldwin. A million thoughts raced through Taylor's mind.

"How? How does he manage this?" she finally asked. "He's just one man."

"How else? He charmed his way into another woman's life, talked her into doing his dirty work for him. We've seen him do this before."

Yes, they had. And watched the bodies pile up in his wake.

"You think Renee Sansom's imposter contaminated the forensics? When would she have access?" Taylor asked.

Baldwin ran his hands through his already disheveled hair. "Remember what you said back there, about the eye being transported to Asheville rather than Fitz actually being moved around the state? They could have staged all of it, right down to the letter. If the Pretender has multiple people working for him, it might not be in his handwriting after all. And then we're off on yet another wild-goose chase."

"But how would the imposter get her hands on the forensics? They intercepted the SBI agents early this morning. Surely that evidence has been in safe-keeping for a few days. They found it last week."

"Hall said the Western Branch brought everything down here for his people to process. They only have one lab for the whole state. We'll have to see when it was logged in and who had access to it, but it's all a waste. Nothing of use." He slumped in his chair.

"Do you think she has a personal connection to him? A lover? Or is she just a tool, someone he met along the road? He seems to have an affinity for finding people to work with. Dial-a-Psychopath, perhaps?"

"No, this was someone close to him. Someone who wanted to impress him. I can feel it."

Taylor took his hand. "Baldwin, are you sure? You're not just…reacting, are you?"

The engines revved, then screamed, and they were pushed back into their seats by the force. The plane lifted off within moments, banked hard left, to the west. When it leveled out and Cici began moving about the cabin, Baldwin spoke again.

"No, Taylor, I'm not reacting. I'm being very, very careful. I've got Kevin Salt running a background check on the real Renee Sansom as we speak, trying to find out why she was targeted. How did she and her team come to be working on this case? Is he recruiting people? And from where? How did he arrange for the plants to be in place so quickly? This took major forethought."

"Well, the Pretender has been off our radar for

almost a year. He's had plenty of time to lay the groundwork."

"Yes, he did. I'll tell you one thing. We can't trust anyone on the outside."

She thought about that for a moment.

"Between your team and mine, we at least have some people we can be sure of. Fitz was so evasive, I got the impression that he didn't want to talk in front of the SBI. He must have suspected something."

"Absolutely. He's smart. He might have seen something, overheard something."

"He's going to be okay, isn't he?"

"He will be. It will take some time, but he will."

They sat quietly for a few moments.

"So we're on our own. Again," Taylor whispered, mostly to herself.

Baldwin put an arm around her, an awkward move considering the seats were positioned so far apart.

"That's just the way I like it," he said.

Nine

That wasn't the truth though. Baldwin didn't like being left out in the cold, and that was exactly where he felt he was at the moment.

Taylor was staring out the window, intensely quiet. He glanced over at her, worried. She was strung much too tight. Avoidance was one of the greatest attributes in her arsenal, and she was employing it to full effect now. The events of the past week were going to catch up with her soon.

He could barely keep up with the insanity himself. The Pretender had weighed heavily on both their minds for the past year. He'd made contact for the first time after the Snow White case had blown up: a letter sent to their home. The letter stood out starkly against his mind's eye, two lines full of threatening portent.

An apprentice no more.
You may call me the Pretender.

He'd named himself: the fundamental sociopathic tool. The ones who named themselves were so narcissistic they were almost always caught. Almost always.

The Pretender had disappeared for a while, then popped back up like a possessed jack-in-the-box. That was when the intimidation began in earnest—phone calls to their home and cell phones, more letters. He began getting involved in Taylor's cases, always on the periphery, but always there. He'd become a malevolent presence in their lives for over a year, threatening, parading, seemingly unlimited in his access and information.

There had been more to the profile that he hadn't shared with Renee Sansom's imposter. They hadn't gotten into the Pretender's vast online network of contacts, other killers, sadists, people who lived for cruelty and discord. Posing as a necrophiliac aptly named Necro90, he'd befriended the international duo of necrosadists, Il Macellaio and the Conductor. He egged them on, planted evidence at one of the Conductor's crime scenes, and made sure Taylor knew he'd done it to help her.

He seemed to love the control he got from manipulating others. Almost as much joy as he got from killing.

They hadn't taken the drubbing lying down. They were fighting back the only way they knew how, with justice, with their own team, their own tools. Finding the man who was threatening his woman was paramount. And Taylor hadn't been privy to everything Baldwin knew.

Kevin Salt, Baldwin's computer forensics expert, had found the Pretender's online signature and had been tracking his movements throughout the web. Kevin could follow him most anywhere; the IP addresses the

Pretender used had been uncommonly consistent for the past few months. Salt documented everything, drew geographical profiles, and found the key that Baldwin was most concerned about. The physical addresses came back again and again to Nashville. The bastard was close.

His influence was spreading again—the attack on the SBI agents had taken cunning, and time. He'd obviously been recruiting people to help him; whether they knew his real plans or not, they were unknown resources.

Now he was ready. Whatever whacked-out strategy he'd been putting in motion was officially in play.

How many people would have to die for the Pretender to be satisfied?

Taylor had seen another mass attack today, and he knew she would blame herself. The Pretender was putting on a bloody show for her benefit, consistently placing the wounded around her, for her to see. Add to that her obvious but misplaced guilt over the shooting of her last suspect, and he was starting to wonder just when the dam was going to break.

He could feel it building, the sense that things were moving quicker and quicker, that the world was spinning one-tenth too fast on its axis. If he didn't grip down, hard, he might go spinning off with it, and that wouldn't do. No, he needed to resolve this, and keep his woman settled, too. Because if Taylor were to come undone, he didn't know if he could stand that. Seeing her in pain made his stomach throb dully, and each time the Pretender poked at her it made his eyes blacken with rage.

The phone next to his chair buzzed discreetly. There was only one person who knew they were on this plane at this moment—his boss, Garrett Woods. Taylor glanced at him; he smiled with what he hoped seemed like reassurance as he answered the phone.

"Hey, Garrett."

"Are you headed to Nashville?"

"Yeah. Thanks for getting the chopper diverted. I'll feel better having Fitzgerald close."

"Sure thing. What's happening there? Where did it all go south?"

Baldwin filled him in on what they knew so far, then asked, "Anything new from Nags Head?"

"Other than the director wanting to know why in the hell a suspended FBI agent sent up a red flag for some rather expensive help after a mass shooting?"

Baldwin groaned. "He found out?"

"Baldwin, son, the whole country knows. It's been on all the news stations. Both you and Taylor were on camera leaving the station."

"Oh."

"Yes, oh. Have you told her yet?"

"Well, no."

"Baldwin, I don't think I need to be the one to break this to you, but I'll try, just in case you're not thinking clearly. You need to tell her. Everything. Now."

He knew that. But he honestly didn't know where to start.

What would she like to hear least? That he'd been suspended while they did a deeper investigation into his biggest failure, the Harold Arlen case from 2004, when he'd made the massive mistake of not turning in his protégée, Charlotte Douglas, when he'd found out she planted evidence at a crime scene? That he'd gotten three good agents killed because he'd been stupid enough to start fooling around with Charlotte? That he'd gotten Charlotte pregnant in the middle of the biggest case of his career? That he'd only found out a year ago that she hadn't aborted the child as she claimed, but gave birth and had seen him adopted? That he didn't know where in the world the boy was, or even what name he'd been given?

How was he supposed to tell his fiancée, the woman who held his heart, that he shared such an intrinsic, intimate link with another woman? He hadn't cheated on Taylor, no, but would she ever forgive him?

He looked out the window, at the stark winter landscape far below. Bleak and barren.

"Yeah, Garrett. I'm on that."

"Seriously, Baldwin. You've got one hell of a woman there. You don't want to fuck it up. So listen to me. I've covered your ass for the day, but that's not going to last long. Get back to Nashville, and get your head down."

"I will. I promise. Has there been any other… news?"

Garrett was helping him search for his son. It had been a year of fruitless starts and stops. He was still getting over the shock of the news: Garrett had found the documents in Charlotte's desk after her death—the birth certificate, with Baldwin's name scratched out in ballpoint pen, and a two-year-old's posed picture. He would be five now.

All Baldwin knew was that the child was a boy. There was no question the child was his, the boy had the same set of the shoulder, the same thick hair, but red like his mother's. He'd inherited his father's green cat eyes.

But he had no idea what his son's name was. Charlotte had put Baby Douglas on the birth certificate; she hadn't even bothered to name their child. He loved the boy, though he'd never seen him. He'd do most anything to get him back.

Pain ran through Baldwin's chest. With the kid's pedigree, would he be a normal, loving child? Would Baldwin's genes predominate, or Charlotte's? Charlotte's entire family was full of horrors: her murderous father, her deformed brother, Charlotte's own sociopathy and eventual psychosis. Did the kid have a chance at a normal life?

Garrett sighed deeply in Baldwin's ear. "Nothing yet. You know I'll call the minute I have something. Now, I have your word that you're going to be a good boy, right?"

"Of course. Thanks for the update." He placed the phone back on its receiver.

Taylor raised an eyebrow questioningly. He just shook his head.

"Nothing new. The news has the story."

"Great," she said. "Everything else okay?"

He lied to her, like he'd been lying. It was becoming second nature.

"Yep, everything's fine. Just fine."

He felt the engines ratchet back fractionally. They were almost home. He took her hand, felt the strong fingers close around his.

Balance. He needed to find some balance.

There was only one way they were ever going to be free, and it went against everything he'd pledged when he joined the FBI. Against the very fabric of his being.

He needed to find the Pretender and stop his heart beating, so Taylor didn't try to do it first.

Ten

The Pretender received the emails one by one, each coming at their assigned time. The pattern harkened back to the discipline ingrained in him by his old master—the Snow White had always wanted a full report as soon as a deed was done, would sit in his dank office with those disgusting cigars, smoking one after another with his bent hands, waiting like a spider in a vast web.

Wretched man. Always bellowing orders, yet too crippled to do his own dirty work. He needed a surrogate to live out his fantasies. When Charlotte had brought them together, for a time it seemed like a dream come true. But that dream quickly turned into a nightmare.

Troy. The name Charlotte had given him, thinking she was being clever. Dead bitch, dead bitch, dead bitch. He felt so much freer out on his own. Running his show himself, learning new and better ways to fulfill his own fantasies. It was like moving from sous chef to owning the whole restaurant, then a franchise chain. He was the master now, with his own acolytes.

But he kept the name. It was easier that way.

The first wave was complete. Tonight would be a second round, the second stage of his plan. It was all going so well. So perfectly.

He played the song, his iTunes set on repeat. Over and over it played, reminding him of his purpose, his goals. He was so lonely. He wanted.

He needed a distraction, so he prepared a cup of tea. The actions soothed him: setting out the thin bone china, heating the water to just below boiling, the delicate green tea measured and placed in the strainer, brewing for exactly one minute before being removed. He discarded the soggy leaves, added a tiny bit of sugar and sat at his computer. He had a new email. His heart sped up when he saw the address. Was she in?

He clicked on the subject line. The message inside was simple. "It didn't work."

He sighed loudly, set the tea in its saucer with a clatter. A curse formed on his tongue. It had been a long shot. That damnable FBI agent was too acute, too sensitive to those around him. He would be on an even higher alert now; penetrating the team would be more difficult. But not impossible. Not at all impossible.

He sipped his tea and debated his next move. He should send a message. Renee Sansom's imposter had failed him, and she needed to be punished. He should put the well-rehearsed plan into action. All it would take was two clicks of his mouse, the directions would be sent, the operative engaged. She'd be dead before nightfall, her accounts scrubbed, all traces erased. No one would ever find the link to him.

There were too many variables, too many players, to allow mistakes to be indulged. If anything, eliminating part of the team would send a very clear message to the rest of them—failure was not an option.

The idea of killing her was so enticing.

He wouldn't be able to see to the task himself, though. At least, not right now. Too bad. She would be a fun toy to play with. A ballsy broad, willing to step into the mix, to kill and impersonate a federal agent.

He really shouldn't eliminate her just yet. She could still be an asset. She was a well-educated forensics master. With a new disguise—a change of hair, posture, contacts—he could utilize her skills again. He hated to admit it, but the truth was he needed her. She helped him play his role.

His finger hovered above the mouse, trembling with excitement.

He weighed the risks. He'd planned several demises for her. It would have been so simple to just discard her, like so many others in his past. The easiest manner of disposal, of course, was to arrange for the car she was driving with her compatriots to swerve away from oncoming traffic, go through the guardrail, land in the icy water below. There would be no time to save her from the freezing water. She'd drown before the rescue crews got on the scene.

Hmm. The idea of her flailing in the cold water…

His finger twitched on the mouse, then he pushed it aside.

He reminded himself that he was no longer a child, that an impulse was just that, a scant fraction of a second of desire that gets compounded into want. Want, want, want. Wanting got little boys into trouble.

But she did need to be punished.

And he left nothing to chance.

Nothing.

His grandfather clock bonged softly, pulling him from his reverie. Half past. The lunch hour was over.

He needed to get back to work. Needed to inhabit the identity he'd created.

He just had so many things to do. So many threads to pull. So many people involved now, hurtling them toward the final moments. It was too late to turn back—the game was in motion. He'd gotten bored with the cat and mouse. The challenge of it all just wasn't enough anymore. He wanted to be impressed. He wanted to teach. But none of this was working for him. It was time to up the ante again.

As he pulled the lanyard over his head, he wondered if Taylor was frightened yet. Brave girl that she was, surely she was starting to feel the strain. He'd told that fuck Fitzgerald to relay his message, to make sure she knew that it was time to play. He was confident the point had gotten across. He'd been very persuasive.

He locked the town house behind him. The ride back to work would only take a few minutes. He wondered what was in store for him this afternoon.

He did love his job.

On his way back to the office, he stopped at the post office, sent the card he'd been holding for three months.

She would be so surprised.

Eleven

Nashville, Tennessee

Colleen Keck looked at the clock. It was nearly time to get Flynn from school.

This was the biggest story she'd seen in years. Her Felon E email had been dinging constantly with new messages: new tips, new confirmations. The fax machine was whirring to life again, people sending diagrams of crime scenes, lists of names. There was something more to these murders, she knew that already. Years of instinct, of assimilating the truth from the annals of crap she had to delve through, gave her a keen sense of story. Plot. Something was definitely up, something big.

This morning's disaster in North Carolina was locked down. A major crime event, too. She wasn't pleased about being shut out, especially since several television news outlets were hovering around, broadcasting minute-by-minute relays of nothing. The only good news was they'd been unable to crack into the scene either. She talked briefly with a reporter from the CBS affiliate who told her the same thing she'd heard on the radio, but nothing new. The names of the dead weren't being released yet.

Frustrated, she called her 911 call-center contact in that area again and heard that next-of-kin notifications were the holdup. Apparently one of the victims' wives was out of town with their kids—Disney World. They were having a hard time tracking her down.

Letting the families know who they'd lost before the world heard was hard in the age of the internet. Twitter was talking about it, but no new information was leaking. Some ghoul on Foursquare had driven to the crime scene and was standing outside the barricades, uploading photographs: "I'm Mayor of the Nags Head Dead!"

She abandoned the shots in distaste. It was snowing softly in Nags Head, the lights flashing sharp off the white ground. Pretty, but not at all helpful in efforting her story.

Colleen felt she had a grip on things again, at least for the time being. The Ativan had helped her refocus. She would come back to North Carolina in a bit.

The news hadn't picked up on her copycat-killer story yet. She decided to go back to that, work all the angles she could find.

She took a sip of Diet Coke and set to work reviewing what she knew for sure, what she'd been able to mine from the various police departments. Last night, in San Francisco, California, there had been a double murder. The crime scene bore the signature of the Zodiac Killer. And late this morning, just a few minutes ago Nashville time, the *San Francisco Chronicle* had received a letter. A coded letter, signed with the distinctive cross inside a circle, the mark of the Zodiac.

He had returned, or someone was copycatting him. Not that there hadn't been false alarms before… Either way, when she hit Publish on this afternoon's blog, she was going to create a firestorm. She was going to beat the papers. The numbers on Felon E would go through the roof. Everyone loved a good Zodiac story. *Everyone but the victims.* She forced that thought away. Feelings like those would cripple her, like what happened this morning. She couldn't worry about the victims or their families now, she needed to report the story.

Not that their loss was any less horrific than the loss in North Carolina, it was just…different.

She clicked the keyboard, the words spilling onto the screen. She'd double sourced this, and it was going to spread like absolute wildfire.

The headline was simple.

The Zodiac? He's Back…

Colleen had no idea what she was about to unleash. She published the story, watched it filter through her systems, then begrudgingly laid her work aside. She turned off the computer to go fetch her son. Her mind was already on the work she'd do as soon as she got home.

The Boston case was up next, then New York. She could work on Boston while Flynn was in his room, focusing on his me time. It had taken her the best part of three hours to source the San Francisco story. Boston would hopefully go quicker since she'd already sent out the emails to her trusted sources. New York, too—her contact didn't work the day shift, so she'd have to wait until after five to speak with him anyway. And the dam would break on North Carolina soon.

Good. She had it all planned out.

Was it really possible? Three serial killers come back to life, all on the same night? Or was her mind treading into fantasy territory? And who was responsible for the carnage in North Carolina?

Were they playing some kind of game?

She shook her head. That was crazy talk.

No matter. She'd get to the bottom of it soon enough.

She pulled on a thin cotton sweater and glanced ruefully at her unwashed hair in the bathroom mirror. A baseball cap was just the ticket. She ran back to the office and dug out her favorite battered FBI cap, the deep royal blue faded to denim after repeated cycles through the washer, and the gold FBI letters frayed around the edges. It fit her head perfectly, and she pulled her hair through the back. She'd scored the cap after a tour of Quantico years back, and Tommy had teased her unmercifully about it. "Cheating on Metro, are you darlin'?" he'd say.

Go away, Tommy, she thought sternly, hoping his ghost would listen, for once. She needed to stay focused. Get Flynn, make him a snack, get him to take a nap. Then back to work.

She fumbled with her keys, still jacked up with excitement and dread, finally inserted them in the ignition. She needed one of those cars with the push button to start the engine. Hmm. How much would that set her back?

The Civic's engine obligingly turned over on the first try, and she put it in Reverse. She realized she was smiling. Good. She didn't do that nearly enough.

Flynn would enjoy seeing her in a good mood. Maybe she should take those pills more often?

She didn't feel the eyes on her as she pulled out of the garage.

Twelve

From: bostonboy@ncr.bb.com
To: troy14@ncr.tr.com
Subject: Pittsburgh

Dear Troy,
Everything is right on schedule. Worry not.
BB

He sent the email, then wondered how long it would take for the delivery truck to be reported stolen. An hour? Fifteen minutes? Despite his research, he didn't know how the specific delivery times were recorded. Were they followed in real time electronically? Or did the drivers upload their information at the end of their runs? The package's tracking number had led him to the correct truck to hijack; he should have asked the driver about the system before he killed him. Hmm. Next time.

Should he deliver a few packages on his way to the kill site? No, he didn't want any chance of his face being seen. If there were regulars on the route, they might ask questions, or recall him when their memories were jogged. And killing strangers wasn't on his agenda today.

No, today he had the pleasure of visiting Miss Frances Schwartz. Frances was a worker bee in a downtown accounting firm, a fancy woman prone to shopping when she felt down. She was horrifically in debt, though her fellow worker bees didn't have any idea. They thought Frances was wonderful—stylish, put together. Just what every woman in her office wanted to emulate.

She'd be arriving home shortly, he needed to get into place. Around the corner from her house was an old parking lot. Empty, with cracked asphalt and no visible video cameras anywhere near. It was the perfect spot to wait.

He was surprised at his energy level. He figured the nine-hour overnight drive would wear him out. When he'd done the dry run, he'd barely been able to keep his eyes open. Must still be riding the adrenaline high from Boston. He had to admit, this was fun. The rush when he killed. The idea that there were others out there that he was competing against. He'd had his doubts about entering the contest, had thought about pulling out several times while the field had been whittled down from fourteen to three. But since he'd made the cut, he figured what the hell. He'd play along.

It gave him something to do, especially since the targets had been chosen for him. His responsibility was to kill them in the manner of the killer he'd drawn, the Boston Strangler, who was a sick fuck, no question about it. He'd researched and planned, run through the scenarios several times. The goal was to make the kills on the schedule provided and not get caught. Getting seen was an automatic disqualification—if a description went out on the airways, he was out. Getting caught, well, that went without saying.

Stealing UPS delivery trucks was no small feat, but he'd handled it effortlessly both times. He was truly fond of this MO. No one looked twice at a delivery truck. He'd posted the packages himself before leaving Boston, to Pittsburgh, Cincinnati, Indianapolis. He'd mapped the delivery system through the tracking IDs, saw exactly when each package was due to arrive. It was simple as pie—package goes on the truck, truck heads out on regular route, truck is intercepted, driver taken out, then the package was delivered. Tied with a big, beautiful bow.

He laughed at his joke. He knew how serious this game was, but truly, it was just a game. If he didn't win, life would go on. He had plenty of money, that wasn't his purpose in participating. He'd spent too many years alone, not knowing how many people out there were just like him. Thank God for the internet. He was able to find all types, all shapes and sizes and predilections. When he saw the ad, he deleted it, then thought twice. Once the idea got into his head, he couldn't help himself. He was bored, and looking for a challenge. And it gave him a chance to meet some people. He'd become too isolated.

He checked his watch. Frances should be home any minute. She always got home precisely at 5:35 p.m. She'd change into lovely, tight-fitting Lycra, drink a protein shake, eat a banana, then head out for either a run or a bike ride. Frances was in training. Biathlon. She was strong. Capable. Not his usual type. Maybe she'd fight back. The thought excited him.

He pulled the electronic pad out from its resting spot, grabbed the bulky box. It was time. Time for Frances to say goodbye.

Thirteen

Nashville, Tennessee

Taylor and Baldwin arrived in Nashville with enough time to get to Vanderbilt before Fitz awoke from surgery. Taylor was exhausted—her day had started at 5:30 a.m., with no appreciable sleep in the past forty-eight hours. The adrenaline from the morning's adventures had drained away, and she sagged a bit against Baldwin's arm as they walked across the tarmac to the parking lot.

"You need a coffee or coke to get your head back in the game? We can stop at Starbucks," he said.

"Yeah, that's a good idea. I'm starting to drag."

"Why don't you let me drive, then? Give you a chance to shut your eyes for a few minutes."

She smiled at him gratefully. "That would be great. Just give me a second."

She opened the back door of the 4Runner and took a gym bag off the seat. She unzipped it and rummaged around, then pulled out a fresh pair of jeans. Baldwin stood in front of her as a shield to prying eyes. She yanked off her boots, shimmied off her jeans and pulled on the new, bloodless pair. That was better. She couldn't have faced another moment wearing Nadis's blood.

She stowed the bag and the dirty jeans, then tossed the keys over. They climbed into the truck and headed toward downtown.

There was no snow in Nashville, just the lingering bitter chill that ate into her bones despite her shearling jacket. She turned the heat up and sat on her hands. They'd been cold all day.

"Do you really think he's come to Nashville?" she finally asked.

The "he" didn't need explaining. Baldwin shrugged. "I don't know. I can't imagine he's going to go anywhere else. We need to get a name for him, a real, legitimate name, not a copy, not a fake. The better I understand his background, the easier it will be to predict what he might do next. He's certainly paying close attention to everything you're doing. We may need to discuss some increased countermeasures."

"Draw him out using me as bait, you mean?" She stared out the window as Baldwin took the 440 split that would lead them onto West End.

"God, no, Taylor. I'm not using you as bait. What I meant was prep a team for distraction. Something to assure us that he won't be able to touch you."

"Using someone else as bait, you mean. Haven't we lost enough already?"

She glanced over, he was staring straight ahead, face grim. She put her hand on his knee.

"It's wrong, Baldwin. We need him to come for me. We need to end this. He's already told Fitz that he's ready to make his play. I assume that's going to happen sooner rather than later, regardless of the bait."

"I don't disagree. But I won't dangle you out there

like a carrot for him to covet. We need you keeping a very low profile."

She didn't answer, just let the cold street flow beneath her, the trees beckoning with dead branches. The longer this dragged on, the more opportunity the Pretender would have to hurt those she loved. She didn't plan to give him a chance to get that far.

Baldwin stayed silent, pulled into the Starbucks drive-through. He ordered them both venti lattes. When the coffees were ready, he pulled back out onto West End, narrowly missing a coed in a Tri Delta sweatshirt jogging up the sidewalk. When he slammed on the brakes, a bit of hot espresso sloshed onto Taylor's hand. She cursed loudly and immediately felt better. Being back in Nashville was going to help make everything okay. Nothing could hurt her here.

The HoneyBaked Ham store had a massive sign advertising their Thanksgiving hams. Her mouth watered at the thought—she was suddenly starving. She sipped on the latte to curb her hunger. She hadn't realized how close they were to the holidays. With the madness of Fitz's kidnapping, then the Halloween massacre, she'd completely lost track of time. She usually went to Sam's for Thanksgiving. She'd have to check and see if that was still the plan. If not, she might have to do Thanksgiving herself this year. She would need to host Fitz, make sure he was well taken care of. Maybe McKenzie and Bangor, too. And Lincoln and Marcus, plus Daphne. Good grief, where was she going to put all of them?

Baldwin turned onto Twenty-first Avenue, then right on Pierce, which led them directly to the entrance of Vanderbilt Medical Center.

She was loath to climb out of the warm truck. When

she did, she regretted it immediately; the wind bit frantically at her cheeks.

Baldwin's face turned pink as a flash-boiled shrimp and he slouched farther into his coat. She realized they still hadn't talked about his hearing at Quantico. She got the feeling he wasn't all that keen to share what had gone down.

They hurried across the street. Inside the building at last. Heat rose in waves. The surgery center was painted a sunny yellow, warm and inviting, quite unlike the gray drabness of the emergency rooms Taylor was used to.

Taylor badged the nurse at the front desk. "We're looking for Peter Fitzgerald."

The nurse took their credentials carefully, checking them against a notepad she had at her elbow.

"May I see your driver's license, please?" she asked politely. Taylor nodded and dug her wallet out of her back pocket—a slim golf wallet she'd bought for her dad's Christmas present several years earlier and instead confiscated for herself. It was easy to carry, and had only the essentials, a twenty, two credit cards, her license and insurance cards. She'd do anything not to be bulked down with a purse. Baldwin handed his own license over. The nurse compared that pictured against his FBI credentials, wrote their names down on a pad of paper, then handed it back and apologized.

"We were under instructions to double-check everyone trying to see Mr. Fitzgerald today."

Taylor smiled and said, "Good. You did good. How is he?"

"He's just out of recovery and back in his room. He's up on the third floor, room 323. The doctor will be seeing him later today."

"Did the surgery go all right?"

"I don't know, dear. Why don't you go on down and see him?" The nurse smiled kindly and focused back on her work.

Baldwin punched the button on the wall and the doors swung wide. They walked the long hallway to Fitz's room in an uneasy silence. Before they reached the door, Taylor grabbed Baldwin's hand.

"Have you ever thought about how easy it would be to kill someone in a hospital? That nurse did the right thing asking for ID, but she could be overpowered in a heartbeat. And once you're past her, look out. You can go anywhere in a hospital without anyone giving you a second glance. It's not safe, Baldwin. He's not safe here."

"Honey, I doubt the Pretender has any more interest in Fitz. His part in this is over—he's suffered, and relayed the message to you. Besides, Lincoln is with him now. If you're that worried, we'll get a permanent guard on him, in addition to all of us."

In her heart, she knew he was right. It wasn't necessarily the Pretender she was worried about. The idea of Fitz, so alone, so hurt, missing his eye, missing his girlfriend, his life upended…she just didn't want him to be by himself. Not now. Not when she couldn't be there 24/7 to hold his hand and reassure him that everything would be all right. The Pretender was done with Fitz, but Fitz would never be done with the Pretender. Not while they both lived.

They took a few more steps, reached the door. She blurted out the question that had been on her mind all afternoon.

"Don't you need to go back to Quantico?"

He stopped, and she saw something unrecognizable flickering in his eyes before he shook his head. "I'm going to take off a couple of weeks. Personal time. You need me right now."

She watched him for any more signs of discomfiture, but he was smiling, the fear she thought she'd seen gone.

"Okay," she said. She didn't want to admit that she was relieved. She wanted him close. She wanted everyone close right now, where she could watch out for them.

The door to Fitz's room opened and Lincoln Ross walked out, his dreadlocked hair subdued. He gave her a big hug.

"Hey, good to see you. Heard you had a rough go of it this morning."

"You could say that."

"I've got to run. I just got called out on a case."

She felt her pulse quicken. "Anything I need to know about?"

"I don't think so. We received a report of a body out in Percy Priest Lake."

"Cold for swimming," Baldwin said.

"No kidding." Lincoln flashed them a smile.

"We need to get some folks to stick around for Fitz," she said.

"Already done. I talked to Huston. She's authorized a four-man shift. The first guy should be here any minute."

"Thanks, Linc. You're the best."

He flashed her a gap-toothed smile. "Remember that come raise time. See ya later." He loped off down the hall.

Taylor knocked on Fitz's door softly, a warning so he could get himself together, then they entered the room. Fitz was lying in the hospital bed, quiet and drained.

His good eye was closed. The missing eye was bandaged similarly to earlier in the day, but the dressing was clean and white.

"Hey there," she said quietly. He wasn't asleep, and turned to her with the ghost of a smile. His voice was raspy from the anesthesia.

"Hey yourself. What happened? Why am I in Nashville? I woke up and Lincoln was standing over me. Thought I was dreaming for a second till the fool opened his mouth." He started to cough.

Baldwin got busy pouring Fitz some water, letting him sip it from a straw before he spoke more. The coughing eased.

Taylor pulled up a chair, touching Fitz lightly on the arm.

"First, how are you feeling? What did the doctors do?"

When he cleared his throat, it sounded like fabric ripping apart at the seams. "Damn anesthesia. I don't know. It was a bunch of technobabble to me. All I picked up was that I'll be able to get a shiny new eye in about a month. Seems everything went just fine."

"Are you in pain?"

"Naw. I'm still high as a kite. I'm sure that won't last forever. Now, what the hell happened?"

Taylor filled him in on the morning's disaster. "We didn't have any choice but to divert you here. I couldn't take the chance that it was some kind of trap, some unfathomable grand plan… I'm still a little bit in shock."

Fitz whistled. "Yeah, something didn't feel right about the whole thing. I figured it was because of the drugs, but I could swear I'd heard Sansom's voice before. And I mean before, before, while we were still on the boat. It didn't make sense that she would be on the boat and be at the police station. I knew she wasn't straight, but there was no way I could tell you. I'm so sorry. If I had, maybe none of this would have happened. I was so confused…"

She took his hand.

"Don't do that to yourself. The fake agents had a very specific plan. If you'd said something, they might have killed us all and been done with it. Now that we're safe and sound, can you talk about what happened? I could tell you were holding back in Nags Head, I just didn't realize why. Now that we're on the same page, do you feel up to giving me some more details?"

Fitz leaned his head back, the cheap, thin pillow crackling a bit as he sank in. He sighed, a deep, heavy, sad noise that made her stomach hurt.

"If you're not ready…"

"No, it's okay. I just miss her, you know? It's my own damn fault it all went south." Fitz's voice was tired, quiet. "Remember we lost our impeller down in Barbados?"

"Yes," Taylor replied. "You called because you thought you saw the Pretender near Susie."

At the mention of her name, Fitz winced. "Yeah. Bastard bumped into her. She dropped everything on the ground. I was watching through the binoculars. Asshole picked up the packages, handed them to her, then turned around and saluted me. He knew exactly who I was. Then he disappeared. The engine part came the next day—we made the repairs and started sailing north. He caught up with us in Miami. There were four of them, but they wore masks, those black things terrorists wear. What are they called?"

"Balaclavas," Baldwin interjected.

"That's it. But these had a skull printed on them, just the lower jaw and nose. Freaky-looking—like a skull with live eyes." He shook his head, wincing slightly at what Taylor knew must be great pain. Emotional or physical, that was the question. She was worried about him. He didn't sound right.

What he should sound like, she didn't know.

"It's my fault. I left Susie on the boat, went into the port for supplies. When I got back, they already had her tied to a chair with a gun to her head."

"Fitz," Taylor started, but he interrupted her.

"No. It *was* my fault. I should have never left her alone." He paused for a moment, then looked away. "Did they… Was she…"

Baldwin put his hand on the older man's shoulder. "No. She died quickly."

That was enough to send Fitz over the edge. He started to cry, something Taylor had never seen him do. Tears of relief, frustration, pain, all coursing down the right side of his face. If the lost eye was crying, the tears were being soaked up by the bandage.

She swallowed hard and squeezed Fitz's hand. He quieted, and she handed him a scratchy tissue. He swiped at his face angrily, sniffed a couple of times. She felt Baldwin moving around behind her, glanced over her shoulder at him. The naked hostility on his face startled her. He hated this as much as she did, but his reaction to Fitz's story was visceral.

"Fitz, why don't we stop now? You can tell me the rest later."

"*No.* I want to finish. You need everything I have if you're going to catch him." He coughed again, the leftover anesthesia clearing from his lungs. "He wasn't there long. He used the name Troy. The other three were really deferential. They knocked Susie on the head and drugged me. The rest is sort of blurry, just bits and pieces really. I wasn't awake when he took my eye, just came to with blood all over me and a wicked pain in my face. He told me what to say to you then I conked out again. Next thing I remember, they dumped me on the side of the road, doped to kingdom come. I don't know how long it had been though. A couple of days? A week? I wandered around for a bit before the cops hauled me in."

Baldwin cleared his throat. "From what we can tell, it was at least three days from your enucleation until you were found, but we don't know when they took your eye exactly. Susie had been dead for a while."

"How?"

"Fitz—"

"*How,* goddamn it?"

Taylor swallowed, then answered him. "They cut her throat."

Fitz blanched under his already pasty skin. "I thought so. I heard them do it, I think. I was hoping it was a bad dream."

He pulled into himself then, and Taylor knew they needed to give him some space. She thought he might have started to doze, his mouth went slack. He looked like an old man, fragile, broken. Her heart felt shredded, and she was careful not to wake him as she got up.

She whispered, "We'll be back soon, okay? We're going to find him, Fitz. I swear to you. We're going to find him, and take him out."

They were quiet on the way back to the truck. Taylor was at a loss. This whole fucking situation was spinning out of control. She couldn't erase the image of Fitz, his battered face, his broken heart, the loneliness engulfing him; she envisioned what he was seeing right now—the white hospital room, the sheets, the walls, all screaming at him. She didn't know how to take on his guilt.

Losing Susie wasn't his fault.

It was hers.

All hers.

She stopped walking, the bile in her stomach rising to the surface. Baldwin pulled up short.

"Are you okay?"

She shook her head, swallowing hard. Good God. She'd spent all this time waiting for the Pretender to make a move, letting him toy with her. Look where that had gotten her. She had to do something. She couldn't sit back and wait to see what happened next.

Baldwin was hovering. The sun would set soon, flashes of gold and red were reflecting off the buildings around them. The sky would turn to fire, and the darkness would come again.

"I'm okay," she managed.

"Let me take you home. You've had a long day."

"No, I can't. I need to go into work. I'm so far behind, I just need to try to…to get a handle on things. I'll bring some stuff home and work on it, okay? You go on home. I won't be long. We can eat. Try to eat."

"Are you sure? I need to do some work myself. I can hang there, make some calls. You're still on leave, they might kick you out."

"No, really, it's fine."

"You need to be alone."

He said it without malice, just a statement of fact.

She worked her face into a smile, met his eyes. Tried to erase the concern in them. "You know me too well.

Yes. I need to get my head straight. Seeing him so hurt, it just about killed me."

"Paperwork will help?"

"Mindless. I just need an hour or so. Okay?"

Baldwin swept her into his arms, pulled her tight to his chest. She shivered, he was so warm. Always so warm. So good, and so right.

"Okay, Taylor. If that's what you want, that's what we'll do. I'll drop you off?"

"Sure. Thank you."

She wanted to take the comfort of his arms and bottle it. Instead she focused on the feeling of safety, the strength in his embrace knowledge that he would do anything for her. It would have to be enough. For now.

Because when she was finished with the Pretender, Baldwin might never look at her the same way again.

Fourteen

To: Troy14@ncr.tr.com
From: crypto@ncr.zk.com
Subject: Denver

Dear Troy,
Long drive. Arriving shortly. Anticipate no delays.
ZK

He was tired from the drive. The thump of the tires on the road was driving him mad. He was too tall for the car. The little beat-up compact rental was a piece of plastic crap. He didn't like to drive. It would have been faster and easier to fly, but he had to follow the instructions to the letter. He'd taken the fastest route—I-5 south toward L.A. then across to I-15 northeast. He drove through the night, then face-first into the sun. He'd lost two hours in Vegas—the victims' house had been hard to find in the maze of sameness that was the Vegas suburbs. But he'd found and dispatched them with the thoroughness expected of him.

Kill 'em and leave 'em. Those were the rules. No playing with the bodies. He was sorry for that. After the couple in San Francisco, the reaction he'd had to the blood, he was curious what it would be like. They wouldn't be moving, right? But they'd still be warm.

It would violate the rules.

Monotony. He turned on the radio for company. He liked the conservative talk shows the best—they got his blood boiling. He'd always dreamed of calling in to one of them and telling the bastards exactly what he'd like to do to them. How he'd take them apart, piece by piece. They had everything—money, drugs, women. That Limbaugh guy had just gotten married for something like the twentieth time. And that English prick Elton John played at the wedding. He always thought Elton John was a liberal—he was gay, after all, flaming, really. Apparently money made everyone mercenary. He knew it worked that way for him.

On he drove, his thoughts racing, the radio spewing.

The sun, sinking like heavy red blood in his rearview mirror, the moon rising heavy and full, an expectant sky, then stars, pinpricks in the ink-black night, peeking from their celestial beds. For hours his headlights mingled with the moonlight, illuminating the path, miles upon miles of empty, lonely road stretched before him. At last the moon bade him farewell. The trees hung low across the pass, the tunnels empty and forlorn.

He rolled across the Rocky Mountains as the sun clawed through the morning virga, the gigantic peaks powdered with snow, the air becoming crisp and sharp. There would be a storm tonight, the rains he'd left behind in San Francisco making their way to higher altitude. He needed to finish the job and move along so he didn't get stuck in town. That would get him off schedule, and he didn't want that to happen. He glanced at his watch to double-check. No, he was still okay.

He stopped in Conifer for gas and a candy bar. He needed the energy. He was getting sleepy. He had another to kill today. He was surprised at how deadening the thought was. Boring, almost. Almost. The first time, back in San Francisco, now that had been something special. He wanted to stay and savor the moment, relive the gun exploding in his hand and the shocked looks on their faces, relish the scents that streamed from the bodies. He had no idea they would smell like that. Burnt offerings, elegantly tinged with copper, and the faintest tang of urine.

But he couldn't stay and relish. He had a plan, and he must stick to it. The letter must be posted. The next targets eliminated. He didn't know if he liked this game. He felt rushed. The driving, the back-to-back deaths. His own senses were out of whack. Not being able to choose his own victims, well, that took all the fun out of it for him.

He'd agreed to play by the rules. The rules meant he wouldn't be caught. The rules meant he could win, then go on his own path, kill his own way. The gun seemed too impersonal, too easy. He really enjoyed using the knife in Vegas. Four more with the gun, and he'd have that freedom again.

He scarfed the candy bar and drank the Coke. Got back in the car and dreamed as he drove.

Freedom. If he won, the money would float him for years. He didn't need much. A small house with a basement would be good, out of the way, with no nosy neighbors. Maybe he'd get a cat. He liked dogs, but they had to be walked, and he didn't like to be seen.

No, a cat would be perfect, a friendly face to keep him company.

If all went well, a few scared, unfriendly faces, too.

Fifteen

Taylor sat in her office and stared out the window. Night was falling fast. She watched the stoplight change, blinking ever so slowly through its cycles. Green, yellow, red. Green, yellow, red. She noticed how the colors altered ever so slightly as the gloaming settled in, the green like freshly mown grass, the yellow becoming nearly amber, the red a livid crimson. Bloody.

It was better than dealing with the seething mass of paperwork, Post-it notes, schedule changes and case updates that spilled across her desk. Her inbox was overflowing, the wood surface was covered in junk. Even her guest chairs had piles on them. She'd only been on leave for a few days—but it felt like weeks and looked like months. She shouldn't be here now, but she needed a quiet place to think.

Baldwin had dropped her off at the CJC, with stern admonitions about what she was supposed to do for the next hour to ensure her safety while she worked, then he left, intent on some beckoning task. Probably arranging for the guards to be put on her. She was worried about the extra attention. Not because of the threat—the Pretender was going to come for her, that was simply a given at this point. No, she was worried about the accountability.

She'd never planned a murder before.

She wasn't going to lie to herself. What she had in mind was cold-blooded, by-the-book first-degree murder. Premeditated. Malice aforethought. Intent to cause grievous bodily harm.

If she were caught, A.D.A. Page would plead her out. It wouldn't even look like manslaughter once she got hold of the case. It would be labeled self-defense. Taylor was a cop, for heaven's sake. Cops killed in the line of duty. And there were few people within her circle who weren't already aware of the Pretender and his threats. So long as she managed the situation, made sure it was her word against, well, his wouldn't count. He'd be dead. No witnesses to exact the moment. Timing was everything in this plan. She simply needed to make sure no one saw her kill the bastard, but the aftermath would leave no doubt that she'd been acting to protect herself. That was the most important thing. That way it wouldn't look like an execution.

Still, it would be murder.

Taking life meant suffering the consequences daily. She knew that from experience. Usually at 3:00 a.m., when sleep eluded her and the ghosts of the men she'd killed sat on the edge of her bed, staring with empty, disapproving eyes, their flesh rotting in spots, bones glistening in the moonlight. Her waking nightmares were her punishment.

What sort of punishment would she receive if she pulled this off?

She was shocked to realize she didn't care. She just wanted the whole thing to end.

What would Baldwin think?

She squirmed in her chair, messed with her ponytail.

Baldwin had killed before as well. He knew what it did to the soul. No amount of forgiveness or justification could fix that dark spot. Would he blame her for taking matters into her own hands? Applaud her? She got the sense he was thinking the same thing, though she would never ask. This was something that she could never, ever say aloud. Not to Baldwin.

She wished she could use a backup piece. She had a few unregistered pieces that fit the bill. She didn't want to sully her service weapon with her blood revenge. *If* she managed to pull it off, she'd still have a job, responsibilities, a life with Metro. She'd have to touch that weapon daily, knowing it had done her bidding, had purposefully tracked a man down and taken his life. She'd never be able to forget. Perhaps that would be a fitting punishment after all.

Long range, or close up? She forced herself to be honest. Close up, definitely. She wanted to look the Pretender in the eye as he died. It was the only way she could be sure.

She ignored the rush of adrenaline that plowed through her. Just the thought of facing off against him filled her with a combination of lust and dread. She really didn't recognize herself anymore. He'd driven her to this, this base desire to end another human being's life. To walk away from every commitment she'd ever made to herself, to the force. She'd sworn to protect, not to indulge in the darkness.

But hurting the ones she loved…that was beyond the pale. The Pretender had chosen this path, and Taylor was the only one who could stop it before too many more of her people got hurt. Fitz, Sam, Lincoln, Marcus, even

McKenzie, they were more than colleagues, more than friends. They were her family, just as much as Baldwin. Maybe even more so.

She just had to find the son of a bitch. Find him, and get a few precious minutes alone. This nightmare would end.

Taylor needed to make arrangements that suited her plan. She couldn't have federal bodyguards looking over her shoulder. She needed insiders. Friends. People who, if challenged, would look the other way.

She picked up the phone and called her old boss, Mitchell Price, at home.

He answered on the third ring.

"Hell-ooo, Miss Jackson! How are you this fine evening?"

"Pretty good, Mitchell. You heard we found Fitz?"

"I did. Went to see him this evening. He's in good spirits, considering. Have to say I've been celebrating the news a bit."

Taylor smiled at the admission, Mitchell did sound a little in his cups. Not in a bad way, just happily tipsy.

"I can tell."

"Am I that bad?"

"Goodness, no. I just know you well enough to hear the fine Irish lilt in your voice."

"Ah. Good. What can I do for you? Have you finally decided to chuck Metro and come join my merry band of thieves?"

"Not exactly. I was hoping to do some business with you."

She heard the music in the background soften, and he coughed slightly. His voice was solemn.

"Investigation or protection?"

"To be honest, protection. Baldwin is freaking out

on me and planning a barricade of FBI agents. I don't want to be...hampered. I have things I need to do, and his phalanx of suits will get in my way."

"You're not planning on going hunting, are you?"

Price always had known her too well. She avoided answering truthfully.

"We're pretty certain the Pretender's next play will involve me directly. I just want some extra backup. After hours. Off-site. My place. That kind of thing. Do you have a couple of folks you could detail to me for a week or so?"

"Only a week?"

"If it lasts longer than that, I'm doing something wrong," she said softly.

Price was silent for a few moments. She held her breath. Surely he wouldn't say no. She was right.

"Okay, Taylor. I've got a couple of guys who might work for you. They're discreet. Quiet. And damn good at their jobs. I save them for our more *private* endeavors."

Private. Right up her alley.

"That sounds perfect. When can they start?"

"Tonight, if you'd like. Give me a couple of hours to wrangle them up."

"Just let them know one thing. The Pretender is mine. They are not to engage him if he gets close, they are to alert me and back off. Okay?"

"Taylor..." His voice held a note of warning.

"I just want to be the one to bring him in, that's all."

Price harrumphed, but let it go.

She hung up the phone and leaned back in her chair, smile gone from her face. There. Step one was in place.

Now she could worry about the second part of the plan.

She'd felt the darkness inside her, writhing like a snake in its warm nest, the deadening of her spirit becoming more and more complete as she grew older. Each death meant more blood on her hands, more pieces of her soul shattered and sloughed away. Why would this be any different? He was a threat, and threats needed to be neutralized. Simple as that. Taylor knew she could do it. She knew she was capable.

She'd left the church years before, but she found herself praying to an unknown, unseen God, the words moving past her lips soundlessly.

Let it be me. Let me be the one to end this.

Sixteen

Taylor awoke with a start. Damn it. She'd closed her eyes for half a second and drifted off.

A wave of emotion cascaded through her. She needed to move, to breathe in the night air, to find him. It was all well and good to dream about taking the fight to the Pretender, but the truth of the matter was, he was probably bringing it to her.

The walls grew too close and she stood, fast. As she rose, her holster caught on the edge of her inbox, dumping the contents to the floor.

"Son of a bitch!"

She looked at the mess, the parallel to her own emotions.

Be hunted, or be the hunter.

When it came right down to it, she knew which path she would choose.

She dropped to her knees and began assembling the mess. She'd gathered the papers and files into three significant piles when her phone rang. She reached up to her desk and pulled the phone to her. An internal call, from the switchboard.

"Lieutenant Jackson," she answered, pushing all the morbid thoughts from her mind.

"LT, it's Marcus. I'm out on a call, and I think you need to see this."

She glanced at the clock, 10:11 p.m. Crap. Baldwin would be mad at her, she wasn't supposed to be here that long. And seeing as she was deskbound, Commander Huston would be very displeased if she went out on a case in an official capacity. But Marcus Wade wasn't prone to histrionics. Steady and smart, he was the one she counted on to see past surface appearances and into the heart of the matter. If he was calling, he actually needed her.

A quick look couldn't hurt anything, and if the Pretender was watching… A shot in the proverbial dark, perhaps?

"It's late. Why didn't B-shift get the call?"

"Lincoln and I pulled it earlier. It's taken us hours to get the body out of the water. He's still in there, tied to something. We've got the OEM divers trying to get him untangled."

That was right, Lincoln had mentioned getting called out to a drowning. And now Marcus was calling… "You have an inkling about the identity of the victim?"

"I think it might be Peter Schechter."

Taylor groaned inwardly. Yet another teenager dead, more parents to engulf in sorrow. That would be nine of Nashville's kids murdered in less than a week, not counting the one she'd taken down. She didn't know how the city was going to recover. She didn't know how *she* was going to recover.

"Is he a part of the Halloween massacre?"

"I don't know. Can you come on out here? I'm at

Percy Priest, a boat dock off Hamilton Creek Park. Sam's just arrived."

"I'll be there in ten. Tell Sam to hang on until I can see the scene, all right?"

"Will do. Thanks, Taylor."

Marcus clicked off. She turned the light out in her office and headed toward the motor pool at a jog. Her boots made sharp clangs against the concrete spiral up into the parking lot. Screw being on desk duty. One of her team needed her.

She grabbed the first unmarked she got to, slid behind the wheel and headed west.

J. Percy Priest Lake was the largest lake in Davidson County, over two hundred and thirteen miles of shoreline, five marinas and thirty-three boat ramps. With trails and playgrounds and fishing and boating, it was a miracle they'd found Schechter's body so quickly. Though Taylor remembered her friend Robert Trice, who used to run OEM, the Office of Emergency Management, the department that conducted water search-and-rescues, telling her that all bodies come to the surface eventually. Robert was gone now, dead too early. She missed him.

Marcus was standing off to her left, talking to Sam. The moon's glow on the water should have been beautiful. Instead it was menacing. She didn't like this one bit. It all felt wrong, had for weeks. She needed to do some serious assessments of her life. Because this was her dream, right? Right? To protect. To serve.

She didn't think she was saving too many lives these days.

She stepped over to Marcus and Sam, who were deep in conversation.

"How'd they find him?" Sam was asking.

"Some guy coming down to tend his boat saw a flash of red in the water, realized it was a puffy down jacket and called 911."

"That's lucky. He could have been submerged for much longer. The cold water might have helped save some evidence."

"The knots that tied him to the branch were elaborate. His jacket is weighted, too, though obviously not enough. He wasn't meant to be found this quickly, I don't think."

Sam pushed her too-long bangs out of her eyes, her brown eyes sharp. "Good thing he was tied to that branch. He would have floated away, drifted down the lake, washed up somewhere else. So, Taylor, how's Fitz?"

"He's as good as can be expected. He's been through a lot."

Sam gave her a critical, assessing look. "So have you. You need to think about taking some more time off. You're still on leave anyway, why are you here?"

"Because Marcus called me. I'm fine, really. I need to stay busy. If I sit around for another day I'm going to go mad. I won't touch anything, I promise."

Sam spoke softly, so only Taylor could hear. "You were hardly sitting around this morning. I heard what happened. Are you okay?"

Taylor nodded. "Yes. Just do me a favor, be aware, all right? I don't want to take any chances. You guys are too precious to me to risk getting involved in the Pretender's little game."

"Not such a little game," Sam said, a grim smile on her face.

They heard water splashing, then a deep male voice rang out in the gloom. "We got 'im!"

All the noise around her ceased. They brought the body out slowly, trying not to lose any evidence, though the victim had obviously been in the water for several days. Covered in the beginnings of adipocere, a thick, gummy wax made of decomposing fatty tissues, the gases in his body had finally pushed him to the point of buoyancy and he had floated to the surface.

The still-folded stretcher crouched like a metal spider on the uneven ground. The 'gators had a bag laid out, ready to receive the remains. With a splash, four men strong-armed the body into place.

Sam immediately beelined for the corpse, tsking in her typically Southern way. Taylor hung back for a moment, watching. She didn't want to interrupt Sam's communion with the dead. Sam shouted back over her shoulder, "Come on, then. I know you want to take a peek."

Taylor edged forward until she was parallel with what used to be the body's face. Trying not to breathe, she leaned in for a closer look. Male, late teens, it seemed. The skin was gray and doughy, wet with water and bloated tissue. Bits of matter stuck in the brown hair. There was too much damage to his face to be able to tell for sure, but she was certain they'd just found Peter Schechter. Gut instinct, maybe, or just process of elimination. He was their only missing person tonight, and this body fit the description they had in the system.

"Looks like him, bless his heart," Sam said. She knew about the boy's profile, everyone did. He'd been missing for five days, long enough that every cop in the city was on high alert.

"Anything leap out at you?" Taylor asked.

"You know better than that, cookie."

"I do, but I thought I'd try."

Sam went to her bag and dug in for a thermometer. "Best get the priest out of bed, though. I don't want to drag this out any longer than I have to, you know?"

"Yeah, I know. Can you ID him tonight, do you think?"

"I have the dental records back at the office. I'll call Mike Tabor on my way, see if he can't swing by and take a quick look. It's late, but Tabor asked to be informed if we found anything. If it's the kid, we'll want to get his parents notified before this all leaks."

"You can say that again." Taylor stepped away, let Sam do her work. Sorrow flooded her. What a waste. What a goddamn waste. At least she didn't get the sense that this was the work of the Pretender. She didn't think she could handle another death on her conscience.

Marcus was taking notes, face pinched in the artificial light. The scent of rotting flesh permeated the scene. Floaters were the worst. Decomposition mingled with dank winter water created an unmistakable miasma especially designed to help turn even the strongest of stomachs, like three-day-old roadkill drenched in a moldy blanket. He gave her a weak smile.

"Sam's going to try to ID the body tonight. Have you called Father Victor?" Taylor asked.

"Yes, just did. He's aware I may need him."

"Good. I'm happy to go back to the morgue with Sam, let you continue running things out here while we work on the identification. You won't have to rush."

Relief flooded his face. It was going to be a late night regardless—splitting up the duties would make things go quicker.

"You sure you don't mind?"

"Not a bit. I'll call you as soon as we know something."

"Thanks, Taylor. I owe you one."

She punched his shoulder lightly. "Yeah, yeah."

She went back to her cruiser, grabbed her cell. She needed to let Baldwin know what she was up to. He wasn't going to be happy about it, but in truth, she was. She needed the distraction. Working a murder, even peripherally, would keep her mind off the one she planned to commit.

Seventeen

Baldwin answered his cell on the first ring. It was Taylor, her voice thick with exhaustion. He took the news and sighed. Another dead. As horrible as it sounded, he was almost glad she'd gotten involved. The distraction would be good for her. There was nothing like Taylor with a new case to solve; she was a force to be reckoned with. One that he loved to watch.

He wasn't watching her now. He was home, waiting for her. He wasn't sure how much he liked that, but if he pushed too hard, held her too close...Taylor would push back if he smothered her. Strong girl. His warrior woman. Despite that, though Taylor didn't know it, there were four highly trained agents on their way to Nashville. They'd stay out of sight, her watchers, ready for any contingency. She would be safe, at least for the time being.

His other line beeped. He ignored it. Instead he listened to the woman he adored tell him she'd be late, for him to go ahead and eat without her. He told her he loved her, and let her go.

Baldwin set the phone down, ran his hands through his hair, making the black bristle stand on end. Scrubbing it helped him think, and he did so violently, accidentally scraping his nails along his scalp.

This had to stop. They needed to find the Pretender. This tightrope walking was going to end badly, for both him and Taylor, if he didn't exert some control over the situation and find a solution.

He knew what that solution was, but he didn't even want to think about it. Admitting it would make it real, and push him even further into the abyss. His ass was already hanging out with the FBI, killing a suspect while on suspension would be the final nail in his coffin. He needed to find a way around. Capture, not elimination. Then he could get back to himself, to his relationship, to his job. He damn well didn't want to let it all slip away, let that fucking bastard take everything he'd been fighting for. It had been too long since he'd felt settled.

He went to the kitchen and poured a mug full of milk, added chocolate syrup and a package of instant coffee. He put it in the microwave and waited for it to heat through. He needed the sugar, the energy. Despite Taylor's assurances, he would wait up for her. She'd be hungry when she got home, maybe for food, maybe for him. He ate a banana and drank his mocha, let the warmth fill him up. The hot mug felt good on his cold hands.

Back in the living room, he checked to see who'd called while he was talking to Taylor. He was elated when he saw the caller ID. Wendy Heinz. At last. Wendy was thc graphologist he'd hired to look at the note from the trailer. *Ayin tahat ayin*—a most literal message.

His excitement grew as he listened to the voice mail.

Wendy's voice had a sense of elation. "I've gone

through the pages you sent me, and I have something you're not going to believe. Please call me as soon as you can."

Hot damn.

He checked his watch—10:30 p.m. Not too late to call, he knew Wendy was a night owl. Despite her long days testifying in court, teaching graphology at the University of California, and writing preeminent textbooks on the subject of criminal graphology, she was working on a novel in her spare time. Spare time meant early mornings and late nights. When she could find some quiet, away from her day-to-day responsibilities.

He dialed her number, and Wendy answered on the first ring, her tone jubilant.

"Dr. Baldwin! I'm glad you were able to return my call so quickly."

"It was a message I could hardly resist. What do you have for me?"

He heard papers shuffling in the background. "A bit more than you're expecting, probably. So you have something to write on?"

"So long as you promise me you won't be analyzing it, yes."

Wendy laughed. "Good one, Doc. Okay, here we go. The letter you sent me was so short that it's hard to make too many impressions from it, outside of the fact that an increasing rightward slant is indicative of poor impulse control and the propensity toward rage. But that's not the good part. I've been doing this for a very, very long time. I've seen a lot of handwriting, consulted on a number of cases. It took me so long to get back to you because I needed to go look at an old case file. There was something about this handwriting that felt…familiar to me."

Baldwin felt a thrill in his chest, his heartbeat picked up. "Familiar how?"

"Familiar in that I thought I'd seen it before. And I was right."

"Wait, you said an old case file. You've seen notes from this killer before?"

"I can't say that with absolute certainty. I brought in another colleague to double-check my findings, and he agrees with me. We're working on the assumption that this *is* the handwriting of your killer. Without seeing him actually write on paper in front of me, I can't prove that it's him. But yes, I've seen it before. Ready for some notes?"

"You bet. Let's hear it."

"In 1995, I was working on a case in North Carolina. A woman who had Munchausen's by proxy, or so we thought. She had a history, hurt everyone around her, her kids, her husband, her friends. She eventually killed her husband, that's when they finally had enough to send her away. She had a short trial, and was sentenced to life in prison. For her sentencing hearing, her middle son wrote a letter to the court, asking for leniency. He was only fourteen at the time. Obviously, leniency was granted—they could have given her the death penalty. She went away, and the kid was suddenly alone in the world. Got placed into the foster system, then in a group home. He started acting out, violently, then went off the radar."

"He wrote a letter to the court," Baldwin said.

"Yes," Wendy replied. "And in my professional opinion, the handwriting is the same as the letter you gave me."

Baldwin knew some about graphology, but only the basics: that it's the study of all graphic movement, can be used to gain insight into the mind of a person. Handwriting, doodles, drawings, sculpture and paintings, all can be examined for indicative personality traits, and, in the hands of a trained professional, it can be incredibly accurate.

He asked Wendy to give him a refresher course in some of the specifics. She was more than happy to oblige. The good news had them both giddy. Whether he would be able to close the Pretender down with the information was yet to be seen, but this felt like the first real step they'd taken toward finding out his true identity. He'd finally made a mistake they could capitalize on.

Wendy was a good lecturer, succinct and clear. "So here's the deal. We can determine both fixed traits, like IQ, aptitude, temperament and identity, and gain insight into ability, attitude, moods, beliefs, motivational levels and physical condition. With a proper sample, there's very little we can't tell about a person. Handwriting is as unique as fingerprints and teeth. We're guided by three basic principles: physical, mental and emotional, and all three of these are readily apparent in our handwriting. But I digress. The reason I recognized the handwriting from the letter in the old case was because it was the first time I'd seen a real, live example of the maniac D."

"Maniac D. Charles Manson had that, if I remember correctly. It's when the stem of the lower case *d* leans really far to the right, correct?"

"That's right. Manson and the Zodiac Killer, hell, even O. J. Simpson has it. It's almost exclusive to psychopaths and murderers. Certainly violent offenders, the most dangerous people. So this letter had the maniac D, but that wasn't all. It was written with what we call an unstable slant. Most people's writing leans in certain directions—they slant right, slant left or write straight up and down, with variations of all three. It all depends on mood, personality and whether the writer is left- or right-handed, but it's generally consistent. His was all over the place. There was no acknowledgment of the rules—though the letter was written on regular notebook paper, the lines were ignored, the margins deviated. We call that left margin the line of society, and he disregarded it completely. The letters were narrow and the pressure on the page so intense that it tore in spots. It didn't take a lot of analysis to see that the writer was tremendously disturbed.

"Highly intelligent, too—the vocabulary was sophisticated, the argument cogent. But the incoherent baseline told me I was dealing with someone who was deranged. I let the judge know, basically banged every drum I could find, but graphology didn't have the cache it does now." She laughed softly. "And that's still damn little. I had a hard time getting them to pay attention to me. The case originated in a very small town in the foothills of North Carolina. He was fourteen, abused and alone. There weren't a lot of programs in place to help troubled children, much less the antisocial son of a murderer. His trail goes cold after his early placements in foster care and the group home. There's nothing else in the file. And now you have everything I have."

"Oh, Wendy. You're just teasing me now."

She laughed, and agreed. "I am. I know you want his name."

"You better believe it."

"Ewan Copeland."

"Ewan Copeland. *Ewan Copeland*. Why does that sound so familiar?"

"His dad was Roger Copeland. Minor league ballplayer, spent the vast majority of his career in the minors, but got called up to the majors for a year. Played for the Atlanta Braves."

"Son of a bitch. I remember this now. Roger Copeland was murdered right after the season ended. They thought his wife did it. This is the same case?"

"That's the case. For what it's worth, Betty Copeland did kill him. She's clinically insane. I'm honestly surprised she wasn't put into permanent long-term psychiatric care. Terrible lawyer. He could have gotten her off on an incompetency plea. Instead she's serving a hundred and twenty up in Atlanta. She committed the murder, and there was no talking the judge out of the facts."

"Is she alive?"

"I don't know. The last time I looked, yes, she was alive and still incarcerated. No parole hearings for Betty. I've included all of her information in the material I've sent you."

"And you're telling me, with a high degree of certainty, that the man who wrote the letter we found in the trailer is the same one who wrote a letter begging for clemency for his mother after she murdered his father?"

"That's what I'm saying."

"Wendy, I honestly don't know how I'm ever going to repay you."

"I'm sure I'll need a favor someday. I've taken the liberty of overnighting copies of everything I have on this to your home address. You'll have it first thing in the morning. I hope it helps.

"More than you can possibly imagine, Wendy. I don't know how to thank you."

"I'll figure something out. Dr. Baldwin, just one last thing. This boy was completely dysfunctional after the murder. The rest of his family was dead. He was totally alone. If he's your killer, he's obviously grown into something we couldn't imagine. I'd just like to warn you to be on your guard. He's a volatile guy."

"*That* I already knew. We've been trying to profile him for a while now, and the profile keeps changing."

"That doesn't surprise me. He had no anchor back then, and obviously never found one."

"Thank you, Wendy. Again, I can't begin to tell you—"

"I know. Good luck."

Baldwin hung up the phone and opened a map of North Carolina on his laptop. It only took a few moments to locate the place—Forest City was just southeast of Asheville, a little more than an hour's drive from the mountain town. Now that they had the North Carolina connection explained, things were starting to make sense. Copeland leaving Fitz's eye an hour from his hometown—was he looking to be caught? Had he grown tired of the game, and engineered the slaughter in Nags Head to lead them to his true identity? It stood to reason; even if it was a subconscious ploy, he would eventually want them to know that Ewan Copeland had grown into the Pretender.

Baldwin calculated, it was only six hours to Forest City. In the time it would take to arrange for the plane to come to Nashville and fly them there, they could drive. As appealing as snatching the plane again sounded, Baldwin's boss, Garrett Woods, was only one man. He couldn't keep diverting the company jet for a suspended agent. Driving was their best option. If they left now, they could be there before dawn.

But he had to wait for the material Wendy was sending. Damn.

He started to pace, toyed with the idea of going anyway, then made the smarter decision. A good night's sleep wouldn't hurt. The line had just gotten a whole lot straighter, and he knew in his heart that they were about to get to the bottom of things at last.

He went to call Taylor, and couldn't contain the smile on his face.

Eighteen

To: tro14@ncr.tr.com
From: 44cal@ncr.ss.com
Subject: Washington, D.C.

Dear Troy,
It's all cool. I'm in town. Getting close now, man.
44

Traffic. Stuck in traffic. Always stuck in traffic. His daily commute was an hour each way; he'd taken a week off to play the game and was so excited not to have to deal with the mind-numbing lemming cars, stacked one on top of the other, crawling along. But here he was on the Beltway, late. Late was not good. The schedule was vital.

Shit, shit, shit. If he didn't make this kill and report in on time, he'd be eliminated.

His leg started bouncing, making the car jerk forward. He managed to slam on the brake just before ramming into the fender of the Infiniti G35 in front of him. Phew. That was close.

The angel shouted at him. *Don't draw attention to yourself. You must be invisible. Invisible. Invisible. Invisible.*

He hated this. He didn't want to be invisible. He wanted to be splashy, huge. Famous. He wanted to have legions of fans, women who wanted to marry him, who sent him their stained underwear. He wanted to be the celebrity of death row. Jail wasn't so bad. He'd done a few years in his early twenties and hadn't thought it was that big a deal. Maximum-security might be a little different, but not much. Jail was jail, man, no matter where you slept and who tossed your salad. He was a good-looking guy, too—the beard made him look like Seth Rogen. The jail bunnies wouldn't be able to keep their eyes off him.

Death row was where it was at. They never really killed people off, not regularly, and not quickly, either. The death row inmates spent twenty, thirty, hell, forty years in play, never having to work, commute, deal with traffic. They had computers and books, three squares a day, time outside to exercise. It was fucking cushy, that was what it was. He wanted in. No more dealing with others if he didn't want to—he could just do something egregious and sit it out in solitary. Yes, this sounded perfect to him. An escape. He didn't care if he ever got out. And losing his life, well, it would be worth it.

You'd be dead, homey. And what would happen to me, huh? Where am I supposed to go if you get yourself electrocuted?

Shut up, shut up, shut up, shut up.

If he stuck to the plan, to the letter of the law that had been handed down, he could have that freedom. He could go on a spree, the spree to end all sprees, the one that would live in infamy. He'd gun them all down—the entire fourth floor of the building would lie in their own blood and sick. But he wouldn't cop out by taking his own life, no, no. He would lean into his lawyer at sentencing and laugh at the judge, show no remorse at his trial. He'd be the biggest sensation they'd ever seen.

That's better. Go to the crazy house. Tell them you've got a head full of crazy. They let you smoke, and fuck in there. Pills galore. The orderlies, you know what I mean? You catch my drift, brother?

Yes, all right. I get it.

The dashboard clock read 8:40 p.m. He rolled down the window, lit an American Spirit. Blew smoke into the chilly fog outside his car. He had to be at the landing by ten if he was going to catch them. Traffic began to move, sluggish at first, then picking up speed. Divine intervention.

He took the exit for the George Washington Parkway, paying close attention now. The park was after downtown, he knew that because of the map. The cars all came with navigation now—that was so cool. Even so, he sometimes got distracted—*bullshit, you just a crazy fucker*—and he didn't want to miss the turn. Even in daylight, assignations were made in the park. But it was totally dark in there now, and he'd have his pick of paths to follow.

He fingered the suppressor, feeling the rough edges where he'd filed it down to fit his gun. This was the fun part. He loved the few moments before he went in for the kill. Wiping the abnormal bastards off the face of the earth was a pleasure; he was more than happy when he was assigned that subsection of the list. More than happy. It didn't matter that he had a few latent tendencies himself, that he fantasized late at night about the center of another man.

You're not a homo, man. Don't worry. Would I let you be a homo? Homey ain't no homo.

The angel started to laugh, holding his belly, rolling back so far that he tipped right off his shoulder. He felt him crawling around his back, trying to get his footing. He leaned back in the seat and tried to smush him, ignored the squeaks.

Fucker.

No one needed to know about his…his…proclivities. That was his secret, one he even kept from the angel, who was climbing back onto his shoulder, mildly out of breath.

Ain't no secrets from me, homey. I know what a trick you are.

Shut. Up!

When he went to jail, where it was expected, then he could indulge. In the meantime, he'd annihilate the abnormal ones who flaunted their desires.

The entrance to the park was on his right. He swerved into the parking lot. Licked his lips. The angel hung on to his ear for balance, and they both smiled. This was getting good. This was getting really good.

Nineteen

Colleen Keck was nearing her breaking point. Flynn was finally asleep. The boy had sensed something was wrong with his mother and insisted on clinging stubbornly to her neck like a limpet all night. She'd had a bitch of a time getting him down, too. He'd wanted to be held. Not be read to from his favorite book, not watch TV, not even have me time. Every time she loosened her hold on him, he began to wail. In the end, she'd left him crying into his pillow, stomach thick with guilt. She asked Tommy's ghost to watch over Flynn, to comfort him if possible. It must have worked—he'd finally drifted off a little past ten.

In between Flynn's crying jags, she'd been fielding calls all evening about the possible sad resolution to the Peter Schechter case. The phone started ringing around 8:00 p.m., a source of hers with Metro who she could always count on to spill the beans. There was a submerged body out in Percy Priest Lake, and the initial description matched the Schechter boy: white, young, dark hair. No one wanted to jump to conclusions, of course, but logic dictated it could possibly be him.

There weren't too many active missing persons cases in the region that met the criteria at the moment.

She had such a hard time with the cases that involved children. Since that was so much of her daily workload, she always felt on edge, but tonight it was worse. The Schechter boy, the Zodiac letter, the reports she'd gotten from her contacts in Boston and New York, all seemed to indicate that copycats of the Zodiac, Son of Sam and the Boston Strangler were back on the scene. So much death, so splashy and forward. These killings were guaranteed coverage. She'd been posting her speculations all day, now all the major media outlets had it. She'd gotten the scoop first, of course, but they were running truncated versions of it now. They published updates every fifteen minutes with no new information, creating a panic. And their reporters and producers claimed the story was their scoop. First on the scene. Typical.

How often do three murders happen on the same night that imitate famous serial killers? Insult to injury, she hadn't even been mentioned for breaking the story. She should send a note to the producers, let them know she'd been first. She needed the media exposure, it would increase the traffic to the site, which meant more money in her coffers. A story like this could generate some serious cash.

She wondered for a minute if Peter Schechter could be a part of the copycat murders, then shook her head. Her imagination was running away with her. She didn't get the sense that he was a part of this insanity. The only major serial killer Nashville had ever had was the Snow White, and he didn't kill boys. No, Schechter was probably a leftover from the Halloween massacre. That made much more sense.

The only thing she knew was to report the truth as it came in. So that was what she was doing. Her headline said it all.

Has Pete Schechter Been Found?

She linked to all the stories she'd done on the case, four in all. She wrote a short bit of copy, expressing sorrow for the family, emphasized that there would be more tomorrow and posted it. Her day was complete.

She poured a glass of wine, moved her laptop computer to the living room. Her work email was under control, not totally empty, but manageable. Her personal email inbox had a zero count. That wasn't unusual. Her friends had been Tommy's friends, and after he died, after the initial outpouring of grief and sadness, she'd slowly fallen off people's radars. Part of it was by design. She liked the isolation, it helped her work the Felon E persona with minimal distractions. But the rest was "out of sight, out of mind." Survivor's guilt only lasted so long before people went back to their own busy lives.

The past was meant to be forgotten.

There were still one or two wives who would send her a note every once in a while, trying to include her in recipe exchanges and the like. She just wasn't interested in those things anymore. Being a part of a family was very different than being the sole head of a family, especially one reduced to the remaining survivors. If you could call them that. No matter what they said, she couldn't shake the feeling that people dealt with her out of guilt rather than a true desire for friendship. It was tiring.

She took a sip of wine. Alone was better. Alone was safe. Alone was…lonely. The blog kept her sane, at least.

Colleen's normal habit at night, before unwinding in front of the television and heading to bed to sort of sleep, was to run through the comments on the previous day's posts. She knew how important habit was, how far behind she could get after missing just a couple of days, so she took another sip of wine, opened her content management system and started. If they were all counted, across the multiple daily postings, she garnered thousands of comments a day from hundreds of unique individuals. Sometimes more, if a conversation started in the comments, which happened most days.

Yesterday's posts contained nothing unusual. She read through them looking for trolls, but all seemed in order. As she was about to exit the program, she noticed that the comment count on the first Zodiac post from this morning was exponentially high, so, yawning, she went ahead and opened it, just for kicks. She usually liked to wait a full twenty-four hours before checking comments, giving people from all times zones a chance to get into the fray, but there were already seven hundred entries. She clicked the link and glanced through them.

One leaped out at her immediately.

I know who you are.

She felt her heart begin to race. She set the computer down, and got up to check the doors and windows. They were all locked up, just the way she left them. She was being silly. There were plenty of freaking whack jobs out there online, always taking a chance to poke at her. She couldn't help herself, she was totally creeped out.

Just to be extra safe, she reset the alarm system, this time on the highest security setting she had, the one that would send a silent alarm to the police station the second someone even touched her door or window. She secured the drapes, checked on Flynn, who'd finally tired himself out and was sound asleep, breathing deeply, his little chest rhythmically rising and falling. Her heart filled with love and dread watching him, so innocent, so pure. She closed his door almost all the way, leaving a crack so she could hear him if he cried out in the night, then went back to the laptop.

I know who you are.

She started scrolling through the messages, fear choking her. There must have been a hundred entries, all with those five words. All left anonymously, between half past noon and 1:30 p.m. today.

She opened her web stats and looked up the IP address associated with the comments. Nashville, Tennessee.

A few more clicks showed her it had come from a private server at a temporary internet hot spot, but that was as far as she could get.

She chewed on her thumb, teeth catching on a hangnail. She worried it until the skin tore away, leaving a fresh bloom of red blood across the bed of her nail. She sucked on the cut until the pain forced her to stop. She'd received threats before, but they'd always been silly, empty, designed to piss her off more than anything else. Always diatribes, rants against her and her purpose. Sometimes family who hated what she was doing, or an irate fan. But nothing like this. For some reason, this felt real.

She checked the other posts she'd done today. It was there. On every post, the samc five words, so seemingly innocuous, that made sweat break out on her neck and her flesh crawl.

I know who you are.

No one knew she was Felon E. No one. She'd been so careful to protect her identity. She'd even started completely separate mail and phone systems for contacts that were meant for the blog. The cell was disposable, only charged when she used it, which was never, and the P.O. Box was registered under a completely different name. Nothing that could be traced back to her, Colleen Keck. Neither the phone company nor the post office had the capability to put two and two together. The only way was if someone followed her to the post office and caught her checking the Felon E mailbox, then followed her home.

Unless there was someone in her system checking her phone bills against her IP address. That was a true long shot; she routed through multiple servers so she wasn't easily traced back and created new IP addresses every time she logged in. She clicked a few keys and engaged a search, was relieved to see that wasn't the case. No one had been in her system. There were no tracks.

So why did she get the feeling that this crackpot wasn't lying?

I know who you are.

She started looking frantically through the rest of the comments, and found something even more disturbing.

A short exchange, buried in the middle of the mess, from one of her regulars, @texasmassacre. It read:

"Hey, did you hear about @kittycrime and @chaosmaster? They got themselves shot out in San Francisco."

The responses varied from horror to smug nastiness. Colleen felt the fear tear at her stomach, a gnawing, aching terror. She checked the forum, saw the conversations going on about the two regular commenters who'd been gunned down last night. She fished through the forum's registration information until she found their real names: @chaosmaster was Ike Sharp and @kittycrime was named Vivi Waters.

She didn't have to check her notes. She knew the names. They matched the names of the victims in this morning's Zodiac killing in San Francisco.

I know who you are.

Colleen didn't know whether to panic or stay calm, but two words escaped her lips with utter sincerity.

"Oh, shit."

She couldn't keep this to herself anymore. She needed to go public. Not on the blog, not speculation and reporting. She needed to go to the cops.

Twenty

The dark water lapped languorously at the bank, and Taylor could hear the small stirrings of animals in the surrounding woods. It was quiet on this boat dock, isolated. That was why the killer chose this place. It was out of the way. Off the beaten path. Private.

A familiar chirping noise came to her ears, playing in the background behind the murmurs and joking conversations of the crime scene techs.

Crickets. Crickets in winter. Surely there was some old wives' tale that addressed that phenomenon? The world was probably going to stop spinning on its axis, or Sam was sure to have a boy, or a cat was going to walk over her grave. She should ask Ariadne, the witch would have the answer. She always did.

Taylor watched Sam get the body into the M.E.'s van, her instructions reverential yet efficient. Marcus was handling the investigation; Taylor didn't need to be at the scene anymore. She decided to stay a few more minutes anyway, feeling a false sense of responsibility. More guilt, if she was being honest. That was crazy, she wasn't responsible, for the Schechter boy's death or for this case, but the simple fact that another kid had died was too much for her.

When was this going to stop? Was it something she'd done, some wrong she'd committed? And why, if the Pretender was so fucking omniscient, wasn't he taking his chance? He'd get off on the thrill of having cops around. She'd walked the perimeter of the crime scene alone purposefully. If he was watching, maybe he'd take a chance. From a distance, in the dark, the best he could do would be a body shot, her vest would stop that in a heartbeat.

She realized she was assuming that the Schechter boy was just a ploy designed to distract her, and sharpened her senses even further. Death was not a finite commodity.

Anger burned through her. *Come on, you motherfucker. Let's go.* The dark greeted her with silence, broken only by crickets and the grunts of the investigators behind her.

Over the past few months, the murder rate on the whole had risen in Nashville. While her team's close rate was still in the eighty to eighty-three percent range, much higher than anyone else's in Metro and across the country, too, the fact that there were more murders to solve meant resources were stretched thin, and emotions running high. She knew the Pretender had contributed to the mess, amplifying the murder rate almost fifteen percent all on his own, but she'd had other cases this year that contributed. Nashville was much more likely to see an uptick in lowbrow crime—drugs, prostitution, gangs—than these unique serial cases. Yet the crazies kept finding her.

Another reason she needed to resolve the problem, and soon. If she eliminated the Pretender, the crime rates would drop. The chief would be happy with her, Delores Norris, the head of the Office of Professional Accountability, would quit breathing down her neck, Fitz would come back to work and her whole team would be back together, and life would go on.

Yes, elimination was the key.

Sam interrupted her reverie. "We're ready to take off. Tabor will meet us there."

Taylor turned to her best friend. "You look tired. You could hand it off to one of the other M.E.'s."

Sam was almost eight weeks pregnant, dark circles riding under her eyes, her face drawn with exhaustion.

"I'm okay. Simon's got the twins, and I'm feeling all right now. I'm on the late shift this week, so that works good. It's the mornings that are getting to me. I'm much sicker with this one than the twins. Hell, I didn't even know I was pregnant with them for a couple of months."

"All the more reason to rest. But I understand. I saw a couple of the guys on their phones. I hope this hasn't leaked out just yet. Keep an eye on that, will you?"

"Sure thing. I'll see you later."

"Wait, Sam. Mind if I join you?"

Surprise etched Sam's face, but she shook her head. "Not at all. I could use the company. I'll see you over there."

Taylor watched Sam stride away and get into the plain white van that served Forensic Medical. She found Marcus, let him know she was leaving, then climbed in her own car. She picked up her cell to call Baldwin again, tell him she was heading to the morgue, and realized the battery was dead. Careless. She never let that happen. But with the quick trip to North Carolina,

Fitz, the murders this morning, she'd just spaced out. Baldwin would be furious with her, she'd get a lecture. She didn't blame him, it was a stupid mistake.

She got out of the car and went to borrow Marcus's cell. She didn't need her flashlight, not with the crime scene fully illuminated. She scooted around the edge of one of the light stands, turning her body to slip past the contraption. Out of the corner of her eye, she saw something orange. She halted, looked closer. The tree closest to her had a pentacle painted on the wood.

She shouted to the nearest crime scene tech. "Hey, Iles, come here for a second."

Iles was capable, smart. Quiet and businesslike. She liked him. He came over to her, smiling, his teeth flashing white against his tanned face. She wondered if he went to a salon or spray tanned, or both. Really, a tan at the beginning of winter? Metrosexual men, she never knew what to think about them. She usually didn't trust guys who spent more time in the bathroom getting ready than she did—with the exception of Lincoln, of course. His fascination with clothes was actually fascinating to her. That man had taste, and style. He wasn't a poseur.

"What can I do for you, Lieutenant?"

She pointed to the tree. "Has anyone looked at this?"

Iles shined a Maglite on the bark, the fluorescent orange practically leaped out in 3-D. Eerie. It had been spray-painted, little drips of orange had run down the tree, puddling in the bark and on the ground below. She leaned in close and sniffed deeply, the acrid scent of acetone filled her nostrils. Not totally fresh, but not entirely dry either.

"No, I don't think we have. You think this has something to do with the crime scene?"

"A teenager dead, and a pentacle at the scene? Either it does, or someone has a very sick sense of humor."

She called to Marcus. He joined them, eyebrows tight.

"What's up, LT? They just found a bag under the tree branch, looks like the kid's backpack. I think we're going to be at this for another couple of hours, at least."

"Did you see this?"

Marcus stared at the tree.

"No, I didn't." He turned to Iles, voice tight. "Get pictures of this, now."

"Why would someone paint a pentacle on the tree out here?" Iles asked. "I thought you shot the kid who ran the Halloween massacre, and locked the rest of them away."

Taylor tried not to flinch in the face of Iles's words.

"Let's just pray it's someone playing a very bad joke," she said.

She drove in silence to Forensic Medical, planning to use the phone as soon as she arrived. It was after hours and the lobby was dark. She used her key card to enter. She was doing her damndest here. From the outside, it looked like another strike against her, running around alone in the dark. She was becoming more aware of her vulnerabilities. It wasn't so hard to lay herself out in the open, ripe for the taking. She needed it to look like she wasn't aware of her surroundings, that she was comfortable enough to let her guard down. And that meant walking a thin line, close to the ones she loved, to draw the bastard out.

She'd been alone for a couple of hours now. Why hadn't he made a play? What in the name of God was he waiting for?

The door unlocked with a snap, and she entered the building. The reception desk was deserted, of course. Kris, the bubbly, vivacious girl who handled the day-to-day management of calls, requests, family visits, was home for the night.

Taylor pulled out Kris's chair and sat at the desk. She reached for the phone, and a picture taped to the top of Kris's computer caught her eye. Kris and Barclay Iles, in bathing suits, hugging, tan and happy. Ah. That explained Iles's tan. She didn't know they were dating. Kris had always seemed to like bad boys; Iles was, well, benign, if she were to be honest. Hmm.

She dialed home, but Baldwin didn't answer, the phone went directly to voice mail. That only happened when he was on the other line, so she left a message detailing where she was, the random pentacle at the Peter Schechter scene and that she loved him. All told, a good message, she thought. At least it ended well.

After taking one last glance at the picture of Kris and Barclay Iles, she crossed the lobby and swiped her card again to enter Forensic Medical's inner sanctum. A long hallway led to the autopsy suite, and she smiled as she passed Sam's office. The door was ajar, a small red Chinese lamp filled the room with soft light. Everything was in its place. Sam was a neat freak, had more than a touch of obsessive-compulsive disorder. Just enough that details were always sewn up, her office never looked like a bomb had gone off in it. It was what made her such a good medical examiner—there weren't too many things that she didn't notice.

Taylor entered the women's locker room, put her hair up in a bun and changed into a pair of scrubs. She didn't want her street clothes anywhere near the autopsy suite tonight—floaters were the worst, and she'd stink for days if she miscalculated.

Sam was already at work, sipping a cup of green tea just inside the door, wearing a full-length lead apron. She wasn't alone. Dr. Michael Tabor, the forensic odontologist for the state of Tennessee, was staring at the illuminated x-ray window box. Stuart Charisse, Sam's perpetual lab assistant, was taking new radiographs of the body, which was still clothed.

Tabor greeted Taylor with a hug. She'd always enjoyed working with him. A regular dentist by trade, he was also one of the most experienced forensic odontologists in the country. His ties to Los Angeles and New York had garnered him nationwide respect, and enabled him to work cases outside of Tennessee. He'd been called to New York after 9/11 to work on identifications. He had spent weeks in New York naming the firefighters, police and other innocent men and women lost in the collapse. Taylor knew the experience had changed him, and she couldn't help but respect how difficult a job that had been.

While Stuart prepped and x-rayed the floater's teeth, Tabor went through the National Dental Image Repository worksheet on his laptop. Though he could look at the two sets of radiographs and tell almost immediately if they had a match, this was an official case, and the procedures must be followed.

On paper, the law enforcement dental identification process seemed simple. Match antemortem dental records to postmortem records through the use of the FBI's huge nationwide NDIR computer database. In reality, the NDIR didn't have much luck making matches. The dental database should have been basic protocol all over the country. But many of the rural police departments found it difficult to populate their databases simply because their victims weren't commonly seen by dentists. The big-city guys were too busy with their caseloads to follow through. It just hadn't gotten to the point that it worked smoothly.

The idea behind it was easy. When a missing persons report came in, the investigator who talks with the family asks if the missing person has been to a dentist in the past several years. If they existed, antemortem radiographs and dental charts would be retrieved, charted and inputted into the database.

If a likely victim surfaced, a forensic odontologist would examine the body, then create a postmortem dental chart using plain sight and postmortem radiographs. The database would work its magic, spit out a match, and notification would be made to the family that their loved one had been found. If it worked.

Peter Schechter's case was a bit easier. Missing for five days, his parents had submitted his radiographs to the police over the weekend. They were in the NDIR system. Tabor already had the comparison radiographs prepped.

Taylor watched Stuart and Tabor work together, Tabor nodding and clucking. He had a good poker face, so she couldn't tell if there was a match yet or not. Sam was filling out some preliminary paperwork. Taylor went to her.

"I didn't know Kris and Barclay Iles were dating," she said.

Sam knit her brows at the interruption, answered without breaking stride in her writing. "Yeah, they've been out to us for a couple of months now. She was the reason he got hired in the first place—she brought his resume to me. He was almost overqualified—he'd made it a couple of years in med school before dropping out. I was a little annoyed when I found out he was actually her boyfriend, but it doesn't seem to affect either one of their duties. I see how well you and Baldwin work together, thought I'd bend the rules a bit and let them have at it."

"You're using Baldwin and me as an example?"

"Of course. Lord knows Simon and I can't work side by side. I'd wring his neck and he'd divorce me. We're both much too controlling. But the two of you, you have that give and take, you complement each other rather than butt heads. It's cool."

Sam was right, Taylor did work well with Baldwin. She worked well with her whole team. Granted, she'd handpicked them, made sure she had personalities that would coalesce, but Sam had a point. It wasn't always easy to work with your significant other.

"It's him," Tabor said.

"One hundred percent?" Sam asked.

"Yeah. No doubt about it. The radiographs are a perfect match. Sorry about that, ladies. I'll get the rest of the paperwork filed in the morning. But for the time being, as far as I'm concerned, you can do a notification." Tabor packed his things, nodded to both Taylor and Sam, then let himself out.

Sam put her tea down. "All right then. Stuart, let's get him undressed."

Taylor watched while they struggled with the wet

clothes. When his shirt was stripped off, she felt a huge pang of relief.

Taylor called Marcus. He answered on the first ring.

"It's Schechter?" he asked without preamble.

"Yeah. Tabor just finished the dental comparison."

"Damn. Okay then. I'll head out to see his parents. Any word on our pentacle? Is Schechter left over from the Halloween murders?"

"There are no visible knife wounds or carvings on the body. I don't think it's related. Keep an open mind though, you never know, but this doesn't feel like the Halloween killings to me. I'm going home now. Let the parents know Sam will be ready for them to do a closed circuit visual identification around…" She looked over at Sam, who held up four fingers twice. "Around eight tomorrow morning. And, Marcus, you go home after you talk to the Schechters, okay? You've had a long-ass day."

"You know it, sister," he said. "I'll see you tomorrow?"

"Sure thing."

"Oh, hey, before I go, any idea about cause of death? His parents are sure to ask."

"Hold on," Taylor said. "Sam, any idea on COD?"

Sam was helping Stuart wash the body, called out, "Not yet. There's some bruising around the neck, but I'll have a better idea by morning. Stall them."

"Did you hear that?" Taylor asked Marcus.

"Yes," he sighed. Notification was one of the most hideous duties of their job. Even though they brought the department's chaplain along, as was required by Metro regulation, watching a family receive the most horrific news of their life, news that would shape their world from here on out, was devastating. None of them was good at it, though it happened regularly in their line of work.

"Good luck," she said, sincerely. "I'll see you tomorrow."

Taylor quit the morgue, casually looking for the watchers Price was supposed to have put on her tail, hoping for one that felt out of place. He'd emailed her their photos so she wouldn't mistake either of them for her target. She spied one of them, a dark shadow lingering around the corner of the building. He saluted her, then melted back into the darkness. The other was out of sight. If the Pretender saw them… No, he'd enjoy that challenge, too.

She got in the car, debating. Looked at the clock, nearly midnight. She needed to go home. They would follow. She would explain to Baldwin that she'd brought her own people on board. He wouldn't be able to argue—she was allowing herself to be protected, after all.

The streets were practically deserted, just her and the watchers following at a discreet distance. She hopped on I-65 south to I-40 west, the Nashville skyline winking at her for the briefest of moments. She loved the city at night, its lights glowing in the deserted buildings like a sailor's succor after months at sea. She felt a calm steal over her, peace, despite the evening's death. Thought about the Schechter case.

The dead had no secrets once she got involved. Her job, her mission, was to ferret out the truth, find the tiniest bit of shame in a person's background and follow that thread to its conclusion. What secret was Peter Schechter hiding? What small transgression, invisible or visible, had he witnessed or caused that ended in his death?

The pentacle—she couldn't help but feel that was a message, not a fluke. Not a joke.

She flipped open her phone and dialed a number she'd recently committed to heart. Only felt a moment's silliness for calling the witch—she'd yet to be wrong about things.

After a few moments, a woman's soft voice answered the phone.

"How are you, Taylor?"

"Ariadne. I'm good. You?"

The question was a bit loaded. Ariadne carried a child, one conceived in violence. Taylor felt the full weight of responsibility, but Ariadne reassured her.

"The Goddess's blessings are upon me, as always. We're doing very well. I'm so glad you found your sergeant. I told you he'd be all right. How are you coping?"

Taylor envisioned the woman, curled on a sofa in front of the crackling fire, her small pale feet tucked beneath her, long, luxurious black hair swirling around her body like a cloak. She wished she felt the kind of peace Ariadne seemed to embody.

"I'm happy he's going to be okay. As for me, well, I'm as fine as I can be, considering," Taylor answered. At least she had been honest. "Listen, we found the boy that's been missing since Halloween."

"He's dead," Ariadne said, a statement, not a question. Ariadne always knew things.

"Yes. There was a pentacle spray-painted on a tree close to where we found the body."

"Were there any markings on the body?"

"None that we saw. I don't think it's related, but I could be wrong."

"Don't second-guess yourself, Taylor. Your instincts are always right."

"You know about the man who has been stalking me. I'm wondering if this was him, trying to draw me out."

"You want to be drawn out, though."

Shit. Maybe this hadn't been the best idea. "Ariadne, I just need to know if this boy is connected to the earlier case."

"Give me a minute."

There was silence, then a sigh. "I don't believe he was a part of the Halloween massacre."

"That's what I thought, too. Thank you. I'll see you soon, all right?"

"Taylor?"

"Yes?"

She could hear the hesitation in Ariadne's voice. "Go careful. You don't want things backfiring. Some situations are…irreversible."

The witch was drowsing again. How she managed to read Taylor's emotions and intentions over the phone was uncanny.

"I will. Have a good night."

"May the blessings of Diana be upon you, sister."

Taylor glanced at the chilly moon and smiled, then hung up, pushed Ariadne's warning from her mind and thought about the timing of Peter Schechter's murder again.

He'd been missing since Friday. Five days. Plenty of time for the Pretender to swing through town and grab him. Maybe he had someone do it for him, like Nags Head. Maybe she'd been hanging around Baldwin for too long, seen too many oddities in her own cases, but the idea of a gang of killers executing a game was all too real to her.

This could easily be connected to the Pretender. She was a cop, she didn't believe in coincidence. A pentacle painted on a tree near the dead boy, not exactly the same, but similar. She had to throw that thought into the mix. The Pretender was a copycat, after all. It was entirely possible that he was simply poking at her, yet again.

But when he mimicked, it was down to the most minute details. This could be a random murder, completely unrelated to either of the cases.

Poor Peter Schechter. Whatever his story, he didn't deserve this.

She was already at her exit. She glided down the silent ramp, suddenly anxious to get home. Baldwin would help chase away the lingering darkness. The streets were quiet in the bitter night air, so it only took her ten minutes.

The lights were burning brightly when she pulled into the drive. She smiled—of course he hadn't gone to bed. She was glad. In the midst of all this turmoil, she needed her anchor. Baldwin was her very heart.

He was waiting for her in the kitchen, a huge grin plastered on his face. He swept her into a hug.

"Mmm, I'm glad you're home."

"Me, too."

"I made you some soup. Chicken noodle." He played with her hair, still smiling widely.

"I can smell it. Are you anticipating me getting sick sometime soon?"

"Of course not. Just helping you keep your resistance

up." He kissed her, softly at first, then with a building passion.

This, this was heaven. Coming home to the man she loved, the warm scents of food and lingering smoke from the fire. Could she give all of this up if she were caught? *Shh,* she told her mind. *Stop thinking about it.*

She returned the kiss, wrapped her arms around Baldwin's strong body. She loved that he was taller than her, they fit together so perfectly. Just as she started thinking less of the warm soup and more of their warm bed, he broke away.

"Not just yet," he said.

"Damn." She ran her hands through his hair. "I was thinking we might..."

"Oh, and we will. But I have something really awesome to tell you first."

"What?"

"Come sit down."

He led her to the table, then went back to the stove and spooned out the soup. He crossed the kitchen carefully and set the full bowl on the placemat in front of her.

"Eat," he commanded. She didn't dare disobey. He had something up his sleeve, she could tell. She dipped her spoon in the smooth golden liquid, let the salt burst into her mouth. Oh, that was so good.

After several mouthfuls, she set the spoon down. "Okay. Tell me. You look like a little boy at his birthday party, about to dive into the cake."

Baldwin took a deep breath and grinned. "I know who he is."

"You know who who is?"

As she said it, she realized. Felt her breath catch in her throat.

Baldwin handed her his notes.

She abandoned the soup.

November 7

Twenty-One

"Tell me again."

The Federal Express truck had arrived at 7:30 a.m. with the package from Wendy Heinz, and they'd gotten on the road fifteen minutes later. They were due in to Forest City at 2:00 p.m. local time, and Baldwin was pretty sure they could shave a good twenty minutes off that if they could keep up the pace. As he drove, Taylor had read him the entire contents of the file Wendy had sent. They were just outside of Knoxville, the sky a stormy gray. Rain was chasing them westward, rain that would turn to overnight snow in the North Carolina mountains. The Blue Ridge, so aptly named, was putting on a show for them, the cobalt horizons murky and amorphous.

Taylor went back to the beginning of the file and started over.

"Ewan was born in 1980, the second of three boys. Mother was Elizabeth, known as Betty, father was Roger. Betty was a native of Forest City. Her dad, Edward Biggs, owned a barbecue joint that passed into her ownership when he died. She was nineteen at the time. She met Roger Copeland in 1977, when he was a successful third basemen for the Richmond Braves, that's the farm team for Atlanta. They got married, had their first child, a boy named Edward, named after her father, in 1978. They had Ewan in 1980 and Errol in 1982. You know, that's strange. There's nothing in here about the youngest child after the trial. I wonder where he is?"

"We'll have to ask around. I'm sure someone will know what happened to him."

"This just gives me the willies. He belongs to someone, Baldwin. He has a past, a life."

"Of course he does. They all do, honey. We only find out about them once that background has turned into a seething mass of hatred, and they lash out in desperation, or desire. But they all come from somewhere. Whether they're a product of their upbringing or they're born with it, they were, at some point, innocent."

She shook her head, ponytail swinging around her neck, and looked out the window. "Ewan Copeland was never an innocent."

Baldwin didn't disagree, but he didn't feel the need to verbalize that. Nature versus nurture: the greatest debate. If Ewan had been born to a mother who hadn't been sick, would he have turned into a normal, healthy man? Maybe played ball like his dad?

Taylor had grown quiet. He reached over and touched her hand. "Penny for your thoughts?"

"They don't come that cheap," she replied, but tossed him a smile.

"Seriously, what are you thinking?"

"I don't need your FBI guys, okay? I hired a couple of Price's men. They're going to stick to me like glue. Are sticking to me like glue."

Damn woman. He figured as much. The blue sedan

four cars back had been on them since Nashville. Not bothering to hide themselves, either. She knew he wouldn't fight her, he trusted Price as much as any of his own people. Devious, manipulative…

"Really. Well, thank you for sharing that."

"No fight?"

"No fight."

"Wow. Okay then. Now I'm wondering when you're planning on telling me what happened up in Quantico."

"I told you—"

"I *know,* Baldwin."

He steered the car around a particularly steep curve, gripping the steering wheel tightly. The gray leather was sure to have handprints denting it after this conversation.

Sarah McLachlan came on the radio, singing "Angel." Fitting for their excursion, he thought. This was their second chance, their big break. The lead that could blow the case of the Pretender wide-open.

"You know what, exactly?" he finally said carefully.

Taylor snapped the radio off. "Oh, please. Quit playing games with me. I saw the note from the graphologist. Would you care to tell me why I have to find out you've been suspended from a total stranger? And why total strangers know something about you that I don't?"

He breathed a huge internal sigh of relief. The suspension was something he could manage to explain. Charlotte, the boy—he just wasn't ready.

"I'm not keeping it from you. I just didn't want to burden you. You've got too much on your plate already.

It will blow over. Garrett is already working to get me reinstated."

"Pray tell what exactly did you do to get yourself suspended? You're their golden boy."

"Ha. If only. You're not mad?"

"I'm just a little surprised you didn't feel like you could trust me with this."

That wasn't a no. He glanced over at her. She was staring at him with that forthright look in her mismatched gray eyes, genuinely confused, and genuinely hurt. She'd sat on that annoyance for three hours; he felt terrible. He should have told her in the first place. He told her that.

"Taylor, I trust you with my life. You know that. This suspension, it's a temporary thing. A power play. There's a special agent named Tucker who has it in for me. It's kind of a long story."

She gestured to the open road in front of them. "I have nothing but time."

It had been horrible having to relive the deaths of his team in front of an adversary at his hearing. To explain it to the woman he loved… He really wasn't prepared, but he couldn't put this off any longer. His life with Taylor was too important, and he'd been stupid to wait at all. She was a tough woman, she could easily handle the truth. Most of it.

So he told her. He explained the Harold Arlen case in detail. How Arlen had duped them all with a tunnel in his basement, how the man had joined forces with a fellow pedophile and created a game of hide-and-seek with the bodies of little girls. How Charlotte Douglas had decided to plant evidence, told Baldwin her plan, and how he foolishly hadn't told anyone the truth. How that omission got him dragged in front of the disciplinary hearing, six years after the fact.

Taylor listened attentively, not asking questions, just letting him unload. She didn't comment when his voice thickened as he described the shooting. In the end, three good agents were dead, and so was Harold Arlen. His seventh young victim had survived. Small consolation to Baldwin, but some consolation nonetheless.

He'd never told her the whole story before. She knew bits and pieces, but he'd always held back the deepest part of the truth, that if he'd been paying more attention, no one would have had to die that awful day. And the role Charlotte played.

She was silent for a moment, then reached over and grasped his hand. She didn't say anything, didn't need to. He felt the forgiveness flowing through their touch, and felt wretched. He didn't deserve her forgiveness. Not until all the truth was out. All the cards on the table.

After a few minutes, she spoke. "It wasn't your fault. You know that. So what else is there, honey? I know you well enough to feel that you're holding back from me. Just tell me. You can tell me anything, and I'll always love you. Always."

She knew him too well. Maybe she was right. Maybe it was time to come clean. He formed the words in his head, trying them on for size. *I have a son. And Charlotte was his mother.* He took a breath. Started to tell her. He truly did. But his phone began to ring, and the moment was lost.

"Hold that thought," he said, then answered the phone with a curt, "Yes."

"Dr. Baldwin? This is Buddy Morgan. I'm the chief

of police down here in Forest City. I understand you're on your way to see me."

"Hi, Chief Morgan. It's good to hear from you. We have cell service again, I think we're actually getting close. We should be in by two o'clock."

"Have you eaten?"

Baldwin laughed. "Honestly, no. We took off like bats out of hell pretty early this morning."

"Meet me at Smith's Drugs, then. My treat. We can eat and talk. I'll fill you in on the Copelands. It's a long story. I hope you've got some time."

"We do. I made a reservation at the Holiday Inn there—we'll be spending the night."

"Good. I'll see you shortly then."

He hung up.

"Chief of police is treating us to lunch. At a drugstore, no less."

"Small towns," Taylor said.

"Taylor, I—"

"It's okay. We have a six-hour drive back. You can tell me the rest on the way home."

Neither one of their phones had been able to get a signal for the second half of the drive. The cellular service was terrible in the North Carolina mountains at the state border. Service restored, both of their phones were beeping with missed calls. They each busied themselves with their respective duties, and Baldwin couldn't help but feel relieved. He'd earned a momentary reprieve, but the truth was coming out, whether he wanted it to or not.

Forgiveness was a tenuous thing. He hoped, for both their sakes, that Taylor had the ability to grant it.

Twenty-Two

The outer reaches of Forest City had succumbed to the homogenization of America. The highway bypass into town was littered with chain restaurants and hardware supercenters, the concrete strip malls colonized by the everystore mentality that permeated all other mid- to large-size towns off just about every highway. The ultimate in impersonal convenience.

Once they got into the heart of the city, things changed dramatically. For the better, in Taylor's opinion. She was surprised to see a traditional Main Street replete with mom-and-pop shops, an old movie theater, the drugstore Buddy Morgan had mentioned, with what looked to be a full restaurant lunch counter, and a variety of specialty stores, including a promising-looking bookstore nestled next to the drugstore, Fireside Books and Gifts.

Baldwin drove slowly, and Taylor stared up the tree-lined median, a small smile playing on her lips.

"What are you looking at?" Baldwin asked.

"I'm waiting for George Bailey to come running down the street."

Baldwin did a double take, then laughed. "God,

Taylor, you've nailed it. This looks exactly like Bedford Falls."

"It does, doesn't it?"

"Too bad that whole movie set was just a creation. The idyllic town square… I always thought it would be fun to live in a small town. Have a routine, eat at the diner every morning, walk everywhere, wave hello to the people who've known you your whole life."

She shook her head.

"Oh, no, not me. I'd go mad with that level of accountability. Nashville is plenty small. Besides, everyone already knows my business."

They got out of the car, and she looked up and down the street. "This is ridiculously charming. I can't imagine Ewan Copeland here. It's just too normal. Too sweet."

Baldwin saw a man in uniform standing in the window of the drugstore, gesturing for them to come in.

"Look, the chief's waiting for us. He's waving from the window over there. Let's go."

They walked past the diagonally parked cars in the median and entered the drugstore. They were met with red vinyl, shiny chrome and the overwhelmingly delicious scent of frying burgers.

"You must be the folks from Nashville," the chief said, shaking their hands in turn, then pointing them toward a booth in the window. He was trim, about five foot nine, with gray hair. His face was lined and weathered, someone who spent a lot of time out of doors. Taylor guessed he was in his mid-fifties.

"What gave it away?" she asked with a smile.

"I know all the folks round here who have guns, that's what. Plus, your faces were all over the news, that brouhaha down in Nags Head. North Carolina law enforcement's had a rough couple of days. Sakes alive. Hopefully the worst is past us now. Unless you brought the mayhem with you?"

"I hope to God not," she said.

"Good. I'm not in the mood to chase bad guys." He smiled wide. He was missing a molar on the right side of his mouth. His eyes crinkled with good humor. Taylor liked him immediately.

They settled into the booth, and a young woman came to take their order. She had a small silver ring in her over-plucked left eyebrow. Her hair was tinted red. Henna, maybe, or cheap drugstore dye. It suited her creamy pale skin and brown eyes.

"The biscuits are good here, if you're wanting breakfast. Burgers are, too," Chief Morgan said.

Taylor's stomach grumbled in anticipatory protest, they hadn't taken the time to refuel on the way down. "I think I'll have the burger, then. Well done, American cheese, please. With fries. And a Diet Coke."

"Pepsi okay?" the girl asked.

"Ugh. Yes, if I have to."

"All we got down here. What about you, sir?"

"I'll have the same," Baldwin said, refolding the small paper menu and sticking it upright beside the napkin holder.

"Make that three then, Amy. Throw some of that thick-slab pepper bacon on mine."

The girl nodded and whisked away. Morgan watched her go. "Amy's family has owned this drugstore since the early 1900s. If you walk along that back wall toward the bathroom, you can see a mural of what Main Street used to look like. All the old storefronts. It's changed now, but a few places are originals. At the very least, the preservation society has stepped in and declared a few landmarks, so there's funding from the county and state to help with the upkeep. The bookstore next door is a perfect example. They did a great job renovating that place. Tallest building in town, don'tcha know."

He folded his arms across his chest. "But that's not why you're here. You need to talk about the Copelands."

Taylor could hear the note in his voice, the mixture of revulsion and sadness. She steeled herself. The story to come wouldn't be antiseptic, printed on the page, open for interpretation. They were about to get the meat of the tale, find the answers to the terror that had haunted her for months. She swallowed involuntarily, mouth suddenly dry. Amy appeared with their sodas. Taylor slipped her straw into the Styrofoam cup and took a long sip, ignoring the chemical taste she abhorred in favor of a caffeine rush.

Morgan ran his finger along his nose, composing his thoughts, then began.

"Elizabeth Biggs Copeland always had problems, from the time she was a little girl. She was the kind of girl folks called delicate, meaning she was totally crazy and full of piss and vinegar to boot. There wasn't a soul in this town who wasn't afraid of her, especially those of us in her class at school. Betty Biggs, you can only imagine the names she was called. She got teased quite a bit.

"She wasn't overtly bad, just…things happened around her. Cats went missing, only to show up days later dead in their owners' yards, bad things done to them. She was suspected of starting a couple of fires. They started off small, dustbins and the like, but as she got older…" He shook his head. "Two of her friends' houses burned to the ground in the middle of the night. The first time, she was about eight, and no one was home. The second, Betty was twelve. A little girl named Tabitha was killed, along with the family dog. Betty'd been fighting with Tabitha at school that day. I can't say that I remember exactly what about. Some boy, probably. Betty had a hard time with the opposite sex in her younger years."

Baldwin leaned forward in his seat. "You say suspected. No one ever prosecuted her for the fires?"

"Nothing to prosecute. There was no proof she had anything to do with any of it. My dad was chief before me, and his dad before him. They were good cops. They didn't have the tools we have now. They had to rely on actual grunt work, investigations that hinged on eyewitnesses, unreliable eyewitnesses at that because, first off, we were children who were scared to death of getting in trouble, and second, we were even more scared of Betty skinning us alive if we ratted her out. We don't have the kind of violence y'all do up in the city. All ours now is drug related—the kids around here have nothing better to do than get high, and they do that well. But back then crime was infrequent, and minor. To have a child accused of murdering her friend, well, that just wasn't going to happen."

"It got swept under the rug, then?" Taylor asked.

"Not exactly. Most folks steered clear of Betty after that. Tabitha's family moved away, the story was only whispered about. It put the fear of God in Betty though, she calmed down, and the strange happenings slowed. She managed to get through high school without any major mishaps. Started dating Roger Copeland her senior year. He was a couple of years older than us, and a god around these parts. A talented minor leaguer with an eye to moving up. He was being groomed, was a damn good ballplayer. No one knew what he saw in Betty outside of the fact that she was putting out. I mean, she was pretty enough, but vacant. Distant. Something in her eyes always gave me the chills.

"Anyway, Betty got pregnant right after graduation. They married, had Edward, then Ewan and Errol. Things seemed okay on the surface. Both her parents were dead by then, the restaurant gave a decent income. Betty settled into motherhood all right, though all three of the boys were always sickly. Strange stuff, not the usual kid sicknesses like chicken pox. No, the boys were always in the hospital, getting some sort of exploratory surgery, or undergoing expensive tests for diseases no one had ever heard of. We'd never seen the likes of it, to tell you the truth. But she wasn't doing anything wrong that anyone knew of. Not obviously, anyway."

Chief Morgan grew quiet. With perfect timing, the food arrived, steaming hot. They all settled into the business of eating. Morgan was right, the burgers were good. Hot and juicy, seasoned perfectly, the thin shoestring fries crispy, just the way she liked them.

Baldwin wiped his mouth with his napkin. "Good choice, Chief."

"I'm glad you like it." He settled his burger back in its greasy wrapping paper. "Where was I? Oh, yeah. So Betty's kids were always sickly. Roger's career wasn't going the way he wanted, he'd been told again and again that his time was coming, but you know how it is. Promises made, promises broken. He was drinking some, quiet-like, on the sly, and took up with a barmaid. Stephanie Sugarman. Got her pregnant, of course. Betty found out. She went absolutely around-the-bend nuts. Threatened the girl, threatened Roger. Made a big stink out of it. Publicly. Roger slunk away for the season, left the girl and Betty and his boys behind. He got called up to be a third baseman for the Braves just a month into the season. It was his big chance, going to the show. The whole town was proud."

He took a bite of his burger, then wiped his mouth carefully before he continued.

"Well, Betty wasn't about to let a little thing like Roger's career keep her from getting her way. She harassed the living hell out of that man. Letters, phone calls. Driving up to his games in Atlanta, pitching a fit when she couldn't get near him. He finally had to file a restraining order against her, and had his lawyer draw up divorce papers. Word was he planned to marry the Sugarman girl. Of course, he never got the chance.

"Betty wasn't going to give up that easily. The restraining orders, the time she spent in jail when she was caught breaking them, none of that stopped her. She fell back on one of her old tricks. Burned the Sugarman girl's house down. Steph was working at the time, over at the Point and Shoot. It was sheer luck that she wasn't killed, too, she was supposed to be at home. The other bartender had gotten sick and Steph came in at the last second to cover her shift."

"What was happening with the boys during all this time?" Baldwin asked.

"They were sicker than ever. I remember my mama went over and took care of Edward and Ewan one time, right before Edward passed. They'd gotten pneumonia, and Betty was locked up. The school called my pops. We didn't have much in the way of social services back then, it was all church oriented, the kindness of neighbors and the like. They didn't have any more money for the hospital, so Betty sold the barbecue place and ran through that money like water on all the medical expenses. My mama took care of them, was able to nurse Ewan back to health. Edward died about a week into it, the docs said his body was just too damaged to handle the bug. He'd gone too long without proper treatment. Tore my mama up. I remember her crying her head off the night he died."

"Is there any chance Ewan could be responsible for his brother's death?"

"Edward? No, not unless he infected him with the bug in the first place. He had fluid in his lungs at autopsy like he'd drowned."

Baldwin raised an eyebrow, and the chief shook his head.

"I really don't think that was the case. My mama was there for the whole thing, she'd have noticed something wrong. They were both too weak to move."

"Okay then. Please, carry on."

"Mama told me that all three of the boys were just covered in healing scars from all the surgeries. Crisscrossed all over their stomachs like fishing net. When Edward died, the youngest boy, Errol, he was real thin, like anorexic thin. Weighed no more than eighty pounds, the doc said. They stashed him in a psychiatric hospital for a spell while he recovered. Probably the only thing that saved him, at least for the time being.

"Anyway, Betty went crazy when she heard about Edward. They let her go to the funeral, but she still had a couple of months left on her sentence. She was in shackles, and poor Roger, he just looked all embarrassed. He blamed her, of course, they got into a huge shouting match, had to be separated. It was a big mess.

"When Betty finally got out of jail, she didn't hesitate. She headed up to Atlanta in a fine rage and found Roger leaving the stadium after batting practice. This was right before the end of the season. Shot him point-blank. Man didn't have a chance. Betty ran, and no one could identify her at first. Took some fine police work from the Atlanta cops. They found a videotape that had her on it two minutes after the shooting, running away from the stadium. Found her in some fleabag motel on the outskirts of town. She still had the gun, so they hauled her ass to jail. It was for good this time. The trial lasted only a couple of days, it was a cut-and-dried case. They thought about seeking the death penalty, but the district attorney up there in Atlanta, he settled for life in prison. I think he knew that it could be overturned if there was a second trial, she was obviously such a disturbed woman. The judge agreed, and she got sentenced to something like one hundred years. They sent her to the Metro State Prison in Atlanta—that's where they handle the long-term psychiatric cases—and that's the last we all heard of Miss Betty."

Morgan dipped a handful of fries in ketchup and devoured them. Taylor patiently waited for him to finish chewing. After a few moments, she asked, "What happened to Ewan and Errol?"

Morgan didn't answer right away. He bent his head hard to the right, then the left. He grunted softly, seeming to enjoy the loud pops that accompanied the violent motion. His chiropractic feat accomplished, he took a toothpick out of his front pocket and wedged it between his lips.

"Well, the boys were stuck back here in Forest City. Ewan was fourteen when his mama went away. Errol had been released by the hospital, his weight was back in a safe range, but he was still so little. Without Edward to watch out for them, they were deemed too young to be left alone. He and Errol became wards of the state. Errol was always a delicate kid, he didn't last more than a year. Killed himself. The group home they were living in was a sad place, full of unwanted or unwilling children. The home's administrator found Errol hanging from a rod in his closet, he'd been dead for over a day and no one had missed him."

"Poor kid. The shame of his family's demise was too much for him. You see that a lot in Munchausen cases, the survivors are unable to cope," Baldwin said. "Unless Ewan had a hand in it."

"Now that one I couldn't tell you. Kid was horribly depressed, it wasn't a huge shock. Though why kill Errol? Or Edward, if that was the case?"

"We're pretty sure he got his start very young, tried his hand at hurting people when he was still a teenager. The death of a sibling at his hand would fit the profile."

"Ah. I get it," Morgan replied. "Well, there's more, might answer your questions. So now we're left with Ewan. On the surface, he seemed like a good kid. He was smart, especially with computers. He went to school every day. Stayed out of trouble. But something was wrong with him, broken. Like he was just waiting, kind of like a snake does when it's about to have dinner. I use to have a boa constrictor. Thing was a tease. It would watch the mouse dance around, let it crawl all over him, and just when the mouse thought it was safe, that's when the snake would attack. Same with

Ewan Copeland. He was just biding his time. Fooling all of us.

"When he was sixteen, he raped one of the girls in the group home. Not your garden-variety date rape, either, he cut her up. Slashed her stomach with a knife. That got him sent to juvie. They kicked him out when he was eighteen. He disappeared from here, and no one has heard hide nor hair of him since."

"Until now." Taylor pushed her plate away. It was a sad story, but she felt no true sorrow for the man who'd morphed into the thing that haunted her.

"A rape that violent definitely fits. And that's the only one on record?" Baldwin asked.

The chief handed over a file folder. "Yep. This is what I could get of his record under such short notice."

Taylor took the file, flipped it open and set it between her and Baldwin on the table. The file was thin, but there was a picture. She detached it from the two-hole punch, angled it to get the best light from the window. A young man, with brown hair, blue eyes, a thin chin. He didn't look like anyone she'd ever seen. She tried to age-progress him in her mind, fill out the cheeks, add some facial hair. She couldn't envision him properly; they'd have to do it for real on the computers. He certainly didn't look like the man she'd seen in the Nashville bar Control a year before. He looked nothing like the composite sketch they'd put together, either.

She tamped down the disappointment. Just because they had a name and a backstory, that didn't mean it was all going to fall into place. That would make this too easy. Nothing with the Pretender was ever easy.

"What about Betty? I'd like to talk to her, if that's possible," Baldwin asked.

"Nope. She's dead."

"Man, our timing is impeccable. That's too bad. What happened to her?"

"The cancer got her. Breast, like her mama. She died six months ago. They sent us a notice for the paper."

The story had taken almost an hour to tell, the sky was just starting to dim. Early sunsets in the mountains during winter. Taylor was anxious to get moving, to see some of the town, to get a sense of what, and where, the Pretender, no, scratch that, Ewan Copeland had come from.

Baldwin sensed her desire.

"Chief, I can't thank you enough for going through all of this with us. I think we're going to ride around a bit before we crash for the night."

"Of course. If there's anything else I can do, just shout. I'll be around all night. You can hang on to that file, it's a copy. I got this. You get hungry again, you might try the barbecue place 'bout a mile down this road. It's new." He pointed to his right.

"Thank you."

They all stood, grabbed their coats and scarves. Taylor allowed Baldwin to help her into her shearling. She saw the waitress, Amy, laughing in the corner with one of the busboys. A thought occurred to her.

"Chief, whatever happened to Stephanie Sugarman?"

"Steph? Name's Anderson now. She had Copeland's kid, a girl. About a year after the kid was born, Steph ended up getting married to the owner of the Point and Shoot. They had a few more, too. There are lots of Anderson kids running around these days. Got them some sweet grandbabies now."

"So she still lives in town?"

"Yeah. Right down the street from here, actually. It's just north, right up from the police station. You can't miss it, it's a pretty house. Biggest one on the street. Three stories, red brick, brown shutters, with a wide white veranda. You might even catch her at home, she babysits the grandkids in the afternoons until their parents get off work."

"What about the daughter?"

"Ruth? She's a sweet girl. Doesn't live here anymore, but visits sometimes. You know how it is when they grow up."

Baldwin shook the chief's hand in farewell. "I take it the Point and Shoot does a steady business?"

"Son, you know it. Keeps us all in high cotton—them with the bar earnings, me with the drunks getting into fights in the parking lot. Y'all be safe out there, you hear?"

Taylor watched the chief amble toward his patrol car, tipping his hat at a couple who came out of the bookstore. What a story. It didn't surprise her though—the Pretender *would* have a mythology. He couldn't have just been a crazy kid, no, the courts would claim he was twisted into being by his psycho mother. It fit his profile so well.

She knew he'd never been an innocent, despite what Baldwin said.

"This file's pretty thin," Baldwin said.

"Yeah. We need to get some more background."

"Let's go talk to Stephanie Anderson. She might be able to give us some more insight. I'll let my team know what we've found, too."

"Okay."

They headed toward the car, Taylor's head swiveling around the shops on the main street. Had they known what evil resided in their midst? And what would the Pretender do when he found out they'd cracked into his background?

And Jesus God, he had a half-sister out there. A sibling. Another potential target.

The thought made her knees go weak. They needed to find Ruth.

Twenty-Three

To: troy14@ncr.tr.com
From: bostonboy@ncr.bb.com
Subject: Indianapolis

Dear Troy,
Mind-numbingly simple. Surely you have a bigger challenge ahead?
BB

He had to admit, the steak lived up to expectation. And the atmosphere in the St. Elmo Steak House, home of the world's best shrimp cocktail, wasn't too bad either. Cozy. Warm. Brick. He liked brick. Liked the looks of the hostess who was stumbling around in impossibly high heels, too, casting glances over her shoulder at him every time she wobbled past. Blond hair, brown eyes. Tight black skirt over one of those button-front pin-tucked blouses that was actually a bodysuit. He had an ex-girlfriend who loved those things. They snapped right at her cunt, perforated for easy access. They could fuck up against a wall and she'd never have to get undressed.

He took a sip of his excellent Bordeaux and sighed. The hostess wasn't a part of the game. He'd have to save her for another time. The job was finished here in Indy. He'd killed a woman named Mary Jane. Sweet Mary Jane Solomon. Mary Jane, the pretty and plain. All tied up with a delightful little bow. She'd scratched the hell out of him, raked her nails along the edge of his arm, but he'd brushed her nails with her toothbrush before he left, and changed into a long-sleeved shirt before dinner. He'd gotten blood on the UPS delivery uniform and had to burn it. Exorcise the DNA demon with fire and toothpaste. Some Indy cop was going to find a naked UPS man and think someone had a uniform fetish.

He laughed to himself. Pretty plain Mary Jane's eyes had lit up when he came to the door. She wasn't used to getting packages; she lived alone, had few friends… by choice, of course. Terribly shy Mary Jane. A stutterer, poor thing. Then he had rung the doorbell. Rung Mary Jane's bell, too. Changed her life forever. Death did that to a girl.

One bite left. The meat was luscious, melting in his mouth, leaving little greasy butter trails running down his chin. He always drowned his steaks in butter, just like dear old mom used to do. It made the meat tender.

He checked his watch, it was only 10:00 p.m. He wasn't scheduled to be in Nashville until noon the following day. He'd gotten ahead of the game, so to speak. He had time for dessert, then a chat with the hostess. Maybe score a number, or an email, or, the best of all possible worlds, she would whip out her smartphone and friend him on Facebook. Reverse look-up the number and he would have her home address. Email and he could track her down on the internet with ease. But with Facebook, he'd have her pants down in moments. These silly girls put all their personal information out there for the taking, their birth dates, pictures of themselves drunk and naked, announcing to the world exactly where they were at all times. They made themselves bait. They asked for it. He loved technology. It made the job so much easier.

He waved to his waiter for the check. It was time to move on to the last portion of the game. Time for his big reward. He was looking forward to a nice calm night. He could swing back through Indy on his way home, see if he couldn't get himself a date.

Twenty-Four

The chief was right, it was impossible to miss the Andersons' house. Not only was it beautifully huge in the Southern style of miniature Taras, there were tricycles, toys, multiple discarded gloves and a small battery-powered minicar parked on the front lawn, damning evidence of a juvenile invasion. Children's laughter rang in the air, shouts of joy that made Taylor's stomach hurt. When was the last time she'd been so innocent and carefree? So very happy?

They pulled up to the curb, watched as a gang of little boys tore around the edge of the house into the dead grass of the front yard. Playing cowboys and Indians, it seemed, all bundled up against the cold.

Taylor smiled. She did love kids, so long as they weren't hers.

She and Baldwin wended their way through the game to the front porch. One of the boys, a towhead with incredibly light blue eyes, stopped to gawk at them. When Taylor grinned at him, he picked his nose and ran off toward the back of the house.

"Charming," Taylor said.

"Little boys," Baldwin replied. There was something

strange in his tone. She glanced over at him. His face was shuttered, he looked lost in thought. He'd been acting weird for two days now, and she was pretty sure it didn't have anything to do with his suspension, though finding out about that had gone a long way toward settling her down. She'd had a crazy moment when he'd looked at her sideways in the car and she wondered, for the briefest of seconds, if he was having an affair. It was a silly thought. Baldwin wasn't the kind of guy to sneak around behind her back, but something was up. She let it go—they had enough on their plates. He'd tell her when he was good and ready.

They crossed the porch and knocked on the door. Taylor could smell a wood fire burning, and was suddenly chilled through. She tucked her hands under her arms. She should have asked the waitress at Smith's to make her a to-go cup of tea or hot chocolate.

The door was opened by a woman with liberal gray streaks running through her dark brown hair. She was of an indefinable age, anywhere from forty to sixty, with either laugh lines or crow's feet surrounding her eyes, and deep vertical wrinkles sprouting from her upper lip like perfectly planted rows of corn, the telltale sign of a lifelong smoker. Taylor blessed her decision to quit the previous year—it was the idea of having those wrinkles that had forced her to stop.

"Mrs. Anderson? Stephanie Anderson?" Taylor asked.

The woman smiled. "That's me. What can I do you for?"

Open, guileless. Maybe there was something to the notion of a small town. She pulled out her badge, Baldwin followed suit with his credentials.

"I'm Lieutenant Taylor Jackson, from Nashville,

Tennessee. This is Supervisory Special Agent John Baldwin, with the FBI. May we come in? We need to ask you some questions."

The woman's face closed, the smile faded. She hesitated for a brief moment, then said, "What's this all about, if you don't mind me asking?"

Baldwin turned on the charm, smiling in encouragement. "We're here doing background on a former student from this town. We won't take much of your time, I promise."

Mrs. Anderson's eyes narrowed, but she pulled the door open wider. "Come in then. I'm just making the kids some dinner. I hope you don't mind if I keep cooking while we talk."

They followed her into the warm, inviting kitchen. It was purely country—oak cupboards with glass insets, cabbage rose wallpaper and flouncy lace curtains, a huge open fireplace at the far end. Taylor crossed to the fire and stood, warming her hands. "That's nice," she said.

Mrs. Anderson's face creased in dismay. "Your nose and cheeks are bright red. I didn't realize it had gotten so cold out there, we had a right nice afternoon. The fire keeps things so toasty in here, and you know how it is with kids. They love to play in the cold, then come in, warm up, and go back out again. I should probably round them up before they catch their death."

Taylor did know. When she was a kid, they'd had a lot of snow in Nashville during the winters. She and Sam would spend hours sledding, then decamp back to one or the other's house to defrost and drink cocoa. She felt almost wistful for a moment, then pulled herself together.

"If you can wait for just a second, Mrs. Anderson,

it would be better to talk without the kids running around."

"Oh. Of course. Certainly." Mrs. Anderson went to the stove and took the lid off a huge stoneware Crock-Pot. Steam billowed off the contents. She took a wooden spoon and stirred, and Taylor smelled chili. Despite the meal she'd just had, her stomach rumbled. She loved good chili.

Mrs. Anderson started chattering about the boys, her grandkids, bragging on how sweet they were. Baldwin looked at the pictures she pointed to on the wall and murmured his approval. They were dillydallying. It was time to ruin the woman's good mood.

Taylor settled on a stool at the wide counter. "Mrs. Anderson, we want to talk to you about Roger Copeland."

The woman's body stilled, though her arm still rotated the spoon in the pot. She sniffed twice, then with great care, she removed the spoon and laid it gently on the counter in a white ceramic holder shaped like a cauliflower. Despite her attempt to keep things clean, some of it spilled over onto the white Corian counter. The red of the chili sauce looked like blood.

"Roger's been dead a long time," she said, soft and gentle.

"We know. We're sorry to have to bring up bad memories."

She smiled. "Oh, they're pretty good memories. I loved that man like nobody's business. He loved me right back. It was terrible, what that woman did to him."

"Betty Copeland," Taylor said.

"That's right. Betty. Mean as a snake, and crazy as a bedbug. He used to say she was a charmer, that she put some sort of spell on him. Then he woke up and saw the light, and it was too late. Three little boys, a nutty wife, a career to manage. He was on the road a lot. That helped. When we got together, he wanted out. He just didn't know how to end it with her. He was scared of that woman." Her soft Southern accent broadened. "Scairt to death of her, really. Looks like he was right to be, don't you think?"

Taylor glanced at Baldwin, who met her eyes and raised his eyebrow. *Something here,* his look said. She agreed. They stayed silent, watching Mrs. Anderson as she chewed on her lip for a moment, lost in thought. A gauzy smile appeared on her face.

"At least I have Ruth to remember him by. Not that I'd ever forget him, of course. But time, it does heal all wounds. He never got to meet her, more's the pity. She's a lovely girl. Smart as a whip. Looks just like him, too. All the good parts. Roger was such a handsome man."

Baldwin sat at the counter next to Taylor. "Mrs. Anderson, do you ever hear from Ewan Copeland?"

Mrs. Anderson clutched her throat. "Ewan? Oh, no. That boy. That poor, poor boy. Wrong in the head, just like his mama. You know he raped a girl when he was only sixteen? How does a young man learn how to do that? How do they even know? Movies, I guess, or those girly magazines. The state, they shipped him off quicker than you could say jiminy, that's the last any of us heard from him."

"So these are Ruth's boys you're babysitting?" Taylor asked.

"Oh, no. Ruth doesn't live here in Forest City. She's not married either, though I nag her about it constantly.

No, she ended up going to school to be a scientist, up in Raleigh. She works for the city up there."

Baldwin shifted on his stool. "Oh? Doing what?"

"Crime lab stuff. Like that TV show, *CSI?* Though she tells me that it's a pack of lies—her job's nothing like that. 'It's drudgery, Mama,' she tells me. 'Nothing cool and glamorous, and we don't get to carry guns.'"

"She's a forensic scientist?" Taylor asked.

"Yeah, that's the right term. Smart girl, my Ruth. I bet she'd love to talk with you, Agent Baldwin. She's always talked about the FBI, getting into the academy. The selection process is hard though."

"Yes, it surely is. Do you have a picture of Ruth?" Baldwin asked. Taylor didn't need to look at him; she could feel that he was practically quivering. It dawned on her why. Oh, my God.

Mrs. Anderson was back to her cheerful self, pride in her offspring's accomplishments overshadowing the sorrow she'd been feeling about losing the girl's father. "Well, sure. Right here in the living room. Come on, you can see it, it's up on the wall with the rest of the family photos."

The formal living room was painted a glossy eggshell-white, the thick red Turkish rug whisper silent on their feet. The family photographs took up the entire back wall, a huge montage of generations. Taylor's heart thudded with every step she took across the floor.

Mrs. Anderson pointed to a picture dead center of the collection.

"This is the best one, here. Taken just after her college graduation, see? She's still wearing her cap and gown. She looks so lovely in blue."

Taylor covered her mouth so she wouldn't swear aloud.

When she smiled, Renee Sansom's imposter was almost pretty.

Twenty-Five

Taylor couldn't get away from Mrs. Anderson quickly enough. She felt like she was going to throw up. They'd nearly been killed by the Pretender's sister. His *sister*. Granted, a half-sister, but still his flesh, and his blood. He'd found her somehow, and manipulated her into working for him. And she'd been worried for her. Jesus.

Looking at the soft, gently lined face of Mrs. Anderson, she was filled with an all-consuming rage. This woman had helped sow the seeds of destruction to the tune of at least seven deaths. She either didn't know her daughter was a psychopath, or didn't care.

Taylor couldn't afford to let the emotions show. She swallowed them down, kept the smile plastered on her face. Felt her nails dig into the skin of her palms. They needed more information. Background. History. Contact information, if they could wheedle it out of the woman. She slowed the beating of her heart and adopted her calm, professional demeanor. But the words didn't come. She was thankful when Baldwin stepped in. He'd sensed she wasn't prepared to speak just yet, and he was a master tap dancer. He poured it on thick.

"Mrs. Anderson, we'd love to talk to Ruth. I'm always looking for qualified crime scene techs. My teams in the BAU have at least one forensic scientist on them, sometimes two. If she's not right for me, I might be able to suggest another spot for her. At least get her an interview or two. The Academy classes start soon. If she's right for us, she might make it in under the wire."

"You would do that?" Mrs. Anderson's eyes were shining. No, she didn't suspect a thing. She was too sweet, too unassuming. She probably didn't know about her daughter, not in a conscious way. She may have felt something was off, or Ruth could have been a fabulous actress. Regardless, she'd birthed a killer. A maniac. Was there something in Roger Copeland's genes that sparked madness? Granted, Betty had a history of instability, but Stephanie Anderson seemed downright normal. Two very different women, Betty and Stephanie. Yet both mothers of killers, with Copeland's sperm the simple common denominator.

She heard Fitz's voice in her head. *If it looks like a duck and quacks like a duck…*

Baldwin was still talking. Taylor forced herself back to the conversation.

"I'd be more than happy to talk with her about it. We're looking to fill these positions rather quickly, so the sooner I talk to her the better. Do you have a phone number, or an email, where I can reach her?"

Mrs. Anderson was beaming now. "Of course I do. Let me get my book. I've got all her information written down. I can't ever remember all those little details. Thank goodness for speed dial." She looked at her watch. "Why don't we try to give her a call right now? I haven't talked to her in a few weeks. She never answers her phone, such a busy little thing."

Baldwin gave her a huge grin. "You know what? Let me make the call. I'd like to surprise her."

"Oh, Dr. Baldwin. You're a good man. Ruth's going to be so happy."

She bustled back toward the kitchen. They held back for a moment, let her get ahead. Baldwin's face changed, the good humor gone, the sharp planes of his cheekbones shadowed. Taylor squeezed his arm, and he whispered in her ear.

"At least we know who the imposter is now. Copeland's certainly kept this all in the family."

"You don't think Mrs. Anderson is shining us on? Is she clueless?"

"I don't think she has any idea of what Ruth's become. But we aren't going to be able to sit on this for long. Mrs. Anderson's bound to follow up with her daughter. And we have to keep Ruth from contacting Copeland. He can't know we're getting close."

"Maybe that's exactly what we need to flush him out?"

"I don't know, Taylor."

"Baldwin, this is a small town. The FBI and a cop from Nashville? It's all over the place by now. If he has any contact with anyone here, he knows."

"I bet he doesn't. I think he wants to stay as far away from this place as humanly possible."

There was a noise behind them, they broke apart.

"Here we go," Mrs. Anderson sang out. "Let's see, do you have anything to write with?"

"Absolutely," Baldwin answered, drawing a small black Quo Vadis Habana notebook from his pocket. Taylor had bought it for him online and he carried it with him everywhere. He needed to order some more, this one was nearly full. He'd developed a taste for the fine Clairefontaine paper, felt like quite the dandy when he felt the perfect ink lay down.

He opened to a clean page and said, "Go ahead whenever you're ready."

Mrs. Anderson recited all the information for her eldest child—home phone and work phone, home address, email. Ruth Copeland Anderson was based in Raleigh, North Carolina, and worked for the Durham Police Department. The traitor in their midst. At least now the fact that all the forensics from the trailer in Asheville and Fitz's boat had been compromised made a perverse kind of sense.

Mrs. Anderson handed Baldwin the phone. "Just hit Memory, then 1. That will call her house."

Taylor watched him mime the motion, depress the buttons only partway, clear his throat. After a few moments, he shook his head. "I'm getting the answering machine. I'll leave a message. Hi, Ruth? This is Dr. John Baldwin, from the Federal Bureau of Investigations. I've just met your mother and she tells me you're interested in joining our team. Please call me at 703-555-5494 so we can talk about getting you in for an interview. Don't forget to call your mother. Bye now."

A nice bit of subterfuge. Baldwin had never hit Dial, she saw the number on the screen as his hand flashed to hit the end button. He handed the phone back. "That's too bad. If you talk to her, let her know to give me a shout. Thanks so much for your time, we need to get going."

Taylor could barely contain herself. She just wanted to get out of there, call Roddie Hall from the SBI, and give him the information so his people could get up to Raleigh and take her down. Assuming Ruth had gone back to Raleigh after killing the agents in Nags Head.

Would her brother be with her? The odds were in their favor. Taylor would bet a hundred dollars that he never, ever expected them to find this small town, to hear of his sad, troubled childhood.

They bid Mrs. Anderson farewell, tried to be polite about it. She didn't sense anything wrong, or if she did, she chose not to see. Taylor suspected that Mrs. Anderson got through a lot of life's little monstrosities by turning a blind eye. It was what all good Southern ladies did.

They took the path to the street.

"Good job," Taylor said.

"I'm getting that phone disconnected right now. It doesn't matter, I can't imagine she went home. If she's got half a brain she's on the run," he replied.

She let Baldwin hold the door to the car, slid into the soft leather seat feeling smug. Mrs. Anderson waved from her wide, gracious porch. Taylor waved back, hoping Mrs. Anderson misinterpreted the cold smile on her face.

We've got you now, you son of a bitch.

Twenty-Six

They drove back to the town square so they didn't raise Mrs. Anderson's suspicion by sitting in front of her house making excited phone calls.

Once they'd parked in front of a large stone block that Taylor identified as a monument to the fallen heroes of the World Wars, Baldwin took the honor of calling the SBI. She eavesdropped as he relayed all the information to Roddie Hall, whose ebullience came through the phone's speakers. He was thrilled to have at least a part of the puzzle solved. He knew the chief of police in Durham, and promised that a tactical team would be sent to Ruth's business and home addresses within the hour. He'd call with updates as soon as he had anything to report.

Baldwin hung up the phone and turned to her with a smile. "God bless Wendy Heinz. If she hadn't put two and two together…"

"But she did. How long do you think it will take Hall to get the juvie records for Ewan Copeland?"

"Roddie said that would be his second call. He'll have to get the district attorney's office involved. He's on it. Told you he was a good cop."

"I'm glad you have friends in high places. You know, it's only 7:00."

He took her hand. "I assume by your tone that's not an invitation?"

"It's never too early to go to bed."

"Hmm. We do have that reservation. Or we could just head back to Nashville instead."

She was getting interested in what Baldwin was doing with her hand.

"Tempting. On both counts. There's nothing like a Holiday Inn to get my juices going. But heading home's not a bad idea either. We could trade off driving so you could get a nap."

"I'm up for it if you are." He showed her that was certainly the case, tossed her a crazy, silly grin that she couldn't help but respond to. They were like disaster survivors, giddy in the knowledge that they'd come through okay. She recognized the feeling, she had it every time a case turned her way. She reached over and ran her free hand through his hair, smoothing it down. He'd been fussing with it, and it was sticking up in all directions.

"You know, on second thought, I'm wondering if we should stay in North Carolina, just in case. Raleigh is only a couple hours north of here. We could head up there instead. Hall could use another couple of trained agents, couldn't he?"

"Taylor, we'd just be in the way. Hall knows what he's doing."

"True." She sighed heavily and looked out the window. "Well, Chief Morgan gave us the address of the old Copeland place. What about we go over there and take a look, see if Hall calls us back in the meantime?"

He sighed dramatically and released her captive hand. "All right. You win. We'll go put a place to the face."

"Thank you, sweetie. I'll make it up to you, I promise."

"Oh, yes, you will," he said, then put the car in gear.

Within five minutes, they arrived at the address the chief had given them.

The Copelands' old house was off a side street, tucked into a neighborhood that was probably nice in the forties or early fifties, but now just seemed tired of putting on airs.

It was fully dark; the single streetlight's meager illumination didn't penetrate the houses' front yards. They had to dig the Maglites out of the trunk to get an idea of the scene. Equipped with the powerful lights, they started toward the little house.

A cracked concrete walk littered with weeds and trash led to the tiny front porch. The house was a small single-story clapboard affair, smaller than its neighbors, with what looked like five rooms—the kitchen up front, and two tiny bedrooms that overlooked the dingy gray porch. Taylor played the flashlight's beam into the darkness. She could see a hallway off what was most likely the bathroom, and a living room beyond. The master, if you could call it that, would be in the back.

They scrambled around the side of the house, shining their lights into the desolate landscape and murmuring to each other. The backyard butted up to the train tracks, with a chain-link fence separating it from the endless black iron. There was a small storm cellar beside the house, the doors painted what used to be blue.

A dog began to bark two houses over and the porch lights on either side of them came on.

"Who's there?" a deep, hurt female voice whispered. "Allen, is that you? You're late." Someone was expecting a date.

"Time to split," Baldwin said, sotto voce.

Taylor nodded and turned off her light. They slunk back around the side of the house as quietly as they could, Baldwin leading in the dark, Taylor following him back up the slope into the front yard.

Another female voice rang out, this time more authoritative, from their right. "I see you moving around over there. I'm calling Chief Morgan. You no good little brats better stay out of my yard. I've got a gun and I know how to use it." A door slammed and the dog stopped barking.

Feeling silly, Taylor turned to yell that she *was* the police and stumbled over something hard. She went down on her hands and knees, the breath going out of her in a whoosh. Baldwin was right there, helping her up, shining the light around in a circle so they could see what she'd tripped on.

It was a metal stake. The kind you hammer into the ground to tie a dog's chain to. She limped the last ten feet to the car and let Baldwin look at the offending shin.

He rolled up her pant leg gently, his palm warm against her sore skin. "You scared me. Don't go falling down like that."

"Then tell these people not to put stakes in the middle of their yard."

The voice from next door spoke again, this time much closer. "Serves you right, sneaking around like that."

Baldwin moved like lightning, his weapon out in a heartbeat and his Maglite shining square in the woman's face, effectively blinding her. She was an older woman with a frazzled gray bun and a white terry housecoat covered in small brown cartoon puppies. True to her word, she carried a Remington 12-gauge shotgun, which she had pointed at them. Taylor hadn't heard the shell jacked into place, either the woman was waiting to impress them—there was nothing like the sound of a pump action shotgun going live, it was unmistakable and threatening enough to stop any smart person in their tracks—or she didn't have it loaded, and the gun was just for show.

Taylor bit her lip so she wouldn't laugh. This was absolutely ridiculous.

"Please don't shoot, ma'am. We're law enforcement. We have identification in our pockets. I'm John Baldwin, FBI, and this is Lieutenant Jackson, from Nashville."

The woman grinned at him. "Well, that's a damn good thing." She lowered the shotgun, stuck out her hand. "Sharon Potts. I'm a nurse, over at the hospital. Let me see if she's okay. Can't help but feel that was my fault, spooking her like a spring horse. You're a jumpy thing, aren't you?"

Taylor just sighed and stuck out her leg. Baldwin shined the light up and down it while the old woman ran her fingers along the broken skin. She hissed in a breath when the woman grabbed her leg and twisted. The nurse stood and brushed her hands down the front of her housecoat, smoothing it out over her hips.

"Nothing's broken. You barked it pretty good, that's a deep scratch. You're bleeding all over this fine young gentlemen's car. You don't need stitches, but some peroxide and a Band-Aid might come in handy. Probably need a tetanus booster, too. You folks have a first-aid kit in this fancy vehicle?"

"Not one that has fancy tetanus boosters," Baldwin said. Taylor could hear the smile in his voice. He thought this was funny, too. Then she drew a breath and sobered. If the Pretender had been lurking around instead—no, she'd have been alerted by her guards. He wasn't going to be able to sneak up on her.

"Smarty pants. Well, you can take her on over to the emergency room. Won't be too busy this time of night," Sharon said. She started back to her own yard, coughing deeply, the Remington slung up over her shoulder, almost longer than she was tall. Taylor felt like she'd stepped into the pages of *Li'l Abner.*

"Wait, Ms. Potts?" Taylor called out.

"Yes, yes, you're welcome," the old woman called back, hand fluttering up in a backward wave, still moving toward her front door.

"No, I…well, yes, thank you. But I was wondering. How long have you lived here?"

She stopped walking and turned around. "Long enough. Why?"

"Did you know the folks who used to live next door to you? The Copelands?"

Potts stared at her for a long moment, the darkness making her face look like a Janus mask, grotesque and unyielding. Then she smiled, and the face turned.

"Hell, you'd best come in. I'll make you some tea."

The tea was plain old Lipton from a bag, but it was warm and there was fresh cream and lots of sugar. Taylor sipped her cup and held an ice pack against her leg with a paper towel. Ms. Potts had fixed her up, but only after she assured her that she'd gotten a tetanus booster just six months earlier. It was required by Metro—like a dog, she had to get all her shots regularly.

Baldwin had settled in at the small wooden dining table looking like a giant. Sharon Potts was about five feet tall, and her house reflected that. Everything felt small, compact and efficient. Clean and homey, nothing superfluous. Just like its owner. Who was quick to share her story. Taylor got the sense that even though Ms. Potts worked around, with and for people all day, she was terribly lonely.

"Of course I remember the Copelands. Laws, there's no one in town who doesn't. It was terribly sad. Betty, she had a sickness. Even growing up, that girl was wrong in the head. Everyone knew it, and we all tried to help. But some kids are just born bad, and there's nothing you can do to help them. I knew her mama, God rest her soul. She was terrified for that child. Loved her to pieces though she never knew what she was going to get into next. Overloved her, really. She was pretty much blind to her faults. But you know how it is, no one can ever tell what happens behind closed doors. I think she let the cancer get her, so she wouldn't have to witness what she'd given birth to. Breast cancer, you see, late stage, and her so young. She was barely forty, died when Betty was seventeen or so. Right before she graduated. That spooked Betty, I think, because her mama was always the one place she knew she could turn when things got tough."

"What about her father?" Taylor asked.

"He was off in the merchant marines." She snorted. "Which is a fancy way of saying no one really knew who Betty's father was. Edward Biggs married Barbara when Betty was about three or so, gave her his name. But by that time he was so busy with the restaurant, and

Betty was such a handful. He died early, and Barbara, that's her mother, Barbara did the best she could. Barb was a good woman. But when she died, Betty had no one. So she took up with Roger Copeland. Got herself knocked up, knew he'd take care of her. Roger was an honorable man.

"They moved in after they got married. It was much nicer then, the neighborhood, I mean. Sweet little place for starting a family. And all he could afford, what with the baby practically here already and whatnot, and that BBQ joint not doing so well.

"Everything seemed normal, on the surface. I've been working up at the hospital going on thirty years now, and I'm telling you the God to honest truth here. Something was wrong in that house. I saw those boys come in with the strangest maladies. And Betty, hell, Betty was an expert. She could have been a doctor. Knew more than I did about these foreign diseases. She spent practically all her time looking through that huge copy of *Gray's Anatomy.* She'd sit on the front porch with a glass of cool tea and read like her heart was about to give out.

"Roger was gone all the time, and those boys, those poor boys. We did what we could, tried to help, to be neighborly. Brought food over, covered dishes and the like, offered to do the laundry. But Betty wouldn't let us get too close. She beat those kids, treated them like animals inside the house, but outside, she played the role of doting mother. They were all cowed by her. Roger included. I think that's why he was so anxious to leave.

"When the boys were sick and in the hospital, she would hover over them and berate us like we were idiots. Insist on giving the medicine herself, things like that.

The winter my mama died was when the oldest took sick. I wasn't here, I had to go and stay up with her at the hospice. I came back and everything was changed. Roger was dead, Edward was dead, Betty was in jail, poor Errol was in the loony bin sick as a cat, and Ewan was here by himself, trying to make ends meet. Then they put him in that home and he just fell apart.

"That slut who Roger got pregnant should have taken in those boys, but she pranced off and married Anderson, made sure she and her little bastard were taken care of. I always hated her a little for that, and I know it's a sin. But if she'd loved that man at all, she'd have seen to his boys. As it was, when Errol killed himself, she was in Myrtle Beach, with her girlfriends. Ewan had no one to help him plan his little brother's funeral. I remember him sitting by the gravesite, eyes just blank. Once he hurt that girl and disappeared, the whole story faded away, into town legend. The house got taken by the bank, and no one's been there since. They never were able to sell it. The walls probably scream."

Taylor felt a chill go through her at the thought, reflexively sipped on the strong hot tea.

"What was he like?" Baldwin asked.

Ms. Potts was enjoying her bit of company on this cold night, and she was a natural storyteller. She bustled around her little kitchen, fixing them some more tea and setting out a plate of cookies. Tagalongs, from what Taylor could see of the box. Her stomach growled in a decidedly unladylike fashion. The nurse just smiled and pushed the plate of cookies closer.

"Ewan? Like his mama, I daresay."

"Like her how?"

She tapped her finger on the table, thinking. "Messed up in the head. He tried so hard. It was heartbreaking, really, watching him struggle. Like he knew what he did was wrong and bad, but he just couldn't help himself. Take the dog. That stake you tripped over? They had a dog when Ewan was about ten. Just a mutt, nothing special. He found him over the tracks, back in the woods. Boyo loved that dog. Slept with him. Walked him. Played with him. And when he shot him, and the dog lay there dying in the front yard, whimpering and bleeding and looking up at the one good thing in its poor little life, he stood over it and cried. I watched him do it. That's when I knew. He was wrong, bad wrong. But he didn't want to be that way, I don't think. He was compelled."

Taylor set her half-eaten cookie back on the plate. "You saw him shoot the dog?"

"I did. I'd just gotten home from my first shift. Heard the shot, looked over. Ewan was standing there, snot running down his face. I remember he looked up at me, and he was so stricken. 'I had to,' he said. 'He was hurt.' But that dog was fine, right as rain. He killed him because he wanted to."

Baldwin nodded. "He equated pain with love. That's what his mother's Munchausen's did to him. The only way you can tell someone how much you love them is by hurting them. Physically hurting them. It brings all the attention to you."

"That sounds about right. Betty did love those boys, no one could deny that. But she hated them a bit, too. She must have. How else could she have kept hurting them, over and over and over?"

Taylor met Baldwin's eyes. They were beginning to have a better understanding of their adversary. Such understanding could lead to sympathy if they weren't careful, and suddenly Taylor felt like they were stalling.

It was time to go. Time to erase this bastard off the face of the earth.

"Ms. Potts, you've been a wonderful help," Taylor said. "Thank you so much for fixing me up. We need to get back on the road now."

With minimal protestation, the nurse saw them out, pressed the extra Tagalongs into Taylor's hand. She accepted them gratefully; she needed the sugar boost, could eat again despite the knowledge she'd just gained and the heavy, late lunch. They promised to stop by again if they were ever in town, then made their way to Baldwin's BMW.

The noose was drawing tighter.

Twenty-Seven

To: troy14@ncr.tr.com
From: crypto@ncr.zk.com
Subject: Kansas City, MO

Dear Troy,
Entering Kansas City now. It's been a long drive.
But don't worry, everything is under control.
ZK

Highway. Again. Gray strips of asphalt that ran on forever. He wished he had more time; he'd get off the interstate and run the roads through the cornfields. *Get your kicks, on Route 66*. Did Route 66 run through Missouri? He thought it must have, but he couldn't remember. He carefully placed his knee against the steering wheel and reached beside him for his notebook. Glancing at the road every few seconds, he wrote himself a note.

Check on Route 66.

It was his way. He was the curious type. Despite his previous troubles, he liked to learn. He didn't have the best memory in the world, so he sometimes had to refresh himself.

Denver had gone so well. It was the best of the three cities he'd been in. It even topped his first in San Francisco. He thought popping his cherry was going to be the highlight of his life, but Denver proved him wrong. It would get better, and better, and better. He was getting more confident. That helped. He chalked Vegas, the flailing and gushing blood everywhere, up to simply being scared. Performance anxiety. He had worried that when the time came, he wouldn't be able to deliver. He'd gotten himself really worked up and the nerves made him pull the knife early. He rushed the big finish. He hadn't gotten a real chance to see the terror in their eyes fade to nothingness as they died.

But Denver…oh, sweet mother of God. Denver was perfection. Cherry Creek Reservoir was hand-built for murder. The meandering paths, the snowy lane. Drops of blood on the white canvas of his world, so elegant. He was not making Jackson Pollock paintings. Wait, was that the artist's name? Jackson? Or Johnson?

He pulled out the notebook again.

One hundred miles to Kentucky. And he was right on time. He bent his neck to the left, then to the right, hunched his shoulders and felt the muscles stretch out. He was so cramped in this car, so boxed in. He needed something bigger to allow his frame to sit comfortably. He had a friend once who'd owned a Prius. He'd lasted an hour in it before his thighs cramped up.

It wouldn't be too much longer now. He was on the last leg of his itinerary.

Their fearless leader had picked the victims so well. Troy had assured him that the girl would respond to the Craigslist ad. Rollerblades. In winter, at that. He wondered how the man knew so much, then pushed that thought aside. When it was time, he would be enlightened. When he won the game, the master would share all with him—the money, the benefit of his years of experience, his real name. They'd been instructed to call him Troy. If he were being honest with himself, Troy didn't sound like the name of a man who could mastermind an operation of this kind. But he'd promised the winner the goods. Winner take all. The million-dollar prize. He could do so much with that money.

And once he'd won, been *chosen,* Troy would hone his new apprentice into a fine, sharp edge, so they could go on killing without ever getting caught.

He wasn't entirely sure of himself yet. The idea of becoming a serial killer had its upside, yes. Truth be told, he just needed the money. He hadn't counted on enjoying it so much.

Troy. Wasn't that the name of that city, the one with the fake horse? All that blood spilled over a woman. What was her name? Hera? No, that was a goddess, Zeus's wife. Halley? No, that was the name of the girl he'd just killed. Helen? Helen. That sounded right.

He wrote it down in his notebook, just in case.

Twenty-Eight

The glowing green clock in Baldwin's dashboard read 8:45 p.m.

He tapped his fingers along the wheel, trying to decide what their next step should be. Head back to Nashville? Head north to Raleigh? They might be smart to stay put, at least until Roddie Hall called them back with news about Ruth Anderson.

"That was a sad story," Taylor said. She had drawn her hair up into a messy ponytail on the top of her head, the ends just wisping against the middle of her back. He loved her hair. So thick it had a mind of its own. He reached over and tugged the holder away, let the mass of it spill over his hand.

"Yes, it was. One of the worst I've heard in a long time. Not a huge surprise though. That kind of abuse, deadly abuse, disguised as loving kindness—it's really no wonder he ended up a killer. He didn't know any other way to interact with people—"

"But that's no excuse."

"No, no, that's no excuse. Plenty of children are abused and don't end up murdering people." He looked over at Taylor. The playful spirit that had bubbled up between them before they talked to the old nurse was gone.

"What trips the switch?" she finally asked.

"If I could answer that, I'd be a very rich man. Every mind is different. You've seen this a hundred times, people who weren't abused do terrible things, people who were abused go on to lead normal, loving lives. We're back to nature versus nurture. I do think there's something genetic to all of this, the predisposition could be there, but the choice to kill is just that, their choice."

"And the odds of one man spawning two killers with two different women?"

"Unthinkable. I don't know of a case like it. Granted, Betty's genes played a part. If I had more time, I'd love to do a historical study on both Roger and Betty's families, just to see. Of course, no one knows who Betty's real father was, so that's hard to track."

She grew quiet, allowed him to massage the tightness in her shoulders.

"Your leg okay?" he asked.

"Yeah, I'm fine. Ms. Potts must be a hell of a nurse. I can't even feel it."

"The Neosporin she applied has lidocaine in it. Numbs the skin."

"Smart."

She captured his hand, pressed his flesh to her lips. Ah, that drove him crazy. She drove him crazy. Though how he could be thinking about sex at a time like this?

His cell rang, making them both jump like guilty teenagers caught necking in the car. Taylor giggled as he fumbled the phone from its holster. Good, she was feeling better. Melancholy didn't suit her.

"It's Hall," he said, and answered with a truly professional, "John Baldwin."

"She's gone, man. Just like you thought. Looks like Ruth Anderson took off at least a few days ago. Neighbors saw her last Saturday, but can't remember seeing her since. We've got evidence galore in her apartment—including emails with directions for the killings in Nags Head. Police chief here in Durham got us a search warrant while we were staging, and we've hit the mother lode. Don't know where she's headed, but we know where she's been. And she's been a busy little bee."

Baldwin popped in one of his favorite CDs by a band called Butterfly Boucher. He keyed the player up to "Another White Dash," his ultimate road-trip song, and hummed along to the words quietly. Taylor had fallen asleep just before Knoxville, and he intended to keep her that way.

Hall was of the opinion that Ruth Anderson was no longer in Raleigh, nor North Carolina, for that matter, because of an email from someone as yet unidentifiable who said to "come to N" if there was trouble.

Nashville.

N could have been anything, but the most logical place that was in the pool of discussion was their town. Returning to the scene of the crime in Nags Head would be suicide, there was still a very active investigative search going on in that area. Ruth's cover had been blown wide-open, and her picture was plastered all over the evening news. Baldwin wondered what Mrs. Anderson would think of his deception, then stashed that thought away. He'd done what he needed to, plain and simple.

It was just about midnight. He would get them back

to Nashville by 3:00 a.m. They'd have time to regroup for a couple of hours before embarking on the next stage of the investigation. Having the sister was going to help them close this case one hell of a lot faster. If they could find her. He called Buddy Morgan and filled him in on the situation, let him know he needed to keep watch at the Anderson home on the off chance Ruth decided to come home, or call her mother. Morgan assured him that it would be taken care of.

I-40 was flowing well, considering the roadwork and multiple long-haul trucks making their way through the mountain region. It was quiet, the moon shining brightly off the snow that crusted the hilltops, the trees marching over the ridges in ragged formation, like soldiers after a wearying battle. He was so tired. The emotional wreckage of the past few days reared its ugly head—his career, his life with Taylor, the threat against her life, the knowledge that his son was out there, being raised by another man—it was all too much. They needed a break. A real vacation, away from Nashville. Away from everything. He could tell her the truth with nothing hanging over their heads, and God willing, she'd forgive him.

Taylor's cell phone began to trill. She shifted in her seat and opened her eyes, the insomniac in her immediately awake.

"Where are we?" she asked.

"Just past Crossville. Sorry, I forgot to turn off your phone. I was trying to let you sleep."

She looked at the caller ID. "That's all right. It's Lincoln." She stretched as she answered.

"Hey, Linc, what's up?"

He glanced over and watched her face in the moonlight. She mumbled "uh-huh" three times, then grabbed her notebook and started writing. He loved how she could go from sleepy mouse to Valkyrie warrior at a moment's notice.

She hung up the phone, and her statement wiped the smile right off his face.

"We have a problem."

Of course they did. "What now?"

"Let me make a call. I'll put it on speaker. You'll get the gist of the issue."

She was already dialing, referring to the number she'd written down in her notebook. She set the open phone on the console and clicked the speaker button. Baldwin heard three long rings, then the call connected. A woman answered, she sounded wide-awake.

"Hello?"

"Ms. Keck?" Taylor asked.

"Lieutenant Jackson? How are you? Call me Colleen."

"Colleen, then. One of my detectives said you'd called in and asked to speak to me personally. Can you tell me what's going on?"

"You don't remember me, do you? We met at a FOP function several years ago. You were only a detective then, but my husband, Tommy, introduced us. It was before he…he died."

Taylor was silent for a moment. "Of course I remember. I apologize, I'm running on fumes. How are you, Colleen? How's Flynn?"

"Oh, good, you do remember. So many people would have just lied."

"Tommy was a good man. Sorry it took me a moment to put it together. So what can I do for you?"

"Lieutenant, Tommy told me that if I was ever in

trouble, I should come to you. He thought the world of you."

"Are you in trouble, Colleen?"

A ghost of a laugh bled through the speaker. "More than I can tell you. Have you ever heard of a blog called Felon E?"

Twenty-Nine

Nashville, Tennessee

"Ruth, Ruth, Ruth. Tsk. I am so disappointed in you."

She squirmed. The wood must be biting into her knees.

"Ewan, it's not my fault. Please believe me. I left nothing to chance. Nothing. There's no way they could follow my trail back to you."

He had to admit, he was enjoying the sheer panic in Ruth's voice. She was expecting to be killed. He didn't disabuse her of the notion. She knew the penalties for failure.

"And yet they did. Now how do you suppose that happened? Hmm? Because it certainly wasn't anything *I* did."

He gave her hair a little tug. She was on her knees facing him, and he had a fistful of brown. She grimaced, but didn't cry out. Strong little Ruth. Willing to do most anything for him. Lie. Steal. Kill. Handy in a sister.

"Answer me, Ruth. What do they have on me?"

Her words came out in harsh little pants. "Nothing. I swear to you, nothing. If they found my apartment it was totally by chance. Someone must have recognized me at one of the crime scenes. They had pictures of us coming in the door from the security cameras. They must have shown them around and someone figured out it was me. I know it wasn't Newt or Harvey. We killed Newt as soon as we got out of North Carolina."

"You killed Newt? I didn't give permission for that."

"I'm sorry. I had to. I was afraid…"

"Afraid of what?"

Tears formed in her eyes. "Afraid that you had told him to kill me, or Harvey. I couldn't take the chance."

"Don't you trust me, Ruth? I'm your brother."

The mongoose to the cobra.

"Of course I trust you, Ewan. But Newt was acting weird, checking his email constantly. I just got freaked out. Maybe he was a plant, you know? Someone from their side, an informant. Harvey wanted to do it, so I said yes."

Look at dear Ruth, showing some backbone. He had to admit, he was impressed. She was smarter than he gave her credit for.

"Have you kept Harvey in check? We don't need any more negative attention. This is my plan, my game. Not his."

"Of course. I told him to lay off."

"Ruth, don't lie to me. I saw a case of a missing boy here in town, from last weekend. I know you were here with Harvey doing reconnaissance over Halloween. You didn't have some fun while you were here, did you?"

"No, no. We didn't."

He pulled harder, felt little bits of hair release at the roots. She whimpered at last.

"Yes, okay. We couldn't help ourselves. He was right there, fresh for the taking. Drunk. You know how Harvey is with drunk boys wandering the streets. I'm so sorry. He won't be found, won't be connected to you. I promise. Harvey took him out of town."

My God. You just can't trust anyone to stick to the plan these days.

He snarled at her, face right in hers, his spit splashing across her lips and nose. "You didn't have the right to make that decision."

She sagged against him, allowing him to yank harder on her hair. "You're right. I will take care of Harvey. I'll kill him tonight. I promise."

Good. She'd gotten the message. He released her hair and she fell to the floor with a satisfyingly loud thump.

He moved to his chair and sat, watched her rub her scalp, then sit up cautiously and cross her legs like she used to do when she was a kid.

"I swear," she said, looking him in the eye.

"What will they find in your apartment?"

"Nothing. Nothing." But she looked away, and he knew there was more that she wasn't telling him. Stupid, stupid girl.

"What do they have, Ruth. Tell me. Tell me!"

She started to cry, wrapped her arms around her body and rocked gently to and fro, a boat cast adrift in an increasingly dangerous swelling sea.

He sucked in a breath through his nose. Losing his temper now wasn't what they needed. Ruth would scuttle off if he showed his true rage, shut down and rock for hours, just like when she was little. He used to follow her home from school, sneak her off into the woods and play. Chess mostly, checkers and backgammon were too easy. She was good at keeping secrets, but if she went on overload, she'd turn off, retreat into that precious, special little world she had and he wouldn't get anything more out of her tonight. And damn if he didn't need her help, one last time.

He softened his tone, bent to her level.

"I'm sorry, Ruth. I've had a hard day. I didn't mean to yell at you." Conciliatory wasn't his forte, and she sniffed and turned her head away. He decided to try a different tack.

"You can tell me. I promise I won't get mad."

She didn't look up. Spoke in a tiny voice. "Promise?"

"I promise."

She wrapped her arms tighter around her legs, like she could disappear into herself. "My laptop is on my desk. I didn't bring it with me. I thought I'd have a chance to go home. Things have been so crazy, moved so fast… Then Harvey decided he wanted to do the boy here, and we got behind on the schedule and had to rush to Nags Head." She broke off, sensing he was about to blow his load.

"Your laptop. With all the emails?"

"Yes."

The emails that led directly to him. Well, it was nearly time to vacate the premises anyway, the last stage of the plan was about to go into motion. Time to let the acolytes make their move. See if they were as good as he hoped.

Ruth had started her industrial-strength rocking. He needed to pull her out before the trance got too deep.

"Ruthie, what if I told you someone needed to die?

Today, as a matter of fact. Not Harvey—you can keep him. I know you like him. Would that cheer you up?"

He saw her eyes slide toward him. Bloodthirsty little beast. He knew the idea of death would get her attention.

"Who?" she asked, voice small and childish.

"Colleen Keck. The blogger. It's time for her to go."

Ruth unfolded from the floor, scooted over to him with a feral little smile on her lips. She looked up with doe eyes for permission, which he granted. She stroked his leg.

"Harvey's already on her. He's been watching her since we left North Carolina. She was the first stop when we got back, I left him at the top of her street, before I came here. He's got it covered."

"No, my sweet. I want you to do it."

"Why? Not that I wouldn't be happy to, of course, you know that. But I thought you wanted her left alive until the very end. You've changed your mind?"

He stood and walked to the window, leaving Ruth crumpled on the floor like a discarded lotus flower. "Yes. I've changed my mind. That's my prerogative."

"But you always told me to stick to the plan—"

"Ruth, no buts."

"I thought I got to kill the other woman."

He looked over his shoulder. "After the mess you made of things in North Carolina? No, Ruth. You don't get rewarded for fucking up."

Rock, rock, rock.

"Don't pout, Ruthie. Keck will be fun. I promise. She's become a liability. Too smart for her own good. She'll figure out the victim pool anytime now. Those perverted, stupid idiots on her site blew the surprise. So she has to go now, before she alerts anyone else. This is a big favor for me, a personal favor. You know what happens when you do me personal favors, right?"

"I get to ask a favor in return."

"That's right. You're such a good girl. Now go. Take care of this pesky bitch for me."

Ruth got to her feet. "Yes, Ewan. If you say so."

"I say so. Take off. I have other things to do. And, Ruth? You know what to do if you're caught."

Her lips turned down and her face got white. "Yes, brother."

He watched her scramble from his apartment and sighed. Maybe he should have given in to the impulse to have her die back in North Carolina? No, what's done was done. Her mistakes would accelerate the plan. While the Jackson bitch was smart, she wasn't a magician. He knew Ruth was telling the truth—she'd tried to keep his secrets. He'd been so careful to cover his tracks. New names every year. New cities. New faces, too. Ruth was the only one alive who knew who he really was, the rest of his family was dead or gone. His mother especially, she was bat shit crazy, didn't even remember she'd had children. He'd gone to see her once, three years earlier. Just to be sure. Her brain was mush, the years of insanity and the cancer drugs had turned it into psychotic cornmeal. She saw devils on the shoulders of her guards, who had to force her to bathe since she'd developed a fear of water. She'd become a regular Medusa, her hair twisted into smelly, unkempt dreadlocks. She'd been trapped inside her own mind.

No, he was safe on that account. He had no concerns about anyone finding out the truth. The bitch was dead.

But he had the final three chess pieces moving toward

him. Which would it be? Who would win the game? Who would be found worthy? Which pawn would cross the length of the board and have the chance to watch him kill Jackson, in the method of the winner's killing profile? He'd chosen his three favorite historical killers for the last. Watching her die by any of their methods would be good fun.

The million dollars was incentive, certainly. They were all highly motivated. If he had to lay down odds, he'd have to say the young lad from Boston was the likeliest candidate. When they'd talked, he seemed calmer than the rest, more mature. More focused. He was independently wealthy, so he wasn't in it for the money. Not like California—he was in debt up to his ears, his house had been foreclosed on, he had no ties, no foundation. And an extra long trip—probably not fair, stacking the odds against him like that, but he was so obviously mercenary. Sadly, his boy from Long Island was riding the edge. He was unpredictable, maybe even crazy. No, he thought Boston was the real contender.

A new apprentice. How very exciting.

He smiled to himself as he watched Ruth drive away. There were words she used to say to him when they were children. They held no meaning for him before, but as he grew older, they finally, finally started to make sense.

Entreat me not to leave thee, or to return from following after thee: for whither thou goest, I will go; and where thou lodgest, I will lodge: thy people shall be my people, and thy God my God.

He was Ruth's God. Just like he was about to become Taylor Jackson's God. Time to finish this. He was getting bored. He understood bostonboy's impatience, sometimes challenges grew tedious. They had to be resolved, or else they were just open-ended tasks. Sisyphean.

He turned from the window and grabbed his lanyard with the laminated badge that spelled out her doom. Strung it around his neck and looked down at the smiling visage, the face that even he barely recognized anymore.

Oh, yes, Taylor. It's nearly time.

November 8

Thirty

Nashville's skyline rolled into Taylor's view, the lights of the Batman Building glowing in the darkness, the new Pinnacle tower with its tiny branding sign, so understated. Blue, red and yellow lights reflected off the Cumberland River as they drove across the Shelby Street Bridge, the colors mingling with the dark water, rippling and shimmering in a seductive dance.

Baldwin drove them straight to her office at the Criminal Justice Center. She'd called the team in, too, rousting them from their warm beds. McKenzie met them in the Homicide offices, yawning, with coffees and a homemade chai tea for Taylor courtesy of his partner Hugh. Baldwin accepted one of the coffees and peeled off from the group, went to one of the interrogation rooms to make some phone calls. Marcus rolled in five minutes later looking like he might not have gone to bed yet. Only Lincoln was impeccably dressed, looking sharp in a crisp white Armani shirt tucked into dark-washed Seven jeans with black tasseled loafers, topped with a dark purple suede jacket.

"Clotheshorse," McKenzie said to him as he handed over the steaming cup of coffee.

"I could help you sometime. We could go shopping. The poindexter look went out a few years ago."

"What, you want to be my girlfriend now?"

"You already have Hugh for that, sugar."

"He's my wife, dumb ass. Husbands don't go shopping with their wives. That's what they save for their mistresses."

"Ouch," Marcus said, laughing. "He got you there, Linc."

"Boys," Taylor warned. "Play nice, or Mommy will take all your toys away. Thank Hugh for the chai, Renn. It's delicious, as always."

McKenzie shoved Lincoln's hand away from his cup of coffee, just saving it from being doused in cream. "I will. He says you owe him dinner."

Taylor smiled at them. She was happy to see McKenzie fitting in so well with Marcus and Lincoln. He was a very capable detective, and she knew he'd earned their respect on that front. He'd earned hers, too, that was why she'd brought him on as a permanent member of the team. But respect and friendship were two very different things. The three seemed to have bonded quite well. Which was good. She could stop worrying about it. Maybe Fitz would come back to Homicide, too. Lord knew she'd take him back in a heartbeat if he were willing. Becoming the collateral damage of a serial killer wouldn't be an easy thing for him to put away; he could take his twenty and run off forever. He'd been considering doing just that when he'd been kidnapped—he and Susie had been on a decision vacation, planning out their future.

She swallowed the lump in her throat. The loss he must be feeling overwhelmed her—she only knew Susie casually and she was torn up about her death. She hated that he was lying alone in the hospital. She just wanted to go back to Vandy and hug him, just so he knew she loved him. Later. She'd go tomorrow. He'd kill her if he knew she was fretting about him instead of focusing on the task at hand.

The Homicide office was crowded with the overnight shift, so Taylor led them to the conference room. As she turned on the lights, her cell rang. She didn't recognize the number, but answered it anyway. There was too much happening to miss any opportunity to learn something new about the case. She vaguely recognized the voice on the other end.

"Lieutenant Jackson, this is Paul Friend. I'm a producer at Fox News—we actually worked together the last time you were on, with Kimberley? During the Snow White case?"

Ah, that was it. Paul Friend had produced the segment, had been the voice in her ear instructing her of breaks and fresh camera shots. "Yes, Paul. How are you?"

"Awake at this ungodly hour, unfortunately. We've gotten an unconfirmed report about a murder victim. Make that two victims. Out in San Francisco. Staged to look exactly like the Zodiac Killer's first kill. A letter was sent to the *Chronicle* and everything. Turns out the victims were participants on a blog called Felon E, and my sources tell me you've been talking to the owner of the blog. We're running the story during the morning show. Would you be willing to confirm for us?"

"Confirm what?"

"That this anonymous blogger knew the Zodiac Killer was picking victims from the blog and didn't share that information with the police, or warn the other participants? Oh, and I should mention, we had another set of murders here in New York that looks strangely like the Son of Sam case. The men who were shot were also frequent commenters on the Felon E blog. And just so happens there was a note left near the bodies that said, and I quote, 'There are other Sons out there, God help the world.' Since I don't think David Berkowitz has managed to escape from prison…"

Oh, crap.

"Sorry, man. I don't know the first thing about it."

"You don't? Because I would think you of all people could understand the need to warn people if a copycat killer is on the loose. Especially since you may know exactly who is responsible. Come on, Lieutenant. Just between us, off the record. After your involvement with the Snow White case, and your attendance at the massacre in North Carolina yesterday morning, it's obvious what's happening. Listen, I've been watching things. I know the Snow White's apprentice got away. He's out there, and he's been quiet for too long. This feels like him. You have to admit that, at least."

"You're making some pretty big assumptions there, Mr. Friend."

Friend was quiet for a moment. "Lieutenant, we're on the same side here. I want to help you catch these guys. See real justice done. Who knows how many of them are out there?"

"I don't know anything. I'm sorry. Seriously, Paul, you're sharing new information with me, not the other way around."

"You don't want to be like this, Lieutenant. You want to work with me. I can help you."

"Really, Paul, I haven't heard anything about it. Sorry. You'll have to double-source somewhere else. Have a good night. Morning. Whatever."

She hung up and turned to the guys. "We need to move, now."

Marcus raised an eyebrow. "You just lied. Naughty, naughty."

"Yes, well, you can spank me later. We need to save Colleen Keck's ass first. Who knows about her calling in outside of us? Dispatch?"

"No one that I know of. Lincoln talked to her, he called you."

"We might have a leak, so pay attention to anyone who's showing an interest in this case. Let's find out what Ms. Keck has managed to uncover."

Thirty-One

To: troy14@ncr.tr.com
From: 44cal@ncr.ss.com
Subject: Charleston, WV

Dear Troy,
Rocking in the free world.
44

"I could do it right here. Right now.

"Fucking McDonald's. Happy, nasty children playing. I've got the AK, it's loaded and ready to go. I could just spray them all. That would get their attention."

Not such a good idea, homey. There aren't enough. You need more. Many, many more.

He counted them—fourteen. His rancor subsided. The angel was right, fourteen wasn't enough. He needed to make it a proper mass killing. Like that rag head down in Texas. He put on quite a show, but the dumb fucker got himself shot and was paralyzed. No, suicide by cop wouldn't work. He didn't want to die, not now, at least. He had things he wanted to do. Books to read.

Especially that, and if he managed a death penalty case, he'd have years to fill.

He loved to read.

I love to read, too. Remember that great one, about the stalker who cuts the woman in half?

"Hush. I'm trying to think here."

No, he needed to make sure he was in Tennessee before he went postal. They killed their criminals dead, dead, dead, dead. And death row was his goal. He giggled. Going postal. That was exactly what he was going to do. *Falling Down,* like Michael Douglas when he lost his shit and went on that righteous spree. That was cool, but Douglas was weak in the end. That was before his facelift, too. What stupid motherfucking man got a facelift?

He'd enjoyed killing those faggots in the park in D.C. They hadn't expected him, the Avenger, to glide up to them and open fire. The look on their faces was priceless. They were about to ask him to join their little party, to be a third. Probably wanted him to be on bottom. Dickwads.

The angel start to rap. *All the little dickwads, sitting in a row. Pow. Kapow. Blammo, and so. You're dead. You're dead. You're dead, and gone-o.*

A thought came to him. A big, beautiful thought. He could find a gay bar. They are always crowded, every night of the week. Oh, imagine that. A whole room full of the abnormal assholes. He knew there was a gay bar in Nashville, a big one. He could go in there, shoot it up. Mow. Them. Down. Oh, my. Oh, that was just perfect.

He got goose bumps, felt them parading up and down his body. His erection was nearly instantaneous. Why hadn't he thought of it before?

The angel was quiet for once, savoring the idea. Fuck the game. Fuck that twisted asshole running it. He was done playing by other people's rules. He was in control now.

He reset his GPS. Instead of stopping in Louisville and shooting the senator's gay-as-a-three-dollar-bill aide like he was supposed to, he was heading straight for Nashville.

Good plan, homey. You're finally getting it.

He lit a cigarette, looked at the bottle of medicine in the console. Rolled down the window and threw it in the trash, followed a moment later by the still-lit cigarette. He was going for broke. No more pretending, no more pills. No more games. Screw the target, that Jackson bitch. He didn't care about her anyway.

I'm coming for you, motherfuckahs.

Kill the gays, kill the gays, kill the gays.

The angel yelled, *Wheeeeeeee.*

Thirty-Two

Colleen couldn't find the place to park that Lieutenant Jackson had suggested, so she went to the underground parking garage across James Robertson Parkway from the CJC instead. She drove down the ramp, surprised at how well lit it was inside. Not bad for the middle of the night.

She positioned the car under a bright light for a little extra safety. She slung her laptop bag over her shoulder, lifted a sleeping Flynn from the backseat of the car, and hurried into the elevator. There was no one around, which made her feel a bit better, but she wasn't about to take any chance. She had one of Tommy's old guns tucked into her jacket pocket. She'd be damned if someone would hurt her or Flynn.

The streets were empty. The Cumberland River shone brightly to her right, the murky dark water lit up by the array of lights on the bridge. She couldn't shake the feeling that she was being watched. A cold, slithery finger of fear slipped under her scarf, and she pulled Flynn tighter to her chest, no longer worried if she woke him. She sprinted across the street and up the stairs to the CJC. She could have sworn she saw a man follow her, saw a dark blur out of the corner of her eye, but then she was at the door to the building. She rang the buzzer, gesticulating wildly to the guard who was seated behind the glass partition. He buzzed her in and she pulled the door shut behind her, felt it latch securely.

"I think I'm being followed," she whispered to the man. "Can you watch out for someone who doesn't belong?"

"I'll do what I can, ma'am, but we don't get a lot of normal folks running around in the middle of the night. Are you Mrs. Keck?"

She only flinched a little bit at the Mrs. designation. Too young to be a widow, too old to be a Miss. And *Ms.* always sounded like a mosquito buzzing out of the person's mouth. At Flynn's school they simply called her Miss Colleen, in that quaint Southern way that kept children on a more formal but still personal level with their parents' female friends. Of course, it was only for the women, she didn't have a single recollection of someone ever saying Mr. Tommy.

The guard was looking at her, perplexed. *Oh, please tell me I didn't say that aloud.* She tried again.

"Yes, I am. I'm here to see Lieutenant Jackson."

"Yep, you're on the list. Sorry about your husband, ma'am. They're waiting for you. Just go knock on that door over there, someone will let you in."

"Thank you." She fought back the urge to tip him, almost laughed out loud. After her years as a journalist, she was so used to handing out the twenties when she was in need of information the reflex was ingrained into her.

Flynn had miraculously stayed asleep during her panicked flight from the parking garage. She blessed his father's genes. Where Colleen would start and wake from the tiniest click or knock in the house's night, Tommy could sleep through a tornado siren going off next to his bed. He was forever sleeping through his alarm. Flynn was the same way: easy to fall asleep, hard to rouse.

Her third knock was answered by a handsome black man, about six feet tall, impeccably dressed. She almost laughed out loud—who looked that good, that put together, at three in the morning? He smiled at her and she saw the gap between his front two teeth. He looked like a rock star, someone she couldn't place. She had his CDs though. Damn, what was his name? Lenny something. She racked her brain. Kravitz. That was it.

He saw her trying to place him and smiled wider. He must be used to the double take people did when they saw him. Of course, that was what most folks in Nashville did—the country music capital of the world attracted a bevy of famous musicians, songwriters and singers, not to mention several actresses and actors who enjoyed the illusion of privacy Nashville afforded. Folks might look twice when Nicole Kidman wandered into Starbucks with Keith Urban and Sunday Rose, but they'd never do anything more than smile politely and say good morning. It just wouldn't be polite to hit them up for an autograph when they were just trying to fuel up on caffeine.

He ushered her inside. "You must be Colleen Keck. I'm Detective Ross. Sorry about all this."

"You and me both, Detective. Have you heard anything?"

Ross closed the door behind them and gestured for her to follow him. "No, nothing yet. We all just got here.

The LT is on the phone to some of her contacts. I think she's expecting you to brief us, can you do that?"

"I can. Is there someplace I could lay Flynn down? I'm not sure I want him hearing this."

"Yeah, we can finagle something. I'll ask one of the shift detectives to keep an eye on him and page me if he wakes up. They're slow tonight. Will that work?"

"You must be a father, Detective."

He smiled at her. "Nope. My mom was a reporter, and my dad worked the overnight shift. I got used to waking up in strange corners of the city. Always felt better if someone was around to tell me she'd be back in a second."

They came to the conference-room door. He took Flynn from her arms and made his way back out of the room.

Taylor Jackson was on the other side of the room, sitting on what looked like a countertop, one long leg dangling beneath her, talking rapid-fire into a cell phone. She must have been sitting on the other foot, she looked like a very blond crane. Two other men were sitting at the table, flipping through files. One was cute, rangy with floppy brown hair, the other more obviously reserved, with blond hair graying at the temples. She mentally dubbed them Frick and Frack. Wondered where the hot guy had gone with her kid. Wondered why she was thinking that.

Colleen took a couple of deep breaths. It was all going to be all right.

Jackson was wrapping up her phone call now. She flipped the cell shut, stowed it in her pocket, and crossed the room to Colleen. She didn't smile, exactly, but her face was welcoming.

"Hell of a thing," she said, sticking out her hand to shake. Colleen took it, grateful for the warmth.

"Good to see you again, Lieutenant."

"Take off your coat, have a seat. Detective Ross took care of you?"

"Yes, thanks. He's just put Flynn down for me. I'm sure he'll be back in a moment."

Jackson cocked her head and looked at her, but said nothing. Damn. She must have sounded a bit possessive of Detective Ross. Strange, she was *feeling* possessive of the man. She'd only met him five minutes before for God's sake. Hormones. Her hormones must be in gear. It was probably getting close to her time; she always got a little horny when nature was about to make a visit.

God, Colleen, get your head in the game. She was getting punchy. No sleep plus a bucketful of stress and a healthy dose of fear did that to a girl. She tried to redeem herself by resorting to her most professional tone.

"So, Lieutenant, what do you have?"

Jackson turned and went to the table, sitting across from Colleen. "Trouble. A boatload of it. I need you to tell me everything you know about the murders."

"Where should I start?"

"How about telling us where you got the information about the killings in San Francisco in the first place?"

Colleen shook her head. "I can't do that. I have sources. If I burn them, they'll never speak to me again. I can't give you their information. I'm sorry."

Jackson stared at her, then sighed. "Okay, we'll come back to that. Why don't you just start at the beginning and share what you're comfortable with?"

Colleen could tell the woman was trying hard not to

be adversarial, but there was the tiniest bit of anger in the soft words. She didn't blame her—of course Jackson would want the names of the sources. But Colleen had no intention of burning anyone if she could avoid it.

"I knew there was something up when I got a couple of emails from San Francisco telling me there had been a murder that looked like the Zodiac. You have to remember, this happens a lot. People love to imitate him, and there are false alarms all the time. But something felt different about this. Right afterward, emails came in from New York and Boston. At first I thought it was some kind of joke, but it felt wrong. So I started digging. The reports I was getting were right on. I double-sourced everything. Two nights ago, three different cities were struck by copycat killers. They imitated the Boston Strangler, Son of Sam and the Zodiac. Yesterday morning, you had a fiasco in Nags Head, North Carolina, that I'm convinced was related."

"*You're* convinced. No one in the law enforcement community was drawing correlations between these four sets of murders, but you, a semi-pro true-crime blogger, immediately recognized a pattern. So you went off half-cocked and posted your theories on the blog, thus drawing the ire of some creep who decided to spook you."

Colleen raised her chin a fraction. She refused to be condescended to. When Jackson said it aloud, she had to admit, it sounded absurd. But she knew she was right. Knew it in her heart.

"Say what you will, but I was right. And that's what I do, Lieutenant. I run a crime blog. Sometimes the criminals I'm discussing read that blog. It's a free world. But here's the important thing—I help the police solve cases all over the country. People have an inherent mistrust of the police, of the system. They think if they tell the truth, or rat on a friend, the police will somehow sweep them into the case. I provide a forum for people to share tips, insight and information with law enforcement anonymously. I'm very good at drawing conclusions. I'm self-trained to some extent, but please don't forget, I worked the crime beat for years and I was married to a cop. A good cop. Tommy taught me everything he knew. And you were one of the ones who taught him."

Jackson gave Colleen a half smile. "Touché."

"Please don't blame me for all of this. All I've done is report the facts as I've seen them. Just like any good investigator would."

Jackson ran her hands through her hair. Colleen was jealous, because the more rumpled it got, the sexier it looked. Her own hair would do nothing of the sort; when it was mussed up, it just looked like she'd slept on it for days.

Jackson put her hair into a fluffy ponytail, then started playing with a ballpoint pen. "No one is faulting you, or blaming you, Colleen. I wish you had come to me before you shared your theories with the rest of the world, yes. But what's done is done. We just want to know what's going on, and why you and the Felon E blog are being used as the vehicle for these murders. We've confirmed that everyone that we know of who's been killed was a participant on your blog. Did you issue some sort of challenge to them recently, a contest or something?"

"Not that I know of. I went through my archives before I came down. I've done a couple of blogs on the Zodiac in the past, especially when they did the movie, but none on the Boston Strangler or Son of Sam. I haven't ever run a contest, that's not my kind of thing. As for a challenge, I don't know what you mean."

"Could you have accused someone of something, or asked your readers to rally around a certain case or victim?"

Had she? She racked her brain and came up with nothing. She shook her head mutely.

"Then why would he decide to use your blog in particular, of all the ones that are out there in the world? Why you, Colleen?"

Why me indeed. A deranged fan? A killer she'd helped put away who'd gotten parole?

"I can't tell you that. I have no idea why. All I know is what I reported, and the fact that my commenters are dying because of it."

"Not because of your story, I don't think. Your blog's been in play for a while. I wonder if you simply stumbled across something you weren't supposed to."

"Well, yesterday's hacking certainly left no doubt that whoever is responsible is aware of the blog, at the very least. There must have been a hundred comments that said, 'I know who you are.' And no one, *no one,* knows who I am."

"*Someone* obviously does. Your contacts know who you are, don't they? Or is everything you do anonymous?"

Jackson had a disconcerting way of leaning forward as she talked, right into Colleen's personal space. It was a good, solid interrogation technique: make the victim feel like they mattered, that you were hanging on every word. Colleen got the sense that very little passed by Taylor Jackson. She paid attention to every word out of Colleen's mouth, but was reading the context, her body language, the unspoken as much as the spoken. Tommy had said she was one hell of an investigator. Colleen understood how that could be the case—she was able to pry information out of the littlest details.

"Everything I do is supposed to be anonymous. I protect my identity as much as possible, especially from my contacts. They call me Felony. It's a private joke—"

"Yeah, on the blog's name. I get it. So if they don't know who you are, how do you get them to talk?"

"Any way that I can. I give them a sympathetic ear, mostly. Some want money. I'm willing to donate a little bit to the cause, twenty here, twenty there. I won't pay up front for a scoop. They have to be willing to share without recompense, I'll only pad their paws after they give me verifiable information. Honestly, you'd be surprised at how many people want to help for free, simply to see the right thing done."

"How many people do you have in Metro?"

Colleen almost laughed. Almost. Jackson's face had hardened; she didn't like this. Colleen couldn't blame her. The idea of her whole department leaking like a sieve might be a difficult point to swallow.

"I don't have anyone in this office, if that's what you're asking, Lieutenant. That's as far as I'm willing to go discussing my contacts. Right now, they aren't relevant. What we need to be worrying about is the fact that the victim pool is my commenters."

"I don't think anything is irrelevant, Colleen. We've already had a leak. One of the news stations in New York called here just a bit ago, asking questions. So first things first. Take down the blog," Jackson said.

Colleen stiffened in her seat. "No."

"Colleen. Be reasonable. You're putting your readers at risk every moment they're still in play. They count on you for entertainment, for news. Let them know they can count on you to keep them safe, too."

"I won't do it. I refuse to be chased off because some lunatic has it in for me."

"Has it in for *you?* It's your commenters he's killing. Your livelihood. Without the fans, would your blog be anything? Of course not. Really, Colleen. Listen very carefully. You're playing with fire. You've got too much to lose. This man will stop at nothing to get what he wants. You are disposable. You don't matter to him. You're a means to an end, and he will use you then kill you when you're no longer necessary to his little games. In the meantime, a lot of innocent people are going to be caught in the crossfire. I'm telling you, we need to take the blog down."

"No. Absolutely not. I won't be bullied into submission by a lunatic, or by the police. If I take it down, it will send a clear signal to everyone in this industry that they can be scared out of business. I have to stand up for all of us."

Jackson paused for a moment, then threw up her hands. "Fine. I'm sorry you feel that way. I suppose we'll just have to take it down for you."

Colleen rose from her chair. Fury coursed through her. "Don't you even think about—"

"It's already done." Jackson nodded to the door, where the handsome Detective Ross stood, a small frown on his face.

"How—"

"Detective Ross is one of the finest forensic detectives in the country. He's taken the site down, set in motion a system to contact your commenters and alert them to look after their safety."

"You can't do that. It's illegal. Client confidentiality."

"Once they leave a comment in the ether, it's public domain."

"No, no, no. It's not. It's a private domain. They have to register for the site. It's only open to commenters who have opted to give me their information, and those are the only ones who can participate in the comments. I have a strict privacy clause in place, drawn up by an intellectual-property-rights attorney, that they must agree to, not to mention the rights of the hosting company and the content management system I use. There is an expectation of privacy by joining my group. You can't contact them without my permission, or a warrant."

Jackson got right in her face. "Please. Give me a break, Colleen. It's just a blog. And if it's that private, the killer is on that list of people. We need those names."

Colleen started to sputter, but Jackson held up a hand. "Don't bother getting outraged. You're lucky we aren't charging you with obstruction. We need to be serious for a moment. Sit back down, take a deep breath, relax and start talking. You came to me for help, remember? Quit wasting my time if you don't have anything to add to the discussion besides bullshit."

Colleen stayed on her feet. "You're a bitch."

Jackson laughed, short and knowing, then grew serious. "Maybe I am. But I'm much more worried about saving lives than us being girlfriends. Okay? Can we stop playing around and get down to business? People are dying, Colleen. You, and your son, are in grave danger. If you won't do it for me, think of Flynn. Think about what Tommy would want you to do."

Colleen was defeated. She recognized the feeling. She'd just been outplayed. She didn't like it, but she had to respect the gamesmanship. For Jackson to use Colleen's dead husband and her living child against her was low, but it had served its purpose. She tamped down her own anger, sat back at the table and pulled a notebook from her bag. Flipped it open. Started to read aloud. Enjoyed the look of pure shock on the lieutenant's face as she started reading off the victims' names and her website numbers, and the Pretender's victim pool grew exponentially larger.

Thirty-Three

Taylor left Colleen in the conference room alternately vocalizing her anger with Taylor and casting coquettish glances at Lincoln. She found a quiet corner at the end of the hallway. The industrial fluorescents were overbright. Or maybe she was overtired. She glanced at her TAG Heuer watch, it was nearly morning. The interview had taken almost an hour, with Colleen fighting her every step of the way. She had enough information to go forward, but something was missing. Specifically, why Colleen had been targeted in the first place. There were plenty of true-crime blogs on the web. Even a couple of other national sites that were run out of Nashville, according to Colleen. So why her? There was something missing, a piece they were overlooking, but damn if she could see what that was.

Taylor leaned back against the wall and closed her eyes. What kind of game was Ewan Copeland playing? Was he responsible for the murders in New York, San Francisco and Boston? There was no way he could possibly be in all three places at once—he could have committed one of the series, but not all three, on two separate coasts. There was only one conclusion: he'd finally actualized his training from the Snow White Killer and recruited a group of apprentices to work alongside him, even going so far as to bring his own sister into the mix. The thought sent chills to her very marrow.

But more people meant more opportunities for leaks, for mistakes. And that might bring her the chance to end all of this sooner rather than later. All it would take to end her nightmare was a twitch of her forefinger. One clean shot, and the world would breathe easier.

She revisited her ongoing fantasy, thought about how she could lie in wait, and kill Copeland the moment she had confirmation that it was really him. She envisioned the setting—Copeland begging for his life, his pleas falling on deaf ears as she stood over him and shot without hesitation. The end.

Getting away from Baldwin and her team to enact such measures wouldn't be difficult. Deception was a part of her job, misleading statements, sleight of hand. She was a magician with real handcuffs.

Everything up to now has been a dress rehearsal, you bastard. I won't let you hurt anyone else I know.

God, she was tired.

"Are you okay?"

Taylor's eyes flew open at Baldwin's voice. He'd managed to sneak up on her. Good grief, had she dozed off standing, like a cow in a field? She nearly laughed at the image.

"I'm fine. You scared me."

"Sorry about that. I thought you might have a headache. Your forehead is all squinched up like it gets when something hurts." He ran his thumb softly across the two little wrinkles that appeared between her brows when she was frustrated or concentrating. Her railroad tracks, he called them, miniature furrows in her otherwise smooth skin. Her mother had good skin, and her grandmother before her. Lots of collagen. They'd both aged well, she hoped she'd get the same chance.

Something hurt, all right. The bleeding edge of her soul where she'd taken the knife and sliced off a piece the moment she'd decided on revenge as the only path to sanity. She tucked it away. There was plenty of time to wallow later.

"I'm good. Just thinking. What's happening with you?"

"Waiting on a bunch of call backs. It's rather frustrating not to be able to *do* anything."

"You're here. That's doing something." She pushed off the wall. "Want a coke?"

"Nothing cold. I need coffee. It's freezing in that interrogation room."

"I need a coke. Sorry you had to suffer. I keep it cold in there on purpose. Makes the bad guys 'fess up quicker. I have a hard time keeping a straight face when I'm in court and they play video of the interrogations. Watching the suspects try to warm their hands with the cuffs on is a source of great amusement for me."

"Taylor, my dear, you are a first-class sadist."

"You know it."

They started walking, shoulders touching. Taylor took comfort in the contact. It reminded her that even though she was alone in this, she had someplace to turn if she backed out, or if she truly needed a safe place to run to.

"How's Colleen Keck?" Baldwin asked.

They reached the soda machine. Baldwin peeled a dollar out of his wallet and put it in, chivalrously handed the Diet Coke to Taylor. She accepted it, cracked the lid and took a long drink before she answered.

"I had to have Lincoln take the blog down, but that's as far as I can go. Colleen is not cooperating the way I'd like. She's more worried about protecting her sources than helping us stop the Pretender. Without her permission to scan the personal information of the blog commenters, I'll have to get a warrant, and warrants take time. I lied a little, told her we were already contacting them, but she's no dummy, she knew we couldn't do that without securing paper first. I left Lincoln in with her, she seems to have developed some rapport with him. If that doesn't work, I thought I'd let you have a go at her, see if she'll soften up."

"What is she hiding?"

"I wish I knew. She's certainly aware of the situation, and she's given me enough so I can start calling the other jurisdictions. She's holding something back, and damned if I know what it is, or why."

"What other jurisdictions?"

"Boston and New York, so far. I just got a call from Paul Friend at Fox News, they're putting the story together. It's only a matter of time before the whole world knows."

"Do we need to bring Hall and the North Carolina guys in on this, too?"

"According to Colleen. She's profiled the cases and feels they're all connected."

Baldwin was silent for a moment. "She's probably right."

"Hell, I know that. Copeland's sister in North Carolina, and some of his other little buddies scattered across the country? He's showing off, telling us how much control he has. And he's two steps ahead of us.

That's the problem. What in the name of all that's holy is a *blogger* doing putting together the pieces of my case before I get a chance to?"

"Your case. You're assuming jurisdiction of the case?"

"Of Keck's portion of it, yes. Keck is my responsibility now. We need to find out how he knows her online persona as Felon E, and fast. I think she's just being used as a tool, because she has a direct connection to me. I was her husband's training officer. Only for a couple of weeks, but that's long enough. I passed the sergeant's exam, got transferred into plain clothes, and he was picked up by another officer. Two years later, Tommy Keck was shot in the line of duty, doing a drug stop out on Interstate 40. The shooting is on video. Keck walked back to the car he'd pulled over, and the driver laughed as he shot him. Car took off, left Keck lying on the side of the road, drowning in his own blood. It was all over the news. Colleen had given birth just a few weeks earlier. He was just back from paternity leave. It was terrible. Just…senseless."

"And now Colleen Keck has become a pawn in Ewan Copeland's game. We should look into her past as well, just in case. Where is she from?"

"I don't know. What bothers me is he's decided to start pulling ancillary people into the game. Tommy's been dead for a long time, and though I've met Colleen, it was only a couple of times, and at his funeral. I didn't even recognize her when she showed up. She looks… different."

"Grief does that to a person."

"Of course it does. But that was four years ago. I wasn't on Copeland's radar then. It wasn't until Snow White reemerged that he caught wind of me. We've always agreed that he saw me on the television at the beginning of that case."

Baldwin tapped his forefinger against his front teeth. "Maybe. Maybe not. We've been assuming that. Assumptions are very dangerous things. Once we add the Kecks into the equation…I don't know, Taylor. You could have come across him much earlier than that."

"No. No way. How?"

"I don't know. But I think we should do a records search, see if we find anything."

"Search what records?"

"All of them. Everything Metro and the FBI has. I think we should go back through your arrest record, and I'd like to put together a ViCAP query as well. You've been his target all along. He's showing off for you. Haven't you ever asked yourself, why?"

"Every day."

"I think we need to think differently about this. We need to pull all the minds together, in one place. Let everyone have a hand in."

"Your team and my team? Or are you thinking a task force?" As she said it, she felt her heart drop. Was he starting to get the idea that she was planning to hunt the Pretender down, was trying to distract her with procedure? She must be more transparent than she thought. Task forces meant layer upon layer of accountability. Accountability took time. Time was a luxury she couldn't permit. Not if she was going to finish things herself.

"Multiple jurisdictions, multiple cases. That might be the easiest way to coordinate. We let them worry about the other states so we can focus on Tennessee. On you."

Crap, he *was* getting suspicious. She played with

the tab on the top of the Diet Coke. "I don't know, Baldwin. Besides, that's out of my hands, I can't make that call. Task forces cost real money. It's way above my pay grade, and you're on suspension, so it's out of yours, too. I'm going to call Emily Callahan up in New York, see if she knows what's going on with the case up there, then report to Commander Huston and drag A.D.A. Page out of bed. Let Julia handle Colleen's privacy protestations."

"Callahan. I've always had a soft spot for her, considering. Tell her I said hello."

Considering the fact that instead of honeymooning in Italy, they'd spent a couple of days in New York with then-detective-third-grade Emily Callahan from the 108th precinct of Long Island, trying to solve the case of the Snow White, the bastard who was the Pretender's maker. He was dead and gone, now, a victim of his creation. She hoped the Pretender would soon follow in his mentor's footsteps.

They reached the break room, and Taylor decided to change the subject.

"Enough of all this. What have you been doing? I thought you'd pop in on me and Colleen."

Baldwin sighed heavily. "I've been on the phone with Kevin. He's been working on Ruth Anderson's hard drive. If there's something to find, he'll get it."

Taylor had always wanted to get Lincoln Ross and Kevin Salt in a room together and set them to work on the same impossible task, just to see who could finish faster. She'd put money on Lincoln, but Salt was worth every penny Baldwin paid him.

"Can you do that? I thought you were suspended."

He gave a rueful laugh. "I am. Couldn't be better timing, either. My team is working directly with SSA

Hall. They flew the evidence from North Carolina to Quantico. Garrett is in charge of things for the time being, but Kevin is keeping me informed. Right now, I'm afraid I'm a man without a country."

"Hmm. A man without a country, yet Kevin was happy to give you the particulars..."

Baldwin smiled. "Well, to his credit, he snuck the call in from the bathroom. I may have to promote his ass when I get my command back. Anyway, it's going to take more time. Ruth Anderson has been in contact with an awful lot of people."

"Surely Ewan Copeland is in her system? Can't we find out where he is from that?"

"They've been covering their tracks for years. It's going to take more than a couple of hours. Kevin's a genius, but he's only one man. And as far as we can tell, Copeland hasn't used that name since he was eighteen and got spat out of juvie. He completely dropped off the radar."

"Right."

"Tell you what. Why don't we head back to the house, take a shower, catch an hour's worth of sleep. You're dead on your feet, I can see your molars every time you yawn."

"I'm not yawning," she said, just as her jaw spontaneously opened, wide enough that her ears cracked.

"Yeah, right. Make your calls, then I'm taking you home for a couple of hours."

She had to admit he was right. These were the in-between hours, when paperwork created lag time, research was under way and information was barely trickling in.

She decided to be smart. She might as well take advantage of the momentary lull. She had no idea when she'd get another chance to rest. They'd call if they found anything relevant.

"It's going to take Julia Page a while to secure the warrant, I'll have Marcus or McKenzie type it up. Callahan won't be in the office for a couple of hours, no sense dragging her out of bed so early. And she's on eastern time, it's an hour later there. Let me tell the boys I'm taking off. A couple of hours of sleep wouldn't hurt. I'll meet you in the parking lot in five."

She watched Baldwin walk away, waited until he was out of site, then started down the hall to her office.

Maybe she could parade through the lot, or wander up the street, see if he took a shot? He wasn't in the building, and so long as she was safely ensconced in the CJC, he couldn't get at her. She needed to be outside, out in the open, marking her scent along the trees, drawing him closer and closer.

If only it would be so easy. No. She'd been in Nashville long enough now that if he were here, he'd know she was back and gunning for him. It was time to start hunting.

Thirty-Four

Taylor had never been happier to see her exit.

She'd thought about getting a condo downtown for years, and with the influx of housing in the Gulch, Terrazzo and The Icon opening with their rooftop pools and private security, she was even more tempted. She'd spent most of her adult life in a cabin atop a hill west of town, and when she and Baldwin got engaged, they'd bought a home together, one that was big enough for them both to have offices, and a beautiful bonus room for her pool table. She loved the house. It was open and airy, lovingly decorated in their eclectic style, but at times like these, when she was hauling herself home, twenty minutes from downtown, she wished she had something closer. Driving, hell, walking a few streets over from the office would be a nice change, especially when she was this tired.

Her insomnia was getting worse the older she got, and she'd noticed that lately her waking hours were tinged with a slight fog. Stress and years of sleepless nights were finally catching up with her. When she did sleep it was due to sheer exhaustion. Not good. Situations like that would take her off her game if she wasn't careful. She would run, run, run then collapse, never getting the right amount of sleep, and to be honest, until now, never really having to. She could do with three or four hours a night and be perfectly fine.

Maybe it was just this case, the horror of what happened to Fitz, the pressure she'd put on herself to eliminate the threat to her life's order, but she was feeling the lack of sleep keenly. It worried her. She didn't want to be anything less than razor-sharp right now. Since she didn't know how long this case would drag on, she really needed to start taking better care of herself. Even the tiniest slip could derail her world, and she couldn't afford any mistakes. Not now. Not when she was so close.

After this case was over, she could always get Sam to give her something to sleep. Or Baldwin, though she hated admitting her weakness to him. She liked that he reveled in her strength. It made her feel even stronger, more inspired. No, Sam was the place to go. Even if it was just for a night, she could recharge the batteries.

Baldwin had been quiet on the way home. She loved their silences as much as their conversations. It was a sign of true love to her that she could be quiet with him, letting the air charge with electricity without ever saying a word. He had a stillness inside of him, a deep inner peace, which attracted her like a fly to honey. She had the same piece of quietude within her, and the two spoke to each other wordlessly, their bodies flowing in a symbiotic dance.

He pulled into the garage and smiled at her. "Go upstairs. I'll meet you there in a few minutes."

She was happy to oblige. She felt her body dragging as she mounted the steps. The sun getting ready to rise, casting meager light through the blinds. She pulled the curtains shut so the room was totally dark, stripped off her clothes and fell naked into the freezing bed. She was asleep before her head hit the pillow.

Baldwin paced the downstairs, making laps through the dining room, foyer, living room, kitchen, dining room. He knew he needed to get some sleep. He was just as deep in the slumber deficit as Taylor was, and she'd been visibly dragging. As tired as he was, his mind wouldn't stop spinning. The idea that Taylor had come across Ewan Copeland's radar earlier than they'd originally thought was haunting him. If he'd known that, he would have approached this case very differently.

He stopped to put the kettle on, maybe some herbal tea would help him relax. He was amped up on caffeine and adrenaline, and pure, unadulterated fear. Losing Taylor was something he'd never be able to handle. He knew that now. The mere thought that he'd miscalculated, that he could have gotten her hurt or killed with his mistake, nearly handicapped him fully. All he wanted to do was get Taylor on a plane, get her the hell out of here. Find some little tropical island where he could buy off the local constabulary to keep them safe and protected, hire a phalanx of bodyguards and nestle down until this bastard was caught.

Not rational, but tempting. Very tempting.

The stove's small burner was taking forever to heat up. He decided to go out and get the mail from yesterday. They'd been gone to North Carolina and he'd not bothered to get it when they first arrived home. He disabled the alarm so the beeping wouldn't wake Taylor and slipped out the front door. Sunlight streamed into his eyes, making him squint. He put his hand to his forehead to block the light—fresh, new sun, first of the day, as blinding as a strobe light.

The mailbox was full, the usual crap. He thumbed through the stack as he walked back to the house. Bill. Bill. Credit card solicitation, two of them, one for him and one for Taylor. Catalogs from stores they'd never shopped. Magazines. He sighed. Just a bunch of junk. He shuffled the edges back together as he returned to the house.

He almost missed it.

If he hadn't tripped on the step and dropped the stack, he wouldn't have seen it until it was too late. It spilled out onto the brick patio, buried between the magazines. A red envelope, with the name *Taylor* hand-printed on the front. It wasn't glued closed, the flap was just tucked into the bottom of the envelope. He used his pen to feed it open. There was a Valentine's Day card inside.

He opened it, ignoring the schmaltzy words in favor of reading the note inside. It said:

Roses are Red
Violets are Blue
Colleen Keck is Dead
And So Are You.

Inside the card was a thin, clear plastic case with what looked like a CD inside.

He dropped everything on the steps and rushed inside the house, slammed the door behind himself, took the stairs two at a time.

Their bedroom was dark, quiet, the only noise Taylor's soft breathing.

She was fine.

He wasn't. He was thoroughly rattled. He watched her sleep for a few minutes, then quietly went through the entire house, clearing closets and bathrooms. No one there. No traps, no tricks. The son of a bitch was playing with them again.

He retreated to the downstairs, did the same sweep, then went back out to grab the mail. It was scattered on the front steps where he'd dropped it. He picked up the card from the concrete, ignoring the words this time, looking at the jewel case.

Using thc American Express envelope balanced against a *Clipper Magazine,* he flipped the case over. There was writing on the CD itself, block letters in black marker. Numbers. Before he could decipher them, he felt his heart rate rise, the hair stand up on the back of his neck. Someone was behind him.

Jesus.

He went very still.

So this was it. Even on high alert he'd been caught unawares, standing outside his own home. The front door was unlocked, the alarm momentarily disabled. Perfect timing. How could he have been so stupid, to let his guard down when Taylor was at her most vulnerable?

Nothing. No shots, no sounds.

He couldn't help himself, he looked over his shoulder.

There were two men standing on either side of him. Big boys, fit, heavy through the torsos, wearing sunglasses and holsters. Neither one moved, nor went for their weapons.

He was still breathing.

Baldwin took his time standing up. He gathered the

stack of mail, then smoothed his pants down. A lapse in his mental judgment, going to the mailbox unarmed, unseeing, rushing into the house, leaving the door unlocked. Caught up in his own mind, so focused that he kept forgetting what was at stake.

The men didn't move.

"Gentlemen," he said finally. "What can I do for you?"

"Is Miss Taylor okay, sir?"

Sir. Miss Taylor. Deferential. His breath came back, he had to force himself not to gust out a huge, relieved sigh. They were on the job. Taylor's guards.

"She's asleep. Who are you?"

"I'm Wells. That's Rogers. Miss Taylor hired us. Personal protection. She missed her call in."

He wasn't stupid, he wasn't going to take any more chances. He should have done this back in North Carolina before things went to shit.

"ID. Now."

They pulled out credentials, pictures that matched their faces, the *P* overlaid with a dollar sign, Price's insignia, stamped plainly on their papers. Everything looked legit.

The bigger of the two shifted slightly, a subtle movement. Baldwin saw that his hand was now resting on the butt of his gun.

"Sir, I have to ask again. Where is Miss Taylor?"

"She's fine. We're exposed. Come inside," Baldwin said.

The men followed him without hesitation, he wondered exactly how forceful his voice must have sounded. They didn't work for him; they worked for her. Maybe she'd told them to follow instructions from Baldwin, too? No, that didn't sound like Taylor. Damn woman, prancing off on her own to arrange her security. Like the FBI wasn't enough. Like *he* wasn't enough.

He composed himself as the two men crowded into the kitchen. They were wide, not as tall as Baldwin but much thicker through the chest and forearms. Strong. Capable.

"Tea?" he asked, motioning toward the kettle.

They both shook their heads. Baldwin assumed tea wasn't exactly the right drink for these two. Battery acid on the rocks, perhaps.

"You'll forgive us, sir, but we need to lay eyes on her, make sure she's okay firsthand. Orders from Mr. Price," Wells said.

"I understand. She's fine, she just crashed. I wanted her to get some sleep. It's been a long couple of days."

"Tell me about it. But—"

"I'm not waking her up so you can satisfy Price's curiosity, you understand?" Baldwin tried to keep his tone pleasant, but he'd had just about enough. Wells recognized the signs of impending anger, weighed his choices, then nodded briefly.

"Give me a second," he said, then flipped open a cell phone. Baldwin heard Price's voice on the other end of the phone. Wells relayed a status update, said "uh-huh" a couple of times then handed the phone to Baldwin.

"He wants to speak to you."

Baldwin took the phone.

"Hello, Mitchell."

"Well, you don't sound as angry as I expected. She told me you called off your dogs. I think she's just scared, Baldwin, and hates to admit it to you."

"You could have given me a heads-up when she called."

"And risk the wrath of Khan? Hell no. That's her business. Her cash."

"You're right, Mitchell. It's her choice who to trust right now. I won't keep you, I just wanted to confirm that these boys were yours."

"They are. Keep safe, Baldwin. Keep her safe for me."

Baldwin clicked the phone off and handed it to Wells, who stowed it in jacket pocket.

"We'll just wait here until she wakes up, sir."

"Fine. Have a seat. She's been out for about an hour, I'm going to wake her up at seven. Try not to break anything while you wait."

They didn't sit, but Wells leaned against the kitchen counter, meaty arms in a pyramid across his chest. His partner, Rogers, was the quieter of the two. He simply stared at the floor as if he found the wood grain the most interesting thing he'd ever seen, looking up occasionally as if asking permission to continue imitating a statue.

Baldwin shrugged and left them to their devices. Damn if he didn't feel good having them around. This was all spinning out of control, the grains of sand shifting through the hourglass faster and faster. He could feel it in the very air that surrounded them, a sense of expectation, of doom. They were hurtling toward the resolution of the case whether they wanted it or not.

He called in to Lincoln and asked about Colleen Keck. She was apparently fine, madder than a wet hen that she wasn't being allowed to leave, but safe, and alive. So the card wasn't entirely accurate. Just another stupid threat. He told Lincoln to take extra precautions, then hung up the phone.

He discarded the mail on the counter and put on

a pair of purple nitrile gloves from the stash in the kitchen's junk drawer. The beef brothers watched him with interest.

The CD jewel case was taped closed. It had been hand-delivered, obviously. No postmark on the envelope, nothing that could be traced. Smart, creepy as hell. He hated that the Pretender knew where they lived, could access their home at any time.

"Hey, did either of you guys watch the house over the past day?"

Wells shook his head. "No, sir. We followed you to Forest City. Damn boring drive, I'll tell you that."

"What, the majesty of the Blue Ridge didn't do it for you?"

"I prefer the Rockies, sir. Those are real mountains. Better yet, insert me through a HALO jump twenty-five thousand feet above the Hindu Kush. That's some fun times."

Wells almost cracked a smile. Almost. Rogers looked interested for the first time.

Mercenaries. Ex-military yahoos, back in the States. Professional tough guys, keeping tabs on his fiancée. He didn't know whether to be furious or grateful.

"Well, while y'all were on our tail, our killer dropped this in our mailbox."

"We should call that in, sir," Wells said, reaching for his pocket.

"Just hold on, okay? Let me see what this is first."

Wells stopped. There was something to be said for career soldiers, they took instruction well.

Baldwin went to the pantry and took out a small toolbox, one equipped for a rudimentary forensic investigation. A to-go kit. He withdrew fingerprint powder and a brush. Prepped the jewel case, then brushed the powder over the slick casing. Nothing. He used a scalpel to slice through the tape that held it open, then took up a fresh brush and followed the same procedure on the inside. It was too much to hope that there would be prints… Disappointed again. Clean as a whistle.

He took the CD from the case and read the letters. It was gibberish. A bunch of numbers and letters, which meant nothing to him. He was decent at codes, it was one of the weird little things he'd picked up, but nothing was leaping out, announcing itself. He ran it through his mental ciphers, still nothing.

He carefully copied the letters and numbers into his notebook, then left the kitchen for the living room. They had a Bose stereo system. He popped the CD in and hit Play. Turned the volume down so whatever was on the CD wouldn't go booming out into the world and wake Taylor.

The strains of some familiar music started, and Baldwin shook his head. What a crude, silly attempt to send a message.

It was a song from the fifties, by the Platters. He'd never thought of it in this context. It was perfect for a stalker.

"Oh, yes, I'm the great pretender…I'm lonely, but no one can tell…you've left me to dream, all alone."

Jesus. He was overcome with rage. This goddamn freak was getting on his nerves.

"What's it mean, sir?" Wells asked. He and Rogers had come into the living room, obviously concerned. Baldwin realized he'd been clutching the jewel case so hard that it had shattered. A small drop of blood dripped off the end of his finger onto the hardwood floor, followed by quicker, more insistent drops. Crap. He'd cut himself badly.

He pushed Stop on the player, ignored Wells and Rogers's offers of help, and went to the kitchen. Grabbed a towel from the drawer and wrapped it around his hand. Stalked back into the living room to see how much blood he'd spilled on the floor. Wondered how many more chances he was going to get.

Thirty-Five

Taylor heard voices, then music. What in the world? She forced her eyes open. Good. She'd slept. She sat up, surprised at how refreshed she felt. Just a couple of hours of rest, but rest it was. She'd dreamed heavily, not her usual dark, murky nightmares, but of a happy, smiling man wrapped in a rust-colored sheet. A monk. Holding out a small, thin piece of string for her to tie around her wrist, his toothless smile engaging and encouraging. "Protection," he'd said.

Protection. Her hand went to her wrist. It was bare.

If only dreams were capable of such powers.

She pulled back the covers, dressed and hurried downstairs. Baldwin was standing in the middle of the living room, bleeding, and two very large men were standing on either side of him. What in the hell were they doing in the house? And why was Baldwin bleeding? Damn it.

"Gentlemen?"

All three of them started. The two bodyguards' hands instinctively strayed to their weapons before they caught themselves. Baldwin gestured to the men.

"Your guards," he said.

She was struck by the coldness of his tone. Something had happened while she was asleep, that was obvious.

She met his eyes for a moment, tried to ignore the frustration and questions in them, then addressed the guards. “Wells, Rogers, we’re fine here, as you can see. Why don’t you wait outside. We’ll be heading back to the CJC shortly.”

“Yes, ma’am,” Wells said. They turned and went to the front door, slipped out quietly. Stealthy, for such large men.

When they were finally alone, Taylor turned back to Baldwin. “What happened?”

“They got the drop on me. I was getting the mail. They seem very capable.” He shrugged, she could read the embarrassment in the line of his shoulders. There was more he wasn’t saying, but she didn’t push. He’d tell her when he was ready; she could feel him struggling with something. When he turned and went to the kitchen, she followed behind. A change of subject was in order.

“Let me see your hand,” she said.

“It’s fine,” he said, but let her glance at it to prove he was okay. She ran the water in the sink, let the blood wash down the drain. It was a shallow cut, but a bleeder. The gaping edges were already starting to clot and crust.

“I think you’ll live, but let me put some alcohol on it, just in case. How did you cut it?”

“We received a gift in the mail.” She retrieved the first-aid kit from the cabinet and went to work. He hissed as she dosed the cut in alcohol, then let her slowly wipe the excess off, apply Neosporin and close it with a large Band-Aid. Echoes of the ministrations that had been performed on her back in Forest City.

"How's your leg?" he asked automatically. Reading her thoughts again.

"It's fine. I haven't thought about it in hours." Which was true, but now that she remembered, her shin gave a throb. "I'll change the dressing on it later."

She brought his hand to her mouth and kissed the bandage.

"All better?"

"We'll see," he said, and the obliqueness of his tone made her take a step back. He really was upset, just keeping it hidden, right below the surface. Was he mad at her? Or was it something else?

"What came in the mail, Baldwin?"

He flexed his fingers a few times, as if testing the binding. He made a fist and didn't grimace. She knew he was okay.

"Our friend sent us a message. Though I'll be damned if I know what to make of it. Come on, I'll show you."

The Valentine's card was on the counter where he'd left it. She opened it with a pen, read the words. Was surprised at how little they affected her. She was becoming inured to his threats. This was just a game to Copeland, just a stupid game. No wonder Baldwin was so peeved. He was poking at them, just trying to get a rise.

She let the card close.

Baldwin led her back to the living room and pressed play on the stereo. Music streamed from the speakers.

After a moment, she said, "The Platters?"

"Yep. There's more. Writing on the disc. He burned it himself, it's not an original recording."

"Let's see it."

Baldwin ejected the CD midwail and handed it to Taylor.

"It's gibberish to me. I don't see any rhyme or reason to it."

At first glance, she had to agree. There were just a bunch of numbers and letters, none that spelled out anything obvious.

"White board," she said, heading up the stairs to her office. She erased everything that was on the board, then wrote down the numbers and letters at the top, enjoying the strange scent of the erasable marker and its small, squeaking scratches as she wrote. She loved her white board.

When she was finished, she stood back and looked at the string.

148NAD77HCBOTM4482901QRE

"What about a VIN?" Taylor asked.

"Nope. Vehicle Identification Numbers are only seventeen digits. That's twenty-four."

"You remember when we used to get actual airline tickets? There was always that huge long string at the bottom that didn't make sense, but it was really the codes for the airports, and the equipments, dates and seat numbers. Maybe that's it."

"Good idea."

They started playing with combinations of letters, breaking them into groups, writing them backward, but nothing was apparent. No call signs for airports, no dates, nothing that made logical sense.

Baldwin was getting frustrated, his hair was standing on end. Taylor smoothed it down, then wiped away all their conjecture, leaving them with the original numbers and letters at the top of the board.

"Let's look at this a different way. He's sending us a message. What do we think is happening, right now?"

"He's playing a game."

"Right. And we know that he has probably recruited people to play with him. There have been three recent copycat crimes that we know of." She stared at the board, mind whirling.

"Break it into threes?" She transcribed the numbers on the board.

148NAD77 HCBOTM4 482901QRE

"Still means nothing."

She had the first glimmers of an idea. "Let me see the disc again," Taylor said.

Baldwin handed it to her. She looked closely at the placement of the letters, then wrote a new pattern on the board.

148NAD77HCBOTM4482 901QRE

"It looks like there's a space between the first string of letters and numbers and the end. If we break that off, then separate them into three sections…"

She scribbled on the board, then stood back and looked.

148NAD 77HCB OTM4482 901QRE

"License plate numbers?" she said, and heard Baldwin suck in his breath. He tapped the computer on her desk to life, fingers flying over the keys as he accessed a database through his FBI identification.

"Damn, you're good. That's got to be it. Let me call Kevin, have him put some elbow grease into this." He smiled at her, his face radiant, and she knew she was forgiven her transgression.

Would he feel the same way if he knew she'd killed a man on purpose?

She shoved that thought away.

She took the CD and put it into her laptop, stepped out of the room so she wouldn't interrupt Baldwin. Went into their guest room, sat on the bed, and hit Play. The song spilled out of the computer, and she listened carefully to the lyrics. They gave her the creeps. Such a simple song, perverted for a psycho's purpose.

The song finished, and there was silence, deafening quiet. She started to press the eject button, then heard something. Leaning closer, she turned the speakers up as far as they could go. There was rustling, like a plastic bag being wadded up, then a cough. She strained to hear more, but there was nothing. Then a deep voice spoke.

"Don't be late, Taylor. We'll be waiting."

The CD spun to a stop.

She froze for a moment. We'll be waiting. We who? Ewan Copeland and Ruth Anderson? Ewan and his copycat monsters?

Her mind flashed back to the white board, to the last set of numbers, the ones that had given her the idea to break them apart from the rest anyway.

901QRE

We'll be waiting.

It hit her like a landslide, and she yelled for Baldwin.

She heard him excuse himself from the phone and rush to the room immediately.

"What's wrong? You're white as a sheet."

"The last numbers. I was wrong. They aren't a license plate."

"What are they?"

"I don't know what the E is, but 901QR has to be 901 Quaker Run."

The significance dawned on him. "Oh, my God."

"That's Sam's address. Baldwin, he's got Sam."

Thirty-Six

To: bostonboy@ncr.bb.com, 44caliber@ncr.ss.com,
crypto@ncr.zk.com
From: troy14@ncr.tr.com
Subject: Game Over

Gentlemen,
My deepest apologies to share this untimely news, but your covers are blown.

Accelerate the schedule and rendezvous at your predesignated final assignment.

Time to come to Papa. And hurry.
The Pretender

Thirty-Seven

Taylor had never felt the level of panic that was cruising through her system. Despite that, she stayed outwardly calm. She picked up the phone and speed-dialed her best friend's cell number.

It went directly to voice mail, a sign that the phone had been turned off. Taylor ended the call, then dialed Sam's house. Simon Loughley, Sam's husband, answered the phone. Taylor could hear the twins crying in the background. She tried to sound as normal as possible.

"Hi, Simon. Sam around?"

"Hey, Taylor. Good to hear from you. No, she has the overnight shift this week, probably up to her elbows in entrails right about now. She has a doctor's appointment this morning, too. She's not supposed to be home until around ten or so. Hey, are you and Baldwin coming to Thanksgiving? No, let me rephrase. Please tell me you and Baldwin are coming to Thanksgiving. Sam can't drink, and you know how she gets when she's pregnant on national holidays."

Taylor fought the rising nausea. *It's okay. She's okay.*

She's at work. Nothing can happen to her while she's at Forensic Medical.

"We'd love to, Simon. We're planning to be there. I've got to run, I need to track her down. I'll—I'll tell her I talked to you and told you we'd come, okay?"

"Everything all right, Taylor? You sound tense."

"Big case. Lots of stress. You know how it is."

"I do. Be good. See you Thursday, okay?"

She swallowed hard. "Of course. Kiss the twins for me."

She hung up the phone and sought Baldwin's hand. He grasped hers, gave it a good hard squeeze.

"Should you tell him what's going on? Simon has a good head on his shoulders. He won't panic."

"We don't know there's a problem yet. There's no reason to scare him for nothing."

"You're right. It's going to be okay. I'll call Forensic Medical, see if I can locate her there." He flipped open his cell phone.

A horrible thought crossed her mind. "Hold on. I have to get Simon and the twins covered. Maybe he's planning to hit them instead of Sam." As she said it, she knew it wasn't the truth, but it was better than doing nothing. She called McKenzie's cell phone.

"Hey there. We got the warrant for Colleen's blog participants." he said, exhaustion making his voice hoarse.

She cut him off. "I need you to do me a favor, okay? No questions. Please go to Sam's house and keep an eye on Simon and the kids. Don't let anyone near them, for any reason. You understand me?"

McKenzie's voice sharpened. "Yes. Are you okay?"

"I am. I've gotten what I believe might be a threat

against Sam, and I don't want to take any chances. Take extra weapons, get backup, but most of all, be discreet. I don't want Simon freaking out on me, okay?"

"He's going to be suspicious. Where is Sam now?"

"I don't know yet. I'm looking for her. She worked the overnight shift. I'm going down there right now. Just get to Simon, secure him and the kids, okay?"

"I'll be there in ten minutes. Call me and let me know what's happening, okay?"

"I will. Thanks, Renn."

Baldwin was ending his call, too. "There's no answer, just the overnight message."

Taylor tried Sam's cell again. No joy.

She shut her eyes and took a deep breath, felt a shattering tranquility course through her. She would not let anything happen to Sam. No. Absolutely not. This was her responsibility, her job. And the opportunity she'd been hoping for. She knew in her heart he wouldn't kill Sam, not yet, anyway. He'd want to torture Taylor first, make her run all over town trying to figure out where Sam was. He wouldn't do anything to her until Taylor could see, could watch. He wanted an audience, wanted her approval, in a sense. Or her fear. Taking Fitz while he was out of town was just meant to get her attention. This was going to be his final showdown.

Taylor wasn't going to go at this willy-nilly. She had a plan. She'd been preparing herself for this moment for days.

She turned to Baldwin. "We need a BOLO on Sam's car. Kris will have the license number in the personnel files. I'm going over there right now to talk to Kris. She'll be there by the time I drive across town. I need to get a hold of Sam's schedule, see what she had going on last night. I'm going to track every movement she made, and I *will* find her."

"I'm going with you."

"No."

"What?" His voice, laden with shock, went up an octave.

"No. I need you to do something else for me. I need you to find out why Colleen is involved in this. I'm assuming she's being targeted, too."

"Sam is designed to draw you out, Taylor. I will not let that happen."

"I have the boys outside, remember? They will stay on me, and I'll be perfectly safe with them. They won't let anything happen to me. You saw that."

"I did, but…"

"Honey, we have to split up. There's too much to figure out. And we don't have any more time. We are out of time."

"Taylor—"

She stopped his protestations with her mouth. She kissed him, fierce and hard. There was a wild violence to it, no regret, no holding back. He responded, wrapping his arms around her and practically breaking her ribs. When she finally pulled away, her breath came in ragged gasps. She let her heartbeat start to slow, then said one word.

"Please."

He looked her in the eye, and understood what she was saying. She felt his arms loosen fractionally, then he released her.

"Okay, Taylor. We'll play this your way. But for Christ's sake, be careful."

"I will," she said. And she meant it. She'd carefully aim before she put a bullet in Ewan Copeland's brain.

* * *

Taylor had a regular pace going now—redial, ring, hang up, redial, ring, hang up. Sam could have forgotten to turn the phone on. The battery could have died. She could have left it in her office drawer. There were many, many innocent explanations for why she wasn't answering. But Taylor knew that wasn't the case. She knew in her soul that Ewan Copeland had her best friend.

She heard Baldwin's BMW leave the garage. She didn't think she was ever going to get him to agree to her plan. But he'd capitulated, for what was probably the first and only time in their relationship.

She needed the key to their safe. They'd upgraded to a 14-gun Sentry safe after the Pretender's first letter, when she knew he was aware of where she lived. Her home. Her most vulnerable place. It was full to the brim and had a double lock, one keyed, one combination, an extra deterrent to any thieves, or accidental discoveries. She had a lot of important things in that safe, she didn't want to run the risk of someone accidentally stumbling across them.

They kept the key in Baldwin's office filing cabinet, probably not the most secure place—even though it locked, they rarely turned the key. It was convenient if they ever needed in quickly. They didn't get into the big safe regularly anyway. It was there to protect their fun guns and a few important documents.

She'd already decided to take the Ruger with her, and a worn 9 mm Beretta. Both were recently cleaned, road tested first at the gun show where she'd purchased them, then out in the woods behind their house. They were reliable, and disposable. There was a Walther PPK in there as well, plus a few others, not to mention rifles and shotguns, but all of those were registered in either her or Baldwin's name.

In the off chance that she was able to get the Pretender alone, away from everyone and everything that she stood for, she needed a throwaway weapon, one that was unregistered, off the grid. All the cops she knew had a few hanging around, for whatever reason. She wasn't dirty, she'd never carried them with her to a scene, never.

But this was different. In this situation, she was dirty. She was going to kill a man, premeditated and in cold blood, and she needed to be prepared for all the contingencies. If she couldn't make it look like self-defense, she'd have to cover her tracks. She felt soiled, sullied in a way she'd never experienced, but shook it off. This man, this killer, was threatening her, threatening her family. Like a rabid dog, he needed to be stopped. He needed to be put down.

She was just the woman for the job.

Baldwin's office was spotless. He had everything perfectly organized, the desktop clean, a small stack of paper filed in his outbox, his mouse pad and mouse just so. She smiled at the precision, the cleanliness. The order of his mind, the very essence of his abilities, laid out in the symmetry and perfection that was in evidence before her.

Just like Sam. The two of them were her anchors, her life. If something happened to either of them…

Nothing would. She was going to make sure of that.

They kept the key stashed in between several of his files. She pulled on the drawer, surprised to feel resistance. It was locked. Using her house keys, she unlocked the cabinet. Rifled through to the spot where the key was hidden. Reached into the file and pulled back the metal. She started to close the filing cabinet drawer, but heard something, like a piece of paper was caught in the tracks. She ran the drawer back and forth, yes, something was sticking out, making a *shurring* noise. It was all the way in the back of the cabinet, past the file she'd just pilfered. She pulled the drawer out fully, extending it as far as it would go. Something was taped to the topside of the cabinet.

She pulled the loose corner, that was what had caught on the edge of the drawer, and felt the paper give way. She backed it out carefully, the tape peeling back slowly. She didn't want to damage it, she knew immediately that she wasn't meant to see this.

But she was feeling reckless, and Baldwin would never know. In case something happened, she wanted to find out what was so important to him to hide from her.

The last of the tape pulled free. She extracted it from the cabinet. Flipped it over. Felt the blood drain from her face, her head go swimmy.

It was a picture of a boy. Maybe two years old. Posed, in a soccer uniform. He had flaming-red hair, the color that would darken into bronze as the child aged. His face was still unformed, the skin pale and creamy, barely freckled, just beginning to show the edges of high, slanting cheekbones. It was the eyes that were unmistakable. They were the clear green of the forest after a spring rain. Bright. Wide. Stunning.

Baldwin's eyes.

She had absolutely no doubt in her mind that she was looking at a child that had been fathered by her fiancé.

Her breath caught in her throat. She felt like she was going to faint.

Baldwin had a son.

Thirty-Eight

Taylor felt her legs begin to give, wisely stepped back from the sharp edges of the cabinet and sat down hard on the carpet, the picture still clutched in her hand.

A son. Baldwin has a son.

This was what he'd been keeping from her. This was the big secret. What he'd nearly confessed to her in the car to North Carolina. No wonder he hadn't been able to articulate his thoughts. How did you tell the woman you love that you have a kid with someone else? More importantly, if you truly loved someone, why would you keep a secret of this magnitude?

Why wouldn't he tell her?

Taylor wasn't sure she could stand just yet. She felt the anger begin to boil in her stomach. How long had he known? From the beginning? Recently? He'd been acting funny ever since he'd gone to Quantico for the hearing and gotten himself suspended—had he found out then? Or had the past two years of her life been a full-on lie?

And who was the mother of this mystery child?

Quick math and some basic intuition gave her an idea. Charlotte Douglas. It must have been. The red hair was the final clue. Unless Baldwin had made it his practice to do it with a bevy of redheads, planting his seed without discretion throughout D.C., which seemed rather unlikely.

My God. He'd had a child with Charlotte, and hadn't told her. And assuming this was a current picture, if the child was only two years old, it must have happened just after Taylor first met him.

Who was this man she was planning to marry? She knew he had his secrets, all people did. She liked that he was mysterious, with murky and unspeakable bits to him. It gave her an excuse to keep parts of herself quiet. She hadn't told him everything about her life. It was better that way. He'd admitted to so much—that he worked for the CIA in a very covert group. That he had been trained early and spoke thirteen languages. That he had planned on being a medical ethicist but instead had been drawn into profiling by Garrett Woods, a Machiavellian man if there ever were one. She knew he was strong, tender, and in love with her. Those things she knew without doubt.

But she had never known Baldwin to be a liar. Or a cheat.

Taylor swallowed back the lump in her throat, amazed at the emotions she was feeling. She had no time for this, no energy to handle his infidelities right now. She needed to find Sam.

She stood, amazed that her legs would hold her weight without shaking.

Took extra care to tape the picture back into its place. They'd have to talk about this sometime soon, but she had to prioritize.

She glanced at her watch, she'd only lost three minutes.

She felt hollow, the scar of knowledge across her heart burned. She opened the gun cabinet, extracted the weapons she needed, tucked them into her bag, closed and locked things back up. All the while, two words ran through her head: *Find Sam.* She felt her focus return, pinpoint and clear.

The guards were waiting patiently by the garage. She nodded to them, then got in the 4Runner and pulled out of the driveway. As soon as she got to the end of the street she opened her cell phone and called Lincoln. He was still at the CJC with Colleen Keck, ostensibly holding her, but in fact keeping her safe.

"Have you heard from Sam?" she asked.

"Not since yesterday. She sent over a postmortem report on the Schechter boy. High BAL, but no sign of drugs on the tox screen. He drowned, but was strangled first, carefully. There was hardly a mark on him. Maybe just enough to render him unconscious. There was water in his lungs, so he was still breathing when he went in the water. Why?"

"Listen to me very carefully. I need you to protect Colleen. Send Marcus to cover Fitz. I'm on my way to Forensic Medical. Sam isn't answering her phone."

"You don't think—"

"Yes, I do. I think he's taken her. He sent me a cryptic message that had her home address on it."

"Have you seen the news this morning?"

"No, why?"

"Colleen's blog is front and center. Zodiac letters were sent to the papers in both Las Vegas and Denver. There was a Son of Sam letter found at the scene in New York, too. Boston PD are trying to quell the fear. Their switchboard is completely overloaded. The idea of a copycat Strangler has that whole town on edge. So the story is totally out."

Son of a bitch.

"San Fran, Vegas and Denver. The Zodiac copycat is moving east."

"Yes. So far there's no doubt, all the victims were regular commenters on Colleen's blog."

"Have there been reports of any other big murders? According to Colleen, there's supposed to at least three of these fools running around. God knows how many more might be in play."

That gave them both pause.

"Nothing yet, but I'll keep checking."

"I'll call New York right now. Emily Callahan should have some idea of what's been going down."

"I'll keep looking for similar murders. ViCAP's going to take too long."

"Wait," Taylor said. "Wait a minute."

"What?"

"Do you have a map?"

She heard clicking. "The United States, at your fingertips."

"Look at the path the Zodiac is taking. Where does it look like he's going?"

"Assuming he's continuing to head east, he's less than a day's drive to Nashville."

"Right. So if the other killers are doing the same thing, striking on their way here, what paths might they take?"

"Boston south could be D.C. Or maybe Philadelphia? Shoot, same with New York."

"Lincoln, you're going to have to start running through the entire eastern seaboard. Stick with major metropolitan areas. Call their Homicide offices and see what's happened in the past forty-eight hours that could match these MO's. Get a couple of people to help you, it's going to take a while. And keep an eye on Colleen. She's as much of a target in this as I am, though I'll be damned if I know why."

"Wc have his real name now, don't we? Have you asked her if she recognizes the name?"

"No, I haven't. God, what an idiot I am. Get her on the speakerphone for me, will you?"

"Sure, hang on just a second." She heard shuffling, then a click. "Okay, LT, you're on speaker with Colleen."

"Lieutenant, what's happening? Why can't I take Flynn and go home?"

"I still think you're in danger, Colleen. Just hang tight with Detective Ross and let us protect you, all right?"

"How long am I going to have to stay here? I have—"

"Colleen, please. I need to ask you something. Do you know anyone by the name Ewan Copeland?"

She heard Colleen's sharp intake of breath. When she spoke, her tone was flat, emotionless. "Why are you asking me about him?"

Jesus.

"Colleen, how do you know him?"

"I can't believe that you would lock me up here all night, then casually throw his name in my face. You're a cruel, horrible woman. I can't believe Tommy told me to trust you. You know exactly how I know him, or you wouldn't be asking. No wonder you didn't have the courage to do it face-to-face."

"Whoa, that's enough, Colleen." Lincoln took her off the speaker. "LT, what in the hell is going on?"

"I don't know, Lincoln. I have no idea." She could

hear Colleen, furious as a scalded cat, hissing in the background. "I hit a nerve, that's for sure. Can you get her back on the phone?"

"Not going to happen, LT. She's packing up her stuff."

"Lincoln, whatever you do, don't let her out of the building. Detain her if necessary. I'll deal with the fall-out later."

She was on Gass now, coming up on Forensic Medical at speed. "I have to focus on Sam. See if you can get Colleen calmed down enough to tell you how she knows Ewan Copeland, okay?"

"I'll do what I can. Keep me posted on Sam, okay?"

"I will. Thanks for everything, Lincoln."

She clicked off the phone, a million thoughts running through her head. She should have asked Colleen about Ewan directly last night, she was just so damn tired, and wasn't putting the pieces together properly. She thought Colleen had come across his path, she never in a million years expected her to actually know the name. Her first instinct was to call Baldwin, tell him where she was and what had just happened. She couldn't bring herself to hear his voice, not now. Not after what she'd learned. She was trying, so damn hard, to tuck the hurt and frustration away. She just needed to lay eyes on Sam, then she could deal with the rest of her crumbling world.

She flipped her phone back open and dialed the 212 area code that led to Emily Callahan's office phone. The call connected and Callahan's voice floated through the ether.

"Taylor Jackson, as I live and breathe. How the hell are you? Are you in New York?"

"Hey, Emily. No, not so lucky. I'm in Nashville, working a case."

"Ah, this is a professional call. Gotcha. What can I do for you?"

That was what she loved about Callahan, the woman was a professional first and a friend second. She always felt like she could let her hair down with her. She'd always been a compassionate, intelligent shoulder for Taylor to lean on. Callahan had been promoted out of Long Island City and was working in Manhattan's 6th Precinct Homicide now.

"Emily, no chance you caught a shooting in Washington Square Park the other night, did you?"

"The homosexual couple? No, it's not my case, but I know the detective who landed it. Why?"

Taylor took a few minutes and filled Callahan in on the situation. Taylor heard her clicking, knew she was going through the case file to see what she could glean.

"Evidence says there was a couple of cigarettes close to the scene that were collected. If they have anything to do with the case there's always the possibility of DNA. There was a note, too. That's been kept kind of quiet up here. A Son of Sam copycat will send the masses into a panic, and that's the last thing we need."

"No kidding. What I'm trying to figure out is where he might have gone, assuming he left New York. You haven't had any repeat performances, have you?"

"Not that I know of. The men who were killed were both married and having a very secret affair. If something similar pops, I'll let you know as soon as I hear about it. You're assuming he's done a one-off and is headed toward Nashville now?"

"Entirely possible. We're working with air right now."

"Tell you what. I'll personally have them send the results from the DNA run to the FBI. I assume Baldwin is on the case?"

"Actually no, but his team is. You've talked to Pietra Dunmore before, right?"

"Yeah, I remember her. Good girl. I'll send it to her, with a rush."

"God, Emily, what can I do to steal you away from New York's finest?"

"Grow a few hundred skyscrapers. Looking at all that blue sky down there makes me nervous."

They shared a laugh, and Callahan promised to keep looking into the situation.

Taylor hung up and turned on her blinker. Forensic Medical was on her left. It was time to get to the truth.

Thirty-Nine

Preston Pylant was having a very bad day. He'd stopped at McDonald's—*nasty screaming kiddies covered in ice cream; who gives their kids ice cream in the dead of winter?*—and had been waylaid by a bunch of cops as he came out of the bathroom. They hadn't even let him finish drying his hands. Maybe they liked that sort of thing, the filthy bastards. Liked the dirty hands, knowing what he'd just done in the bathroom. Now they had him in a small, cold room with paneling on the walls. Who used paneling in decoration anymore? The gays did, they loved their paneling.

The angel had an opinion, of course. He always did.

Shoot them, homey. Shoot them all. Tell them how you feel about being locked up in this pissant room.

Good idea.

"You can't tell me what to do. What do you think this is?" He was yelling, but he couldn't help it. After an hour, they'd tied him down. He didn't like to be tied down. The angel really didn't like to be tied down. They'd done that once to them, in the hospital. The padded sleeves held him straight and flat, no amount of wriggling or fighting would loosen them. The angel would harp on him, all fucking day long: *a little left there, homey, no, more to the right, you're a stupid fucking idiot, homey.*

He didn't want to go back to the hospital. He wanted to go to jail. Death row. That was the goal here. Not the hospital. Anything but the hospital.

The angel was screaming, a long, low build that ended like nails on a chalkboard. He knew what that meant. He really needed to take his pill. Why wouldn't they let him take his pill?

A cigarette. That would work. A cigarette always calmed him down.

The man in the stupid hat was talking again. It looked like a toboggan. He'd had a toboggan once. Used it to slide down the street in front of his house in Queens.

"Sir, you need to calm down. We have a long day ahead of us."

"The dog made me do it."

"I'm sure he did, Preston. Why don't you tell me all about it."

"It's just a game." The angel chimed in at volume, *Just a game. Just a game. Just a game.*

"*Shut up, angel.* See, sir, you don't understand. We're the apprentices. You know, like that rich dude in New York. With the show. And the hair. He tells us who to kill and how to do it, and we follow his instructions."

"Who is he?" the man asked. His name tag said Sergeant Green.

Preston laughed. Soylent Green. He'd been captured by Soylent Green! *Angel, check this shit out.*

"Who is the man who hired you, Preston?"

"Duh, it's Troy. If you don't know that, you're really far behind."

"Troy who, Preston?"

Paneling. Who used paneling these days?

"Preston?"

"Troy Land. Like *Babes in Toyland.* You know? He picked them from that blog, he made us read it so we'd get an idea of what they were like before we killed them. He called it studying the victimology. Can I go now?"

"No, Preston. You need to stay with me. You need to tell me everything you know."

"All I know is the dog made me do it. There's a million dollars at stake if we win. If we kill all our targets, we get a shitload of dough, and get to watch. We all like to watch. You know?"

Homey. Ask about the target.

Good idea, angel.

Preston said, "Hey, do you know Taylor Jackson? Could you introduce me?"

Forty

Taylor felt a weight release from her chest when she pulled into the parking lot. This was all just another false alarm.

Sam's car was parked in her slot. A silver BMW 330ci, the very car Baldwin drove. He'd taken one ride in Sam's backseat and decided then and there to get one for himself. When they were parked in the driveway side by side, Sam's titanium silver and Baldwin's titanium gray glinting in the sunlight, Taylor always teased them about their expensive tastes. "The neighbors are going to think we're putting on airs," she'd told them, more than once.

She was more than happy driving her truck. Practical. That was her.

Sam must have simply let her phone die. Taylor herself had done it herself the other day. All this worry, the tension; she was just on edge, seeing ghosts everywhere. Typical of Copeland, too, to send her off in a rush. He wanted her to react, not to think things through. This was all a game to him, one that took lives to satisfy his sick sense of humor.

She glanced over her shoulder to make sure Mitchell's

men were in place, then entered the building and went straight to Kris. The bubbly blonde was chatting on the phone, obviously on a personal call. She had a smile on her face a mile wide, her finger twirling a lock of hair at her shoulder. Taylor tamped down her annoyance. It was before hours, there was no reason Kris shouldn't be on the phone with a personal call.

When she saw Taylor approaching, she murmured something, and placed the phone to her chest to block the conversation from whomever she was speaking to.

"Morning, Lieutenant. What can I do for you?"

"I'm looking for Sam."

"She's long gone, I'm afraid. She scooted out of here before I made it in this morning. I had some reports to finish, so instead of staying late last night I decided to come in early today and get them done. Did you try calling her?"

"She's not answering her phone. Kris, you're sure she's not here? Her car is out front."

Kris's forehead creased. "Yeah, I'm sure. She was having trouble with the car last night. She was going to run out for dinner at 10:00 or so and it wouldn't start. She probably had Simon pick her up. I'm glad you mentioned it. I should call a tow truck for her. She didn't leave a message about it but I know what shop they use."

Taylor's heart returned to her throat.

"Kris, hang up the phone."

Kris didn't hesitate—the look on Taylor's face must have been enough. She set the phone in its cradle without saying goodbye.

"What's wrong, Lieutenant?"

"We don't know where Sam is. Have you been

in her office, or through the whole building yet this morning?"

She came out from around the desk with her badge out. "No, but let's go look. My God, I hope nothing's happened to her. Did you call Simon?"

Kris crossed the lobby and swiped her key card through the access slot. It unlocked and she yanked open the door to the executive offices. Taylor followed close on her heels. They jogged down the hallway to Sam's office. The door was cracked. Taylor pushed it open. Empty.

"I talked to Simon. He doesn't know either, but don't get in touch with him just yet. He said Sam had the overnight shift, then a doctor's appointment," Taylor said.

"Yeah, her first big checkup. They were going to do an ultrasound this morning."

Oh, my God. Sam. She took a deep breath. *Stay calm. You're going to find her. She's going to be okay.*

Taylor made a mess of Sam's desk looking for her datebook. "Where's her schedule? I can't find her Day Runner."

"It's online now. We're trying to go paperless. She wanted to set an example."

"I assume it's on her computer?"

Kris nodded.

"Pull it up. I need to look at it. Then you go to the autopsy suite, check with whoever's down there now."

Kris sat at Sam's desk, trying to type. Her hands were shaking, little wispy breaths leaking out of her mouth. She was closing in on a panic attack. Taylor finally reached over her shoulder and grabbed her hands.

"Listen, relax. Breathe. We're going to find her. She's going to be just fine. I promise."

There were tears in Kris's voice. "I hope so. She's the best. Lieutenant, I'm sorry, this is taking forever. She shut her computer down last night. She never does that. We always put them in sleep mode, password protected, of course. But she's turned her whole damn system—"

"Shoot, Kris. Stop. Stop typing. Don't touch anything. Back out of here, shut and lock Sam's office and access the schedule from your computer."

Kris listened, stood quickly and turned to Taylor. "What's the matter?"

"You said Sam never turns off her computer."

"No, never. It uses less energy to keep them in sleep mode, it's a part of our green initiative."

"In case we need to dust for prints or Hemascein the area for DNA, we need to keep it as undisturbed as possible."

"Oh, God," Kris sobbed.

Taylor took the girl by the shoulders. "Kris, I need you. You have to keep it together for me. Go back to your desk, bring up Sam's calendar. If there's anything else you think of that might be relevant, tell me. Who she was with last night, too. I need a list of everyone who was on shift, okay? Can you do that for me?"

Kris swallowed hard and nodded.

"Good. I'm going to head over to the autopsy suite myself and have a quick look around, make sure she isn't over there lost in a case. I'll be back in a minute."

More time, leaking away.

Taylor watched Kris head back through the door to the lobby and her desk. She swiped her own key card to enter the autopsy suite. It was eerily silent. The sun shone through the skylights, making the metal accoutrements along the table glow in the early morning light. There was no one there. No one alive, that is.

Panic struck her. She closed her eyes for a moment, braced herself, then slowly walked into the hall, to the stainless-steel door that housed the body cooler. Bodies were kept systematically stored, laid out on the wheeled tables that were used for autopsies, in their body bags. If things got crowded, they could be stacked vertically.

The door opened with a hiss, refrigerated air spilling into the corridor. A row of about ten bodies greeted her, all nestled in their black casings like caterpillars preparing to shed their chrysalis, their souls hardening into afterlife's wings. A slow day.

She tore through them, ripping open the bags, breaking a zipper on the third, glancing at faces, seeing nothing while she desperately searched the chilled bodies for her best friend.

The end of the row now, the last bag. She took three deep breaths, then firmly grabbed the zipper and pulled.

A man. It was a man.

Relief overwhelmed her.

She'd never been so happy to see a dead man before.

Forty-One

Baldwin paced his office nervously, waiting for Kevin to return his call. He hated agreeing to split from Taylor. He didn't like letting her out of his sight right now, not with this maniac so close. He glanced out the window; the bright morning sun disappeared behind a gray cloud that looked ominous. He could smell snow when he'd crossed the parking lot half an hour before. Just what they needed, a storm on top of this mess.

The idea that Taylor had about the list of figures on the CD was proving to be quite fortuitous. A quick search through the databases showed that the numbers the Pretender had sent them were in fact license plates, and all three plates were registered to car rental companies. Kevin was searching through each database with the appropriate agencies, trying to find out where the cars were.

It had been over twenty minutes. What was taking so long?

Baldwin glanced at his phone again, willing it to ring.

Nothing.

He sat at his desk and opened his laptop. Surfed through his news sites. Felt his stomach drop.

Son of a bitch.

The story was everywhere. Headlines screamed:

Serial Killers on the Loose
The Country Is Under Attack
Do You Know Where Your Children Are?
Don't Talk to Strangers
Resurgence of Old Killers Stuns the Nation

He clicked on the last link, just to see what he could glean. Sometimes, the news outlets did him a favor when they picked up on a murder. This time, he didn't think that would be the case.

The story was as sensational as he feared, with frighteningly accurate information.

Anonymous true-crime blogger Felon E has become a victim. Fans who comment on the widely read blog are under attack by the very killers Felon E purports to bring down. Police are keeping the story hush-hush, but sources close to the investigation say the FBI are now involved in the case. Since Monday, at least thirteen people have been killed across the country.

The investigation is centered out of Nashville, Tennessee, being run by a Homicide lieutenant named Taylor Jackson. It has become clear that the Felon E blog is headquartered in Nashville, and the owner of the site is in police custody at this time. There is no word as to whether Felon E is a suspect or is being held legally responsible for the commenters' deaths. These are issues for the new age of online reporting, and the eventual litigation surrounding this case may decide how many websites will use nonprofessional citizen journalists to populate their news sites.

According to the Felon E blog, California, New York and Boston were the first states hit by these elusive copycat serial killers, who imitated the Zodiac Killer, Son of Sam and the Boston Strangler, respectively. The first murder happened on Monday. Independent confirmation has come in that the Zodiac has also committed murders in Las Vegas, Nevada, and Denver, Colorado. Letters were mailed to the *San Francisco Chronicle*, the *Las Vegas Sun*, and *The Denver Post*, all claiming responsibility for the murders of five people in total: Vivi Waters, 18, and Ike Sharp, 19, shot to death in a lovers' lane outside of San Francisco; Colin and Sherry Barker, both 35, stabbed to death in their Las Vegas home; and Halley Marshall, 20, who answered an ad on the popular classifieds site Craigslist for a pair of Rollerblades and was shot to death behind Cherry Creek Reservoir.

We have also confirmed that June Earhart, 34, was killed in Boston in a very specific manner indicating the presence of a copycat of the Boston Strangler. A source who asked not to be named told this reporter that the victim's scarf had been tied in a bow around her neck, though independent confirmation is yet to be achieved. There was a second murder in this style less than twenty-four hours ago in Pittsburgh, Pennsylvania, a stockbroker named

Frances Schwartz, 31, and another strangulation was recently reported in Indianapolis, Indiana, Mary Jane Solomon, 28.

The FBI are looking into the cases, and people across the country are rushing to buy new locks, guns and other items to increase their homes' and loved ones' safety.

The Son of Sam copycat has proved more elusive, his trail not as defined as his compatriots. After murdering Barry Teterboro, 41, and Martin Bass, 50, in Manhattan's Washington Square Park, he moved to Washington, D.C., where his victims, Joseph Conley, 43, and Nicholas Anche, 40, were found shot to death in the Lyndon B. Johnson Memorial Grove. There have been no new murders attributed to Son of Sam's copycat for over a day.

These killers must be stopped, but speculation abounds as to the individual motives and overall scheme of the situation.

The article went on, but that was all Baldwin could take.

He closed the browser and ran his hands through his hair. Gotcha journalism, run with half truths and outright lies be damned, whoever had written that story had a source inside the investigation. At least the story hadn't made a connection to the Pretender. They had managed to keep his involvement relatively private. Fox already had the bones for that part of the story. Since Taylor had been openly named as leading the investigation, it would only be a matter of time before the rest jumped on board. They were out of time.

He couldn't sit here waiting anymore. He needed to

do something. He wasn't used to being on the outside of a case, looking in. Being suspended was making this difficult. Difficult, but not impossible.

He opened his phone and called Salt, who answered on the first ring.

"Good timing, I was about to call you."

"Tell me you have some good news."

"I do. The cars were rented at the same time, online, using a single credit card, which traces back to Nashville, though to a P.O. Box, not a physical address."

"Probably counterfeit then, an assumed identity. What name was used?"

"Troy Land. It's bogus, I can't find anything that matches up. I can't imagine him using his own name. Just in case, I've started a couple of searches. Though if he's sending you the plates of the cars, he's hardly trying to hide himself."

"Exactly. That's why I assume the ID is fake. What about the names of the drivers?"

"I'm almost there. They said they'd be happy to give me the information, chock-full of specifics, as soon as I provided them with a warrant. We're getting the paper now but you know how long that takes. So in the meantime, I'm taking a small peek into the daily database, see who signed for the individual cars. This company has moved to electronic signatures. Assuming they're legible, we'll at least have something to work with."

"Excellent. What else?"

"Confirmations of murders in Philadelphia and Indianapolis that are attributable to the signature of the Boston Strangler copycat. He's using UPS delivery trucks, and stealing the drivers' uniforms to make deliveries. Who doesn't answer the door for a parcel? Three UPS drivers have been found dead so far. There's been a media explosion, too, in case you didn't have your television or computer on."

"Yeah, I saw that. Hard to avoid, considering the victims are being targeted through a popular online site. The minute that hit Twitter, we were sunk."

"Dude, it's a top five trending topic right now. They've hashtagged it #copycats. Honestly, I think it's going to help. So much attention, you know? Everyone is watching. All the law enforcement agencies are on alert. The entire online world is paying attention. His moment in the sun is about to end."

"Excellent. Great work. Keep it up. Can I speak to Charlaine? I'd like her opinion on something."

"I'll transfer you. And I'll shout the minute I have some names, okay?"

"Thanks, Kevin."

"See ya."

There was a long beep, then the phone went quiet. Two seconds later Charlaine Shultz's sweet, Southern voice came on the line.

"Hey, boss! How are you? Please tell me they've pulled their heads from their asses and are letting you back? This place sucks without you."

"Charlaine, dear, thank you. No word yet, but I know Garrett's doing everything he can."

"Is Taylor okay?"

"We may have a new situation on our hands, she's off chasing it down now. Before I go into that, let me ask you something. No one seems to know what Ewan Copeland looks like. There were pictures in the files from when he was a kid, but nothing that anyone can agree upon as an adult. What do you think that means?"

Charlaine didn't hesitate. "It's so funny that you

asked that. I was just working on a theory. He's moved from city to city for at least a decade, right? Holds no job that we know of. His sister is making money, but enough to support herself and her brother as he traverses the country? That would be hard to pull off on a city forensic analyst's salary. There was a small life insurance policy that the baseball folks took out on Roger Copeland, emphasis on the small, so that money has to be long gone. He died over fifteen years ago. The mom was a guest of the state, died about six months ago. Breast cancer. Nothing suspicious, doctors ruled it natural causes. The last visitor she had was three years ago." He heard her shuffling papers. "His name was Thomas Keck."

"Son of a bitch. That's the name of the husband of our celebrity blogger. There's no way he visited Ewan Copeland's mother three years ago, he's been dead for over four."

"Another fake ID. Not a surprise. This Copeland guy is a piece of work."

"No kidding," he replied.

"That's not all. About an hour ago, I started going through the files we have on Copeland's previous crimes. All of the victims were single, and very much alone. The men, the women. He never chose anyone who had people. A couple of his victims were from upscale neighborhoods, we're talking wealthy, high-end places. So I started thinking, maybe he stole from those people. And guess what I found?"

"Dazzle me. Not that you aren't already."

"There's a name that's been linked to the escrow payouts on five of his victims. A lawyer named Roger Anderson. He's the beneficiary."

"Roger for his dad, and Anderson for his sister. Ewan got himself into their wills. Now that's impressive."

"It gets better. The money that was paid into Anderson's accounts was definitely enough for Copeland to live on, for years. Garrett pulled some strings and got a guy from the forensic banking department to get the account information released. He's living on the interest, he's made some very smart investments. All he needs are small withdrawals here and there, on a debit card, and one set of checks. The checks get interesting though, they're all made out to the same person over the course of ten years."

"Who is?"

"A doctor in McLean, Virginia. Plastic surgeon. Specializes in facial reconstruction after accidents, removal of burn scars, those kinds of things. He's on the up and up, a regular Ward Cleaver of a guy. Donates his time to fix cleft palates in South America, does a bunch of pro bono work here in the U.S."

"Charlaine, Ewan Copeland has a mess of scars on his stomach from his multiple surgeries as an young boy. We've known he was hiding something, I've always thought he had some sort of physical deformity that was readily apparent. What if he went to this doctor to have those scars removed, or skin grafts to help minimize them, and got addicted to surgery?"

"Exactly. You know how pain can work for Munchausen's by proxy victims. Pain equals love and acceptance, so even if it's self-inflicted, it becomes a necessity. Body dysmorphic disorder could explain why no one knows what he looks like. He's addicted to changing his surface. His skin, his face, his bone structure. He'd never be satisfied with how he looks, he'd be compelled to continue changing himself. Unlimited budget, an insatiable need for change and a lot of murders to cover up add up to one very sad, sick puppy. Probably with impossibly perfect skin. The bastard."

Baldwin gave this idea a moment to process. "That's why he doesn't care if he leaves DNA behind. He's altered his appearance between major kills. The odds of finding him through photos or witness identifications are slim to none."

"And Slim's out of town. Exactly."

"I assume you're going to talk to the doctor?"

"Already have an appointment, Baldwin. He cleared his schedule when we mentioned the name Roger Anderson. Guess he has an idea that there's a problem already."

"He could be just as much of a victim as the rest of Copeland's dead. Go careful. I'd assume Copeland has a warning system to let him know if anyone comes calling on his doctor."

Baldwin heard Charlaine slap shut her laptop, envisioned her getting to her feet, a crusader on a hot trail.

"Probably. But I'm hoping he's too engaged in his game to notice we've snuck in through the back door."

Forty-Two

Colleen was starting to get royally pissed off. Flynn was fretful, hungry for smiley-face pancakes, though Detective Ross said that leaving the CJC was an absolute no. They were making do with McDonald's that one of the patrols had brought in, pancakes and sausage patties, but Flynn wanted smiley faces, and just about everyone in the Homicide offices knew about it.

She was lost without her computer. Ross had taken it from her when she tried to leave the first time, before he'd locked her and Flynn in an interrogation room. She wasn't under arrest, but she wasn't free to leave, either. She couldn't believe that they thought she had something to do with this crazy killer's game.

Ewan Copeland.

The name made all the hairs on her arms stand on end. So long as she kept denying she knew him, kept playing dumb, she'd be fine. They'd catch him. She and Flynn would be able to go back to their lives.

She tried to quiet her cranky son, and waited. There was nothing for her to do. She worked on her breathing, her yoga breaths. Square. In for four counts, hold for four counts, release for four counts, still for four counts.

She made a game of it for Flynn. *Watch Mommy, baby.* After five rounds, he began to relax. After eight, he fell asleep against her shoulder, his soft hair spiked with sweat. She held him tight against her chest, felt his small body go limp and warm as he slid into sleep. Wished she could go back to his age and do the same thing.

There was a soft knock at the door. It opened slowly and Lincoln Ross stood in the frame, a wistful smile on his face. She felt her heart leap when she saw him. She was crazy, going mad, but when his smile turned from wistful to engaging, she couldn't help herself, she smiled back.

"The pancakes worked, I see," he said.

"I think I hypnotized him," she replied, and he stifled a laugh.

"It worked on me, too. I've rarely felt so calm while at work."

She realized he'd been watching, waiting for Flynn to settle, before he came back to the room. She appreciated that. Ross came all the way into the room, shut the door quietly behind him.

"I need to talk to you, Colleen. Is he totally asleep?"

"He's out. What is it? Can we leave now?"

Lincoln sat carefully in the chair across the table from her.

"Not just yet. Colleen..." He took a deep breath. She got a terrible feeling in her chest. Like something was going to pop.

She steeled herself. She'd already received the worst news a wife could get, that her husband was dead well before his time. The only thing worse would be hearing something terrible about Flynn, but she had her son in her arms, and no one else to worry about. She would be fine.

"What is it, Detective?"

He fidgeted with his hair for a moment.

"Colleen, where did you grow up?"

"Blacksburg, Virginia. Why?"

His liquid brown eyes rested on hers, and she saw his eyebrows twitch, just a fraction.

"Why?" she asked again.

"Have you ever been to Forest City, North Carolina?"

No. No, no, no, no, no, no, no, no, no.

"I don't believe so," she said.

"Colleen," he started. She shifted Flynn, buried her face in his neck. She felt the panic begin to rise in her chest.

"Colleen," Lincoln said again. "Forest City. Do you remember anyone named Emma Brighton?"

They don't know. They don't know. Please, God, don't let them know.

"I've never been to Forest City, North Carolina, Detective." She raised her chin in sheer defiance and looked him straight in the eye.

"I had your prints run, Colleen. I know you're Emma Brighton. I know what he did to you."

The name. It brought back immediate, slavish memories, ones she'd buried so deep she'd actually convinced herself it had happened to someone else. Someone she didn't know. A story she'd heard about, a dreadful rumor, but someone else's rumor. The kind of things she dealt with every day on Felon E, women raped, children dying. The very people she fought for, who deserved her justice.

She felt the pancakes rise up the back of her throat.

The detective was staring at her still, watching. How could she have ever found him attractive? For the rest of her life, she would see those lips form around the name, his pink tongue touching the edges of his teeth as they parted and joined. Open, close, open, close. Emma. Emma. Emma.

She was crying. How did that happen?

"Colleen? Are you okay? I'm sorry to drop this on you. But we had to know. The way you reacted when you heard Copeland's name—"

"Don't you dare say his name to me."

She jerked to her feet.

"I'm leaving. Now."

Flynn started to cry. She didn't care, she just crushed him to her harder and bolted for the door. The detective followed, but she was quicker. She was already out and down the hallway, running blind, her hair in her face, tears shattering her vision.

She hadn't thought of that moment in years. She'd done extensive therapy, working with a system called EMDR, Eye Movement Desensitization and Reprocessing. It was a cognitive therapy that realigned the neural pathways in her brain so she could move forward with her life, leaving the crippled portion of her soul on the therapist's floor, shoved with her foot under the therapist's couch, forever left behind. EMDR allowed her to hear the word *rape* without cringing, without faltering. It allowed her to get married, to find enjoyment, even abandon, in her marriage bed with Tommy. It gave her a new life, one free from the crushing, horrifying memories of what happened that night. It gave her a new name, one not sullied with the stains of violence. She started over, and no one knew. No one. Not even Tommy.

With two words, that fucking detective had undone years of work.

Her arms relaxed. The door was just ahead.

Emma. Emma *Goddamn raped until she bled on the carpet torn open between her privates her stomach slashed forty times with the sharpest blade he could find her virginity her sex her blood spilling on the carpet the ambulance driver screaming her stoned mother's pitying gaze the whole world knew what he had done to her and she'd never escape the pain the screams the blood* Brighton.

"Stop her," she heard the detective yell, but the faces that turned to her were shocked, and that moment's delay was all she needed. She scooted out the door and rushed across the street. She pounded down the ramp to the garage. She didn't even realize that she'd dropped Flynn back in the station, by the door.

She had no idea who Flynn was.

All she knew was she had to leave, to go, to get out. Now.

The car. Right ahead. Keys…she slapped her pockets and found them. Unlocked the door. Pulled it open and sat in the seat.

Emma Brighton.

The face from her past floated to the surface, the sweet smile, the curly hair. A happy girl.

Emma Brighton, before she was debased and defiled.

Colleen didn't feel the blade slide through her throat. She didn't feel anything at all.

Forty-Three

Ewan Copeland scraped at the dried blood on the table with a fingernail.

So much of his life was spent waiting. For his mother to hurt him. For his father to come home. For the bars to his cell to open. For the painkillers to take effect. For the swelling to go down. For the damn woman tied to the chair to wake up.

He had all the time in the world, but really, this was getting ridiculous. He wanted to play. He got bored with waiting after a while. Patience was a virtue, yes, but in his case, he should be given a bloody Oscar for his performances.

He finished removing the red flecks from the table and debated. He'd started an excellent thriller last night, gotten halfway through. He liked thrillers. They moved quickly. Just like him.

Read? Or wake her ass up?

Choices, choices.

He stood, crossed the room and retrieved the ammonia capsule from his bag. He'd pilfered them from work, the perfect antidote for fainting relatives and distraught spouses. He cracked the capsule open and waved it beneath her nose until she began to moan. He placed it upright on the table, he might need it again.

"Hello, Samantha."

The woman stirred, her dark hair shifting against her perfect ivory skin as her head lolled forward. Not quite there yet.

"Samantha…Samaaaaaantha…wakey wakey."

He tapped her cheek with his open palm, softly, not a slap, just a nudge. A little push toward the left. Her eyelids started to flutter, the brown eyes out of focus. She blinked heavily, the lashes soft against her lids.

He tapped her harder this time, on the other cheek, with the back of his hand, enjoying the bloom of red on her perfectly peach-skinned cheeks. Her eyes flew open. He watched them process the situation—he, the glorious one, standing before her, head cocked to the side like a curious puppy, a ten-inch blade in his hand. The fear registered in an instant. An appropriate, intelligent reaction. Of course, he expected nothing less, but still. Fear was good. He liked fear. He wanted to see that same glance bleeding out from gray on gray eyes, but for now, this would have to do.

He did so love the look of a wide, mobile mouth incapacitated with a gag.

"Glad you could join us," he said.

She shrieked behind the gag, and he shook his head.

"No yelling. That's not fair. I'm not yelling at you, am I? Calm down and be a good girl, and you won't get hurt."

He traced her collarbones with the blade, watched as her eyes filled with tears. Sam Loughley wasn't a dumb woman, she knew what was happening. She sniffed hard, her mouth stretched against the gag, then shut her eyes. They always shut their eyes. He'd gone through a stage when he'd tried gluing their eyes open, but the staring started to get to him. It was so much more feminine, more demure, for the lashes to brush against the cheeks, guiding the rivulets of tears leaking down their skin. Crying with eyes open looked... strange. Like dolls. He wasn't a fan of dolls.

"Sam, you know your role in this play, don't you?"

She opened her eyes again, and there was a bit of defiance lurking there.

Good. She would fight for her friend.

"It shouldn't take too long. You've been missed by now. I haven't. I've been planning this for weeks, right under your noses. But Taylor will be looking for you. She's a clever girl, she should be able to puzzle out where we are. I have faith in her, just like you do. So. We're just going to have ourselves a little party while we're waiting. Doesn't that sound like fun?"

The eyes closed again.

He wanted to talk. Now that she was awake, now that he had an audience...he wondered how Ruth was managing. He doubted he'd ever see her again, her or her creepy friend Harvey. The minute he smelled danger he'd probably taken off, out of town, a rat scurrying for the cover of darkness. The boy he killed wasn't meant to be found, not during all of this, yet he'd managed to both screw that up and leave behind a clumsy, ill-timed red herring that no one had fallen for. Idiot. Why had he let Ruth bring the fool along? It was a mistake, one of the few he'd made along the way. He wasn't perfect, after all.

No, he was going to be alone again, for quite some time. He wanted to enjoy the company while he had it.

"Samantha, tell me. What was it like growing up

with her? Was she as strong as she is now? Or were you the strong one? Working with dead bodies all day, I have to wonder. You enjoy it, don't you? Feeling inside them. The smell of the viscera, the weight of their testicles, all those holes. You become one with their bodies. You bring work home with you, too, into your family, your children. You share small bits of every human being you touch with all the people you care for. There is no amount of gloving and scrubbing that can erase what's in your mind. When you fuck Simon, do you think about the blades cutting through the flesh? Do you like that feeling, Sam? The tugging, the cutting, the succulent tissue parting before you?"

The knife was poised above her abdomen now. He edged the tip through her sweater, a bit farther now, into her skin, just ever so slightly. Relished the gasp of air through her nose as the nascent pain ran through her synapses. A trickle of blood wept from the wound, just a scratch, really, and slid slowly over the edge of her slacks between her legs. He ran his finger along it, gathering the red droplets. He stared at the brilliant glow, felt himself become mesmerized. He had to force his eyes away. He wiped the blood on the table, replacing the smudge he'd removed earlier. It looked so much nicer fresh. Like wet paint.

He really loved this woman. She wasn't struggling, or begging. She was stoic.

Hmm. He decided to see just how brave she really was.

Forty-Four

Taylor ran back to the front desk of Forensic Medical, where Kris was waiting for her.

"Nothing. She's not down there. Do you have her schedule up yet?"

"Yes, and I called the doctor—she hasn't shown there. Here, look." Kris got up and let Taylor sit in her chair, pointed over her shoulder at the computer screen.

"It was a normal day. We had intake of three new cases, late afternoon. She was going to post them overnight, began the night shift staff meeting at ten, that's when she realized her car was crapped out. She was going to grab dinner beforehand, and it wouldn't start, so she decided to have someone from staff run out and get something for her. It was a typical twelve-hour shift."

"Was Stuart in last night?"

Stuart Charisse was Sam's favorite assistant in the morgue, a quiet, smart man who was devoted to Sam.

"Yeah, he was in. I think he got off at two o'clock."

"Call him."

Kris wasted no time. She moved to the right and grabbed her phone. She obviously had all the staff numbers programmed in, she simply hit a single button and put the phone on speaker. A sleepy voice mumbled, "Yeah?"

"Stuart, it's Kris. I'm here with Lieutenant Jackson. We're looking for Sam. Have you seen her?"

He yawned loudly. "No. Not since I left. She and Iles were going to get something to eat. She missed dinner."

"Barclay?" Kris asked. "He was in last night?"

"Yeah. Something about his performance review. They decided to do it over Subway, I think."

"Thank you, Stuart," Taylor said, then cut off the phone. Kris's face had gone white.

"Kris, what's wrong?"

"Barclay isn't in Nashville this week. I was talking to him when you got here. He's in Florida. His mom is sick, he went down to help. He goes down there a lot."

Barclay fucking Iles.

"Kris, how long have you and Barclay been dating?"

Kris was wringing her hands, the knuckles white from the force, her eyebrows touching across her forehead as she frowned. "Almost a year now. He's a great guy. You know him, Lieutenant. I recommended him to Sam—he seemed like he'd make a really good 'gator. He went to med school for a while, he's really smart. The rest of the staff all like him, too. He loves Sam. He loves you, too—he talks about you all thc time. You're his hero. He wants to be just like you. I actually got a little jealous oncc, but that was silly. I was just being insecure. But why would he lie to me? What's going on?"

What's going on indeed? Taylor ran back through her memories of Iles. She'd worked with him the first time not too long ago, but he'd been around the department, at the crime scenes, for months. Access. He'd have access to everything—personnel files, schedules, home addresses.

Son of a bitch.

"Kris, listen to me very carefully. I think Barclay may be someone else, someone very, very dangerous. I need you to give me every bit of information you have about him. His phone number, his address. Every picture you have. Everything you can think of that belongs to him. Right now."

Forty-Five

Come to Papa. Predesignated spot. Game over.

Bill Reiser had received the message on the BlackBerry he'd been given just as he crossed into Tennessee an hour ago. He was looking at the Nashville skyline now. He hoped this didn't mean he wasn't going to be able to hit his final target.

He took the exit and swung around onto Ellington Parkway. He was surprised at how quickly the turn came; within five minutes he was on Gass Boulevard heading toward the target.

The navigation told him he'd arrived at his destination.

What the fuck was this? The Tennessee Bureau of Investigations offices were on his right. This was wrong. This was a suicide mission. He was supposed to shoot someone at a federal building?

Bull. Shit. Hell, no. He wasn't crazy enough for that.

He drove past the building. There was one more building on this road, he'd turn around in that parking lot and go regroup. Send Troy Land an email and tell him no way, no how. What did he look like, an idiot?

He turned into the building's parking lot, saw a white van that said Medical Examiner on it and realized where he was. Jesus, this place was a morgue. Great.

He parked for a moment so he could send Troy the message. He was tapping away when he saw a blur of flashing light behind him, looked in the rearview mirror. Plainclothes cops. Shit. Was this private property maybe?

He used his left foot to shove the gun all the way under the seat. *Play it cool, accept the ticket.* He wasn't doing anything wrong. At least not right this minute.

He hadn't done anything wrong in at least fifteen hours.

He watched the big guy approach the car carefully, his left hand on his weapon. He used his right to touch the back of the car palm down. He'd read once that cops do that so their fingerprints were left on the car in case the driver snatches them, or shoots them.

He could shoot him.

He could shoot the cop.

A rush of adrenaline flowed through him. The cop knocked on the window, made the universal sign for "roll it down."

Think it through. Wait to see what the deal is. He probably just wants you to leave. If it's just a ticket, don't be dumb. You still have a game to win. So much money. Erase the past shitty year with one lump sum payment. And you're so close. Don't blow it now.

He pressed the down button for the window. The man was at an angle, nearly behind him. A cold wind whipped in his face.

"Sir? Please step out of the vehicle."

"Why, Officer? What did I do?"

"Step out of the vehicle with your hands up."

Oh, this wasn't good at all. He bit his lip. He'd only have one chance at this. He glanced in the side mirror, the other man had sidled to the passenger side. His gun was drawn.

Bill's heart sank. Troy was right, he was blown. They'd found out. They knew. God, what should he do? There were only two of them. The gun was fully loaded. He would have to be quick.

The cop wasn't going to wait while he made his decisions.

"Get out of the car, now, sir. Show me your hands. Show me your hands right now."

The other voice joined in, slightly lower, more demanding. They were getting twitchy. He heard the decibel level rise. He really didn't have a choice. He didn't want to go to jail. Maybe he could talk his way out of it. No, probably not. These guys didn't look like they were in a talking mood.

He raised his hands up, then slowly used his left to open the door. As he started to step out, he let his right trail behind, like he was using it to boost himself. His fingers brushed the metal of the gun.

"Hands, now!"

Now was right. He whipped the gun out from below the seat and stood, aiming at the cop closest to him. He squeezed the trigger. Saw gray sky. What? He squeezed the trigger again but the shot didn't go off.

Shouting, screaming.

Oh.

He felt the pain now, a searing blaze through his chest. The gravel smelled like gasoline. A flock of geese flew overhead, honking. He smiled. He'd always liked geese. His grandfather had them on his farm, up in Northern California. Thought they were a nuisance. He'd always wondered…

Forty-Six

Lincoln righted the small boy that Colleen Keck, scratch that, Emma Brighton, had dropped on the hard, cold cement in front of the CJC. Flynn was crying, so in shock at his ignominious plop that it hadn't registered that his mother was no longer in front of him.

Lincoln patted the boy on the back a few times, then handed him off to a sheriff's deputy walking nearby. "Take him to the Homicide offices. Now, please. I'll be back in a minute. I have to go after his mother."

The deputy glared at Lincoln but went ahead and took Flynn from his arms.

He ran across the street to the parking lot. He didn't see Colleen, she'd gotten well ahead of him. He had no idea what floor she'd parked on, so he bounded down the first set of stairs and started through the rows. The concrete walls and floor, backlit by powerful beams, glowed in ghostly silence. It was still very early, so there weren't a lot of cars. Or people. He didn't hear any engines running.

Something felt all wrong about this. He drew his weapon, focused his senses. He could smell blood. Fresh blood.

He took three steps toward the scent. From his right, a woman rushed toward him, like a quail flushed by a bird dog. There was no extraneous noise, no shouts of warning, just the quickening of her feet on the concrete, a predator. His mind tried to process the scene: not Colleen; the woman had a knife; she was charging him with the blade extended. He stopped thinking, his training took over. His finger squeezed with the precision of years of practice on the range. Center mass, three shots.

The woman crumpled in a heap at his feet, moaning. The knife clattered to the ground. He shook his head, his ears ringing from the shots. All the sounds were tunneled, like he was underwater. Smeary voices, shouts, clanging echoes.

The shots went a bit lower than he expected, adrenaline making the tip of the Glock drop. Or maybe he hadn't raised it all the way? He'd have to take a look at that on the range, but the truth of the matter was, he'd never fired his service weapon in the line of duty before. There was going to be a shit storm today, that was for sure. Officers didn't usually kill patrons in the parking lot of the Criminal Justice Center. He felt the sweat break out on the back of his neck.

The woman stopped moaning.

He kicked the knife out of her range and bent to feel for a pulse. Thready, weak. Without medical attention, she was certainly going to die.

He didn't see Colleen. And he didn't have his radio, damn it, or his cell phone. He'd rushed out so fast he hadn't grabbed anything; they were all piled neatly on his desk.

There was an old Honda Civic two rows over, alone, in a spot directly in front of the elevators. A dark trail of oil lead from the driver's-side door. The door itself was slightly ajar.

Colleen.

Shouting now, clanging steps on the hard, cold concrete, people coming in response to his gunshots.

He circumnavigated as he ran, coming at the car from a direction he hoped would preserve any evidence. Colleen was slumped in the driver's seat. It wasn't oil; there was blood everywhere, deep and thick, arterial spray. He was afraid she was gone, the wound in her neck was deep. But as he watched, her chest rose fractionally. He drew as close as he could and took her hand, which was still wrapped around the steering wheel, as if she could drive away from death.

"Colleen?" he asked.

"Tommy? Is that you?"

Her voice was raspy. Lincoln reached past her and got her cell phone from the dashboard sticky pad. Flipped it open, called the desk. Made it official. Told them it was an officer involved shooting. Asked for backup, EMTs, everything they could send, Code Three.

Colleen was talking again.

"Tommy, you shouldn't…shouldn't have come. Flynn. We need to take care of Flynn."

Lincoln ripped off his jacket and pressed the fabric to her throat. He shushed her.

"Don't talk, Colleen. Just hang on for me."

Sirens began to blare, he could hear them through the haze. People were close by but he ignored them, focused all his energy on Colleen.

Colleen shook her head, her eyes fixed on Lincoln. "Tommy. I'm glad you're here. I've missed you. You made me so happy. So safe."

She smiled, her face suffused with a glow.

"Colleen..."

She put her finger to his mouth.

"No, no, Colleen, hold on. Flynn's across the street, he's waiting for you. Please, Colleen, don't do this to me. Don't you dare die. Help is here."

"Tommy, I love you."

Her eyes closed gently, and she was gone. He could feel it, the moment when her body lightened as her spirit fled. He didn't think he'd ever forget the exact taste and shape of the moment, how the voices drew closer, how Colleen's eyes were slitted at the bottom, as if her soul needed to be able to see its way out of her body, how the blood was soaked into the dark fabric of his jacket, the dusty scent of concrete mixed with dying blood. Lincoln fought back tears. Fought for a moment as someone pulled on his shoulder, then dropped the jacket and stepped away, let the EMTs go to work. He knew it was too late. It was too late for them all.

Forty-Seven

Taylor was about to step out into the parking lot when she heard gunshots. She drew her Glock.

"Lieutenant, did you hear that?" Kris squeaked in alarm.

"I did. Go inside the main offices, shut the door behind you."

Kris disappeared into the hallway. She'd be safe in there, you needed a key card to get through.

Taylor glanced out the front door and saw her two bodyguards standing over a man. Whatever was happening was over, the threat had obviously been neutralized. She holstered her gun and ran outside.

"What happened?" she yelled. "Who is this?"

Wells turned to her, eyes quiet and cold. "Pretty sure he's one of the copycats. License plate matches. And he went for a gun. I had no choice."

She looked at the man spread-eagle on his back, his face arranged in a soft smile, eyes forever focused on a sky only he could see. Felt nothing for him.

"Which one was he?"

Rogers tossed her the man's wallet. "His license says

William Reiser. I'd assume he's the Zodiac copycat out of California."

"What the hell is he doing here? Making a move on me?"

"We don't know, ma'am. We saw him coming up the road, then stop for a minute in front of the TBI. Then he came up here, parked and took out his BlackBerry."

He handed that to her as well. She pushed the home button and the screen came to life. He'd been composing an email, to someone named Troy.

She scrolled down and saw the message he'd been responding to, felt her skin crawl.

Come to Papa.

He was answering a direct communiqué from Copeland. Wells was right, this was one of the copycats.

"Well done," she said to him, then grabbed her cell and got Commander Huston on the horn.

Before she could even say hello the commander launched in, fast and loud. "Jackson, what in the hell is going on? We've just had a homicide in the parking facilities. That woman you've had Detective Ross babysitting was killed a few minutes ago."

All the breath went out of her in a rush. Oh, God. Colleen.

"How?" she managed to ask.

"We're figuring all that out now. She left the building and was ambushed. Detective Ross shot and killed her attacker. You need to come down here, now."

Lincoln killed a suspect. He must be devastated. He'd never taken a life before. All of her people were getting hurt. Taylor took a deep breath.

"Ma'am, I can't do that just this minute. I need a crime scene tech at Forensic Medical. We've had a breach of security, one of the national copycats got into the parking lot of the building. He was taken down by two of Mitchell Price's men, who I hired to watch my back."

"Another shooting? Christ almighty, Lieutenant."

"I know, ma'am."

"You sit tight there then. I'll handle things here. Be careful, Lieutenant."

"Yes, ma'am." She hit End, then called Kris, who answered on the first ring.

"Kris, everything is fine out here. We need a death investigator. I need to leave. Can you arrange things, come out here and make sure nothing is messed with?"

"Yes. But, Lieutenant, shouldn't you stay—"

"Kris, I have to find Sam. Please. Do this for me."

"All right."

She hung up and looked at Wells. "I need to move."

"Yes, ma'am. What do you want us to do? Come with? There are more of these fools out there, right?"

"Stay here. Call Price and tell him what went down. Give your statement and tell the truth, Wells. You won't be held accountable, he drew first. When you get clear, call me and we'll meet back up."

"Are you sure, ma'am? You'll be exposed. These killers are getting close, too close for comfort, if you ask me." He nudged Reiser with his foot.

"Stay, Wells. Give your statement. That's an order."

"Yes, ma'am."

And just like that, she was free. Her guards had served their purpose, for the first stage of the game.

Thank you for the setup, Copeland. Couldn't have planned it better myself.

Forty-Eight

Baldwin's cell rang as he was leaving his office. He was pleased to see the internal Quantico number, recognized it as Kevin Salt. Baldwin kept walking, answered the phone as he locked his office door.

"Hey, man. You have something for me?"

"I do. And don't worry, we've already gone into overdrive to get this taken care of. Teams have been sent to each house. I've brought in some extra computer staff to start running their files. Charlaine's off to talk to the doctor she told you about. We've got everything covered on the national scale, okay?"

Ah, the power of the office. He certainly missed being the one directing the show.

"Okay. How can I argue with that? Shoot."

"California's car was rented to a man named William Reiser, we're assuming he's the Zodiac copycat. Record is totally clean, he's run below the radar for years. He's a computer programmer out in Silicon Valley, got laid off last year. New York's Son of Sam contestant was Preston Pylant of Long Island—that guy is a nut. He's got a history of deviant behavior, he might be schizophrenic. He's got a record, did some time about ten years ago—assault. His file lists a history of mental illness.

"The Boston Strangler's car was rented by a Richard Cooper. All of the information for him leads back to a Richard Cooper who works for UPS, so there's the connection. There's just one problem with him."

"What's that?"

"Richard Cooper who works at UPS is at UPS now, in Florida. He's been on the job all week, there's no way it's the same guy."

"You're right, the time doesn't fit. Probably a case of stolen identity. That's par for the course with Copeland. He probably just secured the guy new papers so he could work the delivery angle."

"Maybe. But why wouldn't he do that for all three?"

"It's possible that he did, and we just haven't seen it. Can you explore that further?"

"All right. I'll go the stolen identity route and see who's been accessing Richard Cooper's accounts, plus look at the other two. You know, it's possible that one of the killers is more sophisticated than the others and is covering his tracks better."

Just what they needed, another smart killer.

"Make sure, either way."

"All right. There was a double murder in D.C., in the park just off GW Parkway, just short of Reagan National Airport. You know the one I'm talking about?"

"Oh, the LBJ Memorial Grove? Yeah, I know the one. It's a mecca for gay men to meet up, right?"

"That's the one. They've cleaned it up, got the drugs out, at least the most visible ones, but the public sex is still a problem. Two men were shot there last night, and it looks just like the New York case."

"Yeah, I read about it online. So it's officially been tied in now?" Baldwin asked.

"Yes. Two taps to each forehead with .44 caliber bullets. Ballistics are a match."

"Great job. Explain this part to me. You said contestant."

"I did."

"Like on a game show?"

"Just like it. And there's a reason."

"You're killing me, Kevin. Please."

Kevin smothered a laugh. "Fine. Take all the fun out of it. I've got good news. The Tennessee Highway patrol saw the BOLO for the license plates and spread the word. They grabbed Pylant at a McDonald's off Interstate 40 just outside of Knoxville, said he was acting twitchy. He's talking, too."

Bingo.

"What's he saying?"

"Pylant? Like I said, I think he may be a schizophrenic. But he keeps insisting he's a part of a larger game, that this is his big chance. He's a definite spree killer in the making. He was packing more ammunition than the ATF boys take on their training exercises."

"So he's in custody in Knoxville?"

"Yeah. Sewn up. I'll find out what else he's saying and get that to you as quick as I can. In the meantime, at least we know who was where. And it's pretty evident where they were all headed."

"Yeah. Nashville."

"That's right.

"You're the best, Kevin. Let me know if you get anything else."

"Will do. Everything under control down there?"

"To an extent. Being on the sidelines isn't exactly easy for me, you know?"

"I do. Hey, Garrett wants to talk to you. He asked that you give him a call."

"All right. I will. Thanks."

Baldwin hung up with Kevin and checked his watch. Before he talked to Garrett, he wanted to check in with Taylor.

He speed-dialed her number, relieved when she answered right away.

"Wells just killed the Zodiac copycat in the Forensic Medical parking lot," she said without preamble. "But now we know what Ewan Copeland looks like. The death investigator Barclay Iles, remember him? He's our guy. Ewan Copeland has been working at Forensic Medical for almost a year."

Baldwin mentally flashed to the man's face. Wrapped his head around the idea. He'd had open access to Taylor for a year, right in her own backyard. Fear turned to rage; he missed what Taylor said next.

"What?"

"He's been dating Kris. She suggested him to Sam. He's got a full forensic background, though I couldn't tell you how much of it was real. I've worked with him, Baldwin. Shoulder to shoulder. Shared meals, late nights, laughs. I respected him. Sam's been working with him for months. He's been a part of our lives, watching, waiting for the perfect moment."

There was an edge of panic to her voice, not that he blamed her.

"Calm down. Where are you right now?"

"I just left Sam's office."

"Where does Barclay Iles live?"

"With Kris, officially. But you know he has another

place somewhere. She's not seen him for a few days. He told her his mother was sick and he was going to Florida this week. He disabled Sam's car and took her out of Forensic Medical under the auspices of doing his performance review. The son of a bitch has her, Baldwin. I have all his information, but without Lincoln to track him down, I can't go any further."

"Without Lincoln? What?"

He heard her car engine turn over. "I'm heading downtown now. Lincoln's been involved in a shooting, and Colleen Keck is dead. I don't have the details, just that she ran outside and was ambushed."

Everything was falling apart. He needed to get to Taylor.

"I'll meet you at the CJC. Drive carefully. Don't worry, okay? The Boston Strangler copycat is still out there, but the Knoxville police caught another one, looks like Son of Sam. He's singing like a bird. He may know where Sam is. We'll find her. I promise."

"I hope so," she said, then hung up the phone.

He was in the parking lot now. He unlocked his car and slid behind the wheel, turned the heat on high. He was so rattled that it was only after he put the car in gear and started to leave the parking lot that he realized how short Taylor had been. She never got off the phone without saying she loved him. Nor did he. It was one of their sacred things. They were in a dangerous profession; Taylor had once told him that she never wanted to die without telling her people she loved them. He felt the same way—his parents, dead when he was just sixteen, had expressed their love for him before they left for the evening…he hadn't returned their words. The guilt racked him for years. Still got under his skin sometimes.

He dialed her back. She didn't answer.

What in the hell was going on?

Stress. She was just stressed. Her best friend was missing, bait in an obscenely unfair game. Of course she'd be preoccupied.

He left her a message, told her he loved her, then called Garrett.

Forty-Nine

Taylor ignored the phone when it rang again.

She hated lying to Baldwin. Even though he'd been lying to her for God knew how long, she didn't want to be that woman. The one who said she was going shopping with her friends and actually met her lover in the park. The one who calculated a man's worth before she spoke to him. The one who said *I love you* and didn't mean it. She wasn't that kind of woman, yet here she was openly lying to her fiancé about where she was going. And worse, what she'd be doing.

Greater good, Taylor. You know he'd stop you if he was close. You're smart to send him away. To send him where he'll be safe.

And face it, you don't want him around while you commit murder.

When Kris told her Barclay/Ewan lived with her, her heart sank. A separate address would have been much too easy. Of course he wouldn't do that. She sat in her car for five minutes, breathing, thinking, deciding. She had a feeling she knew where he was, where he'd taken Sam. If she were Ewan Copeland, it was exactly where she would go to end things in Nashville. He knew her well enough to know she'd figure that out. The stage had been set perfectly.

She placed a quick call to Julia Page, the assistant district attorney she felt most comfortable asking a favor from.

Julia picked up on the first ring. "Taylor, thank goodness you're okay. I just heard about the shooting."

"Which one?"

"There's more than one? I'm talking about Colleen Keck."

"We also had a suspected copycat in the parking lot of Forensic Medical. He was neutralized."

"Good God. Did you shoot him? Did he hurt Sam? Have you found her?"

"No, I didn't. Jesus, Julia. I'm hardly trigger-happy." Yeah, right. Like she wouldn't have taken the opportunity herself, and enjoyed it. This was who she'd become. Blindly seeking revenge. "I don't know anything more about Sam, but I'm working on it. Hey, Julia, do you have a contact number for Joshua Fortnight?"

Silence billowed through the phone. Julia finally cleared her throat.

"I know the name of the home he's in. He opted for a group living environment when his father was killed. There was no one left to take care of him, and the estate got locked in an escrow fight, and the staff was let go. The estate will be in probate for years. They released enough funds to pay Joshua's medical expenses. We were able to get him well placed, the best we could do, considering. He's at the Guardian facility, off Antioch Pike and Old Harding."

"Awesome, Julia. Thank you."

"Do I want to know?"

"I just need to ask him some questions later. Nothing

to worry about. This whole case ties back to his father, I just need to clarify something."

"Okay, Taylor. Good luck."

Taylor knew Julia had worked hard to take care of Joshua. A victim of Treacher Collins syndrome, he was blind, going deaf, his face deformed beyond recognition. The fact that he was leading a relatively normal, healthy life was a miracle in itself. His mother, Carlotta Fortnight, had died in childbirth. His father, Eric Fortnight, Snow White, dead by Taylor's hand. His sister, Charlotte Douglas, impregnated by Baldwin, slain by Ewan Copeland…

Joshua's history was a bloody one. It was remarkable that he'd survived unscathed—he'd saved his father from his creation by shooting Copeland in the shoulder moments before Taylor and the SWAT team burst through their doors.

The whole saga was much too incestuous for Taylor's liking.

She was already past Ellington Parkway. She whipped it around and took the exit for I-24 East, settled into the fast lane. She could make it to Joshua's group home in less than ten minutes.

Joshua. The innocent, surrounded by tragedy. The lamb staked out for the lions.

He may have the answers she needed.

She was going to find Sam and see her safely away from the bastard. She refused to give up trying to save the innocents around her, to wallow in her failures. There would be plenty of time to mourn the ancillary players once she was finished.

The phone rang again. She might have to just turn the damn thing off so it wouldn't be such a distraction.

She glanced at the screen—it was an international

call. She recognized the number, with its +44 prefix. Memphis.

What the hell? Why would Memphis be calling now? Should she answer? She pressed the button and connected the call.

"How are you, Special Agent Highsmythe?"

His thick British upper-class boys' school accent flew out of her cell-phone speakers tinged with relief. "I'm so glad I reached you. Are you all right?"

He actually did sound relieved, the fool.

"Why wouldn't I be?"

"Taylor, I saw the case on the news. You're everywhere. It looks like things have gone to hell. Please tell me you are taking care of yourself."

"Worry not, Viscount. I'm always careful."

"I've seen you in action, remember. *Careful* isn't what I'd deem an appropriate term for you. You're as dangerous as a courting lion."

She couldn't help herself, she laughed. He'd always had that ability, at least. Even when she was infuriated with him, he could turn her mood upside down.

"Seriously, I'm all good. What can I do for you?"

"I was worried," he said simply.

He was quiet then, and she felt that strange guilt that always washed over her when Memphis revealed his true feelings about her. Memphis had formed an attachment to Taylor, and when he'd been selected to work at Quantico as the liaison between New Scotland Yard and the FBI on counterterrorism, she'd been terribly worried he wouldn't let things lie. But Memphis had kept his distance, and behaved himself. For the most part. Baldwin didn't know that Memphis called her, and that sometimes, when she wanted a laugh, she answered the phone.

God knew she needed something cheerful now, but this wasn't the time.

"I'm fine, really. But I have to go. I'm tracking down a lead and I've just arrived."

"Be careful then, Taylor. You and your chap need to come over to England sometime. I'll show you around."

"I thought you were in Quantico?"

"Back on the Queen's soil now. The colonies no longer needed my expertise."

He didn't sound bitter, but Taylor couldn't help but wonder if Baldwin had seen to that. He was wildly jealous of Memphis, and having him underfoot in Quantico was probably too much of an annoyance, even for a man with Job-like patience.

"I'm sorry about that. I know you were enjoying yourself."

"Yes, well. One can't have everything one wants, isn't that right?"

And boom, he crossed right on over the line. Typical of him, he could ride the edge for only so long. He was trouble, with a capital *T,* and Taylor knew it.

"I'll talk to you later, Memphis. Have a good night."

She hung up the phone and forced Memphis, and Baldwin, from her mind. She must focus on Nashville.

Fifty

Baldwin had been using the Nashville field office for his day-to-day needs for a couple of years. Its biggest advantage was its proximity to downtown, and to Taylor. Morning traffic into town from the east side was usually terrible, and today was no exception. He took advantage of the crawl to call Garrett back.

"It's about time you rang. Don't your minions give you messages anymore?"

"I have no minions. Just loyal, hardworking souls who would never take the chance of contacting me while I'm on suspension."

"Yeah, right. Tell Salt I believe that."

"Things are going to hell, Garrett. Taylor's bodyguards just killed the Zodiac copycat at Sam's office. Sam is missing. Our best lead is dead. Everything is falling to pieces."

"I know that. Which is why I needed to talk to you. I've spoken with the director. We're reactivating you and rescinding your suspension. There's too much happening out there to have our best player on the bench. Try to stay away from the media, but get a handle on these copycat killers and wrap this case. Where are you with things?"

It was about time.

"I've been working the angle with Ewan Copeland, trying to figure out who he is and where he's from. He's been working at Forensic Medical as a death investigator named Barclay Iles. We nailed his sister—she's the shooter from North Carolina. She's from Raleigh, North Carolina—the SBI are on that part of the case. Her name is Ruth Anderson, and she's on the run. Copeland can't be far behind her—he sent Taylor a CD with the license plates of the copycats. He blew their cover on purpose. It was probably just another part of the game, or he got bored. Who the hell knows. And the true-crime blogger is dead."

"I heard. Salt says they have one of the other copycats in custody. I want you to talk to him face-to-face."

"He's in Knoxville, Garrett. I need to stay here. The game in is Nashville."

"The pawn of the game is in Knoxville. You need to get up there."

"But—"

"Baldwin, your return is conditional. The director feels the media attention to the case warrants finding out why three men decided to start pretending to be famous serial killers. We have too many dead, all over the country, and two more killers in the wind. This fool has had direct contact with the Pretender. The director wants answers, and results, and he thinks the key to the case lies in Knoxville. So get up there. That's an order."

"Yes, sir. I'll make plans to get to Knoxville right away."

"Let me know what you find out. And no cameras, you hear me?"

"Got it."

"Good. One other thing. On a more personal note."

Baldwin knew exactly what that meant. Garrett had news about the child Charlotte claimed to have aborted.

"He's overseas. A foreign adoption. That's all I've gotten, but I'm still working on it."

Baldwin felt the breath whoosh out of him.

"He's okay though, right?"

"It's been at least two years since anyone's seen paper on him. With Charlotte's death, all sorts of agencies got involved. You know how the government octopus works. That picture is very outdated. I'm doing the best I can."

"All right, Garrett. Thank you."

He clicked off. The traffic was finally moving. Once he got past the 440 split, things went smoother. He could see downtown clearly. The clouds had retreated, typical Nashville weather, teasing a storm and delivering sunshine instead. The cold sun glinted off the buildings. It all looked so normal. It felt so right.

The idea of leaving Nashville for Knoxville scared the hell out of him. He couldn't leave Taylor unprotected. It was bad enough that they'd split to work different angles of the case. He needed to be with her, by her side, helping her track down Copeland and Sam.

But if he defied orders when he was on such precarious ground, everything he'd worked for all these years would go out the window.

A week ago, he wouldn't have hesitated. He'd have

said to hell with the FBI and attached himself like a limpet to Taylor's side.

But there was his son to consider now, too. Garrett's support in finding the boy had been phenomenally helpful. Could he purposefully turn his back on his boss, his friend—his son, maybe—to follow his own path?

He never thought he'd have to choose. He was going to fail this test, he could feel it in his bones.

He got on the phone to Kevin as he took the exit to swing through downtown to the CJC. Arranged for a chopper to take him to Knoxville. If he had to go, he needed to do it quickly.

The CJC was a mess when he arrived. The roads were closed at the bridge. He had to park on Second Avenue, in front of Hooters, and walk himself in. He did it quickly, worried. There was an ambulance, but the EMTs were standing around, not acting. When he turned onto the street, two fire engines pulled away. First responders were done. Was all this for Colleen Keck? Or had something else gone down?

He felt a moment of sheer panic. Taylor. Where was Taylor? He flipped open his phone to call her and broke into a run. The call connected, then went to her voice mail. Damn it. Did she have her phone off? Or had Ewan Copeland's final piece of the puzzle dropped into place?

The medical examiner's van pulled up to the light next to him. He ignored the red hand telling him to stop and sprinted across the street. Marcus Wade was standing on the corner, talking to Lincoln Ross. Taylor's boss, Joan Huston, was taking Lincoln's weapon from him. But he didn't see Taylor.

He ran up to them. "Where's Taylor? Is she okay?"

Commander Huston turned to Baldwin. She was calm, collected. Sadness tinged her eyes.

"Hello, Dr. Baldwin. The lieutenant is fine, so far as I know. We lost a witness in the parking garage, and the suspect who killed her. Detective Ross was forced to employ his service weapon in self-defense. This is a crime scene, so I need to ask you to remove yourself. This is a local case, it has no bearing on the FBI."

She was right: he had no right to be there, no reason. But Lincoln was his friend, as was Marcus. He didn't want to leave. And where in the hell was Taylor? She should be here by now.

He looked over to Lincoln, who was gray with misery. Marcus was standing next to him, speaking quietly. He squeezed his arm, then nodded to Baldwin.

Without speaking, Marcus walked away, back toward the CJC. Baldwin fell into step with him. They took the long way around the building, to the back entrance, then stopped on the stairs to talk.

"What the hell is going on?" Baldwin asked.

"Chick had a knife and she was inside the zone. Linc had no choice but to shoot her. He's pretty messed up. It's a clean shoot, straight self-defense. Problem is, three people saw what happened, and two of them are dead. He's on leave, he's going to get sent home for the day at least, after he sees the shrink." Marcus slid his key card through the reader. "Where's Taylor?"

"That's what I've been trying to find out. I was hoping she was here already. She asked me to meet her. She's looking for Sam. We think Copeland's got her. I thought you were with Fitz?"

"I was, but when I heard Sam was missing, I got back here pronto. I've got two guys I trust on him. He'll be fine. This day just keeps getting better and better," Marcus said.

"What caused Colleen Keck to blow up?"

When they were inside the Homicide offices, Marcus went straight to Taylor's office and beckoned Baldwin to follow. He shut the door so they could talk freely.

"Lincoln had a set of her prints run. Turns out she was living quite the lie. Her real name is Emma Brighton, and she's from Forest City, North Carolina. Copeland's hometown."

"Taylor said she thought Colleen was tied to Copeland in some way. That she recognized the name."

"That's what Lincoln was trying to get out of her when she snapped. He thinks she was the rape victim from when Ewan was sixteen. She was in the group home with him."

Baldwin smacked his forehead with his hand. "My God. That makes perfect sense. No wonder he was targeting her—he's wrapping up loose ends. She started her life over under a different name. Got married. Had a kid." Another thought hit him. "Her husband's murder was never solved, right? I bet Copeland was responsible somehow."

"It's possible… He was killed on the interstate during a drug interdiction sting—all caught on camera, but whoever did it knew how to shield his face. They knew it was a man, just by the size of him, but that was all they got. The ballistics never matched anything, it was a clean gun."

"That sounds like Copeland. He found his old flame Emma living as Colleen Keck. He knew who she was married to. He used Keck's name to visit his mother three years ago. He spent years looking for her, then decided to systematically ruin her life. At her most basic, she was a witness. We know he's changed his face cosmetically several times since then. He's been posing as Barclay Iles, from Forensic Medical. One of my profilers is serving the plastic surgeon he's been using with a warrant right now."

"No shit?"

"Nope." Another thought hit him. "The blog name. Felon E. *E* for Emma. I wonder if she did that intentionally or subconsciously? I bet after her husband died, she couldn't help herself. But who was the woman Lincoln shot, the one who killed Colleen?"

"That's what we're trying to figure out. She doesn't have any ID on her."

Baldwin stood and paced for a minute. "The clues that he sent us, with the license plate numbers and Sam's address. There was a leftover letter—an *E*. *E* for Emma Brighton, *E* for Felon E."

"Makes sense."

"I didn't ask—how was she killed?"

"Gruesome. Her throat was slit."

It hit him in a rush. "Marcus, we've got to go back out there. I think I know who Lincoln shot in the parking structure. And if it's her, this just became my case, too."

Fifty-One

The man who would be Richard Cooper loved this hotel. He figured he was due for a splurge—being on the road for several days, the pressure of imitation, the stakes, the hunt and the kill—he was simply exhausted. After he checked in, he'd utilized the exercise room, worked up a good sweat, then opened his pores in the sauna, followed by a cool bath with a fine green tea scrub that had him clean and rosy pink. He ordered a clean lunch—organic greens, papaya and pineapple, a small piece of grilled salmon. He felt lighter, emptier than he had in days. Food on the road, in a rush, drive-throughs and greasy spoons, none of this was compatible with his lifestyle. He took care of himself. His body was his temple. He didn't drink or smoke. He rarely, if ever, took medications. He committed to treating his body the way it was meant to be treated, nothing fake, nothing artificial. Fresh, whole foods, things that could be grown, captured or hunted.

Especially hunted.

He set his empty plates back on the cart and wheeled it out into the hallway, so the scent wouldn't linger and spoil his appetite. He closed the door, triple locked it, then went to the luxurious leather chair situated at just the right angle to watch some television. He planned to watch the news then read the afternoon away, perhaps take a stroll, though it was so nippy outside. He was disappointed they hadn't done this in the summer, the hotel's pool was exceptional.

He found the remote stashed in the drawer of an oak side table within easy reach, turned the television on. Thank goodness for cable news, at your fingertips twenty-four hours a day.

His heart dropped as he watched the flashing red Breaking News! banner cross the screen. He turned the volume up carefully. Listened as the anchor described his past few days with stunning accuracy. The whole game had been discovered.

It was one thing for Troy to summon them without warning—he hadn't appreciated that. He'd done a lot of work lining up his kill in Cincinnati, and he didn't like walking away from a plan. But it was a completely different issue to have the media on top of the story.

It was on all the major stations. He flipped through a few times, then caught a name. His name. Not his real name, of course, he wasn't that stupid, but the name he'd been using in connection with this contest. The name he'd used for the hotel.

He forced himself to stay calm. He needed to walk out of the hotel immediately. He'd leave the rental car, he'd already wiped it down, a nightly precaution he took, and take apart the BlackBerry. He'd succeeded this long because he wasn't stupid, though now he was questioning his intelligence in getting involved with a man who was obviously on a death mission. Troy Land, he called himself, though he knew that name was as fake as his own current nom de plume.

He packed his duffel quickly, put on his clothes. Put on the baseball cap he'd used when he checked in to keep his face off the cameras. Decided to take the linens and robe with him; though he'd only sat on the edge of the bed, he might have left a DNA trace somewhere and he didn't need that hassle. He ran a piece of masking tape along the edges of the chair and on the floor underneath. He always ate with gloves, so prints weren't an issue, and he'd washed the silverware in hot water with soap to get the DNA off them, but he wasn't going to take any chances. He opened the door carefully, no one in the hallway. Thankfully the maids hadn't removed the tray yet. He bundled everything together; he'd burn it once he was clear of town.

He didn't like the South anyway. Too quiet. All those birds chirping, and people smiling. They made eye contact here and talked to you, expected an answer back, noticed you if you ignored them, a truly dangerous combination. He needed the dingy city life, too many people with too many issues to give him a second glance. He fit in well anyway, on the tall side, brown hair, brown eyes. Not handsome, but not ugly either. He had no distinguishing characteristics. He got his hair cut at a walk-in place. Shopped at chain grocery stores, though it made it harder to eat the organic food his body craved. The specialty stores had fewer customers, they had a tendency to recognize the regulars. He wanted to be regular, not be a regular.

He'd borrow a car from the parking garage and drive to Atlanta, drop it there. Buy something cheap and disposable from one of the many scam lots, take it to Florida. Miami. A port town. He'd make a reservation to take a cruise to South America.

But he wasn't really going to leave. No, after he'd

laid the trail, he was going back to Indianapolis, to the adorable hostess at the steak house. That was as good a place as any to start over.

Oh, well. The game had been fun while it lasted.

Maybe he'd drive by the target's office, just for the hell of it. Wave goodbye. A shame, really. It would have been fun to watch her die.

Fifty-Two

Taylor wasn't a big fan of assisted-living facilities. It was purely psychological—her grandfather had been an Alzheimer's patient before Alzheimer's was de rigueur, when it was just called dementia and the nursing homes were dark and silent, aside from the moans of pain or murmured recollections that emanated from the mouths of the inmates. It had smelled wrong, she remembered that. She'd been young when he'd passed away, but the stench of the home where he lived wasn't something she'd ever forget. Neglect, and sadness, and rot, mingled with urine and the sweet, yeasty smell of imminent death. That was what she remembered.

So when she entered the front door of the Guardian facility, she was surprised to smell roses. It was bright, and happy. Clean. Smiling faces. Completely incongruous with her expectations.

She went to the front desk and gave them her name, stated her business. A woman dressed in pink scrubs overlaid with purple and white hearts grinned ear to ear when she heard Taylor asking for Joshua Fortnight. He didn't get a lot of visitors.

The facility had a small indoor garden, a greenhouse,

and they grew roses and orchids and a few irises and hydrangeas to boot, which, as the intake nurse explained, kept the patients happy. It gave them something to do. Especially in the cold winter months when they were stuck inside, and their field trips consisted of going to malls instead of the park or the zoo.

Joshua, it turned out, had an affinity for growing flowers. His specialty was the hard-to-manage orchids. Twice a day, he lovingly played his flute for them, though he was getting more and more deaf, a congenital handicap related to his Treacher Collins, and the notes were sometimes a bit sharp.

"Please don't upset him," the pink nurse said. "He's doing so well with us."

Upset him. Yeah, that nurse was going to be seriously pissed off in a couple of hours, when she found out Taylor had dragged poor Joshua back through the worst days of his life. She had no time to sugarcoat this.

It took ten minutes to round him up. He shuffled up the hall on her arm, ruined face turned away. She took him to the greenhouse, beckoned for Taylor to follow. Once he was settled, she smiled, touched his shoulder gently in assurance, and left.

He had his back to Taylor, didn't turn around. When he spoke, he slurred his words, sibilant and soft.

"I remember you," he said, his pale hands embracing the pot of a delicate white orchid. Using his forefinger, he felt the soil. It must have been all right, he nodded to himself.

"My name is Taylor," she said.

"You have a gun. I can sssmell the metal."

"I'm a police officer, Joshua."

"I know. You killed my father."

She flinched. Coming face-to-face with the ones left behind was never easy. Being in the same room as the child of the abhorrent serial killer, who'd mocked her, used her, and finally forced her to take his life, was possibly the hardest thing she'd done in years.

"Joshua—"

"Don't. Jussst, don't. He wasss a bad man."

That won the understatement lottery. Eric Fortnight was a sick, twisted bastard, one who was forced to stop killing only because of a crippling case of rheumatoid arthritis. His body wouldn't cooperate anymore. When he couldn't stand it any longer, when the urge to kill became too much to contain, he'd enlisted his sociopathic daughter to find him a helpmeet. A killer to kill for him. An apprentice.

Charlotte had chosen Ewan Copeland.

"Are you happy here, Joshua?"

"I miss the birdsss." He turned to her now, and she forced herself not to suck in her breath. His face, his poor face, looked like a melted candle. His eyes were where his cheeks should be, one on either side, pointing out and down, so very like the birds he loved. His nose was a pinpoint with nostrils, his chin practically nonexistent. Strangely, his lips were normal, a bit wide, but full and lush, a bright red, his tongue, thickened by the disease, visible inside. Like he'd bitten into a bloody apple.

His features were terribly disconcerting, but Taylor knew he was fully blind, and couldn't see the horror etched on her face. She shut her eyes and did her damndest to keep it out of her voice, too. This man had been forced to listen to too many sighs of fear in his life.

"You had birds at the house?"

"Yesss. A garden. Like thisss. But bigger. And outside. I miss it."

"Joshua, can we sit down?"

He nodded, and she followed him to a small stone bench under a shelf of purple orchids. They sat, and Joshua reached below the bench and extracted a small brown case. Taylor recognized it, it was his flute.

"The flowersss like the musssic. I play for them twissse a day."

"I bet they do," she said, then put her hand on his to stop him from opening the case. "Joshua, I have a friend, a very good friend, who might be in danger. Do you remember the man you shot last year?"

"Troy. I hated him."

"His real name is Ewan. And he's taken my friend."

"Coming home to roosssst. Father alwaysss sssaid he would. He killed my sssissster. He killed Charlotte."

Taylor forced herself to swallow.

"Yes, he did. And now I'm afraid he's going to do the same thing to my friend. I think he's taken her to your old house. Will you help me, Joshua? Will you give me a way in? Will you help me save her?"

"It doesn't belong to me anymore. The bank took it. They can't sssell it, no one wants to live where a ssserial killer preyed. There's a big lock on the front door."

"I know. But I'll make you a deal. I know you were the one who let Jane Macias out of your father's house. She said there was a tunnel, a back entrance, and she described you to me. I never knew if she imagined the tunnel, or if it was real.

"But you helped her, Joshua, because you knew what your father and Troy were doing was wrong. And now it's my turn to stop Troy from hurting anyone else. If I can get in without him knowing, sneak into the house, I can take care of him, and he'll never bother any of us again. If you tell me how to get in, as a thank-you, I'll take you to the park, so you can hear the birds. Would you like that?"

He was quiet, and she could feel him wrestling with the request.

Finally, he sighed, a great, heavy wet sound. "There is a path into the house. Out the back. From my garden. You can go in there. I'll explain how the houssse is laid out, but he'll have her in the attic. He alwaysss liked the attic. You can get in and he'll never know."

Taylor felt a huge rush of relief. She'd hoped for a key, and instead she'd been given the kingdom.

Baldwin stood over the cooling body of Ruth Anderson. Lincoln had done a textbook shoot, three clean shots to the chest. Ruth was sprawled backward on the cement, one leg crumpled beneath her, the other sticking straight out. Baldwin couldn't shake the sense of justification seeing her like that. The last time he'd looked into her eyes, she'd had a gun pointed at him, was still impersonating Renee Sansom of the SBI. Justified. Deserved, really.

He usually hated the loss of life; in this case, he was happy about it. He would have liked to delve into her brain, would have liked to have both Ruth and her half brother Ewan to study for years to come, but her death was a fitting end to her sad, pathetic, psychopath's life.

He wondered if Ewan knew Ruth was dead, and Colleen with her. He'd sent her to kill Colleen Keck, knowing Colleen was at the CJC. Baldwin assumed that Ewan had planned this to a tee, knowing he was sending Ruth into the lion's den would assure that she was either killed or arrested. He'd bet on killed, because he knew his little sister Ruth wasn't the most stable. It was a gamble, but if it went his way, the elimination of Ruth would allow him the freedom to escape with no strings attached.

Ruth had been flanked by two men in North Carolina. One confirmed dead, the other still missing. Could he be the Boston Strangler copycat? Anything was possible at this point. Baldwin made sure to mention that to Joan Huston when she approached him.

"What would you like us to do with the body, Dr. Baldwin?"

"Forensic Medical will be fine, Commander. I take it there's been no word on Dr. Loughley?"

Huston waved to the crime scene techs who had been patiently waiting off to one side while Baldwin examined the body. They sprang into action, breaking out their evidence kits, taking photographs.

Huston pulled him aside.

"Dr. Loughley? Something's wrong with her?"

Oh, Taylor. What are you up to?

Baldwin needed to tread carefully. The last thing he wanted to do was get Taylor in trouble, but he had a sinking, horrible feeling that she was on a path straight there. He calculated his answer.

"Have you spoken with Lieutenant Jackson this morning, ma'am?"

"Just for a moment, after the shooting at Forensic Medical. I told her to stay put and shepherd the scene. She's still on administrative leave after her shooting incident last week. She's not supposed to be working cases. Now tell me what's happened to Dr. Loughley."

"She seems to be missing, ma'am. I'm assuming that

Ewan Copeland is responsible, just like he was responsible for sending his sister Ruth to eliminate Colleen Keck."

Huston snapped to attention. "Then why the hell haven't we been notified? She's the head medical examiner, not some stranger off the street."

"Lieutenant Jackson didn't notify you, ma'am?"

"She damn well didn't. Does her team know?"

Carefully, Baldwin. "I don't know the extent of their knowledge of the situation."

Fury looked good on Commander Huston. Baldwin knew Taylor trusted her; despite their formal relationship, Taylor had always felt she could count on Huston to be fair. Baldwin decided to gamble. Taylor's safety and Sam's recovery were the most important things now. They could mop up her career afterward.

"Commander, I believe that Ewan Copeland has kidnapped Sam Loughley, and the lieutenant is going after them herself. It's gotten personal for her, ma'am."

"Shit. It's always been personal. This man has tried to ruin every aspect of her life, he's hurt her friends… My God, look at Sergeant Fitzgerald, in the hospital, recovering from having his eye plucked out of his head."

He followed when she started to walk, brisk, purposeful steps. "I don't know why she didn't come to me. She knows I'll do whatever I can to help. She's too valuable to lose." She stopped and grabbed Baldwin's arm. He was amazed at the strength in her grip.

"I'm trusting you to stop the lieutenant before she does something stupid. Do I have your word on that, Dr. Baldwin?"

"Yes, ma'am. You do."

"Then take Wade and whoever else you need, and find her. Find them both. Now."

Fifty-Three

Taylor ignored her phone.

A quick glance at the screen told her it was Baldwin again, trying to reach her. She just needed a little bit more time. She wasn't crazy, wasn't a total idiot. When she got to the house in Belle Meade, Fortnight's house, she would call Baldwin and tell him where she was. He'd come lights and sirens, with backup, but it would be too late. She had her words planned out—*she'd heard a scream, knew Sam was inside. She had no choice but to eliminate*—no, wrong word—*shoot the suspect before he hurt Dr. Loughley or her unborn child further.* She ran it through her head like she did her usual court testimony. Dry. Just the facts. Only a few words at a time. Don't answer questions that haven't been asked. That way you won't have to lie.

She would be in court over this, she knew that, though her union lawyer would fight to the finish for her. Baldwin would figure it out soon. It didn't take a genius to see that Copeland wanted to end things where they'd begun, in the home of the Snow White. Symmetry, above all, was paramount to him.

Taking Sam was simply an insurance policy. A

perfectly calculated move designed to bring Taylor directly to him so they could finally go at it one-on-one.

Thank God she'd lost her tail. At this point, ordering them to stand down would have looked much too suspicious. She had planned this moment out, but wouldn't have to execute it. She was going to ask them to stop for some coffee while she took a potty break, and when their backs were turned, take off in her truck out of sight. Hope that they were unskilled enough to allow for an amateur mistake. But now she could relax, and focus on the task at hand.

The light was red, traffic in the turn lane backed up. There was a Shell station on her left. She swung the truck into the gas station, crossed the lot and wheeled out onto Woodmont. She turned left and powered up the hill. Illegal as hell, but it would be the least of her transgressions today.

Her phone rang again and she glanced at it. Baldwin wasn't going to let up.

She felt a spark of anger, pushed it away.

She made her way through the labyrinth of Belle Meade's backstreets to Iroquois, then hurried across Belle Meade Boulevard.

Almost there.

She needed to keep the end in sight. Instead, every time her phone rang and the caller ID said Baldwin, all she could see was the small round face of a redheaded child.

Damn it, Taylor, focus. You're going to get yourself killed if you don't focus.

She breathed in carefully through her nose. Blew it out slowly. Imagined Ewan Copeland begging on the ground.

Better.

Fortnight's house was on Leake Avenue, a massive three-story gray stucco mansion with curling ivy and dark windows. She didn't want to run the risk of being seen, so she turned on Westover and came in the back way, stopping the truck at the neighbor's house.

Joshua had told her if she parked there and walked into the woods one hundred yards, she'd find an overgrown path to her left that led directly to the tunnel off the side of the house. Overgrown would be her friend—she could slink in unseen and surprise the bastard. Though how surprised could Copeland really be, knowing she was coming? The only thing she had on her side was the fact that she was alone. He'd expect her to come calling with a bevy of cops with her, expecting a hostage negotiation, that she'd give herself for Sam's release. He'd think she was going to make a production of it, try to arrest him, to do the right thing and see justice done. She was a by-the-book kind of detective.

And that was where he didn't know her at all. That was the exact opposite of what she had planned. He didn't know her true strength. That love would make her blind to the dangers, that she would throw the rules out the fucking window in a heartbeat if it meant ending this quietly. Without witnesses. Like a reset button.

That she'd been planning to kill him from the moment he'd set foot in her world, taunting her, playing cat and mouse.

She had to force her heart rate down, she was getting angry again. Anger meant she'd make a mistake. She couldn't afford that. Not now.

It was time.

She was in position at the base of the neighbor's drive.

She climbed out of the car, felt the unfamiliar weight of the Ruger under her left arm. She didn't usually wear a shoulder holster. She tucked the Beretta into the second leather holster she'd snapped on to her belt, with it in the back instead of on her hip, where the Glock sat. She untucked her shirt so it would hang loose over the third gun, then shrugged into her leather jacket, the roomy one she reserved for wearing over heavy sweaters. Everything felt good, solid. In place. Right.

Ewan would be watching from the front, and she was planning to sneak in the back. Right up to the attic on the servants' stairs, winding onto the small fourth story, the one that wasn't visible from the drive. Joshua had told her this was where Copeland had hidden Jane Macias, the reporter he'd kidnapped for the Snow White's pleasure. Joshua had snuck her from the house using exactly this same path.

Her cell rang again. Baldwin. This time she answered, surprised at how normal her voice sounded.

"Where the hell are you?" he yelled at her. "I've been calling for an hour."

"Hello, Baldwin." Neutral. *Don't get upset. Don't get excited.* "You know where I am. I'm going after Sam."

"Not fucking alone you're not. Stop wherever you are and let us catch up to you."

"No."

She got back in the truck, she didn't want any of the neighbors to hear an argument and get suspicious.

"Taylor." His voice dropped an octave. She heard voices in the background, assumed he had someone with him. Hell, he'd probably be bringing a SWAT team's worth of people. If this were a normal situation, that was exactly what she'd do.

"Taylor, please. Don't do this. Just tell me where you are. Let me help you."

"Help me? Sure. There are a few things you can do to help me. How about starting with the truth, for once. If you're capable of it."

"What are you talking about? Does he have you, Taylor? Are you talking under duress? Just say yes if you are."

"No, I'm not. I'm talking about your son. The child you so conveniently forgot to mention to me. You and Charlotte's child?"

Dead silence.

"Jesus. How did you find out?"

She put the phone on speaker and set it on the console, started to wind her hair up in a bun. She didn't want it getting in her face while she was trying to shoot.

"That doesn't matter, Baldwin. Not anymore. You know where I am. I have to do this. I have to end it. I can't let anyone else get hurt."

"Taylor, please. Don't go in there alone. I don't want you to get hurt, or do something you might regret."

"Don't you *dare* tell me that. Regret my ass. My judgment isn't in question here. This man has my best friend. For all I know, he's already killed her. He's mine, and I intend to take care of him."

She was being careless now, but it felt too good to stop. "You had your chance, Baldwin. You could have trusted me. Now I know I can't trust you. The only person I've ever been able to trust was Sam. I can't believe I counted on you. My mistake. So I'm going to do this my way. I'm tired of taking direction from you. You know where I am. Come on down, but believe me, it will be over by the time you get here."

Taylor clicked off the phone, ignoring his protestations. The last thing she heard before the line cut out was him yelling at whoever was in the car with him.

She muted her phone and pocketed it, then stepped back outside. It would take them just long enough to get here, hopefully enough time for her to lay the whole trap. Someone would burst in and see Copeland making a move for her, see the shooting. It was as close as she could come, she needed someone to at least think they saw her defending herself.

A risky plan, but it was the best she had. She just needed to control herself long enough to let it play out.

She walked up the neighbor's driveway, off to the side by the evergreen hedge. Joshua had told her they weren't in the city during the winter. He was right, the windows were blank and cold, the drive quiet.

Birds were singing in the distance. Joshua's birds. Her hands were cold, she tucked them into a fist and blew into them. The leaves had all dropped from the trees, which were spindly and naked. They were woven close together so they formed a privacy screen between the houses. In the summer, in full leaf, they would be so thick you'd never be able to see through to the house next door. Now the view was still hindered, but she could see the corner of the great monolith, just to the south.

There was the path.

She crept along it, trying hard not to make too much noise. She didn't need a nosy neighbor seeing her, misinterpreting the situation.

Going in alone went against everything she'd been taught. But this was the best way, the only way.

Joshua told her to look for a rotted log. It was a fake,

a cover for the controls to the lawn sprinkler system, designed to look like it belonged there.

There.

She flipped the log up to see a trapdoor, like a miniature storm shelter. Joshua had told her where the key was hidden, in the interior knot of the fake log. She found it, unlocked the wooden door, lifted it up. Damp must drifted out, the scent of the earth mingled with too much time. She played her flashlight into the hole, saw the small set of stairs.

She glanced back over her shoulder at the ice-blue sky, then took the first step.

The birds stopped singing.

Fifty-Four

Baldwin pulled the car over and put his head in his hands.

"Think," he said aloud to himself.

Where are you, Taylor?

"What's wrong?" Marcus asked. "What did she say?"

"She said we'd know where she was. She's not thinking clearly."

"I'd say she was pretty clearheaded."

"So you heard?" There would be no secrets after this, among any of them.

"The only obvious thing was the words *child* and *Charlotte*. Add to that the tone of fury, and you do the math. I'm a detective, remember? You had a kid with Charlotte?"

Baldwin ran his fingers through his hair. "It's a long story, but yes. One small detail, I just found out about him last year. I've been looking for him ever since."

"Last *year?* And you didn't tell her? No wonder she's pissed."

"Yes, thanks. I should have told her right away, I

know. I was afraid I would lose her, that she wouldn't be able to forgive me. Looks like I was right."

"She's not prone to histrionics. If you'd been up front with her, I'm sure she could have forgiven you."

"I fucked up. Trust me, I know. And now she's off on a suicide mission. Where did she go? Where did Copeland take Sam? It's someplace meaningful, someplace that Taylor would easily guess. From their past, maybe. Goddamn it, she said I know where she is. Where is she?"

Marcus thought for a minute.

"Where it all began. They're at the Snow White's house."

Fifty-Five

Taylor took four quick steps down into the tunnel, then squatted and pulled the door shut behind her.

Dark. Quiet. The Maglite beam bit into the gloom and showed her the path. She moved quickly now, ignoring the scent of rot. If it had been summer, it would have been worse. Instead, it was simply cold, hard, like frozen flesh.

She counted off thirty paces before she saw the door to the house fifteen yards in front of her. She stopped and turned to her right. The key was on the ledge, a foot from the door, right where Joshua had said it would be. She held it in her palm and took a few deep breaths.

No turning back now.

A bit of light bled from the crack under the door. Taylor eased the key into the lock and turned. The door opened silently, no old squeaking hinges, like it had been oiled down for just that purpose. A trap? Maybe, but a chance she was willing to take. A dark hallway led away and up from the entry. She clicked on the Maglite for just a moment and flashed it up the stairs, just so she could see what was ahead of her, then turned it off, shut the door behind her and stepped into the gloom.

She shut her eyes and let the darkness surround her. Acclimated. It smelled musty and damp, the house had been closed up for almost a year. Old air, recently disturbed.

She opened her eyes and saw the silhouette of the stairs. Back stairs. Servants' stairs. Narrow and steep and dark, not at all like the open staircase rising out in the front of the house.

Stairs for those less worthy. Perfect for her right now.

She climbed them slowly, silently, controlling her breathing. Waved a cobweb away from her face. Listened with each step. Joshua had said that Copeland would be in the attic. Four flights up. She was on the second when she heard crying.

Sam.

Taylor forced herself not to take off at speed, but stepped up the pace. Third floor now, and she heard him talking. She stopped to listen, gritting her teeth. She needed to ascertain where he was in the room so she didn't hurt Sam when she came in shooting.

She crept up four more stairs. She'd go with the self-defense plan. She drew her Glock from its holster. She could see the light under the partially open door.

Sam was crying, soft, kittenish mews. She was in pain. Copeland, she assumed it must be Copeland, was talking. About his sister. A running dialog. It sounded like he was pacing, too. Taylor could smell blood, was just happy that Sam was still alive, alive enough to cry. It meant she still cared, that whatever horror Copeland had visited upon her, she still had the presence of mind to find it terrible. Taylor had seen too many women brutalized who were silent, blankly staring out of dull irises.

She crept two more stairs, only two to the door now. She could hear him clearly, talking, incessantly talking.

"You know, Sam, my sister, Ruth, she was a good girl. Personality of a paper cut, but once you got to know her, she was a really sweet, loving, kind girl. She missed her call in, I would assume she's dead. I kind of thought I'd have a moment to say goodbye, that her ghost would come and talk to me. Do you think the ghost of your baby will talk to you?"

Taylor forced herself to bite her lip. One more stair now. The shadow was crossing the doorframe, back and forth. She just needed to listen to his voice carefully, ascertain when he was facing away from the door. That was when she'd make her move.

The last stair, and he was still talking. "My mother was a sick bitch, too, you know that? She used to cut me. Just to see the blood pool. And then she'd beat me when I bled on the sheets. My hands were always red and chapped from all of the bleach I had to use to get the blood out. Look at the time. Where is Miss Taylor? I thought she would be here by now, her cavalry with her. That sweet, nice Dr. Baldwin, riding at her side. Were you jealous when they met? I imagine it must have been hard to give up your slavishly devoted best friend."

"Fuck. You," Sam said.

Atta girl, Taylor thought. She heard the steps move away from the door, the voice grew fainter. Now. Now was her chance.

She kicked the door open and entered the room, gun raised. The room was small and she was quick. He didn't see her coming, turned with a look of pure shock. She grinned wildly—she'd caught him by surprise. She had him. He moved toward her and she lashed out with the weapon, caught him on the temple. She followed with a roundhouse left, caught him square on the cheek. His head snapped back, she heard a crack. She'd broken something, blood bloomed bright on his cheek. His fragile cheek. She got her first unencumbered glimpse of him as he was going down. It was Iles all right. He didn't look anything like the man she'd seen in Control. It was hard to believe that was the same man, it was astounding how much work he'd had done. He had smooth, unnaturally tanned skin, the nose straight and narrow, the chin full and square. She threw another punch toward his chin as he went down.

He grabbed at her legs and she kicked him hard, twice, right in the chest, knocking the breath out of him. She glanced at Sam. Her face was screwed up in pain, the cream cashmere sweater she was wearing bloodied around her waist. She was handcuffed to the chair, her arms behind her. Taylor saw the ammonia—he must have been using it to keep Sam alert while he cut her. She saw the extra blood on her, in between her legs, on the floor beneath her.

Oh, God.

The baby.

She hadn't been in time to save them both.

Taylor turned back to Copeland in a rage. He was starting to get up, she stomped on his thigh as hard as she could, gloried when he screamed. A broken femur would slow him down. He reached for his leg, crying out like a wounded animal, fighting not to pass out from the pain. She stepped back, took a deep breath, steadied herself. Pointed the Glock at the son of a bitch's head. Smiled at him when his eyes got wide.

"Let's play," she said.

Fifty-Six

Baldwin drove while Marcus called it in and got them backup. They weren't taking any chances, but Baldwin knew they were going to be too late. Taylor would do anything to save Sam, including going into the house guns blazing and getting herself killed in the process.

Did she think she would get away with killing Copeland? Was that why she'd been so quiet over the past few days? He should have seen it, should have recognized that she was going to take it upon herself to end the Pretender's life.

If he'd been less worried about himself and his own stupid problems, he'd have seen her withdraw. He could always read her, and he hadn't even bothered. This was his fault. It was all his fault.

His phone rang, Charlaine Schultz's name popped up on the screen.

"Charlaine, what's up?"

"I just sent you the most recent picture of Ewan Copeland. The plastic surgeon said he'd done at least five facial procedures on him in the past ten years."

"We know who he's supposed to be, let me just confirm with your picture. Hold a sec."

He pulled up the attachment, recognized the face easily as the death investigator Barclay Iles.

"That's him. Good job, Charlaine. We know where he is now, I'll let you know how things shake out."

"Be safe, boss."

"I will. Thanks."

They were screaming down West End. Thank goodness they were going against traffic, people were still flowing into downtown, the morning rush hour compounded by the untimed stoplights and joggers, mostly Vanderbilt students getting a run in before classes started for the day. They were at the tail end of rush hour, though, and heading out of town, so they were able to make good time. They passed Centennial Park and the roads cleared. Baldwin ran the red light at West End and Murphy Road. Time. He looked at the dashboard clock, it had been two minutes since he'd hung up with Taylor.

He shared Charlaine's information with Marcus. "It's confirmation, at the very least."

Marcus shook his head, face tight. "I can't believe we've been working with this guy the whole time. What a devious prick."

"No kidding. Go faster."

It would take another five minutes to get to Belle Meade, even speeding through the lights.

He caught himself praying. "Please, God. Don't take her from me. Let me get there in time."

Fifty-Seven

Copeland had the common sense to look scared. Their eyes locked for a moment, and Taylor saw the pain and fear in them. It was perfect. Just like she'd been dreaming of.

He was incapacitated enough that she felt comfortable getting Sam out of there. Without looking away, she said, "Are you okay, Sam? Can you walk?"

Sam was crying. "I don't know. Thank God, Taylor. I didn't think you'd ever get here."

"Did he hurt you?"

"I lost the baby."

The quiet, cracked voice of her best friend nearly tore Taylor in two. Sam was the strong one, the fearless, the good. Taylor had visited this upon her. She'd never forgive herself.

Another death at Copeland's hands. Taylor had to force herself not to squeeze the trigger. Not yet. She couldn't let Sam see her do this. She needed to get her from the room.

Sam's hands were awkwardly handcuffed to the back of the chair. Without looking, Taylor used her key and undid the cuffs with her left hand, a little awkward, still pointing the gun at Copeland's head. He watched her, wary now. There was no confidence in his gaze.

She helped Sam to her feet. She wobbled, then got her balance. She clutched onto Taylor's arm so hard that Taylor felt the bruise begin.

She walked her across the room, stepping backward carefully, the gun never wavering.

"It's going to be okay, honey. I promise. Go out the back stairs. There's a short tunnel. You can get out there—it goes into the garden. Baldwin should be on his way. The front door is locked, so be sure you show him the back entrance in. Go. Go now."

"Thank you, Taylor," Sam said softly. She took the first steps unsteadily, without looking back, her hands cupped around her bloody stomach.

Taylor shut the door behind her. They were alone. She heard the first siren then. Copeland did, too, his mouth turned up in a bloody grin.

"Here comes your boyfriend."

"Shut the fuck up. You don't get to talk to me. You get to listen."

"But don't you want to know why I chose you?"

She hesitated, and he took the quiet as permission to continue. He spat a large bloody wad toward her boot, and she didn't move.

"You laughed at me."

"I've never met you before in my life."

"That's not true. You pulled me over. Right after I killed Tommy Keck, as a matter of fact. You had everyone out on the highways looking for the shooter, remember? I'd already changed cars, you had no hope of finding me. But you pulled me over and questioned me, like a good girl. I asked you to dinner. And you laughed at me, you bitch."

"You've hurt all these people, killed so many, because I wouldn't go to dinner with you? You're insane."

"Not the dinner, no. It was the way you laughed at me, like I was just a piece of shit you'd gotten caught on your boot. Like I was nothing. Like I didn't deserve the opportunity to talk to you. I've been waiting for this moment for four years. For a chance to tell you that all of this is your fault. That you killed everyone. That you dug the baby from your best friend's womb, that you stole the sight from your father figure. All these things you've done to yourself, Taylor. If you'd shown a little courtesy, been a little nicer, I'd have gone on my way and never come back."

Voices now, shouts from the driveway. Reinforcements had arrived. She needed to make this quick. She sidestepped to the window, keeping her eye on Copeland. She took a quick glance out, the window overlooked the driveway. She hoped they wouldn't hear the shots.

Her head was only turned for a fraction of a second, but it was long enough. Copeland attacked her from behind, punching her low in the back. She stifled a scream, whirled around and lashed out with her leg. She felt her boot connect, heard the sickening crunch as his arm broke.

He grunted in pain and collapsed on his side. She kicked him in the ribs again, hard, and heard the breath whoosh out of his chest as more bones gave way.

She felt nothing now but the pure, fine energy of her wrath. It made her strong, omnipotent, yet anchored her cruelly in the moment. She must stop. She must. Her breath came in ragged jags, the veil was lifting from her eyes. It took every ounce of her being to stop her fists, to stop the beating.

Taking back all that energy was a near impossibility at this point. She staggered four feet away, bent over to catch her breath. After a moment she stood up, and pulled the Winchester hollow point round from her jeans pocket. Two strides and she was on top of him again, legs straddling his body, teeth gritted with the effort it took not to smash her boot into his face. He wouldn't look up, just stared at the ground. He was defeated.

Walk away, Taylor. Walk away. He's beaten.

It just didn't feel like enough to her.

She couldn't help herself—she snarled at him, holding the bullet in her left hand. "You see this, you son of a bitch? This is the one you sent me. I've been carrying it with me, just waiting for a chance to put it in your brain. And here's the moment I've been waiting for. The great big bad Pretender, whimpering on a dusty attic floor in the house of the man who made him. You couldn't even become a killer on your own. You had to use the people around you. You are nothing. And this is the end of your story. Some end, huh?"

Taylor ejected the bullet already in the chamber and dropped the magazine into her hand. Inserted the Winchester. Popped the magazine back in. Pulled the slide and smiled as the bullet slid into the chamber. Troy, Barclay, Ewan—whatever the hell his name was—wouldn't meet her eyes, just cowered on the cold floor.

The window was closing. They were still alone, just for a moment. There was no one to see. No one would know. He had lunged at her. She had been fighting for her life, the gun between them. It went off in the struggle. She could do it.

Jesus, God, she *could* pull the trigger and end his

life. She wanted it so bad, she could taste it. Death was metallic on her tongue.

The gun never wavered.

"Get on your feet," she said.

He crawled to a sitting position, then pulled himself up the wall until he was upright.

She watched carefully, there was still some fight left in him. He eyed her, listing to one side, favoring the broken leg.

He finally spoke, his voice strong, mocking, despite the obvious pain. "After all we've been through, you're just going to kill me."

"Do you have another suggestion?"

"You could let me go. I hate for our dance to come to an end. You've been a worthy adversary. It's always been you. If I can't have you, I'd take death quite willingly."

"You will never have me. But tell me one thing."

"Anything."

"What were the copycats about?"

"Oh, them. I like an audience. I promised them I'd kill you using their copycat's MO. And the Boston Strangler was by far the front-runner. He would have gotten the reward of a lifetime, watching me fuck you and strangle you. Too bad. Such a shame that we couldn't see this to its proper end."

She curved her finger into the trigger. Eased the pad of her finger into the metal. Just needed a bit more pressure.

"Yes," she said. "It's too bad he's not here to watch me end your miserable existence. I only need to pull the trigger once. That bullet is either yours or mine. And I've got a few things left on my to-do list."

Point at the heart, critical mass, center shot.

"Goodbye, Ewan."

More pressure. The trigger started to cave. The voice spoke to her again.

This is murder. It's murder, and you know it. What are you doing, Taylor? This isn't you.

Shut up. Shut up, shut up, shut up. This is justice.

How many more pieces of your soul can you shear away and still be capable of living, Taylor? Every bullet, every life, chips away at your soul. He's helpless. He can't run. This is wrong. This isn't the way to do it. It's not the way.

"What are you waiting for?" Ewan asked. "Do it already. I'm tired of this. Do it, Taylor. Do it!"

She felt the anger building in her, the fevered pitch of desire to end this, to end him. To stop all the worry, the pain and the suffering he'd caused, not just for her, but for Fitz and Susie, for Sam, for her unborn child, for the strangers who'd died at this man's hands.

An eye for an eye.

She caught the movement almost before it began. He lunged at her, but she coolly stepped aside and let him lose his balance. He fell to the hard cement floor with a crash, groaning, holding his leg.

"Do it, you bitch," he snarled at her. "Just get it over with."

She eased the pressure back off the trigger.

Felt a calm steal over her.

"No. You're not worth it," she said, then holstered the Glock. She heard a noise and turned her head toward the stairs.

"That was the last mistake you'll ever make, Lieutenant."

She heard the click, spun back just as Baldwin came crashing through the door. Saw Ewan rise on one arm.

Her weapon was back in her hand instantly, and the bullets began to fly.

She started to move to her left, but her legs wouldn't work.

Pain. Pain beyond comprehension. Burning. She reached for her head, her hand didn't move.

Tears, now, she was crying, the cement hard and cold beneath her cheek.

And then there was nothing.

Fifty-Eight

"She's hit, she's hit. Taylor's hit!" He heard the words screaming from his mouth.

It happened too quickly. He'd gotten into that room as fast as he could. They'd found Sam, bloody and crying, in the garden, all her strength gone. She'd told him where Taylor was.

Taylor had turned, saw him enter the room full speed, the look on her face not exactly a smile, more like satisfaction, and relief, as if she were saying, "See, I didn't do it. I couldn't go through with it."

But Copeland was moving behind her. Sitting up fast. The glint of metal in his hand. He had a gun. Taylor must have seen or heard the movement, she turned back to Copeland, her mouth a grim line of fury, her gun moving fast. But not fast enough. Baldwin's logical mind proceeded with the proper response—start shooting. He started to squeeze the trigger. He wasn't quick enough. He saw Taylor go down, collapsed in a heap, not graceful or slowly, just all of a piece, on the floor. Blood pooled beneath her head, and his heart froze.

Baldwin had only a fraction of a second to decide,

the space between the heartbeats—go to Taylor, or put this dog down. His finger never left the trigger. He pointed the gun and squeezed, four times, in quick succession, a tracking line from Copeland's sternum to his forehead. A fine mist of blood, the thump of the body hitting the floor, and he knew it was over.

Marcus came into the room yelling, "Officer down, officer down." He dropped to the floor on the other side of Taylor, frantically feeling for a pulse.

Baldwin couldn't catch his breath. He couldn't breathe—was he shot? No. Too hyped. Adrenaline. A ragged breath finally entered his lungs and the scene in front of him grew clear.

Taylor.

He threw his gun down and knelt at her side.

The entry wound was an angry red hole above her right temple, a little left of center. He felt the back of her head, there was no exit. The gun Copeland had used was four feet away, lying quietly on the cement floor. She mustn't have frisked him, or she would have found the weapon. Sloppy. But the gun was a .22. Small caliber. There was a chance.

"Taylor Jackson, you are not allowed to be dead. Goddamn it, woman, respond. *Open your eyes, Taylor. Open your eyes!*"

Someone pulled his arm, forced him away and held him back while they started working on Taylor.

"V-tach. Shit, we lost a pulse."

"Pupils fixed and nonresponsive."

"Start CPR, now!"

He wasn't breathing, and neither was she. He watched them work on her, hands at his side. Pumping on her chest, the ribs cracking from the pressure, creating a strange concavity. The stretcher arriving, them practically throwing her body on the thin mattress, the crash as they brought it full open and rushed her out of the room. Then she was gone, her hand trailing over the edge like she was waving goodbye.

He was frozen. He couldn't move.

Blood on the floor. Her blood. Taylor's blood.

Something inside him broke in two.

Nothing mattered now. Nothing.

Two Weeks Later
November 22

Fifty-Nine

I can hear the birds twittering.

They sound so happy. The corner of my lip rises, I realize I'm smiling. Smiling at the birds. Joshua's birds. I need to put food in the feeder—damn, always forgetting that. Baldwin must have done it, that's why they're outside the window. Happy little things. Cardinals, from the sound of them.

I'm awake. It's time to get up. This is my favorite moment of the day—first rising, the moments when I'm no longer asleep but my eyes are still closed. Listening to the birds. I always linger in the bed for a few moments, just hearing the day begin. Trying to fathom at which exact moment you know you're awake. Is it when you first comprehend sound? First open your eyes? Or when you realize you're no longer dreaming, that the fresh scent of clean sheets and the warmth of down are tangible under your cheek? I don't know, but I think I'll linger in the moment just a bit longer.

The birds are getting louder. Good grief. They chirp so much. Are they on the sill? Or has one gotten in the room?

I sigh. Nothing to do but open my eyes and see.

I'm fully awake now. Morpheus has been chased away. Goodbye, sweet prince. I'll see you again tonight.

I love it when I actually sleep. I've had horrible insomnia for years, just a few hours helps me feel better. But this, it's delicious. I feel like I've gotten a full night's rest. I can't remember the last time I slept this hard.

My eyes are open at last. Good grief, I must have left the blinds open, it's incredibly bright in here. I shut them against the glare, trying to let them adjust to the light. When I open them again I see a ceiling, not my own. What is it called, when they have those pieces, and holes, like screwed-up cardboard? I have a ceiling like this in my office. Used to have a stain on it—damn, I can't remember what it's called.

There's a television, too, high on the wall. This isn't my bedroom at home. Oh, it's a hotel. I start to swivel my head but something is holding me down. Great. Dream within a dream. I do that sometimes, dream I've woken up and snuggled back to sleep only to have never woken at all. I'll just shut my eyes again, let myself go back into the dream.

That stupid cardinal is sitting on my chest. Loud, nasty bird. Go away. Go away, bird.

Mmmm, coffee. That smells good.

Baldwin searched out a cup of coffee from the nurse's lounge, grabbed the morning's paper. The nurses had seen him enough in the past couple of weeks to remember to leave it out for him. He had his new routine down pat—call the hospital before he left the house, just to see if there'd been any change. After the first week, when he'd refused to leave her room, they finally kicked him out. Bodily. It had taken two security guards. But he knew in his heart they were right. No one knew how long it would be until Taylor woke up. If she ever woke up.

The bullet had gone in at a funny angle. It entered her temporal lobe and lodged just inside her skull. It had been a tricky surgery, and she'd seized on the table. They'd kept her in a medically induced coma for a week, the halo in place to make sure she didn't move her head and undo all their delicate repair work. After a week, they brought her off the drugs. She didn't wake up.

There was no way to know when she would. If she would. Or what she would be like when she did.

He couldn't think like that. He had to believe she'd wake up, that she'd be fine.

He dumped two packets of sugar in the coffee. He needed the extra energy these days. There was so much aftermath when a cop gets shot, explanations, excuses.

There was so much aftermath when an FBI agent who was supposed to be in Knoxville interviewing a suspect is instead found in a Nashville hospital, crying over his fiancée, and his gun is a match to the four bullets that were pulled from a corpse in an attic in Belle Meade. Decidedly not Knoxville.

He was feeling almost cheerful today. Taylor was a fighter. He had been exonerated, reinstated. They were calling him a hero. Saying he'd saved Taylor and Sam from the clutches of a madman.

He didn't disabuse them of the notion. And when the autopsy of Ewan Copeland came back with multiple broken bones and contusions, a collapsed lung in addition to the four bullet holes, he told them Copeland had fought him hard. Marcus backed that story, too.

Taylor needed to be protected now, more than ever. He had no intention of letting anyone know she was the one who'd inflicted the damage on Copeland. He'd shot and killed him, yes, but before Copeland shot Taylor, she'd kicked the bejesus out of him.

That was his girl.

The information they had on Copeland grew exponentially with each passing day. They found his spare apartment, a town house he'd rented in east Nashville. It was bare except for his laptop, a chair and a battered teapot, with a matching china cup. Why he'd left his laptop behind was anybody's guess. Baldwin figured he'd done it so he could show them just how prolific he'd really been. He knew he was going to die, probably welcomed the escape it would bring.

There was only one file on the computer, in Word. It was a journal of sorts, with daily entries. Copeland had discussions with himself, decisions to make. Charlaine Shultz had been right about the body dysmorphic disorder—the doctor had confirmed their theories. Copeland was dutiful about his entries. He'd documented almost five years on the computer—his kills, his surgeries, his plans. His growing disenchantment, his anger.

Baldwin assumed that before that, Copeland had kept handwritten journals. They hadn't found those yet.

Copeland had detailed his displeasure with the pretty cop who'd dissed him four years before, right after he killed Tommy Keck. Every move, every detail was listed. It would take years to unravel, but there were already ten new murder cases that had been solved because Copeland had drawn maps showing where he'd left bodies.

A new ViCAP search linked seventeen rapes together, violent assaults, with one thing in common, cuts to the stomach. Copeland had had his own scars eradicated, but kept revisiting them, over and over, on the souls of others.

Sam was a recipient of some of those scars. Baldwin had seen her two days before. She was getting back to her old self, sassy and bold, but there was a lingering sadness to her that he'd never seen before. Losing her child had been hell, losing her best friend, too, would make her cave in. Simon had taken her away on a small vacation, just them and the twins. To repair her outside. Inside, she'd never be the same. Copeland had taken care of that.

He walked down the corridor to Taylor's room. He had a newspaper in his hands, and his new iPad in a backpack. He'd picked three books to read this week. He'd been reading them aloud to Taylor, the classics. They were going to do *Emma* today, one of her favorites. He thought briefly of Emma Brighton, a poor, frightened girl, a victim. That poor woman. He thought of Flynn, now an orphan.

Like him.

He opened the door.

Something was different.

He saw gray. Twin flashes of gray. Jesus God in heaven, she had her eyes open.

He dropped the coffee and the paper on the floor, ignoring the pain in his leg where the hot liquid scalded through his pants. He leaned over the bed.

"Babe? Taylor? Can you hear me?"

The eyes swiveled to him, and he swore he saw recognition. Without looking away, he depressed the emergency button to summon the nurse. She answered through the intercom with an impatient, "What?"

"Get Dr. Benedict. She's awake."

"What?" All the annoyance was gone. "Is she really?"

"Yes, yes. Now get the doctor." He licked his lips.

Taylor's gray eyes crinkled, and her lip moved on the left side.

"Oh, God, Taylor. I knew you'd wake up. I knew you would. Welcome back, my love."

She started to move, but he laid a hand gently on her chest. It was taking all his effort to hold back tears.

"No, no, don't try to move, you're in a halo. You got shot, sweetheart. Copeland shot you, in the head. You've been asleep for a while. But you're okay, baby. You're going to be okay."

* * * * *

Acknowledgments

Thanks to my great team: my agent Scott Miller, my editor Adam Wilson, and all the rest who make these books come to life: MacKenzie Fraser-Bub, Megan Lorius, Deborah Kohan, Donna Hayes, Alex Osuszek, Loriana Sacilotto, Craig Swinwood, Valerie Gray, Margaret Marbury, Diane Moggy, Linda McFall, Giselle Regus, Heather Foy, Don Lucey, Michelle Renaud, Adrienne Macintosh, Maureen Stead, Nick Ursino, Tracey Langmuir, Kathy Lodge, Emily Ohanjanians, Karen Queme, Alana Burke, Tara Kelly and Gigi Lau.

Thanks also to friends and writers Laura Benedict, Jeff Abbott, Erica Spindler, Allison Brennan, Toni McGee Causey, Alex Kava, Jeanne Bowerman, Jill Thompson, Del Tinsley and Andy Levy for keeping me sane during the writing of this book. Special thanks to the writers of Murderati, and Detective David Achord, for support in all the right places. Lee Lofland and Alafair Burke provided help on the legal bits, Joan Huston and Jill Thompson cast their gimlet eyes on the writing bits. As always, any mistakes are mine, and mine alone.

The real Colleen Keck isn't a true crime blogger, but

a contest winner who kindly allowed me many liberties with her name. The same goes for Preston Pylant, Richard Cooper and Bill Reiser. Thanks for letting me make you naughty, boys.

Extra love to my parents and family, who are my greatest supporters, and as always, to my husband, Randy, who makes my life complete.